Nothing
But
Trouble

SCEPTRE

Also by James Maw and published by Sceptre

Year of the Jaguar

Nothing
But
Trouble

JAMES MAW

SCEPTRE

First published in 1998 by Hodder and Stoughton
A division of Hodder Headline PLC
A Sceptre Book

The right of James Maw to be identified as the Author of
the Work has been asserted by him in accordance with the
Copyright, Designs and Patents Act 1988.

10 9 8 7 6 5 4 3 2 1

British Library Cataloguing in Publication Data
Maw, James, 1957–
  Nothing but trouble
  I. Title
  823.9'14 [F]

  ISBN 0 340 67498 9

Typeset by Palimpsest Book Production Limited,
Polmont, Stirlingshire
Printed and bound in Great Britain by
Mackays of Chatham PLC, Chatham, Kent

Hodder and Stoughton
A division of Hodder Headline PLC
338 Euston Road
London NW1 3BH

Nothing
But
Trouble

SCEPTRE

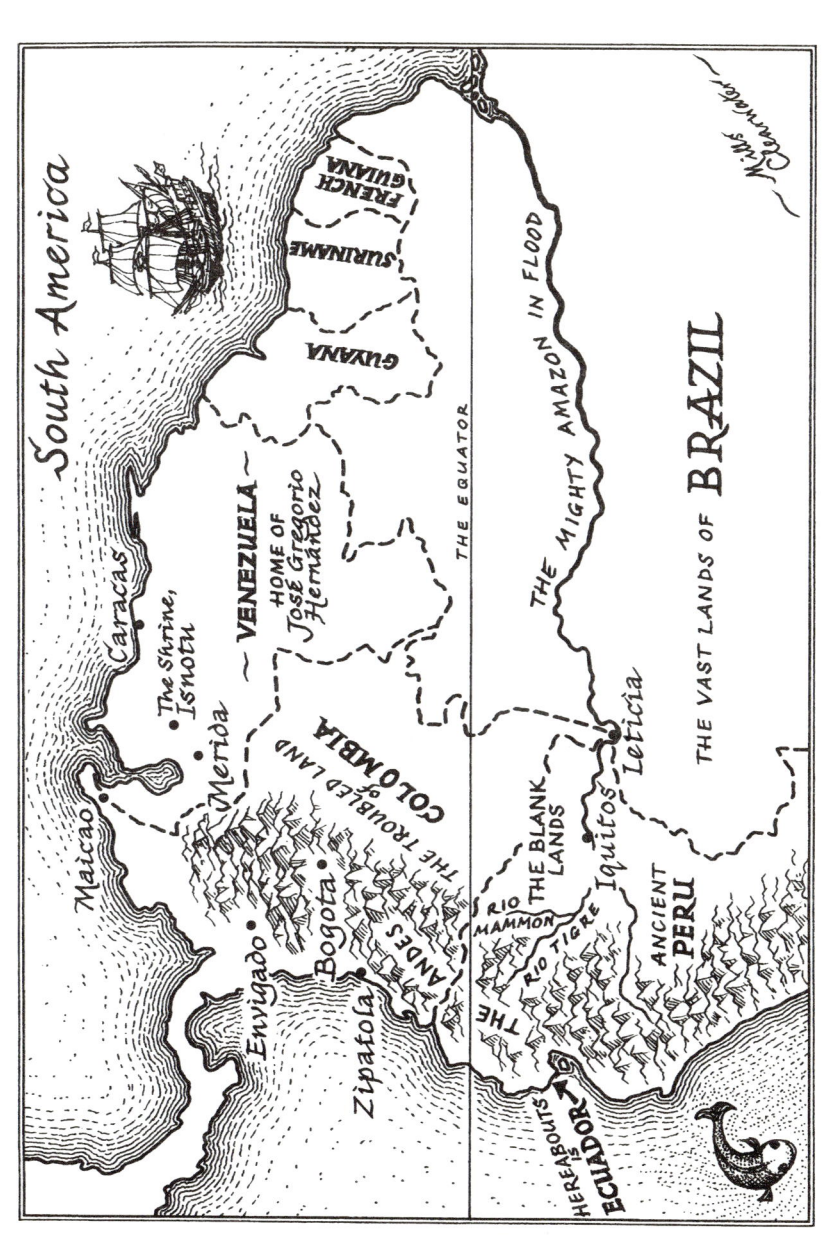

South America

South America

The Shrine, Isnotu
Merida

VENEZUELA

HOME OF
José Gregorio
Hernández

Caracas

Maicao

Envigado

Bogota

Zipatola

THE ANDES

COLOMBIA

THE TROUBLED LAND

FRENCH GUIANA

SURINAME

GUYANA

THE EQUATOR

THE MIGHTY AMAZON IN FLOOD

BRAZIL

THE VAST LANDS OF

Leticia

Iquitos

THE BLANK LANDS

RIO TIGRE

RIO MAMMON

ANCIENT PERU

ECUADOR

HEREABOUTS IS

PART I

Assassination!

The assassin opened up as the newly enthroned Archbishop of Caracas was meeting the Papal Envoy from his plane.

Archbishop Morales had stood there for almost fifteen minutes, bilious and sweating in his number one dress robes on the burning tarmac of the airport; his young chaplain beside him almost fainting from the heat and the ecclesiastical garb. A small flock of nuns, cloister-pale and sticky, with sweat pouring down their thighs, stood around him while the envoy delayed himself at the top of the aircraft steps.

The Papal Envoy: Cardinal Spinoza, wanted to savour the moment. He was going to enjoy being formally met by a radical archbishop whom he'd always despised; a man who had been appointed in a moment of the Pope's tiring mindlessness.

The cardinal eyed the archbishop, plump and flapping in the breeze at the end of a roll of red carpet; a mirage formed by aircraft fuel shimmering from the tail of an Airbus behind him, and it looked to Cardinal Spinoza as if the sulphurous heat of hell-fire had already begun to surround the heretic. These Latin American bishops had been the constant bane of John Paul II's papacy. The Holy Father himself had come here, years before, and famously wagged his finger at them, but it had done no good. They still persisted in their Liberation Theology, undermining the political influence of Rome in Washington. Now, the bastards were actively campaigning for one of their own to succeed to the throne of Saint Peter when the Holy Father graciously called it a day – or Our Heavenly Father did it for him. Which would inevitably be the way. These last few years had consisted of no greater consideration for the cardinal, himself a leading contender for the Big Keys.

The cardinal watched the plump archbishop sweat, his little flock of Clarrisan nuns standing rigid and white-faced around him. He looked up into the sky at the top of the aircraft steps, as if he were taking last minute Divine Instruction, direct from Rome.

Then, in the stillness to which the heat of the open tarmac had reduced the crowd, a lone man broke and ran, and raised an automatic pistol, aiming it directly at the archbishop. Everything appeared to be frozen in time, the soldiers, and the bodyguards, the ranks of police, all stood fixed to the spot, only the gunman moved through the scene; his teeth gritted, his eyes fixed, running like a rugby player broken free from the pack.

One of the Clarrisan nuns screamed, cutting into the airport announcements from the tarmac. Another of the sisters, seeing the assassin, threw herself between the line of fire and her archbishop, covering his chest with her torso and outstretched arms. Her face white, her mouth open but silent.

Then the shots rang out, cracking the heat of the airport. The archbishop dropped his sodden, lace handkerchief.

But the nun who had thrown herself at the portly archbishop was so wasted and undernourished by a life of abstinence and fasting that the fatal bullet passed right through her thin body and into the archbishop's heart. The single bullet killed both of them.

Cardinal Spinoza, the Papal Envoy, returned to the shade of the aircraft.

2 ∫

Oxford University, six months earlier.

It was still dark as Mills made his way into Hall for breakfast on the first day of Michaelmas term. A storm had raged most of the night and the heavy rain clouds were still soaking the city. The quad was awash with water like a medieval sewage system; the buildings were grey and brutally foreboding. The British weather was as appalling and as dogged, and as belligerent as ever.

In the darkness of the wintry dawn he couldn't even find his way around college. The place looked deathly in the half-light, like the location for a movie that had been rained off for the day, and everyone kept back in their hotels. The dark ivy dripped and the lead guttering had broken in places under the weight of water. A weather vane atop a parapet flipped and strained against the elements like a salmon exhausted from its leaps.

Mills shuddered with the cold, and like the weather vane he turned this way and that until he spotted a dim light swinging in the entrance to the Hall.

He'd been told by the porters that breakfast was at seven. He looked at his watch, it was almost five past, and he didn't want to attract attention on his first day by dashing in late when everything was picked over and cold, congealing in that English way. He'd arrived very late the night before, about the same time as the storm, and hadn't met anyone.

One of the porters caught his arm as he turned into Hall.

'As a rule,' he said, 'members of the college do not gown-up for breakfast.'

He stopped and looked down at his sodden scholar's gown. He was cross. 'Oh, right, I'm sorry, sir, I didn't realise.'

'You'll soon get the hang of it, *sir*,' said the porter, smiling at him thinly, obviously rather triumphant that he'd caught out a Rhodes Scholar on his first day.

He went into Hall, rolling his gown under his arm; then he thrust the stupid thing under the bench.

He was the only person there, the Hall was entirely deserted. No-one else was up.

He heard footsteps and turned hopefully towards the door but it was just the porter, shuffling around in his long dark overcoat and stamping his feet on the flagstones to keep warm, like some sort of harbinger of the dread days to come.

He sighed to himself. He still couldn't shake off the regime of the military academy where his parents had sent him in the States to straighten him out. If this were seven o'clock in the morning back at Pierpoint he'd be surrounded by lines of scrubbed and cropped-haired boys, eating in silence, and seemingly in synchronisation; their forks spearing as if to the sway of a metronome. He gazed along the lines of oak tables with ancient silver toasters set on them at intervals. They were fantastic things, gleaming in the half-light, huge and imposing with thick fabric-covered flex; they must have been thirty years old. Piles of white bread stood sentinel beside each of them; bowls of marmalade; curls of butter in bowls of water, jugs of orange juice concentrate; all laid out for a breakfast of ghosts.

Then he heard the sound of fluttering; birds' wings above him in the air; a brief gust of wind like cold breath against his wet face. He looked up – a sparrow that had come in through a sky-light was flying the length of the Hall.

Then there were two more, swooping down on him. A strike of bird shit splattered against one of the masters' portraits, dripping from his left ear as if a big fat pigeon had been perched on his head while he had been sitting for the artist.

Then, as he looked away from the portrait, he saw that the Hall was full of birds, as the half-light brought them into view. They had settled on the tables and had begun pecking their way into the neat, stacked piles of white bread. He got up and tried to shoo them away, but as soon as he managed to eject one lot another bunch took their place. It would only take a few moments, he realised, before all the bread for the toast was holed-through. He felt he ought to do something. The sky-light must have come loose during the storm last night, giving this sudden opportunity to a bunch of avian brigands. He couldn't imagine that the college would put up with this every morning, although, of course, it did, and had done for as long as anyone could remember.

He went along the piles of bread and sorted them, like packs of cards, slipping out the un-soiled slices and loading the toasters with them, pushing them down, one after another, until he'd filled twenty or more.

After they were all full he poured himself some stewed tea from an urn, expecting it to be coffee, and went back to his damp place on the bench.

When he looked up next the birds were scattering, desperately fighting to get out of the sky-light, and the air was blue with rising smoke; the dim dawn-light was cut by the flashes of flame and electrical sparks erupting from the ancient silver toasters. The first one that he'd loaded, on the next table, was fully in flame and he ran over to it and began beating it with slices of bread. He found the flex and pulled it from the wall as the next toaster in line became a small inferno; and then another followed it, until a whole line of them were ablaze.

He began to curse. Orange flickers played against the walls like the ancient echoes of a Saxon banquet. He went over to one of the toasters that was so red hot now it was making weird shuddering sounds and he picked up a jug of orange juice.

'Don't!' called a voice from the doorway. 'For God's sake!' It cut through the smoke and echoed around the walls.

He froze with the jug poised in his hand over the blazing toaster.

At the door stood a young man, sopping wet with stripes of hair running down his pale English face. He was tall and elegant, but water was dripping from his nose.

'You'll start an electrical fire!' he said, rather obviously, taking a step into the room.

'I think you'll find I already have,' said Mills. 'Best possible intentions. I was trying to save your bread, there were sparrows everywhere, you can't see them now, the little bastards, but they were here okay. I didn't realise these old toasters didn't have timers.'

They both looked at each other for a few seconds, neither of them knowing what to do. The young English student stared at him. Mills could see the light of dawn in the quad behind him. Then alarm bells broke into deafening action.

'I suggest we get the hell out of here,' he said.

'What if the whole place goes up?' said the English boy.

These Brits were obsessed with history, he thought.

'My point entirely,' said Mills. 'Let's run for it.'

He grabbed his gown and they sprinted for the quad and dived into a staircase as they heard the heavy boots of the porter running towards the Hall. When the coast was clear they ran into the next quad and leant against the wall. Windows began to open above them. The alarm bells were ringing everywhere. Sleep-headed grads with first-night-back hangovers were looking down to see what was going on. They leant into the ivy, a shake of water droplets showering down on them from the leaves.

Setting off the fire alarm at seven in the morning would not make him the most popular person in college, Mills thought. He sighed heavily.

'God, it's my first day,' said the pale English boy.

Mills shook the water from his hair. 'Mine too,' he said. 'I guess I'll skip breakfast.'

They both dashed for further cover, but in different directions.

The English boy, Jude, had been dreading coming down to breakfast. He'd been up for a few days already but had kept himself to himself, spending his time alone in his room trying to cram through all the books he hadn't read that he felt sure others with better educations than himself would know off by heart.

He was a comprehensive school boy from South London and was nervous about what he might meet in Oxford. Until a week before he'd been working as a welder's mate in a paper mill. He sat in his room again now, miserably towelling his head from the rain. He looked at the old ticking clock. Right now, back at the mill they'd already have been working for an hour. It had got him used to getting up early, much in the way the military academy had done for Mills. In another half an hour, at the paper-works, they'd be taking their first break, sitting on benches, rubbing their heads from the day's first indentations of their welding masks. He'd have a mug of tea in his hand. Daft old Harry would be sidling over, scratching his head in pantomime fashion at the crossword in the *Sun*, asking him for help and embarrassed about the chewed end of his Bic.

He'd longed to escape that place and the day-in day-out life that the Kidbrook Estate had promised him. But now he had escaped it he felt out of his depth, nervous of the future, of the hours and the days ahead in Oxford.

It was three days before they saw each other again.

Mills had gone for a pint to the Bear, with Colin, the gangly physics student with whom he shared his set of rooms. Colin was wearing the same black Megadeath sweat shirt he'd worn for three days. The idea had been for them to get to know each other. So far it wasn't proving a success. While Colin had great enthusiasm for the beer, he had no social graces whatsoever except sucking the froth from the head of his pint through the gingery stubble of his first attempt at a beard, and flicking the beer mats with the back of his hand and catching them in his teeth. Mills looked across the bar and recognised the pale face of the student who'd stopped him pouring orange juice into the toaster, sitting on his own reading the evening paper; a book that he'd got bored with lying face-down in the beer stains. He looked up from his paper and seemed to smile at him.

Mills would sooner be sitting over there with him in silence. He looked at Colin briefly, and put down his pint.

'Look, I'm going for a walk,' he said. 'I gotta get out of here.' He went to the door, leaving Colin behind, mid-way through his matchstick trick.

Jude looked towards the door as it swung and creaked and gusts of cold air skidded into the bar and drops of water from the portal splashed onto the tiles. What a miserable place England could be. He couldn't imagine ever being happy in Oxford.

He slid his pint aside and got up, leaving his paper, picked up his book, pushed the pub door open again and went out into the street. He could see the American just ahead of him, marching resolutely across the road.

He caught him up and put his hand on Mills's shoulder.

Mills was startled at first, thinking it was Colin coming running after him, but Colin was happier with his beer.

'Oh, hi,' said Mills.

'You're the one who burned the college down, right?'

'And a good thing too.'

'The guy I'm sharing a set with is driving me crazy too,' said Jude. 'I suppose that's who you were drinking with?'

'Uh huh.'

'I came to the pub to get away from mine. Anthropology.'

'Is that right? Well anthropology's my subject too.'

'Oh, is it?'

'Yes.'

They both stood there for a moment at a loss for anything more to say.

'I didn't want to share a set with anyone,' said Mills. 'I don't need friends, I get along all right without them. Always have, always will.' He stopped outside another pub, quieter than the one they'd just left. It looked warm, with a log fire. He went in.

Jude stood in the rain for a moment longer, not knowing whether he'd been invited to join him or not. By the time he got to the bar Mills was already ordering himself a pint. He ignored Jude for a few moments more and then turned to him abruptly.

'The name's Mills,' he said.

'Miles?'

'No, *Mills,*' he said, 'as in Dark Satanic . . .'

'And your Christian name?'

'That is my Christian name,' he said. 'So who are you?'

Jude still hesitated about giving his name, because as he said it his eyes flickered and betrayed his sense of nervousness. He'd never liked his name.

'Jude,' he said, finally.

'Jude, well, good to meet you, Jude. You're a Catholic?'

'No, why'd you say that?'

'Saint Jude. You're named after the saint of lost causes?'

'No, no, not after the saint.' He tried to laugh but his awkwardness meant that he just produced a nasal snort that sent a puff of cigarette ash up out of the ashtray on the bar top and onto the head of Mills's pint.

'No, quite the opposite really,' the English boy was saying.

'Uh huh?'

Jude ordered a pint and pulled himself up on to a bar stool next to Mills.

'My mother was a secretary in London in the late seventies,' said Jude, trying to begin a story he really didn't want to tell, and that he wasn't at all sure that Mills wanted to hear. 'One lunch time she had tickets for the Paris Studios, you know? That was where they did the BBC radio recordings. It was in London, not Paris. I don't know why they called it that.'

Mills tried to show an interest, but couldn't really understand why he was suddenly being plunged into the life of a secretary in London in the late seventies.

Jude looked equally lost as to why he had embarked on this story. He was visibly floundering, as if he were trying to conduct one of those conversations you have with a tutor in a foreign language class.

'So she goes along and sits in the front row expecting to be bored because the tickets were free, but the surprise guest was Paul McCartney,' he managed to say finally.

'Is that so,' said Mills.

'She screamed so loud she wet her knickers and couldn't go back to work,' said Jude quickly as if it was a part of the tale that he didn't much like but which was necessary to the overall scheme. He had a decidedly sullen look on his face, as if he suddenly no longer believed this story himself. He'd certainly lost heart in the telling of it, but now he was committed there was no way out but to persevere.

'Did she?' said Mills.

'Yeah, she was only sixteen. She went to St James's Park to dry off.'

'Probably very wise.'

'Yeah.'

There was silence for a moment while they both took long slugs at their beer.

'She met one of the gardeners,' said Jude.

This story could go on for ever, thought Mills.

Jude coughed to clear his throat. 'And they had a shag in his hut,' he said finally, and looked down into his pint.

Mills looked around the bar for a moment.

'Right.'

'And she got pregnant,' said Jude.

'That's bad luck.'

'Yes. So she named me after the Beatles' "Hey Jude". Must have seemed appropriate at the time.'

'Well, Jude, I guess you're lucky she didn't call you "The Fool on the Hill".'

'Yes, I suppose so.'

They both fell silent again. Mills skimmed the top of his pint with his finger, there was still ash in it.

He watched as a shadow passed over Jude's face, leaving as a legacy a nervous tic at the corner of his eye. He was good looking, with black silky hair, and piercing blue eyes, but he had no idea how to present himself. Outwardly he exhibited elegance and precision of movement, but close up everything that quivered nervously beneath the surface rose up in awkward eddies.

Mills's heart sank as he wondered if Jude really was the bastard son of a St James's Park gardener, conceived in a green-painted hut, and it seemed to him that he probably was. Why did he have to do this to other people who were probably okay? Why did he always make them suffer in his company? The guy was only trying to tell a funny story, whether it was true or not, and he'd created an atmosphere that had made it impossible for him. It was obvious that Jude was something of a loner, like himself. He could see the guy was upset, but there was nothing he could do about it now. An analyst his parents had sent him to had said that he was unable to form fundamental relationships. The stupid old fool was probably right, and he hadn't got along with him either.

Jude was now totally silenced. His name had always embarrassed him. At school he'd longed to have an ordinary name. Just to be a Steve, or a John, or a Paul, and blend in: anything but Jude: *the kid with the druggie rock'n'roll mother.*

Mills felt unable to retrieve the situation so he downed his beer and slid the glass across the wood to the barman.

'Well, I'll see you around Jude,' he said, although he didn't really want to go. He got off his stool and walked out of the door, pulling the collar of his Barbour up against the rain.

He walked past the Sheldonian, glancing up at the grim faces of the stone philosophers, and scowled back, equally stony.

Mills had never been good at making friends. His father was a politician and as a child they'd moved him about a lot. They'd left the States when he was nine and gone to Geneva, where his father had been a minor ambassador at the United Nations.

When he was fourteen they'd returned to Texas and his parents had put him in a military academy. It had not been a success. Now he was a Rhodes Scholar in Oxford. If he could have counted anywhere as home, then maybe he could have counted this as exile. Instead, he knew, he was just a prime example of a truly mixed-up kid of nineteen, soon to be twenty. He was used to it now. His parents had spent a great deal of money on professional help for him; they employed people just like themselves. His most recent shrink even had the same voice as his father. Being mixed-up had become a habit, he felt that he'd turned professional at it now, and it was something of a refuge; a place he'd made his own. He'd begun to look out for examples in his behaviour that would get a knowing nod from that ever present hired-shrink who still seemed to bear down on him wherever he was, like an anglepoise lamp.

His parents had refused to allow him to do what he really wanted: just to take a year off and go trekking across South America. It didn't seem a perverse thing to want to do. Other kids were allowed a year out. But no, they said he'd been given too much freedom already. He needed to *knuckle down*. His father had been a Rhodes Scholar at Oxford. It had been formative.

The new solution to their son was to be study. Abroad.

To Mills, Oxford looked like the same old oppressive hierarchy, hard beds and damp sheets; young people showing off to each other and talking rubbish. It would be a place where he was treated as a strange kind of thing; where the neuroses that his family had bequeathed him would stand out sharply. Where his inability to form relationships would be under glaring bright lights. No-one would see anything but the wreckage of his transient upbringing; bits left here and there scattered on disparate shores. They'd see the legacy of his violently entrenched family. They would see the generations of Clearwaters who had all conspired to produce himself: the end of the line.

As he walked through the heavy stone of Oxford he felt the presence on his shoulder of all the Robert Lemuels and Chet Zephaniahs and Earles and Kyles that had carried the Clearwater name before him, handing it down like a torch to each generation, so that the flame was now burning so hot that the hilt was heated, and he was due to drop it.

What kind of disaster would he make of Oxford, he wondered? Would it end with a real attempt to burn the place down? If he was as delinquent as his parents suggested, maybe it would.

Early next evening there was a knock at Jude's door. He'd been sitting at the window looking out through the leaded lights at the lashing rain, pulling at a thread hanging from the curtain. He went to the door.

'Oh, hello, er, what do you want?' said Jude.

Mills looked at his shoes for a moment, then looked up and tried to speak.

'Well, nothing really.'

'Oh, right.'

'Do you want to go to the pub?'

'Er, yeah, sure. If you like.'

'Unless you're busy or anything?'

'Well, er, no,' he said twirling a loose end of thread in his fingers, 'not especially.'

Jude followed him silently down the staircase.

'I was a shit to you last night and I'm sorry,' blurted Mills. It was the first step.

It was approaching the end of their first term. Mills and Jude went to the pub together most nights. They were both uneasy in college, and at first just as uneasy with each other. Neither of them had made any other friends, but very often they'd talk so late into the night that they'd fall asleep on one or other's floor. Neither of them had experienced a close friendship before and their conversation was intense; they had the whole world to discuss, and discuss it they did. Jude talked a great deal about his mother too, who'd spent most of his life staying out until four in the morning and staggering back clutching a bottle of Volvic, and whatever 'bloke' she'd ended up with. They'd invariably finish up on the living room floor in a blue haze of hashish fumes. Sometimes she'd disappear for days, off to Glastonbury, or some endless warehouse party. Jude had learned to throw himself back on his own resources.

Mills never talked about his parents at all but it astonished him to hear the stories of Jude's druggie-mum. It seemed incredible that anyone could have a mother who was only thirty-five. He asked him one night if the gardener's hut story was true and Jude replied that he didn't really know if it was, but that he probably owed his existence to something equally sordid, and that was the way he'd explained his conception, and name, to himself. His mother had certainly given birth to him at sixteen, and in the absence of evidence for any other father, a gardener in St James's Park would do. At least it was the premier park in London. Charles II used to walk his spaniels there.

Before term ended Mills telephoned his parents in Texas to say that if he didn't move out of college, he wouldn't be able to stand Oxford any longer. He was still sharing a set with Colin, who was driving him mad with heavy metal music that only encouraged the problem he already had with body odour. Mills's parents had stumped up some money and he'd found a house to rent on the Abingdon road. Mills asked Jude if he would blow out college too and rent the place with him. As soon as Jude saw the house he felt it was magical. It seemed natural that they should live in it and he congratulated Mills on his find. He couldn't believe how cheap the rent was: no more than living in college. Mills kept quiet about his parents' subsidy. The two misfits moved out of college.

Cudlow Hall was a medium-sized Edwardian stately home that had fallen into disrepair. The grounds swept down to the River Cherwell and just beyond lay the undulating greenness of the Vale of the White Horse.

The house had been bought by an entrepreneurial estate agent who had made his money in repossession sales and had now set about the mighty task of renovation. The old stable wing had recently been completed and made into a very fine house with two reception rooms, a large kitchen, and two bedrooms. It was The Stables that Mills proposed they rented.

On their first morning in the house they looked out of the window, across the lawns down to the Cherwell. There was a layer of mist still hanging eighteen inches deep across the lawn, and as they watched they saw a hare pop his head up above it to get his bearings before he dipped back down and lolloped off, his ears leaving a jet-stream through the mist. They skipped their lectures that morning, wanting to stay in the house, wandering around it, imagining themselves the young lords of the manor.

By mid morning the mist had cleared and it had turned into an unexpectedly stunning day with bright winter sunshine. They took a walk into the walled kitchen garden. Naysmith, the old gardener, was raking leaves up from around the fruit trees.

'Mornin' there squires,' he said, and with the gardener's broad Oxfordshire accent, they really did feel like young squires.

It was a good place to read in, too. Over the following weeks as the frost made the view clear and brittle, they often spent the afternoons sitting each on one of the window seats in the living room. Wading birds would come up from the reed beds and stroll across the lawn on their twig-thin legs, their long bills in the air, like a party of old ladies out for a cream tea. There was a long broad view of the flat, uninterrupted landscape and they could just make out the spires of Oxford in the distance. It was picture-perfect; each of the elements, the broad brush strokes of the changing clouds; the almost musical swaying of the beech trees in the copse, and the reeds by the river; the waders walking through it all like the small historical figures at the base of a Poussin. The only thing this perfect landscape lacked was a signature in the bottom right-hand corner.

It was everything being at Oxford should be: afternoons with a book on a window seat; conversations late into the night; intense friendship. Yet at the end of February disaster struck, after just three months in the house. The haven of the Stables was destroyed, as the weight of Mills's family suddenly descended.

The first indication Jude had was when the television mysteriously failed to work and Mills talked him into not getting it repaired. The radio wasn't working either. Jude really couldn't understand why everything electrical was failing on them. Mills said nothing, he had been quiet for days. He'd been back to the States for Christmas and had been in a peculiar mood since his return. Although they still talked late into the night Mills wasn't saying what was on his mind and there most obviously was something on his mind. Both of them, being natural loners, would have quiet patches and they each respected that. But this was a different kind of quiet.

Then the newspaper that they had delivered didn't arrive for a couple of days.

'I don't get it,' said Jude. 'It's a complete media black-out, like they had in the Gulf War.'

Mills said nothing.

'What is it they don't want us to know?'

Jude walked into the village to talk to the newsagent.

'I'm sorry, sir,' said George, 'but your *Guardian*'s been cancelled. Young Mr Clearwater came in and said you weren't going to be wanting it.'

This was very odd indeed. Mills hadn't consulted him.

Mills didn't return to The Stables until very late that night and plodded up the stairs to his bedroom without speaking.

Jude pushed his door open and found him sitting on the edge of his bed twirling a sock in his hands. He asked him what the hell was going on.

Mills stared at the bedroom carpet for some time, and when he looked up his eyes had glazed over, as if he was going to cry.

'I just can't face it,' he said. 'I just don't want to know. It's going to be the worst thing.'

'What?'

'I really hope he's not going to do it.'

'Who?'

'My father. He spoke to me at Christmas. It's going to ruin everything. They'll make me go home, I know they will.'

He went silent, and Jude thought it best just to sit and wait. Mills smacked his pockets, and looked around the room for cigarettes. Jude handed him one and as he lit it he drew long and hard, filling himself with smoke. Then he blew it out.

'He's thinking about running for president.'

'Really?'

Mills snapped at him, 'Yes, really.' It was uncharacteristic of him to snap these days and Jude felt shocked and hurt by his hard, dangerous gaze. He looked entirely lost.

'Of what?' said Jude, slightly fazed. 'President of what? His company?'

Mills gave him a withering look.

'Of The United States of Fucking America,' he said finally.

'Shit.'

'Yeah, shit exactly. This is going to ruin everything. The press'll destroy my parents' marriage, they'll turn me into Chelsea Clinton, or Amy Frigging Carter. You know what happened to Chelsea when she went to Stanford? They sent Secret Service guys over to the campus, and so they'd blend in, they gave them bikes to ride around on. Can you imagine? I'll never survive it. I'll let them down, I know I will. I'm too mixed-up to be the president's son.'

Mills drew hard and long on his cigarette again, so that the glowing end formed into a spike of ash.

'But it's fantastic, it's terrific, surely.'

'No, Jude, it's not. Just think about it.'

Jude thought for a moment. He realised that he could be sharing a house with the son of the President of The United States of America. A warm glow came over him, he couldn't help it, his face flushed like an embarrassed teenager. He'd already spoken to the man a couple of times on the telephone when he'd called for Mills. They got on quite well he thought. He'd be having regular chats with the presidential candidate, and as Mills's best friend, my God, he'd lord it about Oxford. They'd dine on High Table. He was beginning to tremble with excitement. He wanted to smile and laugh, but Mills's face was fixed and icy.

'Will he win?'

'No, I don't think he's got a chance of even getting the nomination. It's ridiculous. He's going to tear us all apart and get nowhere near the White House. You don't know what American politics are like, the Party tears itself apart through the primaries. No-one is exempt. Everything I do will be under the spotlight. If I get drunk, if I flunk an exam, if I have a one-night stand.'

'Well, perhaps it's a good thing you're in England. Surely that must help?'

'I don't know,' he said. 'In some ways it might make it worse, because my father was a Rhodes Scholar in Oxford too, it kinda makes me a little version of him, doesn't it? It puts expectations on you. The press just love it when a politician's kid screws up. It's bad, Jude, it's bad, and I happen to believe it's a fundamental human right to be able to fuck-up. It was the first right we got for ourselves, Adam and Eve got it in the Garden of Eden. They fucked-up at the very first opportunity. But if I do he'll never forgive me.'

'And he's definitely going to run?'

'I don't know, he was still thinking about it. But if he's going to he'll have to declare pretty soon. I don't know what he's going to do.'

'Well,' said Jude, 'cancelling the papers and blowing up the telly isn't going to make it go away for you. A media black-out has to involve everyone else as well, not just us.'

'That was really dumb, I know. I don't know what I thought I'd achieve. I just wanted us to live in blissful ignorance for a little bit longer. I guess that was my first fuck-up already.'

Jude sighed deeply. The import of the news was now sinking in.

'I'm going downstairs to get the whisky,' he said.

'Yeah, that's a good idea.'

When he came back into the bedroom Mills had his head in his hands.

'This is why you never speak about your family.'

'I know. I've learned not to. He's been a Governor for a while now and so most people only want to talk to you because of who he is. I mean, I didn't go in for the Rhodes to follow in my father's footsteps, I went in for it to get out of the States and away from it all. Damn it, I didn't even have a choice about that. I wanted just to go travelling and relax for a bit. But I came to Oxford. Perhaps dad did the same with his father. *He* was a real son-of-a-bitch politician. I thought maybe I'd make a real friend here, a friend

I could trust because they didn't give a damn what my dad did for a day job.'

'And you did.'

'Yeah,' said Mills, and stood up, and lunged towards Jude and put his arms around him. He buried his head for a moment in Jude's shoulder and then broke away, sweet whisky on his breath but deep sadness on his face. He was beginning to shake, a simultaneous kind of fury and desperation. His hands were flapping about for a cigarette. Jude pulled his pack from his pocket and put a cigarette into Mills's mouth.

'You see,' said Mills, 'I really love my dad. I hate his politics. He's so right-wing, but I love my dad. I guess it's one of those things you can't help doing, even if they don't think much of you. He's a great guy. He really cares, he really does. I mean, he's true blue National Rifle Association and all that, there's not a single thing he stands for I agree with.' Mills tried a smile. 'He's a *Moderate* Republican, you know, he believes in a Woman's Right to get stuck with sixteen unwanted children, he believes in the right to Bear Arms, and that you can't hunt elk without a grenade launcher . . . I wouldn't vote for him, but I love him. He's my dad.' He sounded like he was trying to convince himself.

Mills looked ready to crack. Jude stared hard into his face. He'd never heard Mills say that he loved his father before, and there was a hollowness to the declaration, as if it was a line to cover his disappointment. Mills had always given the impression that there was no love in his family.

'It's just,' said Mills, passing his hand over the flame of the church candle that they'd lit on the bedroom floor, 'it's just that I can never now be *me*. I'll always be *the son of* . . . like some sort of really bad sequel.'

Mills was searching for words. Jude knew there was more to it than this. He looked like a man who was being suffocated, his hands vainly trying to push the pillow away.

Mills glanced around the room, at the candle-light as it flickered on the oak-beamed ceiling.

'This is our sanctuary,' said Jude.

Mills nodded. 'Yeah, *our* sanctuary. So you're not going to suddenly go weird on me?'

'Weird?'

'When my dad became Governor of Texas all my friends, so-called friends, went weird on me and I never trusted any of them again. You just can't help yourself, you always suspect their motives.'

'I won't change,' said Jude, putting his hand on Mills's shoulder.

'Yes you will,' he said, 'we both will. You ain't seen nothin' like it.'

Jude fell into the habit of sneaking into the common room in college to catch the early evening news before cycling home. He got strange looks from the other students; he had a reputation for never going into the common room. He didn't mention his visits there to Mills.

It was in the middle of the following week when, after the usual items about the European currency, and another food-scare, up popped Kyle Clearwater. Jude shuddered and muttered 'Oh shit,' under his breath. There was the figure of Mills's father, standing before a bank of microphones on the steps of his Governor's mansion, making his declaration.

Then, to make matters even worse, up came a picture of Mills. The son in Oxford, a Rhodes Scholar like his father. A gasp went up from the other students and they all turned to look at Jude. The BBC News made quite a thing of it. He didn't know exactly what expression he should have on his face so he just stared fixedly at the screen. He hoped it wasn't a foretaste of things to come.

The moment the news was over Jude left without speaking to anyone and cycled home, deeply worried about Mills's reaction. It was already dark and his headlamp battery was failing. An oncoming motorist cursed at him, then the front wheel squelched on something in the road and he slid off on the black ice onto the verge. He almost knocked himself out as he hit the frozen turf. He hadn't been concentrating on the road at all. Jude got up and looked back to see what had de-bicycled him. It was a dead pheasant that had been hit by a car. He picked it up, it was in pretty good shape for a bird that had managed to get hit twice. Thinking it might make dinner, he threw it into the basket on his bike and cycled on, trying to keep his mind on the mechanics of making a pheasant casserole. Mills would be in a wild mood. He'd be explosive.

The Stables were in darkness. Jude had no idea where Mills was, but he desperately wished he'd been home.

He settled himself in the kitchen with a chopping board and his pheasant, looking out into the courtyard every time he heard a noise, hoping it would be Mills.

He wondered what the next days would be like. Would there really be an onslaught of press people after Mills? Would the rival nominees send spies to disgrace them? All of that seemed hysterical in the extreme but he was worried about Mills. Would he do something truly weird now? Would he flip?

Jude heard a noise on the gravel approach to the courtyard, and looked for the light of Mills's racing bike. Nothing, it was just someone using the driveway to turn around, people often got lost in these lanes on their way to Didcot.

You pluck a pheasant from the breast, working towards the neck. Then you take the cleaver and whack off its head.

Where was Mills? Had he decided to get out of town? Or had he marched boldly into Hall to take it on the chin and show them all? There was nothing but darkness and silence outside the window. It was too cold even for the owls in the copse to hoot, or the usual evening bats to flutter around the casement, throwing themselves like bungee jumpers from the eaves. It was the deepest of February weather.

He slit the arse-end of the pheasant with his Sabatier and began to pull out the intestines, the worst part of the whole operation, holding his breath against the sweet, sickly smell. Its guts spilled out across the chopping board: the liver, the heart and the gizzard; blood leaked across the wood.

The telephone rang. Mills! he thought: Mills pissed and crazy somewhere, and he dashed through to the living room and picked up the ivory-coloured receiver of the telephone.

'Hello!' he shouted.

'Hi, there,' said the voice. 'Is it possible to speak to Mills?'

'No, I'm sorry,' he said recognising the voice, 'I think he must be working late in the Bodleian, or something.'

'Well, okay, that's fine, maybe I'll call again later. How's it going there in your country pile?'

'Fine, fine, sir.'

'You busy yourself?'

'Er, yeah, I'm plucking a pheasant actually, horrible job.'

'You really live, you guys.'

'Oh, er, and congratulations and the best of luck, sir, with the, er, White House,' said Jude.

'Well, thank you, thank you. I hope Mills feels the same.'

'Oh I'm sure he does, sir, I know he does.'

'Well tell him I called and I'll catch him later.'

'Yes sir, I will.'

There was a pause.

'So you tell Mills I called, ya' hear? His momma sends her *big love* too,' he said awkwardly.

Jude was suddenly struck by how much more American Mills's father sounded than he did. He wondered if it was an accent that had been groomed for press conferences and the campaign trail. It was as if he'd picked it off the shelf.

Mills came back half an hour later. He was rather silent, but gave no indication whether he'd heard the news himself or not.

He walked into the living room. Jude followed him, took a deep breath and said: 'Your father called.'

Mills looked over at the telephone, and its ivory-coloured receiver. There were deep red blotches on it from where Jude had picked it up while he was gutting the pheasant.

'Yes, it looks like it,' he said, wearily. 'He wants to know what I've decided.'

'What *you've* decided?'

'They want me to go back home to help campaign. Put the family on show.'

'When?'

'I'll have to go in four weeks, just before the Easter break.'

'You knew he was declaring today?'

'He called me yesterday.'

'Did you see it on the news?'

'No, I've just been cycling around.' Then he suddenly snapped again. 'What is this, an interview?' Then he looked down at the carpet. 'Look, I'm sorry, I'm sorry. I guess this affects you too. Shit, I just can't see me fitting into all of this.'

'You'll be fine, you'll be okay.'

He tried to brighten. 'Well, I guess I'd better start practising my handshake and my fake smile.'

The Easter break came and Mills went back to Texas. Jude stayed on in The Stables. There was no reason for him to go home.

It was a moody kind of day, undecided and uncertain. The English spring had taken full possession of the Oxfordshire landscape; the lawns, and the fields were in their first, and perfect, green. Tortoiseshells were flapping about in the walled garden with their carpet-patterned wings, everything was just as it was supposed to be in an English garden; it was even a little warmer, but it all seemed rather dull and lifeless without Mills. Jude had the feeling of being in the middle of nowhere.

The house was empty without him too. It creaked when it felt like it, and at times, it shuddered. No-one came out to The Stables and Jude was beginning to feel desolate again. He sat in the window seat all afternoon reading, letting a cup of Lapsang Souchong go cold.

When the telephone rang he jumped up.

'How's it going?' asked Mills.

'It's okay, okay. How's it going over there?'

There was silence for a moment.

'It's worse,' said Mills.

'That bad, huh?'

'I can't tell you.'

There was silence again, as if Mills was having to ask someone to stand by him and explain how to use a telephone.

'I'm going mad with it,' he said. Jude tried to sympathise, but couldn't think of anything to say that wouldn't just sound glib and patronising. Mills spoke again:

'Look, have you got plans or anything for the next couple of weeks?'

'What do you mean?'

'The parents have agreed that you should come out to Texas if you like.'

'Texas?'

'Yeah. You want to come? I'll show you the Alamo.' Mills was sounding nervous and agitated, and suddenly speaking quickly now, where just a moment before he'd seemed to have nothing at all to say.

Jude hesitated for a moment. He'd never been anywhere in his life: Texas would be one hell of a start.

'The money's not a problem,' said Mills. 'The folks are paying. There's a flight leaving tomorrow. We can put a ticket for you on the Delta desk at Heathrow. I'll meet you at Austin airport. We'll have a great time. Wait 'till you meet the family . . .'

3

'Hi there, I'm Trooper Dunbar.'

A uniformed officer held out his hand to Jude in the Arrivals Hall of Austin airport.

He took it, bemused, looking around for Mills. The trooper's vice-like grip gave him a sudden shudder of pain that reached right up his forearm to the elbow. 'How do you know who I am?' he asked. Trooper Dunbar smiled, but didn't answer.

'I'd like for you to come with me, sir,' he said. 'And, er, welcome to Texas.'

Jude had been following the campaign in the *Guardian*, whose delivery had now been re-instated. Clearwater's campaign wasn't actually going that well, as Mills had predicted. For some reason, he just didn't seem to be getting the same amount of attention as a character called Lanyon McKenzie, an East Coast senator and the darling of the Moral Right. Lanyon McKenzie was everywhere, from the cover of *Time*, through to endorsements by sports stars. His shining smile was beginning to haunt Clearwater and his team, the *Guardian* had said. He seemed to have a more popular touch than Mills's father, who was somewhat reserved and ill at ease with the drum-banging razzmatazz of the stump.

Jude was very nervous indeed about meeting him, but right now his main concern was whether there was some sort of crisis with Mills himself.

Trooper Dunbar walked him quickly over to his squad car, which was parked outside, and opened the back door for him.

Jude was in a daze. The trans-Atlantic flight had mesmerised him: first the plane itself, which was so vast he felt as if they'd left Heathrow in a street of houses, then the sight of the coast of Greenland, with its perfect untouched glaring whiteness, and icebergs slipping away from the main like cathedrals.

His heart leapt as they hit the highway; it was just as he'd hoped it'd be. There really were restaurants and diners with fibreglass pineapples, and hamburgers the size of caravans, revolving on top. He could see instantly why Mills hated it so much, but he found it intriguing and exhilarating. Everything shone and sparkled; the same could hardly be said of South London. He almost felt a pang of jealousy; everything about Mills was bigger and more exciting.

Trooper Dunbar was wearing a large white Stetson as he drove.

'So you really do know how to wear hats in Texas,' said Jude, in a gambit to begin a conversation and break the mysterious cold silence.

'We sure do, sir. The only time a Texan takes his hat off is at a funeral. And only then if it's his own.'

The Texan state capital of Austin was not mirror glass and sky-scraper-filled like Houston or Dallas, but on a much more human scale, with fine old two-storey buildings and a Capitol just a few feet short of the one in Washington.

As they drew close to the Governor's Mansion he saw the steel cabins that were set up on the grass verges, trucks with antennae, radio masts; there were marquees, and milling around in sunglasses, sipping from polystyrene cups, the press corps. A couple of TV crews were interviewing a smart young guy, sweating in a suit, on a stretch of grass in front of the mansion gates; one of Clearwater's spokespeople.

As they pulled up at a security cabin he looked around him, somehow expecting a flash of cameras, and microphones to be thrust towards him in the back seat.

When the police at the gates saw Trooper Dunbar they waved them through. Jude watched as he drove carefully, and respectfully, towards the white-pillared colonial mansion. It was something like the White House, small and pristine, but as monumental as a wedding cake in a patisserie window. It had been built in the classical style and was surrounded by perfectly kempt exotic shrubbery and evergreen lawns. Trooper Dunbar got out and opened the door for Jude, pulling his bag out of the boot. Jude glanced back at the media circus to see if anyone was watching. No-one was, but that didn't stop him from standing there for a few moments, feeling as puffed up as a peacock on a palace lawn. He felt inordinately important, and he savoured the moment. Then Trooper Dunbar drove off without speaking, leaving him to walk up the steps to the white double doors. He was suddenly alone and the heat instantly formed a sticky damp-course around his shirt collar. As he got to the door it swung open before he'd even found a bell and a young woman stood there smiling. She was dressed in a smart blue trouser suit, her hair impeccable, and on her lapel she wore a campaign button: *Kyle Clearwater: The Clear Choice.*

'Hi, I'm Catherine Sirteema,' she said, her hand sweeping out to be shaken. 'I guess you're Jude, we've been kinda worried about you. Storm warnings in Atlanta I hear?'

'Tornadoes,' he said, dramatically. 'And Hurricane Wendy.'

'Anyways, welcome to Texas, welcome to the Governor's Mansion. They're not here right now but I guess you'd like to go up to your room and freshen up some?'

'Yes, thank you . . . Where's Mills? I thought he'd be at the airport?'

'He's not here right now and the Governor's doing a TV, but they both send their sincere apologies for not being here to greet you in person. They would have been if your transfer from Atlanta hadn't been held up. I'm really sorry about that . . .'

He smiled as he realised that she was apologising on behalf of the tornado and the hurricane. This woman was running *everything*, he could see it in her eyes.

'. . . But they'll be catching up with you shortly I guess,' she said.

She led him into the reception room with its perfectly painted white walls and garish portraits of former Governors.

They passed an open door where a room was filled with people talking into telephones, the walls were covered with pictures of Kyle Clearwater, and everywhere there was the slogan: *The Clear Choice for America.*

'We're all real pleased you could come on out. The Governor hopes he'll catch up with you,' she said, repeating herself as if she was perpetually on automatic. 'If you'd just step in here with me.' They'd stopped outside a small office with three middle-aged women working away in it at computer screens. They each turned to give broad, over-the-top smiles. One of them was drinking out of an 'I Love Kyle' coffee mug. They looked like they thoroughly enjoyed their afternoons here at the mansion. Party volunteers.

'Desiree, could you Polaroid Mr Cornelius?' said Catherine Sirteema, and Desiree jumped up with a camera, and asked him to stand against the wall to be shot. Before he could even run his hand through his mop of jet black hair the flash had gone off and she had produced a developing image of a startled young man with worse than a five o'clock shadow, looking like a cat that had been suddenly distracted while having a paw-wash. His black hair flopped over his face and his deep sapphire eyes looked piercing. It looked, he thought, like the photographs you see of serial killers. She put it into a heat-seal machine with a small piece of card that had been pre-typed, and after attaching a small silver clip presented him with a pass. It said *Jude Cornelius, MANSION STAFF, AUSTIN.*

'We'd find it real useful if you could wear that at all times. Also if you could resist the temptation to take it off whatever the situation, even within the mansion environs. We really don't want to get into a situation where they go walking.'

'High security, eh?'

'Extreme high security,' said Catherine Sirteema, in a tone that suggested she wasn't to be messed with.

'If you should lose it you're to call the security number on the back.'

He wondered how he could call the number if he'd lost the card.

Catherine Sirteema was a very striking woman in her late twenties. He realised that she must be quite high up in the campaign team. He was flattered by her attention and, frankly, overwhelmed by the whole thing so far.

She swept him up a staircase lined with more portraits of former Governors of Texas, generally surrounded by longhorn cattle.

The sound of telephones ringing was everywhere along with

the dull babble of volunteers cold-calling party members to secure their vote. They were reading from scripts and the babble had a decidedly lacklustre air to it. The latest Lanyon McKenzie poll, with his twenty point lead, had demoralised the whole organisation.

Even upstairs there were wires and cables spewing out of rooms and along the corridors, gaffer-taped to the carpet, as if the whole place were the back-stage area of a rock festival. She led him to a room at the far end of an upper corridor, where, mercifully, the cables petered out and there were just planters with palms to fall over in the night. She pushed a door open. There was a four-poster bed. The wallpaper and the curtains were so floral in design that he felt he'd been slipped some mind-bending drugs.

'I'll leave you now to freshen up. Just call 9–7 on the phone if you want to talk with me. May I just say how glad the Governor and Mrs Clearwater are to have you as a house-guest, and I hope we can all make your stay a memorable one.'

'Oh,' he said, breaking into a short, but he hoped respectful, laugh, 'it's already memorable.'

She smiled at him, for the first time a genuine smile. She looked a little tired around the eyes, he supposed from a relentless schedule.

'I hope we'll take time-out to be friends,' she said. Then in a gust of air and the exhausted residue of perfume and toil she was gone.

He looked around the room again for a moment; it smelled of perfectly laundered linen, a smell that he was unused to. He went over to open the window to escape the chill of the air-conditioning, but the window appeared to be bolted down, and even if he'd opened it there was another layer of glass beyond, greenish in colour, bolted onto the outside wall like a screen. He guessed it was bullet-proof glass. Oddly, it only served to make him feel more vulnerable, and he swiftly moved away from the window.

He lay on the bed for a couple of minutes.

The bedside phone rang.

'Hi, it's Mills,' a voice yelled enthusiastically. 'Glad you made it, welcome to Austin. God! I can live again!'

'Thanks. Where are you?'

'I'm in the car, I'll be home in five minutes . . .' The line was breaking up. 'I'll see you then.'

'Sure.'

At the rear of the mansion was a long gallery, known as the Team Room, that looked out over sweeping lawns and the security fence beyond. Jude could see a guard, with a dog, patrolling the perimeter. People sat around the room in small groups, all with sheaves of paper; analysing polls, tweaking itineraries, throwing down sodas and coffee. This room had been reserved for the top executives in Clearwater's campaign, and for the family, where they could catch up with each other, grab a coffee, entertain a sympathetic guest, or just fall exhausted into one of the vast cowhide chairs. The Governor's billiard table had been removed but the green-tasselled shade still hung from the ceiling. It was a hotchpotch of a room, containing furniture that the Clearwaters had brought with them when they moved into the mansion. The 'private' furniture was in stark contrast to the fine antiques in the rest of the residence. The modern furniture looked strangely more dated, locked in the early seventies when the Clearwaters had married. Traditionally this room had been the family room, and it was scuffed and bruised in places. There were pictures around of Mills as a kid. There was Mills grimacing with a baseball bat, Mills with a fish on the end of a line looking at it, terrified. Mills as a baby with his face covered in Jello. Mills as a teenager playing the drums in a school pipe band with his tongue held between his teeth. There was a black and white snap of his mother in a bikini, looking cold but determined to make the best of it on a stretch of Cape Cod coastline. There was Clearwater holding an amateur golf trophy on Martha's Vineyard; Clearwater collapsed in a chair after an election victory. There was a black and white four-shot in a heavy ebony frame standing on a bureau, taken in the 'sixties: a dignified middle-aged man with a boot-lace tie, a woman beside him, beaming in a beehive bouffant as he shook hands with Lyndon B Johnson, the First Lady, Ladybird Johnson, leaning back and laughing. And then a strangely dark and moody photo: Mills as a four-year-old in a dark button-up overcoat, walking with a deeply serious expression on his face across the back lawn of the White House. His small hand was being gripped tightly by Ronald Reagan. Jude stepped back a little as he saw that photograph and suddenly he felt a sense of the great gulf between their backgrounds, and something of a sense of awe. He couldn't help but feel a twinge of jealousy as well. He felt as if he had stepped into another world. Mills had told him so many stories about his childhood but none of them had contained a real sense of this. The photos clearly shared the family heritage; they said: you can never be where we are because we are the generations of power that have made this state – and we have the right to set our eyes on Washington. Even though the atmosphere in the room was much more relaxed than in the rest of the mansion, it spoke volumes about the kind of family the Clearwaters were. They were a formidable political dynasty, a long line of Texan Republicans.

Then Jude came across a picture of Mills as an eight-year-old, looking at the camera rather reluctantly, dressed as a cowboy, and he remembered what he had told him about that time in his life.

Mills's childhood, as he'd recounted it, seemed really to have consisted of only a few isolated afternoons. This was evidently a photograph recalling one of them. It was shot on the hills to the north of Austin. The Clearwaters had been staying out there for a few days on a ranch owned by friends. The people had twin boys of Mills's age. That afternoon the three of them had put on stetsons and holsters and staged a spectacular charge, raining down on another bunch of kids from the top of what they'd christened Cowboy Hill and in the battle Mills had died most spectacularly.

The twins hailed his death as one of the best they had ever seen. It had begun up a tree when he was winged in the shoulder while still firing two cap guns. It had ended with a bullet right in the temples, which he'd illustrated by going boss-eyed and falling out of the tree. He had to grit his teeth against the pain in his arms and the winding in his chest, but as the twins cheered him, it gave him the most tremendous feeling. He couldn't believe his success. Other boys generally just ignored him, because of his moods, and the cold-fish attitude to everything that he'd picked up from his parents.

He liked books, he liked stories, and most of all he liked maps. He'd open up the atlas and guide his pencil slowly over the oceans and the mountains and the rivers. Best of all he loved the Amazon. When he was more miserable than usual he'd guide his pencil along it, and think of the alligators, and the Indians peering through the forest with their blow-pipes. Then he'd get his eraser and rub it out, and slide the atlas silently back into its place on the shelf; in his mind having made a secret journey.

After falling out of that tree, with a bullet between his eyes, he couldn't believe his success. It had happened by chance, and he knew he'd found something that he was truly good at: heroic failure. He never forgot how it felt that day, how his body had tingled with the luxury of the drama; the sensuous feeling of an heroic death.

Later that same afternoon he was dying so comprehensively (it had included having an arrow burned out, a snake bite sucked, and a bullet cut out of his forehead) that when his new friends' mother had called them all over to the barbecue he'd had to break off and complete the rest of his dying half an hour later – aided by the theft of a ketchup bottle from the table for realistic blood.

When they got home, (his father was an up and coming lawyer in Austin at that time) his perplexed parents scolded him for that theft. You do not go to other people's houses and steal the ketchup, they said. That was the moment they first considered therapy for him.

What made a son of ours do such a thing? they asked. Don't you realise that they're really big clients and the fact they had ketchup on the table at all was only as a consideration to you kids?

He remained tight-lipped and they looked at him as if they didn't understand him at all. And he felt them move away.

A couple of days later he was with his mother in the First Interstate Bank in downtown Austin. Without any warning whatsoever the Jesse James gang burst in and held the place up and shot Mills in the back.

It caused quite a confusion in the bank. Mills was spread-eagled, face down, on the cold marble floor, having taken a rope barrier down with him. He heard the voice of a teller bearing down on him asking if he'd like a glass of water, his mother's yelping suppressions of hysteria panting in the background. Nothing would induce him to open his eyes. He lay there, frozen, his arms splayed across the marble, trying not to breathe.

In the weeks that followed his parents spent a fortune on all manner of medical tests on him. If only their doctors had known that the TV was showing reruns of *Rawhide*.

It was probably, from that time, when he'd finally confessed that he was *only pretending*, that his parents made up their minds that he was nothing but trouble. He was *disturbed*, they agreed, a social embarrassment.

From the age of nine to thirteen he spent his time making himself unpopular at the American school in Geneva, while his father was posted at the UN. It was there that he added to his other difficulties by developing a peculiar accent. He really didn't sound American, not Texan anyway. In fact he could adopt a whole range of accents at will: French, German, English. But mostly English. His accent made people look at him strangely, unable to work out where he came from, and consequently where he was coming from. It put people off, and it became a shield.

On the Clearwaters' return to Texas, when he was fourteen, a solution was found in the Pierpoint Military Academy, Fort Worth. They guaranteed to straighten him out, turn him back into an American.

There was a picture too, beautifully framed, of Mills in his Pierpoint Cadets uniform. Jude smiled as he stared at it: the blue tunic with brass buttons, the white peaked cap and the razored hair. The serious face of a boy standing before a firing squad.

In his last year at the academy his parents attended the Veterans' Day service. All the cadets were decked out in their uniforms and white gloves. Kyle Clearwater had been elected Governor of Texas two years before and they were the guests of honour.

Mills stared up at his mother and father sitting on the stage with the commander, dreading the address his father was to give after the school song.

The opening bars of the song boomed out from the organ

as everyone stood. Then, at the point where the first verse should have begun, there was just the sound of parents and cadets fluttering the pages of their hymn books. Some fool of a boy had got into the hymn book cupboard before the service and painstakingly removed from a thousand hymnals the page that the song was on. It would have taken hours, real determination, and a deep hatred of the academy.

His parents realised instantly who the culprit was.

Jude was sitting in one of the cowhide chairs, wishing he had a book with him, when the door opened and standing in it was Mills, looking bemused and frustrated. His eyes flashed around the room for a moment until he saw Jude looking up and smiling. He came straight over, giving out sighs of relief and shrugging his shoulders.

'It's great to see you! They been looking after you all right?' he asked, breathlessly.

'Sure, sure. It's great. Texas is stunning, I can't get over how hot it is. My head's spinning with everything. Are you okay?'

He looked agitated and slightly unsure of himself as if they hadn't seen each other for years instead of just a week.

Mills laughed. 'I'm sorry,' he said. 'I don't know how I missed you at the airport. It's chaos here. Nobody tells me anything.' He flopped down into the seat beside him. 'Well, anyway welcome to the Wasps' Nest. Let's get away from this rabble. You want to have a beer outside?' He leapt up again, he'd only been sitting down for a matter of seconds; he was hyperactive; he didn't seem to know what to do with his hands. He looked around at his father's cohorts as he led Jude out on to the verandah where wooden fans revolved gently, swishing amid the sound of crickets and birdsong. 'Mom and dad are really looking forward to meeting you,' he said. He stopped to breathe for a moment as they hit the air.

Sitting, sipping at a glass with the ice quietly ringing against the crystal, was an elderly woman in a lounge-chair, dressed as a teenager, in ill-advised bright colours that clashed with her heavily applied make-up.

She was drinking a greenish white cocktail, a highly potent Mint Julep. She looked as if she was slightly sozzled, and building up a real head of steam. She was smoking a cigarette, which gave Jude hope that he might be able to smoke as well. No-one had been smoking inside. Because of her garish summer clothes, her teased hair and a complexion that had a few tucks in it here and there, he found her difficult to date. She was probably approaching her mid-seventies. She wore false eyelashes which buzzed like the wings of dragonflies as she peered up at Mills in the midday sun.

'And who may this young man be?' she asked in a refined, but gravelly nicotine-edged drawl.

'He's my friend from England,' shouted Mills. 'The one I told you about. He's arrived.'

'I'm a bit deaf,' she shouted up at Jude with a smile, 'that's why he yells at me,' and a couple of birds scattered from the lawn and landed in a nearby ceiba tree. 'I went deaf at fifty-eight, because I'd heard too much bullshit, but that's politics. You're here to help with Kyle's campaign?'

'No he's not,' Mills shouted. 'He's a guest. He's a friend, he's not a volunteer.'

'Thank God for that. I can't get in my usual room,' she said, looking up at Jude with a play for sympathy. 'It's full of Goddamn' phones. Who's gonna be the greatest President this country ever had?' she called. Jude smiled, amused. Then she began punching the air, and slapping the armchair again, the Mint Julep spilling everywhere. Mills turned to Jude, smiling patiently.

'Grandma went to a rally last night in Houston and danced 'till two with half the crooks in the oil business,' he said, trying to explain her high spirits before lunch.

'Where's Kyle?' she said, 'where is he?'

'Dad's not back yet. He's doing a TV.'

'Well flick it on, flick it on,' she said, trying to pull herself up out of her chair. 'Let's see what he's got to say for himself today.'

'No, Grandma, it's a pre-record.'

'Pre-records . . . *pre-records*,' she said with sudden venom. 'I told him when he was running for Governor he shouldn't do pre-records, they cut 'em up and make him look like he's fishin' without a pole.' She turned to Jude. 'TV people are the *lowest*, believe me. They can flip you over quicker than you can a drowned catfish. Thank God when Earle and I were in the business they didn't have tape, they didn't have pre-records.'

Mills turned to Jude and smiled. 'They'd only just invented TV,' he muttered. He had an affinity with his grandmother, that was obvious. Perhaps it was from her that he'd inherited his rebellious, critical streak. Sitting out here on the verandah she seemed to have been marginalised by her family too.

'It's okay, Grandma, it's KC-MBG, they won't cut him up,' said Mills.

'KC-MBG? What's he doing on that little shit-ass station? He should be doing *Larry King Live*.'

'He's done LKL.'

'What's happened to my Mint Julep?' she said, her face falling, shaking her head in shock, and betraying her age as she stared at the empty glass she was still clutching.

'It's all over your dress,' said Mills.

'What do you expect me to do, suck it out?' She began flapping her frock to dry it in the sun.

Mills smirked and went back through the French windows to refresh his grandmother's glass. She took out a cigarette – her last had been doused by her drink when she was punching the air with her campaign cry. She patted the lounge-chair beside her. Jude sat down. There were cannas and orchids, and other blazing blooms at their feet below the verandah. The birds were back on the lawn, stamping the ground for worms around the sprinklers. It was a grand place, and Jude breathed in as he stared out across the lawn. He sank comfortably into the lounge-chair with the hot sun on his face.

'So,' she said, 'whadda'ya think of my Millburn?'

'He's great,' said Jude. 'And a real good friend.' It was the first time he'd ever heard his full name. No wonder he'd shortened it. How on earth had his parents inflicted him with that?

'You reckon he'll make President one day if my boy Kyle screws this whole thing up?'

'I reckon he could,' he said to please her.

'Good. I'm hedging my bets. I got it covered each way. We've been four generations trying to get to the White House. Thank God my late husband, Earle, isn't here to see all this going on. He could never stand being overshadowed by Kyle. God, he used to whip his ass as a boy if he ever done well at anything.'

'Really? If he did well?'

'Sure, he'd find some excuse for some other thing. But he'd whip him.'

Earle, Jude realised, was the guy in the boot-lace tie shaking hands with LBJ in the photograph, and this was the woman with the beehive laughing with Ladybird Johnson.

'It's quite a circus out there, all the media and everything,' he said.

'That ain't nothing, young man, you wait 'till we've knocked out Lanyon McKenzie, then you'll see something. It'll be a real roll. They won't be letting me have my Mint Juleps then, in case I have to be on the TV. If I do they'll have me hidden in a back room.'

'Surely not.'

'No, too damn right they won't. I bin in politics all my life, my husband, stubborn SOB, was a senator. Me, y'see, I play the character part. Everybody's dippy grandma. You smoke cigarettes?'

'Well, yes I do.'

'Good, so I guess you'll know how to light this one for a lady.'

She waved a Winston at him that she'd been attempting to light without any success from a heavy onyx table-lighter that didn't appear to have any gas in it. Jude pulled out his plastic disposable and lit it for her. He expected her to offer him one, but it didn't seem to occur to her.

'Sacrifices, that's what running for office is all about.'

'I'm sure it is.'

'What would you know?' she said, and then smiled at him. 'What I mean is, what would anyone know? Politics can destroy a family, young Millburn says this, no family should have to have their trash can gone through. You know that? They've been through the trash cans here, those reporters. In my husband's day they just used to presume that all politicians were crooks, but now – now the bastards want proof as well.' She chuckled to herself. Jude didn't really know quite how to respond. He guessed she was a veteran of the ladies' clubs of Texas, but he doubted that it was a gag from one of her old luncheon speeches. She seemed to have gone through a life of politics and come out the other end, yelling.

There was something about her flappy little ears and the sparkle in her deep blue eyes that reminded him of Mills. She had a magnetism about her, and an independence of mind.

'It's good to see Millburn invite a friend over,' she said warmly. 'I've never seen him invite a friend to the mansion before. We were beginning to think he was ashamed of the place.' She laughed. 'So you're real close to our wild boy?'

'That's right.'

She nodded her head slowly, and then leaned in closer to him so she didn't have to shout. 'So tell me, Jude, are you a homo?'

Jude flushed and his throat dried. 'Well, er, no. We just share a house that's all.'

She nodded her head slowly again. She hadn't heard a word he said. Grandma couldn't think of any other reason for her famously solitary grandson to be sharing a house with anyone.

'Let me give you some advice, Jude,' she said, 'while you're in this house don't say Jack Shit about being a homo. We're Republicans of the old sort. Even the new sort would run you out across the lawn with your tail on fire; entertaining though that'd be, we ain't got time for it this afternoon. You got me boy?'

'Yes, but we're not gay . . .' Jude said, as loud as he dared.

'I guess a lot of kids only want to know Millburn because he's got money, eh?' she said.

'Mills has money?'

'Sure he's got money. My Earle left him money in a trust fund that he gets when he's twenty. How old is he now, d'you know?'

'He's twenty.'

Grandma thought for a while and dropped cigarette ash all over her dress. 'So I guess he's got money,' she said, and laughed again. Then she took Jude's hand and her bony knuckles gripped around it. 'You a good friend to my boy?' she asked.

'I hope so.'

'He's not all bad, don't let 'em tell you he is.'

'I won't.'

'Well, good for you. Where's my smoke gone?' It seemed to have disappeared into thin air. Jude looked down.

'It's on your dress. I think it's burning through.'

'What the hell's the matter with this dress?' she said, throwing her arms up into the air and staring down to where she was smouldering.

Jude thrust his hand into her lap and pulled the burning cigarette away.

'Well, I see you've got acquainted,' said Mills standing behind him with a tray of drinks.

He handed Jude a beer, he had a soda. As he returned to the verandah he sighed again and flopped down into a lounge-chair, as if just crossing that room was like making a dash across no-man's-land.

When Grandma finished her cigarette she declared that it was too damned hot to be outside any more and Mills helped her back inside.

Grandma went off to her room, full of Goddamn phones, to change into something that wasn't scorched and drink-sodden. They sat down in chairs around a coffee table.

'Who are all these people, what do they do?' asked Jude, in a gambit to make conversation since Mills had gone suddenly quiet.

'That's Elliot Hudson, dad's campaign manager,' he said pointing out a svelte forty-year-old in jacket and tie. 'He's a truly fearsome operator. Everybody calls him the Mastermind. He's talking with one of dad's Rebuttal Gang . . .'

But before he could finish, the double doors opened and in came Mills's mother, Anne Clearwater, followed by the Governor, still holding out his hand to be shaken, as if it had become automatic, and fixed in that position. His forearm looked like it was in a splint.

'Well, here they are,' said Mills. 'That's them.'

It was an odd way to refer to your own parents.

Elliot Hudson stood up, as did the guy from the rebuttals office, and Jude found himself standing up as well. There was something so regal about the Clearwaters that he couldn't help himself. More strangely, Mills had stood up too.

He watched as they went straight over to Elliot Hudson,

and the Governor sat down. Anne Clearwater sat beside her husband as if they were joined at the hip. Jude studied his body language for a moment. He sat with his hands loosely crossed over his left leg, and his voice was low and deliberate. He weighed up every sentence before he spoke. He came across as a rather conservative, refined, man. A handsome man in his fifties, statesman-like but still youthful, perfectly poised for the office of Chief.

'Come on,' said Mills, suddenly brightening. 'They really want to meet you. Come over and say hello. But for God's sake don't let dad get you onto the subject of British foreign policy. He loves anything British, he'll have you talking for hours if you let him.'

Mills pulled him by the arm and took him across the room to his parents.

'Dad, Mom, this is . . .'

'Not right now,' said his mother.

Mills stood awkwardly for a moment.

'Let's get a coffee, or something,' he said to Jude. 'Or you still got your beer?'

'It's on the table.'

They returned to the cowhide chairs. Mills was trying to put a brave face on it. His father hadn't even turned to look at him.

'I don't know how I missed you at the airport,' said Mills. 'Gave me a real shock. I thought you hadn't come.'

'I was delayed.'

'I know, two hours in Atlanta. God, airports are boring places to waste time in.'

'So you were there all that time? You *were* at the airport?'

'Sure I was. I must have been in the John or something when you got in. What did you do, get a cab? I was worried about you getting through the security, which, quite frankly, is beginning to verge on the ridiculous. As is everything around here. I never seen so many paranoid people.'

'It was okay, I got here . . .' He was going to explain about the trooper but Mills was talking nervously again.

'It's what I really can't stand about being here. It's been driving me mad. I thought I was going to explode. This never was much of a family home, but now, well, look there's nothing of a home left at all.

The door opened again and Catherine Sirteema came in with a sheaf of papers that she handed to Clearwater, then she came over to where they were sitting.

'Hi there, guys,' she said.

'Hi, Catherine, I want to introduce you to my friend from England. This is . . .'

'Yeah, we met. You settling in okay, Jude?'

'Sure,' said Jude, patting his staff pass as if he already felt part of the whole thing, and drawing attention to the fact that he hadn't lost it yet. Catherine reminded Mills that he had agreed to give an interview to a Young Republican journal. The interview was in ten minutes in the mansion house drawing room. Mills sighed heavily.

'Don't worry about it,' said Catherine Sirteema, 'I'll sit in on it with you.'

Mills's eyes flared. 'It's okay, I can handle it,' he said.

'It's no problem,' she said. 'I'll sit in.'

Jude went up to his room to lie down on the bed for a while. He was exhausted and wished now that he had slept on the plane. He stared at the clamouring wallpaper, at the bulletproof screen at the window that tinted the hue of the blazing sunshine. His eyelids flapped and lowered as the flowers on the curtains seemed to take on the faces of the people he'd met.

There was a sudden tap at the door, then a second knock. He pulled himself off the bed. Opening the door he saw Anne Clearwater standing there.

'I thought I'd come up to see that you're comfortable,' she said.

'Thanks, yes, thank you, Mrs Clearwater. It's very kind of you to invite me.'

'Have you found the laundry drawer?' she said. He was silent for a moment, long enough for her to walk into the room, cross it and open a drawer.

'Towels,' she said, laying her perfectly manicured nails on the luxuriant cotton. Then she turned to look at him.

'We're glad you could drop everything and come on over,' she said. 'I hope we'll not be too hard work for you.'

'No, not at all.'

Anne Clearwater had raven black hair and stood a full five foot ten. In the seventies, when she met Kyle, she was something of a minor tennis star in America. She still had an athlete's way of moving, with economy and directness. In conversation, as in tennis, she took the shortest route to return the ball. On the political wives' circuit she was known as someone still eminently capable of delivering a forehand smash. Lesser women could barely compete. She was good on strategy, and with Kyle, she had learned to play a long game. They had drawn up a plan for their lives very early on in their marriage, and all of it had led to this single point in time. The only hiccough had been Mills.

She was convinced of their victory. On the court, she knew, if you let the notion of defeat enter your frame of thinking, then you would be defeated. You would be that lonely object making the longest walk: the walk from the net after the handshake to the dressing room, while the cameras were turned on the victor. It is the knowledge of defeat, she would often say, that determines your drive for victory. Kyle had no experience of defeat, and it troubled her. But then this was why she had married him, she couldn't countenance marrying anyone but a winner. The alliance would have been unequal.

People found her cold, and cold she was. It came, perhaps, from her rigidly disciplined adolescence. She'd had no time for boys, or the movies, or dances, or any of those trivial social occasions where young people of her class fumbled with the basics of learning how to get along with other people as awkward as themselves. Her time was spent on the court, very often alone, returning balls from a mechanical tube that shot them at her from across the net, and hitting serve after serve.

She was serving now.

'Mills has not had the easiest of home lives,' she said. 'You can understand we are incredibly busy people here. I worry how he has settled in at Oxford. It is not as if we can just drop by and visit. Tell me, how is he liking the university?'

Her question was so direct, yet with so many implications, that Jude didn't know how to reply. A 'fine' or a 'great' wouldn't do it.

'I'm not really sure,' he said, honestly. 'It's such an unnatural environment to settle in to.'

Anne Clearwater looked surprisingly satisfied with the answer. Satisfied, he supposed, that he wasn't going to bullshit her.

'He's unhappy?'

'No, he's not unhappy, but I wouldn't say that either of us are leading a wildly exciting social life. Mills's head is generally in a book.'

'Mills's head has always been in a book. I do wish he'd be more active.'

Jude smiled. 'For some people,' he said, 'myself included, having your head in a book *is* being active.'

She looked him in the eye, and nodded. She approved of the answer, the young man was standing his ground.

'I was never an academic,' she said. 'Do you think Mills will run the course at Oxford?'

'I don't see why not. He's pretty settled at Cudlow Hall.'

'Cudlow Hall?' she said, shaking her head.

'Where we live.'

'Oh, yes, yes of course. Where you live. May I ask you an enormous favour?'

'Certainly.'

'May I telephone you from time to time, just to see how he is? I often feel he hides his feelings from me.'

Jude felt uneasy.

'Of course,' he said.

Mills's interview was running late and so he'd come upstairs to see how Jude was getting on. He arrived at his open door just as his mother was leaving. He looked perturbed. 'Towels,' she said briskly, and hurried down the stairs.

That evening the Clearwaters gave a reception in the mansion for local businessmen. Mills heaved a low growling sigh as Jude and he walked into the state room where about a hundred and fifty people were gathered. He was still smarting from being summarily dismissed in the Team Room . . . ironic in itself – and he was now dreading another brush off. It was not only hurtful, but embarrassing in front of his friend. He'd even posed for the cover of *The Young Republican* earlier, and given a fictitious interview about their family life to please his father. Why did he still allow them this power over him? They made him feel like a kid at Race Day missing the start of the sprint because he was searching for the non-existent faces of his parents in the crowd.

The moment they entered the room Jude could see where Clearwater was by the flock around him as he pressed the flesh. There was an air of tangible excitement as he and Anne Clearwater toured the room, accepting the grateful fawning of their fellow Texans. This was the closest that the independently minded Texans came to having their own royalty, and they let it show in full.

Jude was impressed by everything that evening: by the ranks of crystal champagne flutes; by the heavy oil paintings, in pre-Raphaelite style, depicting long horn cattle; his critical faculties were temporarily suspended by the grandeur of it all.

So many people had attended the reception that the doors were open onto the terrace of the state room and the hot night, and the heavy smell of the blooms entered the room in waves. As a waiter approached them with a salver he could smell the starch of his tunic.

Mills grabbed a couple of beers from the waiter. 'Thanks George,' he said.

'How's it going, sir?'

'Just great, George, just great.'

'We're up another point today in Delaware, I hear sir.'

'Are we really. Ain't that something, *Delaware*.'

Everyone was glossing over the fact that he was down an average of eight all across the Eastern seaboard. Senator Lanyon McKenzie was having a major bash with his sportstars in Washington tonight. It had been all over the early evening News.

The waiter smiled deferentially and withdrew.

Most of the men were drinking beer or bourbon, and the women had glasses of champagne clipped to their buffet plates with plastic drinks holders. It was quite a balancing act with all that heavy jewellery hanging from their wrists.

'Let's get out onto the terrace,' said Mills. 'So we can smoke.'

It was obvious, as he took a great arc of the room, that he was trying to avoid the circle of people surrounding his father.

But as they had almost made it to the outside air Clearwater's voice suddenly boomed out in their direction.

'Millburn!' he called. 'Come over here and meet these good people.'

They went over, and as they arrived so did a broad, fixed smile on Mills's face.

Clearwater was smiling too and he put his hand lightly on his son's shoulder. 'My son,' he said. 'He's been out with me on the campaign trail too.'

'Certainly have,' Mills said. Everyone was smiling at him. The businessmen spotted immediately that Mills's accent wasn't entirely Texan, in fact, not very Texan at all. Clearwater read their faces expertly and continued. 'And he's following in his old dad's footsteps and studying over in England. Oxford. A Rhodes Scholar, aren't you, son?'

'Yes, sir.'

'Is that so, sir?' one of them said. 'That's like their kinda Harvard and Yale rolled together, I hear. I guess you get a real clever education in England.'

Mills smiled painfully and nodded.

The Governor turned to Jude. 'And this is an English friend of ours who's studying at Oxford too.'

Jude nodded to everyone, and a strange rush of pleasure overtook him. He couldn't quite place what it was, but he enjoyed the sensation of the Governor presenting him as a 'friend' of the family. Emboldened by this he turned to the man who'd spoken.

'You certainly have the most beautiful state,' he said.

'You like our Texas, huh?'

'I certainly do sir. The friendliest, most welcoming people I've ever met.' He was going a little far now, but having begun, couldn't stop himself.

'Well, that's the way we lark to thank of it too,' said the man's wife, a woman with so much teased hair that it looked as if her hairdresser had held her fingers in the plug socket. 'May I just sayee that we *love* your accent, I kurd listen to y'all night. Wish I hid an accent myself.'

'It'd be a dull world if we all sounded like the BBC,' he replied and everyone laughed, sounding even more like the BBC now that his accent had been remarked on.

'I'm fascinated by the Brits,' said the woman. 'We were over there Christmas, wonderful time. No people in the world like you Brits, you're a one-off.'

'We're an island race, madam, but then, from what I've seen so far, so are you Texans!'

This went down very well indeed, and the woman clapped her hands together in delight.

Clearwater smiled at Jude, approving of the way he presented himself. Jude looked smart, he thought, looked as if he had opinions, said what he thought; focused. Perhaps some of it would rub off on Mills.

'Well,' said Mills, 'I guess we'd better leave you good people to talk business and go and see if there's any hot young home-girls in the room.' It was an attempt at a full-blooded, Texan thing to say, but there was a silence for a second as they turned to look at him. Then they laughed, they laughed because he was the Governor's son. Clearwater glanced his hand across Mills's back, but it was a rather fumbled gesture in many ways, betraying the fact that in private they were never so affectionate as they were being here, on display.

Mills and Jude revolved back into the throng. *Hot young home-girls?* repeated Jude.

'And what is the news from the BBC?' muttered Mills, stung by the conversation. He grabbed a drink from George and threw it down. 'Let's get out of here. Go and see Grandma on the verandah.'

'She hasn't collapsed yet?'

'No. She gets a second wind about this time. On a good day she can get drunk three times if she puts her mind to it.'

They walked down the staircase.

'Your father seems really pleased that you're out campaigning with him,' said Jude. He could see the simmering disappointment, and perhaps a little bitterness, on Mills's face. 'He really lit up when he called you over . . .' Jude was floundering.

'Sure,' Mills said, flatly. 'I'm a campaign accessory.'

'Oh come on, he enjoys introducing you, it's obvious.'

'He was bored with their conversation that's all. Wanted a diversion. He doesn't work well one-to-one.'

Mills took a bottle of bourbon with him and settled down on the verandah to get drunk with his grandmother. 'You here all on your own?' he asked her.

'No, I'm far from being on my own at my age,' she replied as she looked out across the lawn and raised a glass to it. 'How's it going up there?'

'Same as usual.'

There was a touching closeness between the two of them, as if they took refuge in each other. She'd managed to keep most of the booze off her dress tonight, but the alcohol inside her had made her rather quiet and philosophical.

Mills shook his head and turned to Jude.

'I can't believe I missed you at the airport this morning. I was standing right there.'

'It was okay. The trooper was a bit bloody frosty at the start, and I can't imagine how I'd have got through the mansion gates in a cab.'

'Trooper?' said Mills. 'What trooper?'

Jude focused on the illuminations amongst the plants in the garden. The bourbon, and his fatigue, were taking their toll. 'The one that met me.'

'A trooper met you and drove you to the mansion?'

Mills stood up for a moment and leaned against the rail. Then he snatched up his whisky, drank it and slammed the glass down on the table.

'Damn them,' he said. 'Fucking damn them all. Sorry, Grandma.'

'That's okay Millburn, you go ahead and curse.'

He dropped himself back down into his seat. He was agitated again. 'It figures. You know what the bastards did to me?'

'No?'

'The bastards paged me to information for some spurious call from Catherine Sirteema. You know, I reckon that was when you were coming through. That's how I missed you. They deliberately got me away. They won't let me do anything of my own. Now look at it, they've pulled you into their own nightmare. They're all paranoid. I see now why my parents were so keen to have you come over. So they could check you out, get you on their side against me.'

'Surely not?'

'They did it before. When I was at school, when dad was going through re-election, one of the other guys at Pierpoint was snitching on me. Making phone calls to them.'

He held his head in his hands for a moment. 'I know what they're trying to do: they're trying to get you on their side to keep me from *fucking up*, and tarnishing their perfect-family-thing.' He nodded towards his grandma and lowered his voice. 'Me and her are like the Devil's bookends either side of the Family Bible.'

Mills looked at Jude very seriously.

'I can trust you, can't I?'

'Of course you can.'

'You won't go over to their side?'

Jude looked out into the garden, suddenly feeling guilty about his conversation with Mills's mother, and the way he'd probably played it all entirely wrong just then up in the state room. The evening was heavy and humid, there were biting insects in the air. He really hoped that he wasn't going to be pulled into the maelstrom of this family.

4

The Clearwater campaign had rented an office in Washington that was given over entirely to what they termed 'Deep Research'.

Most of the staff at the mansion house knew nothing about its existence. It was staffed largely by former investigative journalists and security experts who had installed themselves in a rather anonymous building overlooking the Potomac. The building had a reputation as a location for shortly-lived commercial enterprises. Companies came and went from the address and no-one took particular notice. You could run any sort of operation out of such a building as this, and no-one would bother you. On the first floor was an outfit that imported cheap spy holes, for the front door, from Korea. They sent reps out to the old folks, frightened them with local crime statistics, and sold them the spy holes. There was a finance company just below that offered unlimited loans secured against your house, your car and your Great Aunt Agnes. The rest of the place was tele-sales and mail-order sex toys. And of course, Deep Research.

Dale Warnock worked there, a thirty-five-year-old who had already lost his hair and was going to fat. Privately, at home in the evenings, he practised step aerobics. But he still ate out of the deli on the corner when he returned home late from The Warren, as the inmates of the Deep Research building called it.

Dale Warnock had been digging for several months now. Digging around a young woman, a twenty-two-year-old called Dionne Mary-Belle, who worked as a junior manager in an hotel in Zanesville, Ohio.

That morning he had been looking out of his window, staring at the Potomac, when Dionne Mary-Belle telephoned him.

Her voice was quivering on the end of the line, almost as much as Dale's normally solid hand was shaking with expectation as he held the receiver.

'I'm ready to talk about it,' she said.

'You are? To the press and everything?'

'Sure,' she said. 'The bastard has made me suffer enough, I don't see why I shouldn't give an upset to his plans. But, listen . . . listen, I'm doing this because I just can't stand hypocrisy, I hate hypocrisy . . .' her voice finally cracked and she began to gasp.

'We all do, Dionne, we all hate hypocrisy. Okay, Dionne, now listen to me, listen to me carefully. You have to be sure that this is just you doing this, that you haven't been coerced in any way. You don't feel any coercion do you?'

'I don't know,' she said, her voice still shaking. 'It's a big deal, I know it's a big deal, but no, you haven't pushed me. This is me doing this. It's just me.'

'That's good, Dionne, that's real good, and it's real important that you say that. Now, it has to be you who makes the approach. It's simple, it couldn't be easier. You just call this guy we have ready at the *Washington Post*. They won't push you, they'll be real easy. But it can't come from us here, it just can't, you understand?'

'Yeah,' she said, her voice more steady now, 'I understand.'

'But don't do anything until I call you back. These things have to be timed. Just let me make a call to my boss in Austin. I'll be right back to you. You okay, Dionne?'

'Yeah, I'm fine.'

'I'll call you back.'

He put the phone down and called Elliot Hudson, Clearwater's campaign manager, directly.

'We've got him,' said Dale Warnock. 'Young missy Dionne is going to cum all over the *Washington Post*.'

It would change everything.

The next few days followed a similar hectic course as Jude's first day there. Clearwater would generally spend much of the day flying out of state to return in the evening for local fund-raisers; there were barbecues for four thousand people where dozens of cattle were roasted whole; there were addresses to veterans; trips in hot-air balloons and day care centres to be opened. It rather begged the question who was governing Texas.

As the week wore on Mills became more frayed by it all. His parents had hoped that the presence of his friend would calm him down, distract him a little, and while they agreed that Jude certainly was a Godsend, nothing seemed to stem the discomfort their son felt about it all.

Towards the end of the week Mills noticed a definite shift in the mood of his father's inner circle. Elliot Hudson had a new-found skip in his step. His father and Hudson, and a new guy that he hadn't seen before, Dale Warnock, were forever in some kind of secret enclave when they returned to the mansion in the evening. Everyone speculated about it in the Team Room, waiting for the white smoke. A whole new tranche of TV ads had been commissioned and there was a new energy in the air.

Then on Friday morning the Dionne Mary-Belle affair broke in the press, and like the final twist of the microscope lens, the terrible virus that his father's Deep Research team had cultured, came into focus. Mills was shocked by the brutality of it, and while the campaign staff whooped and cheered at the news bulletins played into the Team Room, Mills took himself out on to the verandah to drink with his grandmother. His father had always been known as a 'clean' politician, and if there was one thing Mills could respect him for it was this. There were no skeletons in the Clearwater cupboard: he'd never stupped an office girl; never got involved in real estate, and had, as they say, no distinguishing marks. But now it looked to Mills as if his father was playing dirty. It shocked him.

America was gripped by the Dionne Mary-Belle story.

She had got pregnant at High School when she was seventeen years old. She'd wanted to marry her boyfriend Joe, a young Italian who'd just failed to get into the army, two years older than herself.

Her parents had been against the marriage. Then Joe disappeared, he telephoned her to say that he was going travelling for a while. She didn't believe that he'd made this decision on his own. She could hear the tears behind his voice as he called her. With Joe out of the picture she was left to face the full wrath of her father alone.

He forced her to abort the child. He even sent her to a private clinic out of state. Now she only returned home for family photographs, she said. She still wished she'd had her baby. 'Whatever you think of what I did at seventeen,' she said on every news bulletin, 'at least I didn't destroy a life, it was my father who did that.'

The newshounds fed like writhing maggots on the body of this sad domestic story.

She was Dionne Mary-Belle McKenzie, the daughter of Senator Lanyon McKenzie, Clearwater's rival. She had been silent for five years.

Everyone in the mansion was mightily pleased.

Before McKenzie declared his candidacy, he must have felt he'd cleared things with his daughter. He'd set her up in a nice house, supported her. It was forgotten, he must have assumed, a youthful mistake. She probably even thanked him now. He really hadn't had any comprehension of the silent well of resentment boring inside her.

Overnight McKenzie lost the support of the Right and the Moral Majority. Pro-life demonstrators stood outside his campaign HQ with placards that read: 'Hypocrite and Murderer'. Clearwater's tired old family values message was in the ascendant. His chief rival's candidacy for the Republican nomination was over. It was swift and brutal. Even McKenzie's own campaign team denounced him in shock. They were stunned that he could even have considered running with such a notch as this on his card. Although he would probably have discussed it with his senior staff early on, they all obviously believed that Dionne was on-side. Now in public they declared him an amateur, and attempted to save their own skins for future campaigns. But they knew they were finished too. They knew that in their business the rats that swim away from the sinking ship can never get far enough before the draught of the plunging vessel sucks them under too.

Clearwater went for McKenzie relentlessly, and his ratings soared. Suddenly Clearwater was the shining knight coming to the rescue of his Party. There was a charisma about him now that no TV slots could buy. People were wearing his face on tee shirts in the street.

More importantly, Clearwater had found the message that the people wanted to hear: The Plain Truth. Clearwater assumed the role of the Great Defender of The Family. In a country where there were forty per cent single parents, and Family Values were, in reality, acrimony, alimony and domestic violence, the irony was not lost on Mills. He was so close, at times, to letting it slip that Mr Family wasn't himself too much of a father.

His father, he felt, had happily destroyed McKenzie's family. Mills was bracing himself. Now that his father was the front runner the full glare of the spotlights would be on them all.

Suddenly the race for the White House had come alive, the people had seen a drama played out on their TV screens which had caught their mood. And as Clearwater knew, all elections are won on mood, not policy.

Overnight the press corps camped out on the front lawn tripled in size, as Grandma had predicted.

Mills went up to his bedroom and reached down a book from a shelf still stacked with volumes from his childhood. He sat on his bed and slowly leafed through the yellowing pages. It was the atlas he had as a boy. Every map in the atlas was thumbed, there were small traces of jam in places, where he'd sat with it at the tea table. A couple of raspberry pits remained, obstructing the Panama Canal. There was sand in the cracks of the pages from when he'd taken it on holiday, to check where they were. The marks of his pencil journeys were on every page, and he could see himself now, as a small boy, slowly moving the pencil in imaginary voyages and explorations. He turned over to a ragged page, the one that had most fired his imagination: a line curling down from the Andes mountains to the uncharted jungles of the Amazon basin. The line ran from where the Amazon river was born in the mountains, to where it got lost in undiscovered land, before it became the greatest river in the world. It still thrilled him to see those places on the map where there was nothing, no roads marked, no towns, even the rivers were unnamed and stopped abruptly; the two thousand rivers of the Amazon basin that had defeated the cartographers. Places where no explorer had ever been. Great areas of unknown blankness were still left in the world.

That night Mills and Jude sat drinking in the Team Room after everyone else had gone. There was a heaviness to the air, the hurricane had swirled across the gulf damaging small craft in Atchafalya Bay, Louisiana, and had now made landfall in Texas at Galveston. It was one o'clock in the morning and Clearwater was in his study listening to the reports from the coastguard; he was tired but if there was to be any kind of natural disaster he'd have to be on top of the situation. If the coastal stretch sustained any damage he would need to get down there at first light; it was worth it alone for the photo-opportunity.

'I wish the billiard table was still here,' said Mills, looking forlornly down at the indentations on the Team Room carpet that the casters had made over the years. The absence of the billiard table seemed to distress him all of a sudden.

'We could have had a game.' He was looking up now at the tassled shade that still hung from the ceiling. 'Do you know how to play it?'

'It's bagatelle with sticks.'

'Is it?' said Mills, thoughtfully, but it was clear that he was trying to keep his mind off other things. He flopped back down into a chair.

'I'm going to have to talk to my dad,' he said, gravely. 'It's incredible, you know, because he and Senator McKenzie were real friends this time last year. Dad was even playing with the idea of endorsing him before he decided to run himself. I remember seeing Dionne around a lot when Dad was running for Governor and McKenzie was helping out down here.'

'You really think your dad's had a hand in this?'

'I can remember it, five years ago, when she got pregnant; my parents whispering. I guess Lanyon must have confided in my dad at some stage.'

'Really? It's a tough old game isn't it?'

'It's the worst kind of betrayal. Why couldn't they have fought this out on policies? He's probably one of the few people who knew about it. Desperation's made him dump on his friend; he's pushed his head into the mud.'

He laid down his drink, and looked at his watch.

'You're tired, Mills. I've never seen you so tired.'

He shrugged his shoulders and stood up. 'I'm going to call in on him before I go to bed.'

'You sure?'

They turned off the lights in the Team Room and at the first landing Jude went on up to his room and Mills turned towards his father's study, a determined and slightly fractious look on his face.

'Let me know how it goes,' said Jude. He walked on up to his room.

It was absolutely the wrong moment for Mills to walk into his father's study; Clearwater had enjoyed a heady couple of days and now he'd been thrust back into the role of Governor, with a hurricane at the door.

As Jude opened the door he paused and heard Clearwater screaming at his son, and for the first time in his life, Mills was yelling back.

Anne Clearwater was coming towards him along the corridor. More than her husband she'd sensed the way things had been steadily heading to match point.

'What is going on here, Jude?' she asked. 'What's eating into Millburn?'

'The McKenzie business has upset him.'

'He should be pleased. His father doesn't need him screaming at him right now. Is there anything you can do to maybe calm him down a little? We really would both be so grateful.'

'Well . . .'

'I feel it would be so much better coming from you. Perhaps you might like to suggest a trip up into the hill country tomorrow, or down to San Antonio. You'd have fun down there.'

They both listened for a moment as the yelling increased. Anne Clearwater was almost shaking with anger, but calm under pressure was her stock in trade.

'Well, yes, certainly, if you'd like me to. I could suggest it,' replied Jude uneasily.

'Oh yes. You've been a tremendously calming influence on him already. We do appreciate your being here.'

Anne Clearwater was fully expert in manipulation and she

had a way of making Jude feel flattered and honoured by her attentions. It was so hard to resist her.

'We do wish that Millburn would feel more a part of this whole campaign. I just can't understand why he is fighting it.'

'I'll do the best I can,' he said. 'I promise.'

Anne Clearwater looked suddenly startled. The argument was over downstairs now and Mills was unexpectedly up the stairs after his father had ejected him. He was heading towards them; he'd caught the last part of their conversation.

Mills glared at Jude, shook his head, and barged past. Jude's heart sank. It looked very bad indeed.

Anne Clearwater called after her son but he walked steadily on.

'Do the best you can,' she said, and, walking away from the situation, returned to her room. Jude stood there bemused. It did look as if he had gone over to their side, and in some ways he realised that he had, all because he didn't want to appear rude in Anne Clearwater's own home.

Jude knocked gently on Mills's door but his friend refused to open it. He pleaded for a while but there was just a deathly silence from inside. Hopefully, in the morning, he might have calmed himself. He had no idea how he could defend himself against what would look to Mills like some kind of plot.

The next morning Mills was late down for breakfast. Clearwater had already left for the Galveston coast, a couple of beach huts had come down and there was just enough flooding to justify the TV crews.

By ten-thirty Jude was getting worried and went upstairs to knock on Mills's door. There was no reply so he tried the door handle that had been locked the night before. It was unlocked now and Jude opened the door.

Mills had gone.

Jude sat around all morning. Every half an hour or so Catherine Sirteema passed through the Team Room and shrugged her shoulders. Grandma was out on the verandah taking the sun and he shuffled out there to join her.

'You're looking a bit awkward, boy,' said Grandma.

'I feel it. I don't know what to do. Maybe he's gone back to Oxford. It wouldn't surprise me.'

Jude was sitting with a soda when Anne Clearwater appeared at the French windows.

'This is typical of Millburn,' she said. 'Just so typical.'

'Where do you think he can be?'

'He used to do this as a kid. We thought he'd grown out of this by now,' she snapped.

'There was a time he sat in a cupboard for two days living off cookies,' said Grandma, chuckling. Anne Clearwater scowled at her, Grandma was a liability too.

'Well, don't worry Jude,' said Anne, 'just make yourself at home. He'll show up. He'll be back when he's hungry.'

How little you understand your own son, thought Jude. He's not a family pet that goes off for a bit and comes back at meal time. It was going to be a long day waiting, and as each hour went by the prospect of their reconciliation hung ever more above him like a low dark cloud. Mills had finally *flipped* as he'd always known he would.

PART 2

South America!

5

An hour had passed since the assassination of the archbishop on the tarmac at the airport and the news was just reaching the people of Caracas. The radio station had made a brief and confused statement about the carnage.

Mills's taxi had taken him to the Hotel Catedral, next to the Plaza Bolivar. The flight to Venezuela had been the first one leaving for anywhere in South America that morning. He'd witnessed the shooting from the window of the plane; it was a rude start to the new day and, already considerably shaken by his own actions, he was further confounded by the events around him. They had been made to leave the plane very quickly but Mills had looked back and seen the archbishop's blood being doused on the tarmac, and the facts of the killing being immediately eradicated. They had been rushed through, without even a stamp in his passport. They wanted no witnesses, no-one was asked for a statement. He was pushed through with the rest to the taxi rank, and within seconds his pack was slung on the back seat, himself along with it, as they headed on burning wheels along the pockmarked road to Caracas. He was glad at least that he'd got away before the TV crews arrived and maybe caught him on tape for all to see back in Austin. Nevertheless it was a bad start to his longed-for anonymity.

As he stepped out to look around him, the bright sunshine made the whiteness of the classical façades of the Presidential palace, and the Ministry of Justice building, look blinding. They looked like the pure and upright buildings of a perfect government, the home of politicians who were nothing less than angels on earth.

He began to walk across the plaza. It was a tremendously heady feeling; as if he'd suddenly gained the ability of flight; or had trepanned himself.

Bolivar, the hero of the nation, sat on his black horse in the middle of the square where every morning at eleven the military band played and enormous fresh floral wreaths were laid.

'Whatever you do,' said the matronly woman on the front desk at the Catedral, in English, 'don't walk passed the Liberator's statue with a back-pack on. They will throw you in jail for disrespect.' But Mills was more worried about being suddenly snatched in the street by emissaries of his parents; he was in such a hyper-state that anything seemed possible to him.

Outside the palace the Presidential guards stood in garish pantomime costumes, – red and yellow tunics and beavers with curtain tassels – but cowering in the exuberant shrubbery were soldiers in full battle gear, their automatic weapons sticking out through the bushes.

Mills started across the square. Elderly gentlemen in white suits and Panama hats strolled beneath the shade of the palms, rolled newspapers under their arms, tapping their canes. It could have been the nineteen thirties. It was a very different pace of life; it was leisurely, calming; a place where you could stop in the street and give yourself time to think.

An evangelist was preaching to a crowd of men. Years of preaching in the plaza had made him permanently hoarse and the more his voice cracked and broke, the more grandiose were his gestures, and the more forcefully he pounded his hand on his black, floppy Bible. Old men and women shuffled about with lottery tickets fluttering on sticks, and from up in the shade of the royal palms jet black squirrels ran down to take nuts from a boy.

It was midday and the great bell of the cathedral began to ring out. A small shaggy black bird sat on the ledge of the bell tower, and after each ring he pointed his head in the air, opened his throat and whistled, as if he thought he was solely responsible for calling the capital to lunch. But when the twelfth chime had sounded the bells continued to ring, tolling out the mournful news of the archbishop's death. The bird looked confused by the extended chimes, and he launched himself as if in panic from the ledge, and began circling the tower. The people in the plaza who hadn't yet heard the news looked up, and began turning to each other. They looked suddenly nervous and frightened. Was it a state of emergency? Had their President, – at 86 – the oldest head of state in the world, finally been called to account?

He wondered what kind of state of emergency there would be back at the mansion too. This would really give them all a start. He thought briefly of Jude, but found it too painful. From the very first day he'd arrived he'd been plotting with Mills's mother. He regretted now ever having made a friend; he should have taken his own counsel; he'd learned long before now that they always let you down.

Mills was halfway across the square when he heard a voice behind him.

'Hello my friend, you remember me?'

He turned his head back to look. There was a man in his forties in smart cream slacks and a safari shirt, holding out his hand.

'I don't think so,' said Mills. He was relieved to see that it was a Venezuelan. 'My first time in Caracas.'

Now that was a mistake, he knew, admitting straight away to the first hustler that came up to him that he was new in town.

The man beamed wildly at him. 'Then pleased to meet you, sir,' he said. 'I am Jorgio, and I will be your friend here in our wonderful capital.'

'Well that's a kind offer, but . . .'

'It is the least I can do. I consider it my civic duty to give the best impression of our wonderful country.'

Mills stepped up his pace, and Jorgio skipped behind him. The man's tourist English was good, if a little formal.

'There are so many wonders to see, respected visitors like yourself do not wish to have missed out on all that is most *typical*.'

Yes, thought Mills. And getting hassled is pretty *typical*. If, that is, this man was a hustler. Surely they couldn't have got through to Caracas already and found someone to bring him back?

Suddenly he felt someone prod him in the back and he jolted with a start. He looked behind him again. It was a grubby-faced boy with a wooden box.

'You want shoe-shine. You want shoe-shine, sir. I give you *especial* price only for you.'

Jorgio raised his hands in the air and rounded on the boy.

'Shoo! Shoo!' he shouted. 'The gentleman does not want his shoes shone. Are you saying the gentleman's shoes are dirty? You insult our country's guest. Be gone!' Jorgio smiled at Mills. 'You see, sir, I am your best friend in Caracas.'

But the shoe-shine boy didn't go, he merely fell in behind Jorgio as the three of them walked in a line across the square.

'May I suggest that perhaps we enjoy a coffee together?' said Jorgio. 'Caracas has many fine coffee establishments, but those most superior are known only to a select few. I am one of those few who will be most certainly able to effect an introduction for you to the manager of the finest coffee house.'

Mills looked at him in disbelief for a moment. The man was educated, his features were dignified and refined, he looked as if he had, at some time in life, taught at the university, or run a bank. He'd certainly had money in life. Now he was here, in the plaza, leaping on young back-packers like himself. It didn't seem possible that the man could have entirely overcome the indignity of it.

The shoe-shine boy had made a sudden dash forward and pinched him in the back to get his attention.

'Such fine bells, such a fine tower,' said Jorgio plaintively. 'And such clear weather we are blessed with today. Perhaps you would prefer lunch instead, at a fine brasserie, I am only too happy to effect you an introduction and be your guide to the mysteries of the *carte du jour*.' As he said this an old woman, all hunched up, and a wizened looking man, a rival lottery seller, cut across the square and appeared in from of him. They shook their fluttering sticks at him muttering, '*Señor! Señor!*'

'Be gone!' shouted Jorgio. 'The señor does not want to buy your unlucky slips of hope. The gentleman is above such base pursuits as your lottery!'

The elderly couple fell in behind the shoe-shine boy. Mills thought he probably looked like a burlesque version of his father when he came into the Team Room and everyone followed him about with urgent pieces of paper.

'I was only reading in the newspaper this morning,' continued

Jorgio as if the lottery sellers had interrupted the meaningful conversation of old acquaintances, 'that the price of gold on the global markets is no longer to be trusted.'

Suddenly the old woman thrust a handful of nuts under Mills's nose, causing them all to stop for a moment.

'No! No!' screamed Jorgio. 'The señor is a busy man today. He does not have the time to stop and feed the squirrels!'

The old woman and the man leaned on their lottery sticks for a moment, panting. It was worth stopping him for a moment just for the rest and to get their breath back. The shoe-shine boy had jumped down to his feet and one of his brushes was already on his left sneaker, though how he proposed to shine sneakers was a mystery.

They walked on.

'The only truly reliable commodity for investment these days is emeralds,' said Jorgio, reaching into the top pocket of his shirt. 'And it just so happens that Venezuela has been blessed in this respect. Such a wonderful jewel.' He grasped Mills lightly by the arm. 'Of course, this isn't information we should impart to everyone. It is not in our best interests to spread it about as if such business knowledge were butter on a roll. No, my dear friend, this is information we shall keep to ourselves. Are you agreed on this?'

'Sure,' said Mills. 'If anyone asks me I'll say emeralds aren't worth the price of glass.'

'Exactly! Exactly! I can see you have a mind as sharp as a knife. Look,' he said, unfolding the piece of tissue paper in his hand. In the fold lay six medium-sized emeralds twinkling in the sun.

'I think I could let you have, say two or three. But then, why don't I say to myself, "Jorgio, this man has a head on his shoulders. This man is as bright as these emeralds themselves. He will make such a bargain with me that I will find myself bereft of all six of them". Will you hold one up to the light?'

He put an emerald into Mills's hand. Mills gave it straight back.

'Look, I'm sorry. But I don't want emeralds, I don't want lunch, and I don't wish to meet the manager of a coffee shop.'

'Ah!' said Jorgio undaunted. 'But do any of us really know? Very soon they may be just the things you do want to do.'

'If you don't mind I would just like to go for a walk, *on my own.*'

'A walk? And what a pleasant walk we are enjoying. But I should caution you, sir. This is not a day for walking, no. Today there is nowhere to walk to in Caracas. Just as here, in the Justice Ministry there is no justice, and here in the government building, I fear there is barely any government. As your friend I must advise you of this.' Every time the man used the word 'friend' there was a dull thud in Mills's chest. Jorgio leaned in closer, and as if it were advice on gilt-edge bonds, said, 'Today there will be riots on the streets. Your perambulation will be most definitely curtailed. There will be soldiers and gas attacks and explosions and shootings. Who knows, it may even wake up the old President in his palace!'

'Look, it's been great having all your company like this, but I really want to just wander.'

Jorgio shook his head. 'Another young man, like yourself, once said that to me. I bade him farewell, and watched him turn this very corner here on the edge of the plaza. Within seconds he had fallen down a cavern that had opened up in the street. It was two hours before ropes could be purloined to effect his rescue. When he was brought up, the rats were hanging on to his trouser bottoms. When we walk aimlessly who knows what lies ahead?'

'I'll watch out for manholes, riots, and the CS gas,' said Mills. 'You mustn't worry too much about me. I'll be fine.'

'Have you seen the state of my shoes?' said Jorgio. Mills looked down. The man's swollen feet had burst the uppers away from the soles.

'For a proper conduct of business, I feel a man should have shoes that will remain on his feet. I'm sure you agree. Would you give me one American dollar?'

Mills shook his head. Here was a man with disintegrating slip-on shoes and six emeralds in his breast pocket. Mills knew that if he were to get US dollars out in the plaza he'd immediately be surrounded.

'Look,' said Mills. 'I'll consider your emeralds. I'll be here in the square tomorrow. I haven't been to the bank yet.' He had no intention of doing either.

'Excellent! Excellent!' cried Jorgio. He reached into his pocket again and gave him his business card. 'Produce this card and you will receive the very best of service in Caracas when they appreciate we are friends.'

'I'll do that.'

'And what time shall we meet tomorrow? I shall come to your hotel, it is no bother.'

'Six a.m.,' said Mills.

'An early start, excellent. The Hotel Catedral is it not? We shall take coffee, we shall peruse the morning's newspapers and discuss the state of our troubled world.'

'Well, goodbye,' said Mills.

'Goodbye, my friend!' he said, clasping him with both arms. 'Enjoy your walk in our wonderful city!' Mills was already walking away. 'Welcome to Venezuela. When you hear the bullets be sure to duck!'

He turned the corner by the Justice Ministry. All the government buildings were pristine white, with fountains and flowers. They were in marked contrast to the rest of Caracas which was universally pot-holed and shell-pocked, with decaying tenements stacked like egg boxes.

He could hear singing and laughing from the next street. He turned down to see what was going on. Suddenly a rush of people, hundreds of them, came running out from a side street, yelling, and dropping their placards. He got carried along with it, and suddenly found himself at the front of the surge. Then, as they came to a wide boulevard, another flank of demonstrators rushed towards them. Mills was caught on a traffic island. They were surrounded by soldiers and riot police. The soldiers had perspex shields, and at their sides they had swords in scabbards. Secured to their trouser belts there were canisters of CS gas. They were engaged in pushing back a small cabal of press photographers.

The people began to chant, a man was leading them with a loud-hailer. The placards seemed to be accusing the government of everything from corruption and vote rigging to sodomising pigs and goats. It settled into a stand-off with the soldiers reinforcing their lines. There were three times more troops than demonstrators.

The people were holding up placards with a picture on them. He looked closer. They all had pictures of Charlie Chaplin. They seemed to be saying *Charlie Chaplin for President.* It was extraordinary.

Then the soldiers drew their swords and brandished them in the air. The blades flashed in the sun.

There was a *whooah* of derision from the people, and they flapped their pictures of Charlie Chaplin. What kind of army would use swords in a riot?

From a fourth floor window two office workers were looking down. Then one of them turned back into the room and returned with the office water-cooler which he balanced on the ledge. Everyone laughed. The two men waved, smiling to the crowd, then they pushed it over the edge. It hit the pavement below with a mighty *boom* and soaked half a dozen soldiers with the spray. Everyone cheered. Mills punched the air with delight. This country was going to be *real fun.*

Then a soldier took aim with his rifle and fired two shots. The men, still with their arms up in the air in triumph, flew back into their office, their white sleeveless shirts reddening with blood, their colleagues screaming as they landed dead on the floor.

The people howled, and some fell to their knees crossing themselves. Then the CS gas began as the canisters thudded and rolled in the crowd. Everyone began running in a swathe down the boulevard, and Mills was taken along with them.

An hour later Mills was in the Candelaria, a district a mile to the east of the Plaza Bolivar, and the streets leading back to his hotel had been blocked off by the military. The Candelaria was the old Spanish part of town, filled with shabby markets and sudden futuristic hotels, as well as office blocks that looked like they had been experiments in a World's Fair.

He sat down in a small square in front of a church. Around the square trinket stalls were selling plaster figures of Charlie Chaplin, and they were doing a brisk trade. The bells that had been ringing across the city had been silenced now, only those on the far outskirts, that the military hadn't yet reached, could still be heard. A pall of smoke was rising in the distance, towards the centre.

The day was at its hottest now and he took himself into the church to cool off. The pews and the aisles were filled with people, some prayed, some just sat and muttered to each other. The priests dashed about, appearing from doorways to the side and conducting hasty conferences with each other. They didn't know whether they should offer a Mass or not. The people were looking disconsolate, slightly panicky expressions on their faces. If they made a formal gesture, thought the priests, maybe it would offend the military, maybe their congregation would spill out of the church and riot.

The smell of incense wafted over him and he felt guilty about the man with the emeralds who'd followed him across the square and tried to warn him about the threatening insurgency. The least he could have done was to give him that dollar for a new pair of shoes.

As he began walking out of the church he passed a side chapel around which dozens of people were placing candles and fingering their rosaries. He stared into the darkened chapel. There on the wall, behind a flat grey slab of a tomb, was a portrait of a man. He was wearing a bowler hat, a suit, and he had a moustache. It was the picture he'd seen on the placards in the riot. It wasn't Charlie Chaplin at all, though he looked remarkably like him. He had the same soulfully sad dark eyes and boyish face. But his suit was considerably neater, he wore a stiff shirt collar and a tie. A rather dapper touch was given by a neatly folded handkerchief in his breast pocket.

He read the inscription on the tomb

Dr José Gregorio Hernández. 1864–1919.

He stared up into the eyes of the portrait again; they seemed to draw you in. Unlike those eyes in portraits which people praise because they follow you around the room, these were quite the opposite, they fixed you to the spot. For a moment Mills couldn't move. This church was evidently some sort of shrine to the man; this smart looking doctor from the beginning of the century. He looked at the supplicants' earnest faces again. They were definitely praying to him, there was no doubt.

The eyes drew him back in.

For a saint, as Mills supposed he was, the man was rather an odd one. He'd never seen a saint before with a moustache, for a start, or a smart suit and tie. Weren't saints supposed to have beards? Or at least be pale and wan and half clothed? This man looked like he knew a good pair of shoes when he saw them. He was the kind of saint that looked as if he'd once owned a gramophone; and with the crowd he'd drawn today, he was something of a politician too.

Mills was intrigued. There was something deeply trusting about that face, but right now, amid all these people who knew who he was, Mills felt that the face was singling him out. A tingling sensation ran up his back as he felt sure he saw the lips on the portrait move; trying to speak to him. Perhaps he'd been walking in the sun too long.

He went back out into the harsh light of the square. At one of the trinket stalls he bought a couple of the Chaplinesque figures, a little glass shrine that lit up with fairy lights, and a pendant of the doctor on a length of leather twine.

He was sitting down on a stone banquette, sipping a guava juice, when he heard a voice behind him.

'Hello there my friend!'

He turned around, there was Jorgio, dark patches of sweat in lumps across his safari shirt.

'Have you been gassed?' he said brightly.

'No, no. I managed to get away, just sort of ran with the crowd.'

'Ah,' said Jorgio, flopping down onto the seat beside him. 'In this city sometimes you just have to run like shit. Still, it keeps us all fit I suppose. Good for the lungs.'

'Being gassed?'

'Well, no, but avoiding being gassed certainly.' He was a man who evidently had the ability to make the best of things. 'So everyone is down at the Candelaria. Nothing doing in the plaza at all. No-one. Vamoose. Shots ringing out, cars burning. A terrible interruption to business. They've forced us all down here. I wonder if it will be reflected on the stock exchange?'

'Very likely.'

Jorgio pulled out a filthy handkerchief from his pocket. With it a used metro ticket, that he was intending to use again, fell out onto the ground. He wiped the sweat from his forehead.

'Hot,' he said, and offered Mills his filthy rag.

'I'm okay, thanks.'

'I wonder,' said Jorgio, 'if there is to be a State of Emergency? Have you heard anything about a State of Emergency?'

'No, nothing.'

'No, nor I. But usually they begin like this. A little tension in the air. People gathering here. Hushed voices. A little smoke above the city. The sound of those infernal sirens. Then there's curfew. They wake the President up and he signs a decree to send us all to bed early.' He sighed deeply. 'What to do?' he said.

'Is this because the bishop was assassinated?'

'The *arch*bishop,' said Jorgio. 'They shot him dead this morning at the airport in a rain of bullets, a terrible tragedy for us. It was mayhem and slaughter, many priests and nuns killed, they say. They are trying to destroy the church, the people's faith. They didn't want him to be Pope.'

'Who?'

'Who knows?' said Jorgio and pulled his dirty handkerchief out again. He looked down at the plaster figures of Dr José Gregorio Hernández that were lying on Mills's lap.

'Ah, I see you have made some purchases.'

'Yes.'

'Very providential in these times, may I say my friend? You are invoking José Gregorio's protection. Very wise.'

'You believe in this man?'

'Believe? He is my life, my soul. It is on him I model my whole demeanour.'

'Would you like a coffee?' asked Mills. 'Get into some place a little cooler? I'd like to know who this man is.'

Jorgio looked quite shocked. 'A coffee?' he said. 'In a coffee shop?'

'Sure.'

Jorgio looked down at his watch and sucked air through his teeth. He wasn't really sure that he had the time for coffee. If there was an *emergency* he might be *needed*; although for what and by whom he hadn't quite worked out yet.

The coffee shop was deep and narrow with polished mahogany walls; ancient grinders and roasters rotated behind the counter, where a painfully thin man flitted about nervously and erratically between the customers. He acted as if he constantly overdosed on caffeine, which he probably did.

'In this shop,' said Jorgio, 'I am afraid there are only forty-two strains of coffee to chose from. I would not normally frequent an establishment with less than fifty, but the superior establishments are largely unable to serve us at present, due to the fact that the military are standing in our way to them brandishing swords. It is unfortunate, but these things happen. What coffee would you like?'

'Arabica,' said Mills.

The coffee came in the smallest of cups, and Jorgio insisted on carrying them, pinching the tiny handles, right to the very back of the shop.

Jorgio drank half of his tiny cup straight down, pulling a painful face as if he hated it. Then he drew the sugar bowl over and heaped in spoon after spoon until the level of the cup was back to the top. Then he sipped it gently, with small slurps of pleasure, like a hummingbird transfixed before a bloom.

'I frequent fifty-three coffee shops in Caracas on a regular basis,' said Jorgio. 'And this is number seventeen. So we could have done worse under the circumstances.'

'You've made a league table of the coffee shops?'

'Yes. I have been asked many times to publish it, but a lifetime's knowledge is not something to squander among the masses, is it?'

'How do you rate them?'

'Oh, there are many facets, many facets, I would have to publish a book to explain them all. I couldn't possibly just tell you over coffee. There is, of course, the aroma from the street that first attracts you, and inspires your senses with the integrity of the establishment's roasting facilities. If, for example, an establishment were to be sited, say, next to a monger of fish, then everything would be dashed from the start, would it not? A gentleman simply wouldn't walk in. If I were to take a visitor to such a place he would rightly consider me an insensitive fool with no knowledge of coffee drinking. His entire day might be ruined. I would very soon be out of a job.'

The man behind the counter had indeed greeted Jorgio warmly when they walked in, and had abandoned the other customers to serve them. It was very likely, Mills realised, that this really was Jorgio's occupation: he took people to coffee shops for a living. The emeralds were a sideline, they wouldn't be his anyway, he'd just be on a small percentage. His real job was drinking coffee, although it didn't appear that he actually liked it very much.

'The ambience of the interior, of course, is paramount to the enjoyment,' he continued. 'I must match my visitor to the clientele of an establishment exactly, so that he is at ease with the company he will keep there. We would not, for example, wish to be among the mayhem of screaming children whose mothers had broken off from their shopping. Or with the young men of the financial district whose mobile phones beep in the air, and for whom the coffee is just an occasion to escape their frantic terminals. We would not want to be in an establishment where the morning's street cleaners had come for a wakening shot and left their greasy thumbprints on the counter. No, we would not. And then, of course, there is the taste of the coffee to consider.'

'There is,' said Mills. He looked up around the walls, all of which were hung with fine old maps of Venezuela, browned with the fumes of the roasting machine and the strong local tobacco. Jorgio had matched him to the place exactly. It was a talent, a gift.

'Who is José Gregorio whatever-his-name-is, then?' asked Mills.

'José Gregorio Hernández. You do not know him in America?'

'No, we don't know him.'

'A mighty man. A truly mighty man,' said Jorgio, and Mills could see that he was building up to an oration. 'He was South America's greatest physician. A brilliant man. The professor of medicine at Caracas University until his appalling death in 1919.'

'He was killed?'

'In the most tragic circumstances, in the most appallingly tragic circumstances,' said Jorgio, taking another dignified sip at his cup of coffee-flavoured syrup. 'He was loved by all in the country; he was a Robin Hood of men. He brought all the latest medical advances to us, working tirelessly day and night, but still he found time to treat the poor for no charge. He was the most devout of men; Mass every day; a friend to the bishop. The President: the dictator Gomez, was jealous of him because the people loved José Gregorio more than they loved him.'

'How did he die?'

'Tragic. Hit by the first Ford motor car to enter Caracas.'

Mills took a sip of his coffee.

'He was sitting enjoying his lunch in a restaurant when a man came and begged him to save his mother's life. He went back to his pharmacy to collect the life-saving drugs, and as he stepped into the road . . .' Jorgio had adopted the grave voice of a man speaking an elegy, '. . . his hat fell off. As he bent down to pick it up he was hit by the American car.'

Mills half smiled. What a fantastic sense of bloody reality these people had to make a saint like this; when normally they should be stoned, or beheaded, or burned at the stake, or pierced with arrows; this one was martyred by the Ford Motor Corporation of America. Run down by a symbol of imperialism. There was a perfection to it; a thoroughly modern South American saint. This was just the kind of thing that he thirsted after as he pored over his atlas as a child: the excitement and the unconventionality of foreign places.

'Forty thousand people attended his funeral here in Caracas. Gomez, the President, was on the other side of the country when the Ford struck him down. He cabled: "Do not inter him until I return, by presidential command." Every day flowers are laid in the street where he was killed. From the very day of his funeral all of Venezuela prayed to him. Then in 1962 he appeared in an operating theatre at the university and took over from the surgeons. And Venezuela was exalted, our Doctor had returned to us! And today he is revered by everyone, by the Colombians, the Peruvians, the Brazilians, the Panamanians.'

'But not by Ford, I bet,' said Mills. 'Would you like another coffee?'

'No, thank you. One is all I enjoy.'

Mills paid and they left. As he was saying goodbye to Jorgio in the street, – he'd walked him back all the way to his hotel, and had negotiated with the soldiers to let him through – he offered him some money for a new pair of shoes.

'Oh, no, sir. I couldn't possibly take money from a friend.'

There were maps on the walls of the foyer of the Hotel Catedral as well, and he ran his finger along the thin brown line of the Andes mountains until he found the highest peak, Pico Bolivar. It rose above the university town of Merida, the jewel of Venezuela, and where he wanted to head for as soon as he could. The place where the waters of the Amazon were born.

He went over to the desk to pick up his key. The matronly woman was sitting, asleep, her knitting needles and a thick skein of red wool sliding from her lap. He coughed and she opened her eyes.

'Señor!' she said. 'Will you be having requirement of our fine dinner in our restaurant tonight?'

'Well, I guess so, around about eight or nine?'

'Ah, this may not be possible tonight.'

'No?'

'No. There is to be curfew. Everyone at home by eight.'

'Oh dear. What time's last orders?'

'Four o'clock.'

He looked at his watch, it was four now.

'Because of the curfew our chefs have to go home now or they won't get through the roadblocks in time. Best they go soon.'

'I see.' He glanced back at the map on the wall.

'Are there any flights from the airport tonight?'

'We can telephone. Where do you want to go?' This was excellent news for her, seeing that he was the only guest in the hotel, he'd paid in advance, and he hadn't even yet slept in the bed. It'd be a neat solution to their staffing problems. A few more guests like this and the hotel might become a going concern.

'Merida,' he said. 'I need to get to Merida tonight.'

She called. He sat in the old leather chair for the interminable time it took her to get through. It was as if they were still laying the cables as she dialled. Then suddenly she shouted to him: 'Señor! Señor! Your credit card please!'

He handed it over and they booked the ticket, which after the long wait was all conducted in a sudden rush.

The woman put down the telephone and smiled.

'When does it leave?' he asked.

'Half an hour ago. I will call you a taxi.'

'Well, what's it going to do, turn back for me?'

'Oh, no, señor, half an hour ago is only the official time. That is the time of the flight you must give when you get to the airport, or they might make a mistake and put you on the one before. Which is going somewhere else.'

He shook his head, certain that there was a logic to this somewhere.

'All flights in a big mess again today,' said the woman.

The taxi came and he headed off back to the blood-soaked airport. It had been a heady five hours in Caracas. He'd drunk one cup of coffee and witnessed three people being shot.

The confused departures board was announcing that the hour-long three-thirty flight to Merida would be leaving at five and arriving at half past four. If you could ignore the carnage, it was a lovable kind of place.

6

The town of Merida, with its heavy cathedral above the clouds, is set on a natural rock terrace in the Andes foothills, sixteen hundred metres above sea level.

Where the terrace drops to the River Chama, the town dramatically ends, and looks up and down at the same time, like a dignified, but confused, elderly gentleman lost in the street. Above, the Andes rise thousands of metres in lush cloud forest; but the peaks of the *cordillera*, the great jagged spine that runs the length of the continent, are so high up beyond the snow line that they can't be seen from the town.

The edge of the terrace is overshadowed by the gargantuan iron wheel of the *teleferico*; built by French engineers in the nineteen fifties to power the cable car, the highest in the world. It looks ancient now to visitors, as if they are about to be hoisted in buckets to the maw of some disused mine.

It was nineteen degrees centigrade, truly temperate, as Mills ambled through the park. If this town were in Europe, if it were in say, Switzerland or Bavaria, he thought, it'd be a spa town. It would be filled with ridiculous baroque follies, drinking fountains and Victorian sanatoria making a good business as drying out clinics for celebrities. The visitors to the town would be walking along just as he was now, a little thoughtful, breathing deep of the clear air, savouring the view; smiling and nodding to the locals as they took their evening stroll.

He stopped at an ornate little drinking fountain staffed by cherubs, one of whom had lost his wings and the other his dick. The water was crystal clear and as pure as any he'd ever tasted. He splashed his head under the spout.

The light had faded on the mountains now, and even the foothills of the cloud forest had disappeared, but Mills stood and stared at the blackness. The town held a solitary peace after the clamour of Caracas, and he was glad to be there, in a place he'd imagined from maps, and populated with people from travel books. Tomorrow he'd board the cable car and go up there, to where the air was crystal, and the landscape unmarked by man; to walk alone for a couple of days in the unblemished silence.

Everywhere the townspeople were strolling out to enjoy the air, and have their shoes shined in the square. The cathedral was hosting a requiem Mass for one of the town's dignitaries. Everyone was dressed up and applauding the bishop as he made great sweeping gestures with his arms, and spoke of the magnificence of the deceased man.

Mills stood at the cathedral door for a few moments. What a way to go, he thought: children playing in the aisles, the great and the good of the whole town bursting into spontaneous applause. The elaborately carved coffin was sitting like a gilded Doge's barque about to be launched; as if death was the mighty man's next great adventure; setting off like Columbus. But there seemed to be an air of expectation and mild hysteria among the people, as if they were using the occasion as a chance to voice their feelings about the assassination of the archbishop too.

Mills walked on and stopped outside one of the small offices open on to the street that sold mountain tours to the visitors.

Inside, a young Venezuelan man was sipping a mineral water. He had a soft oval face and long slender fingers curled around his glass like a fine piece of filigree. He looked so placidly content with the evening it seemed a shame to disturb him. He was reading an engineering manual.

The walls of the office were covered in maps, mountain charts of the peaks and the passes, and photographs of happy Australians and Germans sitting in the backs of jeeps, or standing proudly surrounded by ropes and ice-picks at the summit of Pico Bolivar.

'Señor, good-evening,' said the young man, nineteen or

twenty years old, with a freshly starched shirt and an honest, keen face. 'You are interested in taking a tour?'

'Uh huh,' said Mills, staring at the charts on the wall. 'I want to make a trek across the mountain here, stopping off at some of the villages. Can you give me some information?'

'Of course, I can. My pleasure, sir.' But there was a half-smile on the young guide's face. Mills didn't look like a trekker or a climber, he was too smartly dressed and there was a smell of fresh soap about him. He didn't look as if he'd ever been on a mountain before.

Mills stared closer at the map on the wall. 'Is this where people go?' He was looking at a pass, high up by the summit of Pico Bolivar.

'Yes, señor, but now it is very quiet on the mountain. The cloud comes down early in the afternoon. You should really be here in September.'

Mills was still staring at the chart, a faraway look in his eyes.

'It will take two days to make it over the pass and back,' the guide told him.

Mills could hear from the tone of the young man's voice that he had looked him up and down and didn't reckon him to be suitable material for the mountain. It didn't surprise him.

'It is not a country stroll,' the boy continued. 'It is not for casual hikers.'

'Is this where Bolivar marched his army over when he liberated Venezuela?'

'Yes, señor, that is where he made his heroic march.'

It was an episode in history that Mills had enjoyed since a boy. There was Bolivar, a member of one of the richest Venezuelan families, returning to liberate the land of his birth from the Spanish. He was nearing the end of his life, dying from tuberculosis, with his army of Irishmen and Englishmen that had been starving in Europe when they were disbanded from Wellington's forces after the defeat of Napoleon, needing one more fight, in a strange continent, because that was all they knew how to do.

'I'd like to make that journey,' said Mills.

'Sit down,' said the mountain guide, allowing himself a laugh now. 'You'd like a coffee?'

'Sure, a coffee would be great.'

'I have a party going up there in two days' time, some Australians and some people from Berlin. Very nice. You could join them.'

'No, thanks,' said Mills. 'I wasn't thinking of joining a group. I want to go on my own.'

The guide raised his eyebrows.

'It is possible,' he said, 'but it isn't wise.'

Mills shrugged his shoulders.

'Do you know anything about altitude sickness?'

'The altitude can be a problem?'

'Oh, yes, sir,' he said, pouring the water from the kettle into two cups of instant coffee. 'Even water boils at a lower temperature up there. Much the same happens to your blood, the brain is starved of oxygen in the thin air. People can go very strange. Delusions. First you find it hard to breathe, and then your arms tingle. You must walk very slowly, and rest, every ten steps you must rest. If you don't you will encounter the delusions, and the terror of the monsters of the Andes.'

'Sounds quite a trip.'

He handed him a coffee. 'They say whatever demons are inside you, the mountain will bring out.'

'Oh dear,' said Mills. 'Do you ever have casualties?'

'Well . . .' the guide looked hesitant. 'You have to respect the mountain, of course. We do find people who have not crossed the pass before nightfall and have got very cold.'

By 'very cold' Mills realised that the guide was reluctant to use the phrase 'frozen to death'.

'I heard in my hotel,' said Mills, 'that you find them naked.'

'Naked?'

'Yes, people go mad and strip off.'

The tour guide cleared his throat. Perhaps he could persuade him to join an organised tour after all.

'Well, yes, this is true. As we search for them, first we find their back-pack on a ledge where they have just abandoned it. It may contain everything they need to survive on the mountain, but in their delusion, they have just thrown it away. And then we will find their jacket, their water bottle, even their climbing boots. Then we see them, trashed and frozen against the rock where they have stripped naked, because the fancy has taken them, and they have just launched themselves over, through the shale and the snow, thinking they can fly, and died. Their faces, I can tell you, their faces have the strangest expression. They look so happy.'

Mills nodded. It sounded a bleak place indeed and his heart began to race. He had the overwhelming desire to push himself into that environment where no-one could reach him. He too wanted to strip on the mountain, but not his clothes.

'You're a tour guide, right?' he asked.

'Yes?'

'You tell this to everyone. Doesn't it put customers just a bit off?'

'I don't know,' he said. 'I've only just started here. The professors at the university have all been suspended by the government. Us students have to do something to live. I was born up there, in the village of Los Nevados, I have seen smashed gringos all my life.'

Mills walked back over to the chart on the wall and peered at the endless wastes of rock and ravine that led from here to the pass. 'So you recommend that I'll have to start pretty bloody early in the morning, I suppose, to get to the first village on the other side by dark?'

'Yes, you must start early.'

'How many hours walking is that, six or seven?'

'Yes, er, five, six or seven. It depends.'

'It doesn't sound too bad.'

'I would suggest, however, that we get someone from the village to meet you at the top station with a mule. We can send a message with one of the boys tomorrow.'

'No thank you,' he said. 'I don't get on with mules.' He gazed at the snaps and the carvings of condors.

'I'm not very good with heights, either,' he confessed, shaking his head and sniggering at himself.

'What about a trip to Los Llanos?' said the guide. 'It sounds perfect for you. We go by jeep, three days, to the great plains in the south of the country. Great sweeping plains with *gauchos* on horses with their cattle, and coypus all over the pampas. Thirty-five dollars a day, all meals and beer included. And it has the advantage of being absolutely and perfectly flat for hundreds of miles. We have a lot of fun, a whole bunch of us in a jeep, trekkers from many countries. We camp out and light fires and make a party. You would like it very much.'

'No,' said Mills, reflectively. 'I really don't think I would.'

There was such a distant look in Mills's eye that the tour guide suddenly became worried. Mills seemed to be going out of his way to make things harder for himself. Then a small shudder went through him, and he wondered if the guy was a *suicide*.

A shadow had passed over Mills's face too. He could see an image in his mind of himself as a kid, dressed as a cowboy, up in the low hills above Austin; preferring death to winning the game.

'Are you really determined to do this trek?'

'I am.'

He shook his head. 'Then you've got a real problem, sir.'

'I have?'

'Yes, those shoes.'

Mills looked down at his feet.

'You cannot possibly cross the pass in those. Buy yourself a pair of boots, at least.'

Before Mills left the office he stood for a few minutes more in front of the chart on the wall: all his journeys had been made more in the imagination than in reality, solitary journeys by pencil, afterwards erased.

Mills left the shop and a few minutes later a thirty-year-old American walked in. He had a very impressive camera with him, but there seemed to be something more on his mind than just booking a tour.

Finally he said: 'That kid who was just in here, the American, where's he taking a tour to?'

The guide was surprised by the question and wondered why he was being asked. He knew that Americans liked to stick together but the young guy had hardly looked like the type you'd want to hook up with.

'The man who just left, you mean?'

'Yeah, that's him, with the blond hair.'

'You want to know where he's going?'

'That's right,' he said casually and pulled out a twenty dollar bill.

The guide laughed. 'I can't take that!' he said. Then he became a little nervous.

'He's not taking a tour,' he volunteered, it was probably best.

'So what's he doing here in town?' asked the photographer, still smiling broadly to put the young man at his ease. He hadn't expected to have his twenty dollars turned down. Everyone else around here was only too happy to take his money.

'He wanted to take a walk up over the pass, over to Los Nevados.'

'When's he going, tomorrow?'

'Yes, I think so, first thing.'

'Right, thanks, thanks. I'll see you around.'

He was relieved when the man walked out of his shop.

Mills went back to his hotel on the Park Las Heroinas and sat outside with a beer. The photographer settled himself down at a table across the street and ordered a beer too. As Mills lifted his beer bottle to his lips, so the photographer echoed his movements.

7

In The Warren, Dale Warnock had been disturbed by a press agency guy who'd called about some interesting photographs from Venezuela that had just come his way. He wanted to wire them through.

'Okay, wire 'em,' said Dale, not too bothered.

But now that he looked at the electronically produced black and whites as they lay on his desk, still warm from the machine, he got the agency guy on the phone. The man was saying that his client down in Venezuela, who'd been snapping the riots after the shooting of some bishop or other, was willing to blow them across every front page in America for the regular rate. Dale Warnock took a deep breath and tried to remain composed, but he sounded instead like a man constantly struggling to unstick himself, on a humid day, from the seat of a vinyl chair.

Business, he knew, would have to be done well above the regular rate if they were going to keep these snaps to themselves.

Governor Clearwater was sitting in his captain's chair in his big new office in Washington, the new campaign headquarters in the capital. He'd chosen the building because it gave him a view of Pennsylvania Avenue and the White House. It spoke of power to be, and it concentrated the mind to stare out of the window, and see how close it was.

He was savouring the end of the day. By anybody's reckoning it had been a pretty fine day. His campaign was like a stately galleon now, in full sail with the silver nailed to the mast for the first man who sighted land; which in this instance was the

White House lawn. He was riding so high in the polls that it would take an act of God to sink him. And God seemed to be voting Republican this time.

'Governor, sir . . .' said Desiree's voice on his bat-phone, 'half an hour 'till your flight back to the mansion.'

He was a *natural* they said now. He savoured the pleasure of having brought his life and career, and the black arts of politics, together in such a consummate moment. Although he was not a man given to public displays of emotion, when he was alone like this, he allowed himself to indulge just a little. He thought about the sun room on the top of the White House, and how he'd extend the half sized golf course at Camp David to eighteen holes.

'Governor, sir,' said the bat-phone, 'it is twenty-five minutes to your chopper on the roof, and the Washington staff are gathering to well-wish . . .' He was going back home for the night before setting off to contest the Iowa primary.

Clearwater watched himself as he came up on the News Channel: cheering crowds, good sound-bites from a speech he'd made that morning. The editors were obviously on his side for the primary. With no opposition to speak of from his own party now, he knew that he had to use the primaries as part of the presidential campaign proper. He could forget internal party politics now and go for the Democrats.

The sound was down on his TV. He really didn't watch it any more, he had a whole department to do that for him. His job now was to do the serious thinking: to shape the presidency in his mind *now*, before he took the job and was too busy to think about it.

He thought back over the years, of his long time in this business, his years in the Capitol, his years in Europe. He thought of the sacrifices he'd made for this moment. The offers of sex he'd had to turn down; the money he could have made on the side. Anne had been making sacrifices in recent months too. She found it hard not to be the champion of the court, the centre of attention, as she had been in her tennis years. She'd had to stand beside him in this campaign, like a ball-girl waiting to catch wayward shots and return them for him to serve again.

Then he came over hot as he thought of Mills. There was still no news. He slapped his hand on the desk and heaved an irritated sigh, mentally reaching for a horse-whip. He froze for a moment and then he buzzed through to Catherine Sirteema's office.

Catherine came through the door almost immediately, breathless from the dash from her desk: white shirt, sleeves rolled up; a good girl, he thought. She was thorough and business-like, held her own with the tough guys. Kinda sexy.

'Sirteema,' said Clearwater, gravely. 'Catherine, is everything all right?'

'Yes sir,' she said confidently. 'Everything seems to be fine.'

'Is there any news of him?'

'Not yet, Governor, but we expect to have something by tonight. We'll have some kind of fix by the time you're back in the mansion.'

'Right, okay.' He sighed irritably again. It was just typical of Mills to be the only blip in an otherwise perfect campaign. My God, that boy better have his tail between his legs when he returns, he thought to himself.

Sirteema went back to her office. As she pushed the door open she saw Elliot Hudson, the campaign manager, standing there ashen-faced and with a blood vessel twitching on his forehead.

She sensed immediately that something had happened to Mills.

Hudson seemed unable to speak. He just stood there slowly swaying from side to side.

'We got a real big fucking problem in your department,' he said finally. Then he slapped down a handful of black and white photographs on her desk.

'Shit,' she said as she saw them, and the blood drained from her face too.

There was Mills, in the middle of a rioting crowd of South American insurgents, in the centre of Caracas, giving what looked like a Black Panther salute. He was holding his fist aloft amid a bank of revolutionary-looking banners and people caught in mid-shout.

They were the photos of the moment when Mills had punched the air and cheered as the water-cooler was thrown from the office window. The agency stringer who'd taken them hadn't recognised Mills until he'd got them up on his screen, and had begun cropping the image ready to put them on the wire. He'd hoped that there might be some interest in them after the assassination of the archbishop, but when he saw what he had as a bonus he wondered how much more they'd be worth to the Clearwater campaign, and held them back. Only that morning he'd seen a picture of the kid, standing by his father, on the front page of *USA Today* that he picked up at the Press Club. He couldn't believe his luck.

'Your boy Mills,' said Elliot Hudson to Catherine Sirteema, 'is a fucking loose canon. Do something about it or I will.'

He walked out of her office.

Catherine sank down into her chair. After what the press had made of Dionne Mary-Belle McKenzie, they couldn't afford a wayward kid too. The whole thing would begin to unravel. The public had got a taste for this campaign now. They were following it as if it were a TV soap and the press was thirsty for more scandal on which to expend their purple ink.

'Miss Sirteema,' said Desiree poking her head round her door, 'the Governor would like you to join him downstairs for a celebration glass of champagne.'

'I'll be there in a moment,' she said, slowly, wondering how she was going to tell Clearwater that Mills was in South America.

8 ∫

Early the next morning Mills walked across the park towards the *teleferico*. The cable car was swinging there, empty in the morning breeze and mist. It looked like the sort of thing Mills remembered from the state fairgrounds of his childhood, but the cables, in the heavy grey of morning, appeared to stretch into infinity.

'Impossible,' said the attendant when he indicated that he wanted to embark.

'It can't be, I need to make an early start.'

The attendant shook his head; it was as if the appearance of the young tourist had brought the gloom of the mountain swirling around his head.

'Impossible without five people. It is regulation. No have at least five people, no worth us going for the money. You think the mountain will pay us?'

Mills sat at the small open air coffee bar drinking sugar-sweet espresso and looking around to see if anyone else turned up. He really did feel like a kid at a theme park who'd failed to make the minimum height requirement for the ride he wanted to go on.

The cable car wasn't going to set off until eleven o'clock, when it had to go anyway to deliver some maintenance workers. This would only give him an hour and a half to be defeated by the incline of the track before he would have to turn back to catch the last cable back at two o'clock. After that there was a chance the cloud would come down and he'd be lost up there for the night, and add to the toll of frozen gringos with strangely happy faces.

The photographer was sitting on a bench in the park watching.

He watched Mills as the hours rolled by and the cable car hung there swaying like the sword of Damocles. The kid looked troubled this morning, from time to time he seemed to be muttering to himself as if he were plotting something. He looked restless too and would keep getting up and walking away from his coffee and then returning again to sit down and sigh. He frequently shook his head and his mood seemed sombre.

At eleven o'clock Mills boarded.

There wasn't going to be another car and so the photographer realised that he was going to have to share it with his prey. He jumped in just as it was due to leave, and sat at the back with his face turned away.

As the cable car began it lurched over the edge of the natural terrace and plummeted for a good twenty feet. Mills felt his stomach come up into his mouth. He hated heights and he absolutely hated contraptions like this. The sweat was forming on his forehead.

He looked down where the Rio Chama was splashing over limestone rocks below, miniature cattle were grazing on its banks, small homesteads with bright terracotta roofs drifted trails of wood smoke to replace the mist that had hung there when he'd first arrived.

As the car got to the first station, a thousand metres further up, the town below looked like a white serving dish piled up with butter beans and parsley. It looked as if it had been set on a dining table that was covered with a green baize cloth hanging in drapes to the floor. The air had already begun to chill. The un-manned cable car was playing a dramatic soundtrack of Mahler, but the tape had stretched. The music matched the swaying, lurching motion of the compartment as they began to catch the updraught from the valley.

The photographer stole a brief glance at his subject and snapped back again to the view. Being so close made him uneasy. He was only ever relaxed at the end of a long lens.

They changed cars for the run to the second station. Mills stared down into the lushness of the Cloud Forest, a place of vast trees protruding from the permanent grey clouds. Then as the presence of timber subsided they entered the *paramo*, and the sheer walls of the El Toro peak.

The sight out of the front of the car was of sheer brutal rock. The trip to the third station was another country again. The cloud was far below them now, the temperature dropping as they rose, beneath them only barren rock, scattered with cactus.

It wasn't until Mills left the cable car at the four thousand metre point that he began to feel strange and unbalanced, as if he'd misjudged the end of an escalator. Cacti the size of up-turned umbrellas grew by the track side. He began on the first kilometre of the path that led towards the pass, another thousand metres further up. From there he could see the snow-line, and back down a thousand metres, the level of thick white that shielded the cloud forest from view. He felt as if he was leaving the world behind him. A weight began to lift.

The sight of Pico Bolivar was beautiful but terrifying. The peaks of the *cordillera* spanned the skyline with black and rugged serrations, like the magnified teeth of a two-handed saw. It looked impossible to cross. Mills was excited. This was a place where the Amazon was born, thousands of individual river sources that flowed down to make the mighty river. High up there he was on the roof of the world in a terrain as strange and ominous as the surface of Jupiter.

Stretching out, across the ravine between the path and the snow-capped peak of Pico Bolivar, were the old cables that once went further up towards the summit. The red battered cable car was still there, swaying in the turbulent updraught, halfway across the ravine. It looked as if it had broken down midway and had been abandoned to its fate: the tourists dead inside.

He was more confident now of the track ahead and set off too fast. All he could think of was the thousand feet he had to climb to the pass, which couldn't even be seen from the track yet.

He was glad that he'd be alone on this walk, that was the way he wanted it to be, and the desolate landscape matched his own mood. To die up here would be a pure act. As his body froze beneath the summit, where the ancient Incas left their sacrificial victims, it would be, he thought, a natural death; without violence; a calm and solitary re-absorbtion into nature.

Yellow and purple flowers grew by the track side, and it was now suddenly, perfectly silent. He couldn't even see the town below any more. There was nothing but mountain. All he could hear in the stillness was the sound of his own heavy breathing.

The track turned right, around a ridge. The air was very cold now and bracingly crisp. As he turned the ridge, he saw the black lakes sparkling below, and above and beneath him there were sheer rock sides, like those in a quarry hewn by blasts of dynamite; but these were fashioned with millions of years of shattered eroded rock: the debris of deep time.

After the turn in the track the way became progressively difficult, and it already looked to him to be impassable, but he was determined to get above the snow-line. He'd already fixed his eyes on a rock promontory where he intended to sit and look out across the perfect white.

Here, at the footstool of the pass, the path was already made up of just loose shale looking like storm-shattered roof slates that glistened and shone in the burning sun.

He thought of those boys, the Uruguayan rugby team, The Old Christian's XV, whose plane had crashed in the Andes in the seventies, and who had been forced to eat the corpses of their friends. He shivered from the cold. He hadn't imagined it'd be cold.

The altitude had affected Mills now and he was feeling very strange. The frailejon cacti clung to fissures in the rock, their white luminescent tentacles swaying like deep sea anemones transported to a reversal of their element. Peculiar things, and part of something unknown to him. He found he had stopped walking and was staring at one, imagining it to be dancing for him. His head was spinning, his heart was beating fast, his breathing was erratic. He staggered on and as soon as he could get a sufficiently firm footing he sank down onto his haunches to rest, and to regain his equilibrium.

In the absolute silence his panting was amplified. He looked back down towards the cable station.

He looked at his watch. He still had time to return to the cable.

He began to feel so sick that he wondered if he'd ever acclimatise at all. The air felt oxygenless and he was gasping at it in gulps, like a carp landed on the river bank, with staring eyes and every muscle in its head working as if in spasm; gills flapping mechanically like an early attempt at flight.

What was it that the tour guide had said? He tried to remember. He'd said that whatever demons were in you, the mountain would bring out. It was a thoroughly invigorating prospect and he imagined himself on his way to the Hall of the Mountain King; or on the brink of the cliff with the Gadarene swine.

He thought of the people who'd stripped off their clothes and rolled naked over the edge. It was incredible how the thin air thrust you so quickly and so comprehensively into an altered state.

He managed just another ten feet before collapsing down onto his haunches again. All he could think about now was his un-planned and inevitable fall over the bleak promontory of black hard rock.

He could hear his father's voice from a time when they were in Switzerland and he'd tried to get Mills to go climbing with him. He'd said it would toughen him up, teach him team work and discipline. There was no greater responsibility than having another person's life in your hands, he'd said, at the end of a nylon rope. Mills had refused to go. He didn't want to learn team work, he wanted to be left alone. But he'd prove to his father now that he could climb a mountain if he chose, and alone. He amused himself briefly by conjuring up an image of his father depending on him now, just over the edge here on the end of a nylon rope.

He made a few more yards, and collapsed again. For the next hour and a half he continued in this lonely, determined way.

He managed a few more feet and then he saw the pass above him, marked with a distant wooden cross.

He gasped. This time he laid himself down on the loose shale.

His breathing was worse now, and his vision was shifting and flickering. Rocks appeared to be moving to the left and to the right as if the mountain were shuddering, or shivering in its self-imposed cold. It seemed to be participating in an hallucination.

He wasn't far below the snow-table and the glaring whiteness against the sheer faces of the black rock seemed to oscillate; almost a strobe effect on the eyes.

He got up again, and pressed on. The track was now just a ledge about six feet wide that snaked its way above a sheer drop. After that it very quickly reduced to three feet, and the drop increased to a thousand. He moved inch by inch, pushing his face into the side of rock; and then he couldn't go any further. He eased himself down the supporting rock face, burning his fingers on the granite as he pressed against it so hard.

When he got to his knees he slowly tried to slip off his jacket. It had become a burden and he wanted to free himself of all encumbrances.

All that filled his mind now was the tight feeling of the restrictive garment, and the need to rid himself of it, like a turtle intent on prising off its own shell between a fissure in the coral.

He lowered his jacket in front of him and slowly, deliberatingly, lowered his head on to it. He closed his eyes.

He thought of his bed in the posada down in the town. He tried to concentrate his mind on its pattern and its threads, and the images of llamas and capybaras that were woven in. He imagined himself asleep. He wondered if dying in a place like this would be like the onset of an exhausted sleep when you were too full of fatigue for your body to be able to properly shut down its senses.

He stayed like this for fifteen or twenty minutes, pondering the newspaper headlines. Then as his breathing improved he found the strength to sob. It was a luxury he hadn't been able to afford before, for fear of edging himself closer to the drop, and ending everything suddenly and ill-prepared. He thought of the story that Jude had told him about his grandmother's suicide. How she'd walked to the end of the jetty at the harbour in Littlehampton, and before she'd thrown herself in to the current at the mouth of the river Arun, she'd taken off her fluffy slippers and placed them neatly against the jetty wall. 'It was,' Jude had said, 'her way of marking her point of departure.' It was the first time he'd allowed himself to think of his friend since he'd left Austin, and he quickly erased his image from his mind.

It was obvious to him now that he must have strayed off the track. He knew that this was his last chance to give up and return to get the last cable car back down.

He heard the loudspeaker system from the cable car calling the passengers back for the trip down. It was two o'clock. The last cable was going now.

With no more cable cars it meant that no-one at all would be passing on the track in either direction. There would be no-one here on the mountain but him.

He gripped the rock beneath him, fixed. He couldn't find the strength to go up, and there was nowhere to go down. His head sank into the shale, and he stayed solidly in this position while the minutes rolled by, and silence took the mountain again, as the cable car departed. He squeezed his eyes tightly shut.

He wondered if this ledge, as it went up, got slimmer. If the three feet reduced to two, and then to one, and then slivered away entirely, leaving him just with the thousand feet drop.

He pushed his head further into the polyester darkness of his jacket.

Suddenly there was a roaring of air above him that cut the deathly silence. His heart hit his chest like a bare fist on a leather punch bag.

It was a bird, a great mighty bird, full of muscle and ferocity. Wingspan nine feet. He looked up as it swooped past him again. He could see into its deep black eye; its wings splayed condor-like at the tips; some kind of eagle. The wind blew cold and buffeting, but he could feel the rush of its wing beats against his face.

He was so frightened of the bird that he pulled himself up.

I've stumbled into its eyrie, he thought. It's going to swipe me off the rock. Its eggs are here, the creature wouldn't even let me sit here and freeze.

He was moving again, he was moving on, around the next angle of the ledge. As he walked his eyes were fixed on the spot immediately in front, focusing only on the two small spots where his next footfalls would be placed. No sense in looking down, no sense in getting a scale of the thing. He was heaving again, struggling to breathe, but at least it deadened the sound of the bird.

On, and around another sharp curve.

The ledge had widened, it was largely loose shale, but was now six feet wide, and widening all the time. And then a second ledge approached from beyond, and met this one, so that there was now just a gentle incline, of about thirty degrees, at the side of the track before the precipice, and the drop.

But then, just as suddenly, and as violently as the eagle had attacked, Mills's stomach erupted without warning. From fear, from the altitude, he didn't know. It was a battle to keep his thinking clear.

He vomited violently across the rock face and lost his footing on the shale. He fell and slid, like a curling-bowl across ice, his own weight taking him down the thirty degree slope towards the precipice.

He howled with the injustice of it, at least a person should be allowed to expire in their own good time.

Silence.

Silence except for slates of shale slipping away from beneath his boots, and then silence again as they dropped over the edge to shatter a thousand feet below. He was lying face down on the edge. He counted the time it took for the slipping shale to hit the ravine below in the way a child frightened of the storm counts the seconds between the lightning flash and the thunder, to confirm his dread that the storm is moving closer.

The force of the vomiting had caused streaks of tears on his face, but now real tears began, but without any sound to accompany them. He knew he could no longer afford the release of shuddering sobs in case the movement of his rib cage inched him closer to the edge. He was now entirely possessed by fear; every bone and sinew of his being was made of it.

Inch by inch he made it back to the wider track. Pressing his palms down hard on the plates of loose rock, as if they could adhere, like the underside of an anemone. He even sucked against the dusty rock with his mouth full open, trickles of blood from the scrapes on his nose and forehead running into his shirt collar.

Back on the track his mind was like a calculating machine now: ever active but unconscious of the merest sense, an essential digit missing.

Somewhere in these haphazard thoughts he wanted to take off his clothes. His arms and fingers were tingling, and as he walked he could feel sharp metal pins being slid latitudinally into his forearms. His brain was scrabbling for oxygen in his blood.

A while later he was staring up at the wooden cross that marked the summit of the pass, at the height of the *cordillera*. He stared for some time; he was lying curled up on the rock in the foetal position.

He'd made it to the pass but all it had rewarded him with was a seemingly sheer drop the other side, and a view of swiftly gathering cloud. It was bleak and cold up there in the hissing wind, and the cross made it seem more desperate still.

He vomited again and blood began to pour from his nose. It splattered the rocks around him and his clothes. He felt as if he was expelling all the impurities from his body, the extra weight that had slowed him down on his way, and the rock received it as if it had become suddenly permeable to his bile.

He watched the cloud pass across the opposite rock face. The mountain was going to be blotted out by a high storm.

He wiped the blood and saliva from his chin with his sleeve, and then laid his head into his arm.

So this is it? he muttered. Now the cloud takes it, the light fades, the night comes on, and I am frozen to the rock.

He curled himself into a dip in the shale and closed his eyes, accepting the situation as best he could.

He tried to picture a small parade of people coming up the path behind him. He listened to their steps as they lost their footings on the shale.

First came a small boy, who arrived and squatted down beside him in the gloom, sitting silently on his haunches. Squashed onto his head was a red felt cowboy hat, and around his waist a holster with a shiny silver cap-gun.

Then a twelve-year-old in scarf and mittens, grey and cold, with the fine droplets of mist from the lake at Geneva giving his face a bleak and sullen appearance.

Through the gloom, sitting on a rock, there was the fifteen-year-old, melodramatically suicidal, in his crisp blue military tunic; the pages of the Pierpoint Academy Song gripped in his hand, newly torn from the hymnal.

Then there was the young Texan, in a white linen suit and

Stetson, standing uneasily, apparently embarrassed by what he saw.

'Oh God,' muttered Mills. 'What are we about to do?'

He looked through the scattering patches of cloud and he saw Jude there too; he was looking down at them with a fake smile and his thoughtful, plotting, expression.

Mills dismissed him with a wave of his hand and he dissolved back into the greying gloom.

Then the other figures began to disappear too, but badly, like in a TV special effect. As the cloud began to clear, his eyes began to focus on the cross that marked the top of the pass and the shrine that had been built beneath it. In the small alcove of the shrine he saw the remnants of the candles that had been burned there; it looked desolate and hopeless, but his eyes fixed on it nevertheless. Then he saw the small besuited figure with his moustache and trilby hat; he could even see the handkerchief in José Gregorio Hernández's top pocket. He stared at him until he couldn't keep his eyes open any longer.

It would be dark by six, until then, he'd sleep, and then the cold night would come on.

He thought he heard the sound of birdsong above him; the singing and twittering of dozens of little birds. Slowly he raised his head from the rock, splattered with blood from his nose. He looked up into the empty sky, there were no birds.

Then he heard a snort and the clatter of a horse's hoof. He looked around him, with one eye – the other was sealed with bile where the wind had blown it back in his face.

Above him were two young boys, one of about thirteen, the other of perhaps nine, sitting on fine chestnut mules. The elder boy held a cardboard box dangling from a piece of string. The carton was punched with holes. The boy was taking a carton of tiny exotic birds across the mountain to sell.

They stared down at Mills, open-mouthed. They had an expression on their faces which showed that they thought he was the ugliest-looking gringo they had ever seen, surrounded by the pebble-dash of sickness on the bare face of their mountain territory.

Mills felt strangely embarrassed as they stared down at him.

The older boy got down from his horse, reached into his saddle bag, and pulled out a bottle of bright green liquid.

'Altura,' said the boy and knelt down to pass him the bottle. Mills took a swig of it. It tasted like *ouzo* and was probably about forty per cent proof. It seemed to rush around Mills's head for a moment and then push at his ears.

The older boy, wearing a beaten straw hat with red ribbons, helped Mills up onto his horse. He felt that he could do nothing but comply. He looked down at the small dip in the shale that he'd made his own.

As they prepared to set off over the top of the pass Mills glanced back at the shrine. There was a small posey of fresh flowers laid at José Gregorio's plaster feet. Someone had stopped to make a prayer there that day. Mills found himself smiling back at José Gregorio. The boy with the ribbons on his hat caught Mills's expression and smiled too. He bent down for a moment and pulled up a small purple mountain flower blooming in the crevasse of the rock. He took it over to the shrine and placed it at Hernández's feet. He came back, laughed, and slapped his horse's arse.

As they drew near the edge a view of endless sweeping mountainsides opened up. Mills closed his eyes and listened to the humming birds beating their wings against the cardboard of their box.

They began to descend. Mills started to feel that he had overcome a hurdle greater than the mountain.

Mills stayed on the Andino boy's horse for five hours. Sometimes the trail would look impassable but the horses would quicken their step, suddenly breaking into a hectic kind of canter on the rocks, and launch themselves up the mountainsides, almost throwing him off. The horses appeared to have a kind of internal map of every twist and obstacle and a determination to survive the terrain. Some of their fellows could be seen bleached and skeletal in the ravines below.

His palms had become red raw where he gripped the reins, and his blisters had split. His father had tried to make a horseman of him on their return to Texas, and now, he almost wished he'd gone along with what he'd regarded at the time as a kind of masculine nonsense. His nose and the skin of his cheekbones were burned; the sun was deceptively strong; and he was saddle sore, the leather had cut into him and he could feel the stickiness of blood in the crack of his jeans.

But he was alone, and that was the main thing. The Andino boys didn't speak at all. Even the small scruffy dog they had with them was silent and trotted along beneath the lead horse, dexterously avoiding the hoofs, to shade himself from the sun. It was a long walk for a small dog, but not once did he stop to pee.

It was dark when they made their last descent into a small mountain village still above the cloud-line. The one street was angled at almost forty-five degrees and the horses slipped into the gulleys cut into the street by new rainfall. Some of the houses were lying derelict and where the whitewash had fallen away the mud from which they were constructed had been moulded into soft, sculptural shapes by the rain.

He wondered where the people were, out in the sloping fields perhaps, or moving goats or llama to lower pasture. In the entire village there was not a single Coca Cola sign. It was a rare place in the world. There were no restaurants or bars either, just a solitary small bust of Simon Bolivar, dressed as a Roman senator, in the small cobbled square. A single tree stood by a padlocked church with a squat tower. That was the centre of things, at the bottom of a single street of low, windowless white washed dwellings. But the air was as crystal as a chilled draught of spring water from the source.

The Andino boys led him to an abandoned travellers' lodge, perched precariously on a ledge at the very edge of the village. Then they left him, with a shake of the hand, and went off to sell their box of birds, still singing with as full a throat as when they had begun their journey.

He lay down on the straw mattress of the mud-walled cell, with iron bars at the single slit of a window. There was the remnant of a candle by the bed and as he lit it, and the flame played against the darkness of the walls, he saw two soft brown eyes looking down at him from a portrait above the bed.

As he lay there he felt as if he'd come through a very dark long night. He tried to evaluate how serious his suicidal thoughts had been. At the Academy there were suicides and then he'd regarded it as the most ultimate of selfish acts; a way of lashing out at parents and friends in a moment of deranged self-absorption. In the last few days the activity of his own mind had been dramatic; but then, so had the events surrounding him: the shooting of the archbishop, the riot, and now the rescue on the mountain by the soulful and silent Andino boys with their scruffy dog and the box of singing birds.

He looked around the mud cell. He was away from everything now; he'd made his rejection of the Wasps' Nest; it was a matter now of trying to decide what to do about it. The walk, and the ride, across the mountain had been like a great mumbling sentence, a stream of consciousness that had ended here in a definite full-stop.

He thought about what he should do next. A great blank stretched out before him.

In the morning Mills sat for a while and looked out across the valleys. The morning cloud tripped over them, pouring like a waterfall as the cold air pushed the mist over the peaks, and the rising thermals brought them back up again like a celestial pillow fight in slow motion.

He could see a distant figure coming up the track from an outlying hill farm. The man was lugging a bag of camera equipment. As he came closer Mills could see that he was an American or a European. He had the sourest expression on his face and looked as if he was cursing under his breath.

Mills decided to set off back to Merida. When the horse had brought him into the village he'd seen a beaten up old jeep beside the village store. He made for the shop.

The shop sold beer, rice and, peculiarly, knitted woollen hats. The storekeeper agreed to drive him back later in the morning when he set off for supplies.

It was early evening when they drew into Merida by a circuitous route that had taken most of the day. Mills went to his hotel, washed and bound up his blistered hands. He was hungry now and he went into the restaurant beside his hotel for something to eat.

He pulled a stool up to the bar and sat down uneasily, the long jeep ride having aggravated his saddle sores. He ordered a beer and the *comida corriente*, usually a watery soup with a single piece of meat, followed by something indistinguishable with rice and tough, fried bananas.

Three stools down a young back-packer was sitting miserably watching the head of his beer roll slowly down the bottle neck and over the label. He'd studied Mills as he awkwardly took to his stool and after a few minutes he turned to look at him again. Then he spoke. Mills thought he said: 'You want a beer?' but he couldn't be sure, the boy had a strange way of speaking that didn't involve opening his mouth or moving his lips.

Mills pretended not to hear him, but the guy came over. He looked as forlorn as Mills himself.

The guy raised his bottle up to him and mumbled 'Yes?'

'I just ordered one,' Mills said, finally. 'But thanks.'

The guy introduced himself anyway. His name was Tomas and he came from an island in Freishan Germany. 'Nationally known as the birthplace of idiots,' he confessed, mumblingly, with a self-effacing smile.

Mills nodded non-committally and turned to stare at his own beer bottle.

'This,' said Tomas, looking around the restaurant, 'is a terrible place.'

'The soup's pretty watery,' said Mills, making a half-hearted effort with the conversation. The guy didn't look as if he was going to be too demanding.

'I mean the country,' he said. 'I mean the whole country. I arrived a few days ago from Caracas. That's a terrible place too. It's all terrible.'

'I know,' said Mills. 'I was there.'

'You were?' said Tomas keenly. It was obvious that he hadn't spoken to anyone for days. 'You know what they did? They shot the archbishop.'

'Yeah I know.'

'And there were riots.'

'Yes.'

'And look what they did to me,' he opened his mouth wide for the first time. 'I lost a tooth.'

'Yes, it looks like you have.'

'They shot the archbishop at the airport.'

'I know. I was there. I saw it.'

'You did? You actually saw it?'

'Yeah. Have they arrested anyone for it yet?'

Tomas shook his head. His cheek was slightly swollen from where he'd received the blow that had knocked out the front tooth. 'It is incredible,' he said, a little more confident in his speaking now that he'd explained about his missing tooth. 'The whole country seems to be under suspicion. The police even stopped me. Strange isn't it, I've never been in an airport that has so much security, but did they manage to capture the gunman? No.'

'No?'

'It was a *conspiracy*,' he whispered, and looked about him even though the bar was empty. 'The government themselves, in my opinion, had him shot.'

'They did?' said Mills incredulously.

'Oh for sure. People thought he might be the next Pope. So they shot him. That's what I think. Two Belgian guys I met told me.'

'Well, that has to be a fact then.'

'Yes, I think so,' he said sadly, looking back at his beer bottle.

'You're back-packing?'

'Well, yes. I'm making my journey across South America. Are you?'

'I guess I am, I suppose.'

There was such a desolate sadness about the young German that Mills found that he didn't mind his company after all. He liked the fact that he'd lost a tooth and was having a tough time in the country. He appealed to his current state of mind.

'It is a very hard country to travel on your own,' the German continued. 'I hate being on my own.'

Tomas had dreadlocks, which appeared oddly incompatible with his painfully pale skin. He looked as if he'd embarked on a campaign of rebellion against his parents and authority, and society at large, but he'd only got as far as the haircut.

'It's no place to be on your own. Where have you been?' asked Tomas.

'I just jeeped it back from a village over the mountains.'

'You did? What is it like?'

Mills didn't quite know how to reply. What do you say about giving in so quickly to being rescued when you had been debating the notion of freezing yourself to death, that can leave you with any dignity in the re-telling? Before he could answer, Tomas was already staring back at the beer, gradually growing flat in his palm.

'I wanted to go up there in the jeep, but it is so expensive. I planned for four months' travelling, but when I got to Caracas they robbed me of nearly everything at the airport when I arrived.'

'Really?'

'Yeah, they cut through my back-pack with a knife. Got all my travellers' cheques. I didn't realise until I got to a hotel. When I told the police I had been robbed they fined me for breaking the curfew. I think there will be curfew here tonight too.'

'You think?'

'Uh huh. This is no place for a holiday. I just want to go home. I think I must just have bad luck about me. There must be something in my face.'

As he stared down at the bar-top, with this almighty gloom descending on him, Mills was aware of a man coming into the bar and approaching the counter beside him. Then he heard the sound of metal clunking down onto the wood. Tomas was studying the label of his beer again and feeling sorry for himself.

Mills turned to look at the man. He was a big guy in a shiny jacket, unshaven with a thick dark moustache and deep menacing eyes. Mills turned away, but out of the corner of his eye he could see the sawn-off shotgun he'd laid on the bar-top. Then he called to the barman, who came running out from the back, sweat on his forehead from when he'd been seasoning the watery soup.

The gunman grunted briefly and motioned towards the cash till.

Slowly, Mills tried to move away from him, inching away from the guy on his stall; trying not to make any sudden movements, moving closer to the German.

'No-one I've met here has had an easy time of it,' continued Tomas. 'I heard about another guy in Caracas who'd been thrown into the back of a van by two guys the moment he came out of the airport. They made him hand over his wallet and his credit card, and then they drove him to a cash-point machine.'

The barman was frantically counting out a roll of notes from the till. He handed it over to the man with the gun. The guy grunted again, and Mills could smell the acrid aroma of his underarms as he motioned to the till again. It wasn't enough.

Oh God, thought Mills, I'm in a hold up that is going to turn very nasty, and I'm sitting next to the Bad Luck Kid.

'When they got him to the cash-point they put a gun to his head,' continued Tomas, 'and said "tell us your *Pin* number". But he couldn't remember it, he was so scared . . .'

The gunman was stuffing the rest of the money into his inside pocket.

'. . . Finally he remembered it, and then they drove him to a dark part of town and dumped him. They made him shake hands with them and said, "Thank you for doing business with us sir". That's kind of chilling, I think.'

The gunman was now demanding a large whisky from behind the bar. Mills had managed to slide his stool a little closer to Tomas now.

'When I came here I thought I'd be, you know, riding around in jeeps; maybe rafting; seeing all the animal life. Hanging out smoking grass. I didn't think it would be bad like this. I'm just so scared all the time, aren't you? You look nervous too.'

Mills listened as the guy drank down his whisky and spat on the floor. Mills didn't seem able to speak and Tomas stared at him for a moment. Then the gunman pushed back his stool and walked out of the door.

Mills expelled a lungful of air and briefly held his head in his hands. He looked up at Tomas.

'You didn't see that?' he said to him. 'You didn't see the guy with the gun?'

Tomas smiled. 'Yes, I saw him,' he said quietly. 'It was Rodriguez, the doorman, getting his night's wages. He did the same last night.'

For the first time in several days Mills laughed out loud.

Tomas finished up his beer and announced that he had to be going. 'I don't want to get caught out after curfew again,' he said. 'See you around, maybe.'

Mills sat for a little while longer and then found that he, too, was staring at the label on his beer watching the suds roll down. He suddenly felt terribly alone. He was sad that Tomas had gone. He began to consider the fact that, surprising as it was, even he was wanting company; some human exchange.

He paid up, rolling off a wad of low denomination Bolivars to the sweating barman and walked out into the street.

The Park Las Heroinas was filled with unkempt shaggy palms and a crazy attempt at a fountain made from brightly coloured bathroom tiles. Around it, the cheap guest houses, like the one Mills was staying in for two dollars a night, were sited. Above was the wheel of the cable car, where the young people of the town gathered in the evening. Feeling that he needed company, Mills wandered by.

The town kids parked their cars and opened their boots where they had cool boxes with drinks, and ghetto blasters blaring techno. Mills strolled into the park and settled down on a bench, watching the squirrels run up and down for snacks. He reached into his pocket and pulled out his grandfather's hip-flask. He'd taken it as a keepsake, but tonight it was filled with gin that he'd bought duty free on his flight out.

He watched the locals. They were so smartly dressed they put the back-packers to shame. The guys were all in crisply ironed shirts and designer jeans, standing around in groups. Every now and then one of them would inch towards a group of girls, formally ask her if she'd like a drink and then invite her over to dance at the back of his car.

Mills sat there for half an hour or more, taking slugs from his hip flask, participating in their *paseo* vicariously.

Then the polite and gentle atmosphere was cut by the sound of whistles blowing, and the squirrels were running back up into the trees. The ghetto blasters were silenced; the kids were scattering, leaping into their cars and driving off into the darkness. They disappeared up side streets, and the park was cleared in minutes as if it were a practised manoeuvre. As their cars screeched away polystyrene cups sploshed on the cobbles as they flew from the car windows.

The police, with their batons and shields, were heading towards him in a flank out of the darkness. Tomas had been right about the curfew.

He could see the white of an ankle sock catch the light as a girl ran into an alley and he followed her, lurching into the darkness as the gin swilled around his brain and the hot damp night made him heady, like the fumes of a laundry.

Lights were going off in the houses and the blue flickers of the television sets were shutting down. Everyone was making out they were asleep or away. Mills could hear the riot police, obviously intent on starting one, clamouring in their hard boots in the street below. Above, at the end of the passageway, he saw the lights of two police motorbikes bearing down on him. He threw himself into the doorway of one of the houses, but then panic began to overtake him, and he dashed across the street to where the doorway looked deeper. Then he found himself zig-zagging back towards the park, the motorbikes behind him. He took a sharp right and as he passed the doorway of one of the tour offices it opened briefly, and with one single gesture, a hand pulled him in and switched off the light at the same time.

He was plunged into silence and darkness, all he could hear was the sound of his panting breath again, as he'd done on the mountain.

'They're a bit lively tonight,' said a woman's voice with an English accent.

'Certainly are,' he managed through his breathlessness. There was a powerful smell of rum in the air. He could hear whoever it was feeling her way round the edge of her desk. Then he heard the creak of a canvas chair as she sat down.

'There's a stool behind you,' she said. 'Better make yourself at home or the bastards'll take you for everything you've got. You're here to chill out in the mountains, I take it?'

'Uh huh. Bit excitable at the moment, isn't it?'

'It is.'

'Well, thanks.'

'It's nothing.'

He felt for the wall behind him, and the rough plaster came away in his fingers in flakes. The office smelled of tropical damp. Stabilising himself against the wall he slid down until he found the stool. He placed his hands around it. It was a tree trunk.

'You're working late, I guess?' he asked.

'Yeah, just doing my bloody paperwork. I've been putting it off all month.'

'How's it going?'

'Great, these figures look great to me,' she said laughing. The darkness was impenetrable. The only illumination left in town was the torches and the headlamps of the police.

Then a small red glow lifted slowly in the air, and he heard her inhale. The red tip of her cigarette glowed in a succession of pulses like the twinkling lights of a radio mast.

'The name's Jenny, by the way,' she said. 'And this is Cordillera Tours. How's it going?'

'Mills,' he said. 'Thanks.'

'You want a slug of rum?'

'Sure.'

He heard her twisting the metal top of a bottle and feeling her way around the desk again. He watched the red glow of the cigarette come towards him and then felt her hand on his forehead, looking for his mouth.

The rum burned as it seared down his throat and sploshed over his chin.

'Cheers!'

'Cheers,' he replied. 'Bottoms up.'

The desk creaked as she perched herself on the edge. Then he heard a drawer opening and something heavy, like a gun, landed on the desk.

'You just got into town?'

'Three days ago, I was in Caracas.'

'That's what started all this,' she said, and sighed. 'After the shooting the police have got really nervous. Though what they think a load of kids having a dance in the park has got to do with the price of fish, God only knows. They are totally up their own arseholes right now.'

'That seems a fair summation.'

She laughed. 'It's a summation all right.'

Mills pulled out his hip-flask. He didn't get on with rum. 'You want a drink of this?' he said, shaking the flask.

Her hand found it in the darkness. She unscrewed the top and then there was silence. He heard her gulp, and then gulp again, longer and harder.

'Ooooh,' she said, and gulped again. 'Ooooh, gin!'

'You like gin?'

'I haven't had gin for, oh God knows how long it is since I've had gin. It costs a fortune over here, imported. God, I could close my eyes and reckon I was in the Bull's Head in Stowmarket.' She took another long gulp. 'Reckon we've got a darts match tonight, get in the pork scratchings . . .'

'Sorry there's no tonic.'

'Sod the tonic. After six years, sod the tonic.'

He heard the neck of the flask hit her teeth. Then she handed it back.

'Thanks, you can come again.'

'You work here? You live in Venezuela?'

'Been here for six years. I married a Spaniard. Come from Suffolk originally.'

He took a slug of the gin as well.

'Suffolk? No mountains there.' He could hear her fingers scrabbling around on the desk for something. 'I saw them shoot the archbishop, I was at the airport,' he said.

'Shit, were you? It's you they're after then I bet.'

'You think so?'

She laughed. She'd found her lighter again and lit the heavy church candle that she'd taken out of her desk drawer.

'There we go,' she said. 'We can see each other now.'

She was a woman in her thirties, with a handsome face, tanned and with muscular forearms from where she'd spent her time hauling on ropes and wielding ice-picks.

Mills pulled out his hip-flask and offered it again.

'Cheers,' she said. 'Nice flask. I could do with one of these when I go up there. Where d'you get it?' She held it in her hands for a moment. 'To E.C.' she read from the engraved plate. 'That you?'

'No, my grandfather.'

'From L.B.J. Who's that?'

'Oh just some old guy my grandfather used to hang about with.'

'Nice, nice flask. Mind if I?'

'Go ahead.'

She took another slurp, this time a little less enthusiastic now that they had illumination.

She pulled herself off the desk and handed it back to him.

'What's that round your neck?' she said. The tone of her voice had changed, she sounded startled.

'It's just a pendant I picked up in Caracas.'

She inspected it. 'It's not just a pendant. My God, good job the police didn't get you. Good job I pulled you in here. You know who that is?'

'It's a picture of José Gregorio Hernández.'

'Too damn right it is. It's the Doctor. This is weird, you know. This is truly weird. You believe in José Gregorio?'

'Er, well, I went to his tomb, during the riot.'

'You've been there? This is *weird*. I always wanted to go there. I want to go to José Gregorio's tomb.' She drew on her cigarette. 'He's just so amazing. Everyone believes in him. He's done the most incredible things. People *see* him, you know, they really see him.'

'Yeah? He was killed by the first Ford motor car to enter Caracas, is that right?'

'Well, I don't know about that. I don't know if that's true. They like to say that because they don't like America. No offence, obviously, but they don't. It could easily have been the second or the third car. Who knows? That's the politicos, they try to use him.'

'It's a big cult thing?'

'It's massive. It gets bigger every day. It's *weird*.'

'You believe in him?'

'Of course I believe in him. I pray to him every day. I always pray to him.' She was looking at the flask. Mills handed it to her.

'God, it's so good this stuff,' she said. 'But it's weird, you know, because I was sitting here, praying to José Gregorio, and then I just got up from my desk for no real reason. I walked over to the door. Then I heard you running down the street outside. I pulled you in without really thinking about it. And there you are with José Gregorio around your neck. It's *weird*.'

She seemed entirely electrified by having seen the pendant.

'They're going to make him a saint,' said Mills.

'I hope so. But they got a real problem with it. There's all this voodoo and stuff involved and that, apparently, makes the Vatican uneasy. His devotees, you see, well a lot of them anyway, you know how they worship him?'

'How?'

'Well you have to climb a mountain, just up a bit on the coast from here, and stop at all these shrines. At every shrine you have to sit down and pray while drinking a load of alcohol and smoking a cigar.'

'And the Vatican have a problem with that?'

'It's a difficult thing for them to get their heads around. I pray to José Gregorio because of my little boy. My little boy has a hole in the heart.' She reached her hand into the top of her blouse and pulled on a string. The string came out of her blouse for some time, and then on the end of it was a pendant. 'I wear him,' she said, 'next to my heart to *remind* him.'

Mills smiled. 'I'd like to know more about José Gregorio,' he said. 'I keep seeing him everywhere I go.'

He offered her the flask, but the gin was gone. She brought out the bottle of rum again.

'Well you're in the right place,' she said. 'You know where he was born? Isnotu!'

'Isnotu?' he repeated, it sounded like *is not you*.

'Ah huh, it's just up the road. God, I'd love to go up there. I don't know anyone who's gone up there, but I hear they've built a shrine and everything, in the house where he was born. I'd really like to run a tour there, but, well you tourist guys aren't interested are you?'

'I'm interested, I'd like to go.'

'I could organise a trip for you,' she said. 'It'd be a real trip. We got this young guide we've just taken on, Carlos. He's got a jeep. He could drive you over there. He'd be keen. When you get there you can light a candle for my boy.'

The gin had got to them.

'Sure I will,' said Mills. 'I'd like to go.'

'You go there,' she said, 'and you'll be the first tourist they ever had as far as I know. It's really not a place that's on the map yet.'

The gin, the heady atmosphere of the police raid, and the notion of being off the map were irresistible. By the time they'd finished the rum Mills had agreed that she should send the young tour guide over to his hotel the next morning to discuss the trip to Isnotu.

In many ways Mills was beginning to feel a sense of release in just handing himself over to events; to following the moment, wherever it led.

Early the next morning Carlos came knocking at his door. He was a boy of eighteen who'd just started at Cordillera Tours. Like the other guide Mills had met, he was waiting for the government to allow the professors to return to teaching at the university.

'It will be a most wonderful thing to go to Isnotu!' said Carlos enthusiastically. 'José Gregorio is so important to us. You are going to write about him, yes, in English?'

'Well . . .' Carlos looked so pleased Mills didn't like to disappoint him, he seemed to have presumed he was a journalist, though where he'd got that idea from Mills couldn't fathom.

'All my family pray to José Gregorio, but I don't know anyone who has gone to Isnotu. It will be an expedition. We will go in the jeep. It will take three days. It is up, up, up, far along the Trans-Andean Highway. Very off a beaten track. It is in Trujillo where they have the biggest statue of the Virgin Mary in Venezuela. And it's big, I've heard it's very big. This will be *some* journey all right. Big travelling for me. I am very pleased. It will be my first major expedition. It is good I have the jeep. We couldn't do this without a jeep. When do we go . . . ?'

'Well . . .'

'Tomorrow. I drop everything. Tomorrow. I will come with the jeep at six o'clock in the morning.'

That evening, over his watery soup, Mills talked to Tomas, the miserable German.

'You heard about those Belgians that were staying in your hotel?' Tomas said.

'No?'

'They got arrested.'

'Broke the curfew huh?'

'No. They had seven kilos of cocaine under the seats in their caravanette.'

'They'll be in Venezuela for a little longer than they planned then.'

'They will.'

'What are you going to do?'

'I have to wait,' said Tomas. 'I have to wait three more days until my parents wire me some money, then maybe I go to the beach. Maybe I just go back home. I don't know.'

Mills thought for a moment, then he invited him to meet him the next morning at six and come in the jeep to Isnotu. He didn't really know why he'd asked him along, but he felt better for it. He began to suspect that he was missing Jude and was trying to replace him.

The grey of dawn had not yet departed and the iron wheel was silent as Mills stood on the edge of the park, listening to the creaks of the cables. It was quarter past six already, there was no Tomas in sight, and there was no Carlos with his jeep. The coffee shops were opening up and the trails of wood smoke from the frying of the morning *arepos* were drifting across the town.

Then at half past he heard the sound of Tomas running down the middle of the street. He had a small kit bag with him and was carrying a bottle of water.

'I'm late,' he said breathlessly. 'I didn't think I'd make it. Those bastards in my *posada* tried to charge me two dollars for the use of the soap in my room. We had one hell of an argument about it I can tell you.' He looked around him, up and down the empty street. 'Where is your big expedition?' he asked.

'I've no idea.'

Tomas offered him a swig of his water. 'Is it all off?' he asked, forlornly, but not especially surprised.

Mills stood silently for a few moments. Then they heard a roaring sound, mixed with choking as a beat-up old bronze coloured Ford Mustang lurched towards them and stopped, as it hit the kerb, on the other side of the street. The door flew open and there was Carlos waving wildly. He marched across the road.

'Big problems this morning with the jeep,' he said, trying to put a brave face on it. 'My father, he very pleased we go to Isnotu, everyone has always wanted to make the pilgrimage to Isnotu. So last night he strip down the jeep. To make it tip-top. But this morning *phut*.'

'Phut?'

'Si, very small *phut*, some smoke. Then nothing. But there is Daniel.'

Mills looked across to the wreck of the Mustang and waving cheerily from the driving seat was a kid of sixteen, trying to keep the engine running. Carbon monoxide was billowing out of the back where the exhaust pipe used to be.

'My brother,' said Carlos. 'He will drive us in his new car.'

'New car? It has to be twenty years old.'

'Yes, perhaps a little more,' said Carlos, still bravely smiling.

The Mustang was quite a creation. It had white painted wheels and on the bonnet were the remains of lurid orange flames that had been painted on by a former owner.

'But you said it's a really tough road, only a jeep could make it?'

'We will pray to José Gregorio!' said Carlos. 'He will get us there.'

'He's a surgeon, not a mechanic,' said Mills. 'And I'm not sure he'll be impressed if we turn up in a Ford.'

They walked over to the Mustang. 'Whatever you do, sir, say nothing about the car. It is my brother's first car. He loves it very much. It makes him very proud.'

'Isn't he worried about taking his pride and joy up on the Trans-Andean Highway?'

'Oh yes, sir. He's very worried indeed. We must be an encouragement.'

It was a little worrying however, that Carlos knelt down by the car and offered up a prayer before they set off.

The road out of Merida had a pretty good tarmac surface, but belligerent bands of bullocks would wander onto it and sit down. While Carlos persuaded the bullocks to clear out of the way, by prodding them with sticks and luring them with swathes of grass, Mills enjoyed the scenery. The trees around the road were dripping with Spanish moss, and the Rio Chama was twinkling in the morning sunlight. It took several attempts to get the Mustang started again, but when it did start, they were engulfed in a cloud of petrol fumes.

'It is probably not a good idea to smoke,' said Tomas, miserably from the back.

The road into the mountains around Merida was one of the oddest in South America. A great many of the towns along the way were built in the nineteenth century by German settlers. The sight of small Rhineland castles, and entire Teutonic towns, was something of a shock to Tomas. But instead of being delighted by its idiosyncrasy, as Mills was, all Tomas could say was: 'My God, I could have stayed at home.'

After four hours the Mustang started to splutter badly.

'Look where we are!' said Carlos. 'At the point where the road becomes the highest road in the whole of South America. Is something, no?'

Everyone was feeling pretty sick now from the petrol fumes, and conversation was less of a priority than breathing. Suddenly the car lurched into the side of the road, there was a final groan and it went silent.

They got out. The cloud had come down and it was like a bleak day on Dartmoor in the dead of winter.

'If you can imagine,' said Carlos, still trying to please, 'the view from here is spectacular.'

Tomas lay down on a flat rock, holding his stomach and looking ready to throw up. Mills sat by the roadside with Carlos.

'The car,' he said, 'has to have a rest for twenty minutes. It is the altitude. The petrol all is *fizzy*. If we don't stop it will go *phut*.' He looked towards his brother for a moment, who was sitting sadly behind the wheel with his chin slumped onto his chest. He looked like a relative holding vigil by the death bed. Then Daniel stuck his head out of the window and shouted a few short sharp words to his brother.

'He's not happy,' said Mills.

'No, he says we have killed his car.'

The Mustang rolled into Isnotu just before sunset, with three wrecked and sickly passengers, but Daniel feeling quite triumphant.

It was a small town with just a single main street lined with shacks selling plaster casts of José Gregorio. It was hot and dusty and as the white painted tyres rolled over the pot-holed road people stood in their shop doorways to watch. Then, as the children saw Mills's face peering out, and Tomas with his dreadlocks, they began running after the car, whooping and whistling.

They came to a halt outside the entrance to the shrine. There was a grotto made of rocks turned black by candle smoke, and a small white church with exuberant stained glass. There was a canopy covering a statue of the Doctor, in which he was shown looking down benignly with a bottle of pills in his hand. The town had the feeling of a port in the tropics, but, of course, without any water; everyone seemed to be waiting around for a boat to come in, forever ready with their bale-hooks.

As they got out of the Mustang they were immediately surrounded by jabbering children and inquisitive shopkeepers. They may well have been the first cargo boat to have made landfall here in years. The people stared at Mills's blond hair and blue eyes, and couldn't decide what was more astonishing: that; or the weird hairstyle of the other boy; or the sudden appearance of this fabulous looking car with flames painted across its bonnet.

A young boy had run to get a bucket and a sponge and was tugging at Mills's elbow and pointing to the Mustang.

'Carwashing!! Carwashing!' he yelled. 'One dollar!'

'Two dollars and the car's yours,' muttered Tomas. They brushed the kids aside and began to walk over to the shrine. A dozen kids formed a cordon around the Mustang, hopeful of a minder's fee. There was no need for the locals to have any other transport than mopeds or mules. There was nowhere to drive to here, and so Daniel hung back for a moment smiling proudly as the townsfolk admired his vehicle.

The shrine was closed.

10 ∫

It was early evening and Grandma was sitting on the verandah of the mansion when Jude came out to find her. She patted the lounger beside her, and pushed the ashtray over in his direction knowing that he'd come out for a smoke. He had looked entirely lost as he'd mooched about the house for the last four days, every day expecting Mills to return.

Some of the volunteers had done their best for him, taking him down to the blues bars in Sixth street, driving him out to see Lake Travis. They'd even taken him down to San Antonio the day before to visit the Alamo, but nothing was shifting his black mood. He was blaming himself for Mills's departure. He'd have liked to have felt angry with him for deserting him, inviting him over and then abandoning him to this limbo; but he knew he had let Mills down badly.

The Clearwaters were away in Iowa now and much of the team had gone with them. He wandered around the house like a ghost, continually asking if there was any news. No-one told him anything, they just repeated the mantra that the Clearwaters were very happy to have him there; that he should treat the place as his home; and that he should stay a little longer in case Mills returned. It was Catherine Sirteema's belief that his presence would temper the hostilities.

'You young people can be mighty awkward when you put your mind to it,' said Grandma.

'I'm sorry,' said Jude. 'I don't mean to be.'

'I don't mean you. I mean our Millburn. He's a real awkward son-of-a-bitch if you want my opinion.'

Jude tried to smile. 'He's that all right.'

'Always has been. He was born with a knotted brow. This time he's sure got under his father's skin. You reckon there'll be a lynching party when he gets back?'

This time Jude did smile. Everyone else in the Wasps' Nest spoke of Mills in hushed terms, as if he was dead. Grandma had a way of cutting straight to the chase. She was the only one here who could relax him. She looked out across the garden.

'What tree d'you reckon they'll pick?'

'I reckon,' said Jude, 'they'll choose that cedar out front so the press can get a decent shot. Do the press know yet?'

'Nope. It's all being *managed*.'

Jude poured himself a drink. Now that Grandma was left to her own devices she'd got into the habit of bringing out a whole pitcher of mint julep, stacked up with ice. He was rather touched by the fact that she'd started bringing another glass out with her too and their relationship was such now that he could just help himself. She seemed to appreciate having a smoking and drinking partner. No-one on staff smoked or drank and Grandma heartily disapproved. Campaign air, she said, should be blue with smoke and at the end of the day the staffers should get smashed. Otherwise the stress would kill them, and that wasn't healthy.

It was turning into a beautiful evening, with flocks of birds passing over on their way to their roosting grounds down by the Colorado river.

Jude was especially thoughtful. He'd just spent a bit of time in Mills's bedroom upstairs. From an inspection of his wardrobes he'd evidently taken very little with him. His bedroom was still that of a teenager; remnants everywhere of his itinerant life between the mansion and the Academy. Lying on his desk, in front of a pristine games console that looked as if it had never been touched, was his *Time Life* atlas of the world. Jude had picked it up and slowly flicked through the pages. It fell open naturally on the section devoted to the Amazon river.

'I know where Mills has gone,' said Jude, finally, pouring another drink for Grandma.

'Is that right?'

'Yes.'

'You feel real bad about all of this don't you, Jude?' she asked.

'Yes, I suppose I do. If I hadn't have been standing there in the corridor like that after his row with his father I don't think he'd have taken off. He'd have just gone to get the whisky and we'd have got blasted.'

'You don't know that. He's always been impulsive. I remember once, when Kyle was first Governor, he called from that terrible Pierpoint place to say that he'd been kidnapped and the people holding him wanted a million dollars.'

'He did?'

'Uh huh, that's what he did all right. His father was real mad, called the state troopers, everyone.'

'And what happened?'

'What d'ya think? His father refused to pay. Sad, isn't it? The kid was only trying to see if his parents loved him.'

'Yes, that's sad.'

'And it's one thing we never had a speciality for in this family. We none of us had any love for each other. Poor old Millburn was in the Academy laundry cupboard with a mobile phone for two days.'

'But you love Mills, Grandma,' said Jude.

She laughed out loud. 'Damn it,' she said. 'He's far too like me for me to love him and for it to make any difference. As you get older, kid, you'll find out that chalk only really wants the love of cheese.'

The both took long cool pulls of their drinks, the ice ringing in the crystal tumblers; the birds squawking above; the light fading across the lawn.

'He's gone to South America,' said Jude.

'Sure. That's where he wanted to go for his year out they wouldn't let him take. Kyle wouldn't have it, of course, that was the big row they had before this one. It was obvious to me the moment he disappeared that he'd head down there, head over the border. It's the best way he's got of really aggravating Kyle. You got to understand that here in Texas we really hate our southern border. Oh God we hate the guys over the fence.'

In the atlas Jude had seen the route that Mills had drawn. His final destination was a town called Leticia, far down in the Colombian Amazon. And this time the route had been marked out in black ink. The indentations of former journeys made by pencil could be made out on the page as well, and, generally, they all had return routes to Texas marked. The ink route had no such provision.

'You want to go down there too and make your peace?' asked Grandma.

'I think it's the only thing I can do. I can't just sit around here.'

'But you *want* to go?'

'Yes, I really want to go.'

Grandma refreshed his glass. Then she patted her handbag mysteriously.

'Well, let's keep this between ourselves, and I'll see what I can do. Someone's got to bring peace to this family.'

11

The main square of Isnotu was deserted as Mills and his troop marched across it. It didn't look as if it had been swept for some time, the ground was covered with locus pods. There was an old hacienda that served as town hall, police station, health centre and anything else vaguely municipal. But in the entire building there was just one elderly man dozing behind the reception desk. They'd been told that it was the only place in town where they could get a meal.

There were half a dozen tables set out for dinner in the foyer and the old man perked up as best he could, astonished by their appearance, and passed them a handwritten menu that was frayed and smudged with thumb-prints.

As Mills and his friends sat drinking beers, waiting for their meal, the old retainer went out back and telephoned his wife. She arrived ten minutes later, walking through the foyer smiling to them and nodding excitedly. With her she had her smaller children, her sister, her aunt, her sister's mother-in-law, and a few friends. They came through like a procession; all of them carrying the items that would be needed: boxes of vegetables and meat, cooking oil in fearsome looking flagons, pots, pans, bottles of butane gas and a couple of little stoves; as well as the family's small dog that didn't want to miss out on the scraps.

Mills ordered more beers, and they listened to the gales of laughter coming out from the police chief's office, which had become a kind of field kitchen for the evening. Mills felt like quite a host and their spirits had certainly lifted. Even Tomas was smiling.

Mills thought for a moment about his self-imposed ordeal on

the mountain and it seemed now as if it had happened a long time before. He was beginning to feel free. There was no point in running off if you didn't leave it all behind, he reminded himself. He determined to begin enjoying his journey, it might, after all, be his last burst of freedom for a long time.

During the meal the town's children began to arrive. At first they just hovered in the doorway, but then they became bolder, gradually inching in until they surrounded the table. Every time that Mills or Tomas spoke they fell into fits of laughter.

'Carlos, what do they want, money?' asked Mills.

'No, no, Chief, they just want to hear you talking in the foreign language.'

Carlos had taken to calling Mills Chief to compensate for having got them lost more than a few times on their way into town. He'd also confessed that this was his very first job for Cordillera Tours. He'd never guided anyone anywhere before, and so, he felt if he elevated Mills to *Chief* then his own lowly position would somehow also be drawn up with it.

While they were eating, one of the children approached the table. He had something cupped in his hands.

'He has a present for you, Chief,' said Carlos.

Mills held out his hand to receive it and as he did so a cricket almost five inches long leapt from the child's grasp and flicked straight into Tomas's dreadlocks. It struggled there for a moment.

Everyone laughed and cheered as the grasshopper freed itself from Tomas's dreadlocks and sprang onto the floor, and then up onto another table. The old retainer came rushing at it with a rolled up newspaper, but every time he took a swipe it beat him to the next table. Then the other children, who'd also brought presents of extraordinary flying bugs, let them all off, carried away with the excitement of it all. Gigantic insects were ricocheting everywhere and circling above them, as the old man growled at the children, swatted with his newspaper, and the dog got so excited it howled and did a sort of back-flip with a moth in its mouth. It would sneeze from the dust of its wings for the next half an hour.

Then as suddenly as the eruption had begun, the room fell silent, except for the buffeting of moths and insect rasps, and the sneezing of the dog, as everyone turned to look towards the door.

Standing there, perfectly still, and dressed in white like an apparition, was one of the nuns from the shrine. She was carrying a torch and she walked slowly over to the table.

She spoke in Spanish and Carlos, somewhat in awe of her, stuttered as he translated.

'She says, you are the American who has come to see the shrine. She is sorry it was closed when you came today. She says do you want to see the shrine tomorrow?'

'Yes, I would. Thank her for me. I'd like to see the shrine tomorrow.'

'She asks if you have a special interest in José Gregorio Hernández.'

'Yes I have.'

She nodded happily, and then she held out her hand to be shaken.

'She says, are you the American journalist we have been expecting?'

Mills was perplexed for a moment.

'Thank her for her help,' said Mills.

'She says the priest has sent her over. He is looking forward to meeting you at the shrine tomorrow. At eleven-thirty, will eleven-thirty be a good time to meet?'

'A very good time.'

Mills sat quietly for a while after the nun had gone smiling back out into the night with her rubber torch. Their saint, he could see, was very important to them. It was not something to be played with. It was a story they were desperate to have told in the wider world. He could hardly have been the kind of mouthpiece they'd hoped for, he thought, but he could try, he could certainly try. He wondered what his father would think of him if he went back to the States and started publishing articles about a bizarre South American doctor credited with miracles. Would he be amused, or would he merely repeat his usual mantra: *when are you going to get interested in the real world?*

This aside it crossed his mind, however fleetingly, that perhaps he would quite like to be a journalist. Leave Oxford and become a journalist. It would surely be a life that would offer a certain level of independence. He had never realised before that he could possibly make the situation his father had put him in work to his own advantage. A slow smile began to cross his face.

The figure of José Gregorio Hernández had begun to genuinely fascinate him, ever since his eyes had seemed to look right through him from that plain dark chapel in the church in Caracas. It was an inexplicable feeling. He woke the next morning with the distinct impression that during the night he'd dreamed of him; he couldn't recall anything of the dream, but he had a lasting sense of having heard his voice in the night. It made him feel strangely detached.

It was coming up to eleven-fifteen the next morning, the sun was already strong in the sky, when Mills, and his friends, walked to the shrine. Daniel wasn't with them, the whole thing bored him; he was giving the local sixteen-year-old girls trips around town in the Mustang, and acting the big-shot.

The statue of José Gregorio with the concrete canopy was all that was left of the house in which he had been born. It was entirely covered with small marble and cast iron plaques, as was every other building around. They gave thanks for José Gregorio's *favor*. Some of them would have a picture showing the miracle; a group of people in a bus, screaming and waving their arms; a car caught precariously on a mountain edge; a bandit firing a gun at defenceless women. Some of the miracles were more prosaic, and the plaque would simply read: *Gracias Dr J.G.H* and carved into the marble on either side would be a representation of a bleeding arm, or an enormous pair of feet, with the word *miracle!* inscribed in Spanish beneath.

In the church the stained glass windows all showed images of José Gregorio. There was even an image of him, with his trilby hat, his waistcoat, and his pocket handkerchief, rendered in wrought iron to form the doorway. It had the feeling of a South American Graceland about it.

Beside the church was a single storey building, entirely covered in plaques, that served as an office for the priest and his nuns.

They went in. Around the walls there were reproductions of oil paintings about the life of the Doctor, some of them rather gruesome, especially the one of him being hit by the Ford. The artist had chosen to show José Gregorio with his eyes cast up to heaven, but his arms and legs were sprawled like a puppet with its strings cut across the bonnet of the car. And then there was his hat. In the painting it was forever fixed halfway between his head and the ground, and the pills, in a little pot, were flying everywhere. There was something chaotic about it, something of the atmosphere of the meal they'd had the night before when the crickets and the bugs and the sneezing dog had reduced things to vaudeville.

The office had a couple of desks and behind them sat two nuns, bashing away at old Remington typewriters. They were elderly, but rather rosy-faced, and they looked as if they'd been in this office here, running the whole thing, since the typewriters were bought. They sat happily thumping away.

The nun who had come to the town hall got up, smiled and went to fetch the priest. It still seemed unfathomable to Mills that they should be taking someone like him seriously but he was rather enjoying their attention.

There was a woman in a bright floral frock there too and as soon as they had walked in she had started talking to the nuns. She seemed to want to talk to Mills, but the nun was trying to silence her.

Then she sidled up to Carlos and began talking to him.

'She wants to know if you're the American that's come,' said Carlos. 'She says she's seen José Gregorio.'

On the night that Mills had met Jenny at Cordillera Tours he'd been excited by the prospect of maybe meeting someone who'd actually seen the Doctor. It was rather overwhelming. He was pleased he'd made the trip.

The woman had taken Carlos's hand, so that he couldn't get away, and began telling him her story. She was a Colombian, she said, but had come to live in Isnotu so that she could dedicate the whole of her life to Hernández. Carlos was nodding as she gabbled away in Spanish, he looked excited by the encounter too.

'First time I saw him', she said, 'was when I was giving birth to my second child in nineteen-sixty-three. All that time ago, it doesn't seem possible now. But it was a miracle and so it seems just like yesterday to me.'

'Yes, it must,' Carlos was nodding.

The priest had still not come, he was held up in the school.

'They had to give me a Caesarean,' the woman told Carlos, 'and I was very young and very frightened and when I looked up he was standing there, and he says to me not to worry, he will guide the surgeon's hand. And I said yes, José Gregorio, I will pray to you always, and I will make my observance, and I will bring a plaque for you to Isnotu.

'And then in nineteen-seventy my neighbour's house was burning down, and the roof of my house had caught fire too, and I ran with all my children out into the street. But there was no-one to help us, no-one with buckets, and I knew my house would be destroyed. And then I remembered my picture of José Gregorio, that I have always above my bed, and I ran back into the house. Full of smoke. All the rooms, I said to myself, have clouds in them. The heavens have come down. And as I took the picture from the wall I saw his eyes come alive. And his face moved. It moved! And he spoke to me from the picture, and he said, do not take me down, leave me where I am and your house will not burn. And I put him back, and when I looked around the smoke was clearing. And my little girl was standing there and she said, *mama, mama,* the fire is going out!'

Carlos was looking at Mills with a strange expression on his face.

'She has seen the Doctor twice!' he said. Then the nun who had gone to fetch the priest returned and cast a glance at the woman.

'I was very ill again three years ago,' the woman continued, with her nails digging into Carlos's forearm. 'My bowels were dominating my life. I was sickly pale and weak and there was nothing left inside me . . .'

Now that she'd got everyone's attention she slowly rose to her feet, bringing Carlos with her, and addressing Mills directly, even though she was speaking in Spanish.

'The doctors were no use,' she said, 'nothing they prescribed me made any difference. Bottles of this and bottles of that. Terrible pink gunk, and then blue, or green. But no difference. In the end they try me with one more prescription and I go to my pharmacy and I say, hello Señor Esteban, again it is me. And

I give him my prescription. But then he comes from out of the back and he says to me, what is this writing here? Who has written on your prescription? This is not Dr Ortiz writing this, look. And I looked and the writing hadn't been there before, I didn't see it before. And so we walk here to the shrine and we hold it up to one of Dr José Gregorio's prescriptions that are framed in the museum, and the writing is the same. And so I take those pills as well, and I am cured. Or else would I be able to be standing here talking to you today, without suddenly dashing away? See, I am standing proof!'

She was still talking when the priest came bursting through the door, sweat on his brow from where he'd dashed from the school. He saw her and waved his arm and shouted in Spanish, '*Oh do shut up, woman.*' It didn't need translating. She sat down silently on a chair.

The priest took Mills's hand and shook it warmly. He was a man in his late sixties, bristling with energy, with a broad welcoming smile. His name was Father Leonardo and his eyes twinkled behind his glasses. Like the nuns he was dressed in tropical whites, with small cloth-covered buttons running down the front of his cassock. But despite the plainness of a priest's equatorial garb he certainly made up for it with his haircut. His head of auburn hair was raked over in a great flop, and the vivacity of its colour looked largely chemically supported. He was charismatic, but like a great many successful priests, Mills suspected that a streak of vanity ran through him. Father Leonardo looked as if he could be quite an entertainer too, his gravitas came from authority rather than sombreness; he looked like a pretty dab hand with the microphone. He knew the value of publicity, and of big public events; he jealously guarded the reputation of his saint.

'Why don't we take a walk outside, young man,' he said, steering him with his arm towards the light of the door. 'I want to show you the museum I am building.'

'How long have you been the priest here?' asked Mills.

'Since the beginning of it all,' he said. 'When I came here there was no church, no shrine, there wasn't even a house for the priest. And as for the town of Isnotu, there was no road. There was no mains water, nor electricity, nor even a school. We have had to build all this.'

He looked out across the piazza proprietorially.

'You're not Venezuelan?'

'No, they got through four different Venezuelan priests in a single year here in nineteen-sixty-two. I am Spanish. I couldn't believe it when I came here, I had to live in one of the villagers' huts with his family. Then one day someone arrived with one of these plaques that you see everywhere, and it all began.'

He was pulling a key out of his pocket as they approached the door of a windowless hall built beside the church. He unlocked the door and showed Mills into a large single room, hung with oil paintings and containing a few meagre objects of José Gregorio's life. He led Mills over to a photograph of José Gregorio's massive funeral in Caracas in 1919.

'He must have been very famous for forty thousand people to attend his funeral,' said Mills as the priest spoke about the great event.

'Ah, yes. Possibly the most loved man in South America since Simon Bolivar. A far more charismatic figure than, say, Perón. And people began to pray to him from the very day of his funeral.'

'I don't understand this,' said Mills. 'Why did people begin to pray to him spontaneously? What sparked it?'

The priest laughed. 'Ah, you have to understand the way people are here. For example, my housekeeper, Maria, she prays to her Aunt Clara if anything gets lost in our house. And you know why? Because her aunt was a very nervous woman, very panicky, with a weak heart. Whenever her uncle lost something her aunt would get into such a terrible state of fear and frustration about it she would turn the whole house over and make such a mess that whatever was lost, could now never be found. Then she would break down in tears. Eventually in one of these nervous rages, of course, she suffered a heart attack and died. So when something is lost in my house my housekeeper prays to her aunt in heaven, and says "Aunt Clara, you know how upset you get when you can't find something . . ."'

Mills laughed.

He was staring at a picture of an old colonial house framed on the wall.

'José Gregorio's birthplace,' said the priest. It was unrecognisable from the plaque-encrusted construction that now stood in its place.

On the wall was a large oil painting of the young Hernández receiving his medical degree at the University of Caracas. In the front row were his parents, dressed in the high society clothes of the day, all silks and stiff collars. Then there was a painting of Hernández at home when he'd become the most famous doctor in the continent. There he sat, playing the piano, knocking out a popular song, surrounded by his young male friends, singing along.

'He played the piano?' asked Mills. It seemed, again, bizarrely incongruous in a saint.

'He liked to dance too,' said Father Leonardo. 'Come here.' He led him to the end of the hall, where, behind ropes, were José Gregorio's three most treasured possessions, lovingly preserved at the shrine. Mills smiled broadly. There was his bed, his piano, and his wardrobe. All of them made from plain dark wood, but rather elegant for all that.

'He liked to dress well,' said Mills.

'Oh yes, he loved his clothes. You may have seen that from the figures of him that the pilgrims buy, sometimes he's in a dark suit with waistcoat, and sometimes he's dressed in a white suit and hat, often with a green ribboning around the lapels and the cuffs. There's a rather fabulous four-foot white plastic version of him on sale at the moment that ingeniously lights up from inside. Quite a thing to see. He was a very dapper man. Looked after himself, never married.'

'And will the Vatican make him a saint?'

'It is very close now, very close indeed. Recently I almost feel as if I can sense his election to beatification in the air around here; as if the place is changing, turning into Holy Ground. But, in these last days, I'm sad to say, it has become a contentious issue. Unfortunately we had a great ally in Archbishop Morales, but he has just been assassinated.'

'I know,' said Mills. 'I was there. I was on the Papal Envoy's plane when it landed in Caracas.'

Father Leonardo suddenly looked shocked. 'You were?' he said, and unhooked the ropes that protected the furniture. He walked over to José Gregorio's bed and sat on the edge. 'You were there?'

'Yes, I saw it all. It was mayhem.'

Mills sat down on the bed too.

The priest looked at him very deeply for a moment. 'Why have you come here? Why have you come to talk to me?'

'I don't know,' he replied. 'I really couldn't say. It's just that everywhere I turn I seem to come across José Gregorio. He was there when I was rescued on Pico Bolivar, and I suppose I could have very easily died up there. I feel I owe him something, but I don't know what.'

The priest nodded slowly.

'This is the way it is when you are caught up by him. I never expected to spend my life here, building all of this.'

'No?'

'Tell me,' he said, with deep seriousness. 'Are you working for someone?'

'A newspaper, you mean?'

'No, no. There is a nervousness in the country right now. Some people do not want to see José Gregorio's cause advanced any further in Rome, others do. The backing of the American cardinals would be a great aid to us, but many people think that if we were to have a Latin American saint, then it would give us a dangerous feeling of nationalism. A pan-American feeling of nationalism that could be, perhaps, destabilising in a continent that is already politically tinder-dry. Have you come to spy on me? Are they trying to close me down?'

Father Leonardo was a refreshingly direct man. Because of his authority here he held the belief that even the most devious of men would find it hard to lie to him.

'I promise you I'm not spying on you. Do I look like a spy?'

'I've no idea what they look like, I imagine they can seem as unlikely as my saint does to some people.'

'Why would they want to close you down?'

'Why did they want to kill the archbishop? Who knows who orders these terrible things? All I know is that when Rome chose the first non-Italian Pope for four hundred years his home country Poland was transformed. They had an identity in their hearts again and felt as if they had returned to being a nation in the world not just part of a bloc. Communism quickly ended there. The raising of José Gregorio to beatification, and then canonisation as a saint may be seen by some as a precursor to a Latin American Pope. Imagine! An anti-conservative candidate to the throne of Saint Peter! There are many in America who wouldn't wish to see that, and I include in America our own southern continent. But this, of course, is all politics, and I try to stay out of human mysteries and concentrate solely on the divine, which are quite enough to be going along with.'

'Tell me, when did you come to Venezuela? You must have been very young.'

He stood up and walked slowly over to José Gregorio's piano.

'I was twenty-eight and at a seminary in Barcelona,' he said. He laid his hand on the ivory keys and played a chord.

'Incredible isn't it?' he said, staring into space. 'In all this damp heat, it's still in perfect pitch.' Then he turned to Mills and smiled. 'I believe José Gregorio wants you to tell this story. His hand is at your back.'

When they had come into the museum the priest had locked the door behind them, now he took the key out again as they walked towards the door. The priest opened it onto the midday light.

'You must come to my house for lunch,' said Father Leonardo. 'It's just a short way up the hill. You'll hear an even finer story there. Bring your friends. We have Don Emillio Guzman lunching with us today, our great Colombian benefactor. Now he has a story to tell that is much more miraculous.'

12

Father Leonardo's house was just above the town and looked down on the single main street. It was Spanish in style, with white-washed walls and a small L-shaped courtyard, where the dining table was set.

Through the archway Mills could see Don Emillio's black Mercedes parked on the road where his driver sat buffing his nails. Don Emillio himself was a large man, he sat at the head of the table, and every time he spoke he laid his hand heavily on the table top as if he were addressing his business associates.

'Don Emillio is a friend,' said Father Leonardo. 'He is going to build a bell tower here for us. Whenever he is in the country, he stops by and we have a long lunch like this, with the excuse of going over the architect's drawings.'

Don Emillio laughed. 'The Father loves to build!' he said, his fingers and his rings slapping the table. 'What will he do when he has finished building Isnotu? What will it be next, Leonardo? An airstrip for the pilgrims?'

'José Gregorio International,' he said laughing.

Don Emillio looked like the kind of man who had made a vast fortune through dubious means and now sought the favour of a priest in his maturing years.

The two nuns came to the table with the first course; river fish in garlic and oil, avocados and tomato, chorizo sausage and baked corncobs; all served in Catalonian earthenware bowls.

Father Leonardo pushed the bowl of corncobs away from him and the nuns laughed. In his first year here, he explained, he'd lived on nothing but corncobs and he couldn't bear to look at them. They were the only part of God's creation, he said, that he despised. They reminded him of grenades.

It was simple but delicious food and Tomas and the boys ate as if they'd just been released from prison. They'd flagged down Daniel during their walk here, and now he was sitting next to the priest, reeking horribly of petrol.

The nuns were named Sister Boniface and Sister Ignacio, but the priest called them Sister Bon and Sister Ig. They called him Father Leo. Don Emillio Guzman was Don Emi.

The atmosphere of the lunch was one of familiar jocularity. Mills watched the nuns go back into the kitchen where he supposed the housekeeper who prayed to her Great Aunt Clara whenever she lost anything was to be found. Then the nuns came back with salsa and a flagon of lemonade, and Sister Bon had a file tucked under her arm. She handed it to the priest.

'Ah, good,' he said. 'You have finished it.' He smiled at Mills. 'We have been typing up some notes that might be of use to you, just little things about José Gregorio's life that you may find of interest.' He passed the file to Mills, who opened it and flicked through the pages with their Remington typewriter print. The 'e' character was full of dust, or more likely simply worn out by overwork, and hit a great many of the words like a splodgy black bullet hole.

He nodded in thanks. The priest was a generous man. He looked around him in pleasure. There was bougainvillaea grow-ing all around the walls; the fallen blooms scuttling about in swirls on the flagstones and occasionally fluttering down from the whitewashed wall and onto the table. It was hot and Father Leo had unbuttoned his cassock at the bottom and again at the top.

'Don Emi is building the bell tower here in thanks for a miracle,' he said.

Don Emi shrugged. 'It is the least I can do,' he said. 'José Gregorio gave me a gift more precious than gold and I repay him in concrete.'

'Can I ask what the miracle was?'

'He gave my son back his sight.'

'For the Vatican to canonise a new saint their investigators have to first examine two cases of miracles. Don Emi's son is one of the cases that has been selected for investigation,' explained Father Leo.

Mills nodded gravely. He thought of the woman who'd been talking to Carlos in the nuns' office that the priest had told to shut up in such a peremptory fashion. Carlos had told him on the walk up to the priest's house that she had seen José Gregorio no less than sixteen times. She had been married to a notorious drunk in Bogota, she told him, and her friends said that she sees more of José Gregorio than she does her own husband. All shrines must attract such people. Mills wondered what was so special about Don Emi's son.

'You must come to my house and meet him, talk to him,' said Don Emi. He passed his card down the table. It bore his name and his address in Envigado, over the border in Colombia.

'I would like to very much,' said Mills, putting the card in his top pocket. 'I will come.'

Mills looked down at the table for a moment, and then he pulled up his napkin and wiped away the oil from the fish he'd eaten, which was running down his chin. He was still a little troubled by the fact that they were expecting an American journalist, as Sister Bon had said when she came to the town hall. They couldn't imagine for a moment that he was that journalist. For all the saintliness, and the atmosphere of miracles, these were men of the world. They were both, in their way, businessmen. And evidently they were making some kind of investment in him.

'Our friend here,' said Father Leo turning to Don Emi, 'was present at the assassination of Archbishop Morales.'

'You were?' he said, visibly shaken. 'It is a very bad thing all round. Very bad indeed. I have heard several reports of what took place. They say it was carnage, many many people killed.'

Mills shook his head. 'This simply isn't true,' he said. 'I heard that said in Caracas only hours after the shooting. But I promise you, it wasn't like that at all.'

'But this is what they said on the television,' said Don Emi, and Father Leo was nodding.

'I promise you, no.'

'No? But there were Sisters, and military, and six or seven people killed.'

'Well, I don't know who's managing the news, but that isn't the way it was. Of course, they got all us guys that were on the plane out of there very quickly. They didn't even ask for a statement.'

Don Emi was shaking his head from side to side. 'I don't understand it,' he said.

'I believe it is as we thought,' said Father Leo, sadly.

'There was just one gunman and he ran out right in front of the military and nobody did anything. I mean, I saw it, we'd been kept so long before we de-planed that there was nothing else to do but look out of the window at the archbishop shuffling about at the end of the red carpet. I wanted to see who was getting off. I thought maybe they had the Pope up there in first class, the service had been slow enough back in economy. But as that gunman ran, I tell you, not a soldier even moved for his gun. No-one did anything, it was as if they knew it was going to happen. The only person who did anything was the nun. She had time to throw herself against him. That's how she got shot. It was carnage, yes, but it was one bullet carnage.'

At the end of lunch Father Leonardo came round the table and asked Mills if he would like to take a walk in his garden, 'to aid digestion'.

They left the others drinking coffee and sampling the powerful but sickly dessert wine that Sister Ig had produced from the kitchen.

The garden was a cultured wasteland of jungle plants clumped together around gravel walkways.

Mills stopped beside a banana plant and stroked its limb-like stem while he thought. 'You seem so sure of all of this,' he said. 'Tell me, why did you came to Isnotu?'

The priest nodded his head and laughed a little. It wasn't just to escape Sister Ig's home-made dessert wine he'd taken Mills into the garden.

'I have often wondered that myself. I was sent here by the head of the seminary I trained in. I never knew why he sent me here, but a couple of years ago, just before he died he came here himself and told me the whole story. We had just begun the campaign for José Gregorio's beatification and I guess he knew it was important that his side of things should be recorded. It is all in the notes the sisters have been typing up for you.

'It started back in nineteen-sixty-two,' he said, 'in Barcelona. For three days the principal of my seminary had endured sleepless nights; it wasn't the heat; the fan over his bed was working perfectly and there was a cool breeze from the sea. He wasn't troubled particularly by anything that he knew of. He just didn't sleep.

'On the third day, he collapsed suddenly while he was reading his breviary in the middle of the afternoon, and as his head lay on his desk, sweating into his desk blotter, he dreamed.

'The dream was more vivid than any he had ever had. He was dreaming about one of his students. About a young priest of twenty-eight years old. A young man he was about to recommend to Rome.

'The truly odd thing about the dream was that nothing really happened in it. It couldn't be called a spectacular, or revelatory, dream. He seemed to be still half-conscious when he had it, he could hear the sound of the bougainvillaea blooms fluttering outside his second floor window as they blew in through the grille and collected in swirls on his polished floor.

'The dream was so realistic, he said, that it was just a mirror of the day that had left him so exhausted and longing for sleep. It consisted of nothing more than a very ordinary seminar on the Pauline doctrine of the authority of the church.

'The next day my principal excused himself from his annual lecture on the observance of the Feast of San Pedro. It was an un-heard of gesture and caused consternation among the faculty. I remember it well. That morning he had received a letter from an old contemporary; a friend with whom he'd been ordained thirty years before in Barcelona. The letter begged him to send a young priest to take on a difficult parish in the Andean hinterlands of Venezuela. In the last year the parish had seen four priests come and go. None of them had been able to stand the place for more than a few months.'

Father Leonardo sat down under the shade of one of the banana plants. He began to talk about how Venezuela had just begun to enjoy the new wealth of the oil boom discovery beneath Lake Maraicaibo. It was the nineteen-sixties; the young

South American priests were ambitious, and those that weren't were ambitious for another thing: this new Liberation Theology with its volatile blend of Marxist ideology and political ferment amongst the intellectuals. His principal's old friend, who was then a bishop in the far flung state of Trujillo, Venezuela, needed a solid young priest who could endure the hardships of a rural *campesino* parish with no prospects, material or ideological; someone who could be a father to the poor. He was desperate and hoped that a young priest, trained in the forthright orthodox catholicism of the seminary might feel a calling to the tropics. Could his old friend help?

'The night after receiving that letter, my principal fell asleep at his desk. He slipped easily and naturally into sleep but not without another odd dream. This time he was himself a student again, but strangely not a student of theology. He saw himself sitting in a large anatomical theatre as a young medical student. He was listening to a charismatic professor of medicine enthusing his students with the innovations of modern science. The professor was smartly dressed, dapper in fact, in the costume of the early part of the twentieth century. Again, the dream was so realistic that when the Doctor called for questions at the end of his lecture, the principal was able to raise his hand and ask quite coherently: "Yes sir, can you tell me why I am dreaming this?"

' "Yes, certainly," replied the professor. "It is because your mind is so full of doctrine and church history since you accepted the post of principal that this is, perhaps, the only way you can be reached. Next question?"

' "Yes," said the principal, "I have another. What is it that you want?"

'The professor seemed almost impatient, but he turned to him and smiled. "I want you to send me your best student, your *best*," he emphasised, and turned away.'

Father Leonardo heaved a great sigh. He pulled himself up from the shade of the banana and they walked on until they reached where a couple of hammocks were slung under the shade of almond trees. Mills and the priest settled into one each; Father Leonardo continued his account.

'When he woke,' he said, 'his arm was numb from the pressure of the desk and the weight of where his head had laid on it, he found his hand was lying on his old friend's letter on the desk.

'For the next two days he slept badly again. He was aware of his debilitating exhaustion, he'd found himself tottering as if drunk through the cloister, and he saw the whispering behind the hands of the senior members of the faculty.

'He grew tired of breathing through his pillow in the night, hoping that if he deprived himself of all senses it would lead him into sleep. When he glanced at his shadow in the courtyard it seemed to be out of step with him, flickering like his eyelids that were tired of the light.

'He knew he had to call the young father to come and see him. I was that father. He saw me that afternoon in his private rooms.

'I came in, eager to hear what the principal had to say. I knew we'd be discussing my future, and I was hoping for Rome.'

The priest paused for effect for a moment. His years of preaching here, and of building up the myth of José Gregorio, had given him a strange way of speaking; everything was recounted like a homily. But his voice was so resonant, and the garden so supremely peaceful, that Mills could have listened all afternoon.

They could hear laughter from the dining table set in the courtyard. Don Emi's roar echoed against the walls; Sister Ig's wine was kicking in.

'There was a jug of lemonade on the table, I remember. It was topped up with ice from the new refrigerator that the seminary had just purchased. The ice glinted in the sun and I glanced thirstily towards it. It was a hot day in June. But when the principal poured the glass for me he couldn't stop his hand from shaking. When he came to visit Isnotu he told me that he didn't know how he was going to explain his reasons for asking me to come to this dreadful parish. "I am so glad, Leonardo, that you are here," he said. "You asked me to come," I replied. His hand shook even more as he pulled the jug back towards himself, and he didn't have the strength to pour another glass. A sudden sea breeze blew in a flutter of bougainvillaea blooms.'

'Like they do in your courtyard here,' said Mills. He glanced at Father Leonardo. The priest's eyes were glazed over; he visualised the day back in the nineteen sixties as if it had been that morning. He looked like a man who had been waiting to tell this story for a very long time.

Father Leonardo snapped himself back into full consciousness and continued. ' "I have had a letter," my principal began, "from a most revered bishop, asking me to recommend to him a young priest for a parish that is in his gift." He looked across the old wood of his table at me. "He is looking for a priest of proven resourcefulness," he said.

'That was the moment at which I began to worry. "A challenging parish," he said, trying to smile.

'I brightened up then. By "challenging parish", I thought he must surely mean Rome after all.

'He knew that what he had to say had to be said quickly, and directly, without any beating around the bush whatsoever, or my hopes might be raised to such an extent that it would be cruel to bring them so resoundingly down to earth again. So he stood up and walked slowly towards his window, and looked out onto the street while he collected his thoughts. Across the way an old man was lighting a cigarette in the shaded doorway of a hat shop, eyeing up girls as they passed. He said he felt suddenly jealous of that man's simple life. He turned back to look at me and blurted out the words. "South America". I was astonished. "The parish of Isnotu in the diocese of Trujillo have especially requested you. Your undoubted talents will most certainly be valued there." Then he turned away towards the window again, unable to meet me in the face.

'When he did look back, he said I had a perfectly untroubled expression on my face.

' "Wherever Mother Church wishes to send me, is where I shall endeavour to undertake God's will," I said, as young priests do. "Shall I be going soon?" I must have seemed very self-righteous, and I was, insufferably so. It was then that I looked up to his bookcase. I took down a beautiful atlas from its shelves, and leafed through the index.

' "There's no Isnotu," I said. "I'll try Trujillo." I remember looking up and smiling as I found it, and turning back to find the page on the map. Then I stared at it for some time. Finally I looked up at him.

' "Why?" was all I said. The principal couldn't speak. I held my head in my hands for a moment. "Why?" I muttered again. What have I done? I was on the verge of tears. Have I done something to offend?

'But his hand was shaking worse, there was sweat on his brow, and then he broke down.

'I was very shocked by seeing him cry. "I have been plagued by dreams. Dreams that tell me to send you there", he said. I raised my eyebrows, I couldn't believe what he was saying. He shook his head. He knew that if people thought he'd begun to believe in dreams he'd be a laughing stock, finished at the seminary. He'd never become a bishop. "I can't explain it", he said. "But I can tell you this, based on what has been revealed to me, when you get to Isnotu, you too will have a dream. And in that dream, you will be told what is required of you. I can tell you no more", and with that his head hit the table. I tried to shake him awake, but the poor man was exhausted.

'And that is how I came to be in Isnotu,' he said, and sighed.

You're a lucky man, Mills wanted to say, to have your life decided for you at twenty-eight; the rest of us just thrash about looking for clues, screwing the whole thing up.

They began the slow walk back down to the house.

'Did you ever have that dream when you arrived in Isnotu?' asked Mills. Father Leonardo laughed again.

'I had been here for six months,' he said. 'Living with a family who had a smallholding, growing coffee and maize. Most of the time I helped them in their fields because I felt rather redundant. I didn't have a church, or a school, or anything to be priest of. So I helped in the fields because I thought I was a burden on their resources. And, apart from occasionally reading the last rites, which they appreciated, I was no help to the place at all. It was humbling, and I cursed my existence here. I felt like a spare-part, sidelined by the church, you know? I couldn't see any way I could get a mains water supply, or a school built – a church was at the very bottom of my priorities – though I would have liked one. It's the very least a young priest expects. So in that first year I cursed my old principal and his dreams. I thought maybe he'd lost his marbles and I was a casualty; sending a bright young theologian like me to end up working as a peasant in the fields. Then one afternoon, after a year of this hardship, the man in whose house I was living came out across the maize field to speak to me. He was waving and I put down my machete. "There is a man here," he said. "He is very dignified, he is wearing a black trilby and a fine suit, with a moustache, trimmed like they have in the city." "Is that so?" I said. "What does he want?" "He says he wants to see the priest, he has something for him." So I walked back across the fields, and sitting at the one table we had in the shack was the man, just as he'd described him.'

'Really?'

'The absolute image,' said Father Leonardo, laughing again. 'Although, of course I knew not one thing about José Gregorio at that time, not what he looked like or anything. On the table the man had a heavy object, wrapped in brown paper. "You are the priest of Isnotu?" he asked me, and I said that I was. "I have brought you this token in thanks for a miracle," he said, and unwrapped a marble plaque. It was the first of all those thousands you see around you here. As he walked away I ran after him, I couldn't have looked much like a priest to him, in my rough trousers and ripped shirt and straw hat for the fields.

' "What brought you here?" I asked him. He stopped and turned and said "I have prayed to José Gregorio all my life, since the day I saw him buried in Caracas as a boy, and the night he saved my grand-daughter's life on the operating table in Merida I had a dream which told me to come here to Isnotu and find his priest. So I thought, I can't go without something to take, and my son is a stone mason, so I asked him if he had a small piece of marble that was no good for anything. He gave me that piece and I carved it. I have written a thank you to José Gregorio."

'There was no expression on the old man's face, he simply walked back to the track to wait for mules to the next farm, the next town. Heaven only knows how long that journey had taken him from Merida by foot and mule, with his slab of marble. But you see, he had promised José Gregorio he would do it. I wept as I held that piece of marble, but I had no idea what I should do with it. That was the afternoon I decided to stop cutting corncobs and be something of a priest. I was pretty angry too, I can tell you, when I realised that the old man had had the dream that was promised to me. José Gregorio knew I needed humbling.'

They got back to the house and joined everyone still sitting at the table. The atmosphere was relaxed in the afternoon sunshine. The telephone was ringing and Sister Bon went off to get it.

'You will come?' said Don Emi to Mills. 'You will come to Envigado and meet my son?'

'Yes,' Mills said. 'I would love to.'

Sister Bon came running back from the telephone and spoke to Father Leo. He listened intently. Then he stood up and addressed them.

'We have a problem, gentlemen,' he said. 'The priest from the next town has called. The military are heading this way. There's rather a lot of them and he says they have just passed through his town without stopping. They can only be coming here.'

Don Emi was already pushing his chair back.

'You go,' said Father Leo turning to his friend. 'You don't need to suffer their over-enthusiasm.'

'I do not.'

'You have the file I gave you?' said Father Leo turning now to Mills.

'I have. Will you be all right? What's happening?'

'We have been expecting it. I'm sorry, but you see, wouldn't we look odd?'

'Odd?' said Mills.

'To our nervous military. A Colombian businessman lunching with José Gregorio's priest and a young American. Take the lower road, go out of town for two miles, it's just a dirt track but you'll find it, there's nothing else. May God bless your escape.' The priest almost seemed to be enjoying the drama.

Don Emi laughed. 'See you in Envigado,' he called back to Mills, and made for his car.

Tomas and the two boys were getting up from the table. 'Your Mustang had better start,' Tomas muttered to Daniel. Daniel spoke to his brother, not having understood anything that had transpired.

'What's he saying?' Mills asked Carlos.

'He says he's meeting a girl in town later.'

'Well, he'll have to drive back some other time.'

'I'm so sorry our lunch has been curtailed,' said Father Leo. It had obviously been his intention to make quite an afternoon of it. Mills held the priest's gaze for a moment, and then offered him his hand. 'Tell me,' he said, 'are the soldiers going to shoot you?'

'In thirty-eight years I've never been able to fathom this country. You know what to do, take the lower road and you'll avoid them.'

'Tell me one thing,' said Mills. 'How did you know who I was?'

Father Leo looked down for a moment, like a small boy who had been caught. 'Your face has been in *USA Today*.'

'And you read that out here? You knew who I was the moment I hit town?'

'Yes,' confessed the priest. 'Although I don't generally read the American newspapers. I had a call from your tour company yesterday. She's English, she reads *USA Today*.'

'I see.'

'She just wanted you to have a profitable time here. Now you must go. Five minutes and they will be here.'

Mills couldn't feel angry about Jenny's call because, on reflection, he had made no effort to hide who he was. He'd handed over his credit card to pay for the trip that night when they were drinking the rum, and that would have confirmed who he was at Cordillera Tours. He'd stupidly presumed she was entirely out of touch with the wider world. He sighed.

'Tell me one other thing,' he said. 'Were you really expecting an American journalist?'

'Oh yes. When your friend Jenny called it was also because someone had come into her office looking for you, said he was your friend, and asked where you were. She had told him you had come here, and then thought that maybe he was a pressman, he had cameras with him. She called me, both to encourage you in the support of José Gregorio, and to warn you about the pressman. I have been wondering how to tell you about this. I didn't know until I finally saw you this morning if you were going to turn out to be one or the other.'

Father Leonardo walked them out to the Mustang, and Mills turned back to him.

'One more question,' he said. 'All these people have seen

José Gregorio, thousands of them, but have you? Have you seen him?'

Father Leo laughed.

'For thirty-eight years I have served him here,' he said. 'I've cut corn, picked coffee, built a road, a school and a church. Every day I meet people he has appeared to. So have I, José Gregorio's best friend in the world, ever been rewarded with seeing him?' He laughed again. 'No. No, not once. Not once, not so much as a dream.'

Mills had the priest's typescript gripped to his chest.

'Now go,' said Father Leo. 'His hand *is at your back*. Don't let us down. We are glad you came.'

The Mustang started first time and they roared off, the dust still settling from Don Emi's Mercedes as they took the two miles to the lower road.

Mills looked at his watch. About this time, he thought, the military would be bursting through that little archway and spraying the place with bullets and the bougainvillaea blooms would echo the splatters of blood on the priest's white cassock.

'This is very bad news,' said Tomas, suddenly, and sullenly from the back. 'These back roads and dirt tracks are riddled with guerillas and thieves. We'd have been better taking the tarmac road. Anyone around here will kill us for our shoes. Maybe we'll be kidnapped. Why has your picture been in *USA Today*? What did the father mean about the press? You are wanted by the police?'

'Long story,' said Mills, killing the subject dead.

As Tomas sank back into his seat Daniel pulled a half melted chocolate bar from the glove compartment and offered it to Mills. Mills smiled, it was a kind act. He took a chewy bite and offered it back to Carlos, who'd been explaining the state of play to his brother.

They drove in silence for a few miles, dust billowing up so that they had to close the windows and endure the petrol fumes. Mills began to think about this mysterious pressman who'd wandered into Cordillera Tours claiming to be a friend. He tried to recall the faces in the small crowd when the priest and he had left the museum. It seemed that the tabloids had tracked him down already and wanted to make something of it, though he couldn't imagine what. He'd have to be a great deal more circumspect from now on.

Daniel was doing a very good job, hitting the pot-holes in the dust track at speed so that they just seemed to glide over them. They were in shade now, the road was narrow, slicing between the maize fields, the plants of which swayed a foot or two over them.

'Oh God,' said Carlos suddenly. They all looked up. Daniel instinctively slowed the car.

There was a roadblock.

It was a makeshift thing, made from palm fronds and branches, hastily thrown together, but it blocked the road entirely. There was no-one manning it. It just stood ominously barring their way.

'They are in the maize fields waiting,' said Tomas, sticking his camera under Daniel's driving seat.

'Well, drive through, drive through, just bust it all apart,' shouted Mills. 'Carlos, tell your brother to drive through.'

Carlos said nothing.

'Are you so stupid?' said Tomas. 'My God, I've had a bad time here but it's sure worse with you. We bust that roadblock and they will shoot us dead. They will spray us with bullets. They are going to rob us. Maybe kidnap, who knows. We haven't got a chance here.'

'Bust through it,' said Mills. 'Tell him to get some speed up. It's our only chance, we can't just give in to it.'

'I don't know what to do,' said Carlos. He had begun to cry. 'This is my first trip, I don't know what to do with guerilla roadblocks.'

Tomas put his head in his hands and began to sob.

Daniel brought the car to a halt in front of the block.

'For God's sake!' screamed Mills. 'Why did he stop?'

There was silence. A long silence.

'They're in the maize fields,' said Tomas, speaking through his hands, where his head still was. 'Are you going to pray to your José Gregorio now?'

Mills looked around him ignoring Tomas's sarcasm. There wasn't much to see in this overshadowed narrow stretch of road.

'It's you,' said Tomas. 'They want to kill you. It's because of you, whoever you are.'

Mills watched as the maize stems began to part on either side. There were a lot of them, a dozen or more. Then he saw the first face appearing, clad in a black wool mask, advancing through the undergrowth with the butt of a gun before him.

Tomas pushed his face between his knees. 'Why did I come here?' he sobbed. He listened as Mills wound down the window.

'Bugger off!' Mills shouted in his Anglified accent. 'Your roadblock's crap.'

There were twelve of them now around the car. They had guns carved from bits of wood.

'Carlos, tell them to bugger off,' said Mills again.

The oldest of them, and obviously the leader of the gang, and about ten years old, approached the Mustang, looking as fearsome as he could.

'One American dollar!' he demanded, brandishing his wooden gun.

'Carlos, tell them I won't pay.'

Carlos, considerably relieved, translated his message to the boy, a smile beginning to spread across his face.

Mills opened his door and got out of the car and stood in the road with his hands up.

Slowly Tomas raised his head to look. 'My God,' he muttered. He leaned forward and called out of the window. 'The fucking Venezuelan military are on their way here and you're fucking about in the road. Get in the car for Godsakes.'

'They'll just have to take me hostage,' said Mills looking back to Carlos. 'Can you tell them that?'

Daniel had begun to laugh. Carlos leaned out of the window and told the children that they had a prisoner.

'Tell them they'll have to tie me up with string,' said Mills.

Carlos translated and the boy, the one with the wooden gun and the balaclava that his mother had knitted him for the cold mountain weather, said that they didn't have any string.

'In that case,' said Mills, 'tell them that they'll never grow up to be proper bandits if they don't remember to bring any string.'

The young boy with the wooden gun looked hurt.

'Tell them they'll just have to hold me here and torture me horribly,' Mills shouted back to Carlos.

The young boy began to get impatient, and made a demand. He shouted at the car.

Daniel began to laugh, and he shouted back too. He said that if all they wanted was a dollar for him to be returned, he'd give them two dollars to keep him.

There was laughter all around. Only Tomas remained silent.

Finally Mills was marched back to the Mustang, and he made a short speech, translated by Carlos.

'If you want to grow up to be guerillas, or major criminals, then you must go back to school and not play truant like this. Father Leo has built you a very good place to learn how to tie knots. So stop bumming around.' Then he reached into his pocket, gave the boy five dollars, laying his hand on his head.

'Oh God,' said Tomas, 'now he thinks because a priest has blessed him he's a saint too.'

The kids whooped with joy, and Mills got back into the car as they dismantled the roadblock.

'I guess,' said Carlos, 'that they have been watching too much TV during the state of emergency. It must be the latest game around here.'

'Poor little bastards,' said Mills.

As they got back onto the road Mills's thoughts returned to Father Leonardo. Their laughter at the roadblock had been largely of the nervous kind. They were all worried about the journey ahead.

13 ∫

They didn't inform Clearwater about the 'salute photos' that had been taken of Mills in Caracas. He had to look untroubled for the Iowa primary. But there was real nervousness behind the scenes among the three people who knew about them. And Catherine Sirteema was very uneasy about Warnock.

Warnock was a happy man. He was even dressing better, wearing real wool now instead of shiny man-made fibre suits. Alice, his wife, had said: 'You see what good suits Governor Clearwater wears? You see how he wears a tie? He don't have it halfway down his chest with the buttons undone so everyone sees his string vest. He don't wear brown shoes with black trousers.'

She was right. This job was Warnock's meal ticket. His work on the Dionne Mary-Belle story had put him right at the centre of the campaign, and now he had this rear-guard action to fight over Mills. What had begun as a clandestine appointment, working in The Warren, was now becoming crucial to the campaign. He couldn't believe his luck. He was beginning to taste success; Clearwater would be so indebted to him that he could see a very fine post for himself in the new administration when Clearwater won. A minor player suddenly thrown into the front line. Maybe, even maybe, he'd become the President's press spokesman, on TV every day, his future assured. He was almost dizzy at the prospect.

So Alice, his wife, was right. Clearwater wouldn't want me walking around the White House in brown shoes he thought. A man who wears brown shoes, said Alice, expects to step in shit.

Elliot Hudson and Catherine Sirteema met late that night in Hudson's hotel suite. The meeting was strained.

'What is that sleaze-ball Dale Warnock doing hanging around?' demanded Catherine. There was an anger in her eyes that she rarely displayed in public, but with Elliot it was different.

He wished she didn't despise him as much as she did. He wished they didn't have to be stuck in the habit of being mean to each other in front of everyone else, just because of their history.

Hudson went over to his hospitality bar and opened the fridge.

'Come on, Catherine,' he said. 'I know it's tough at the moment. But we're gonna win here tomorrow night, let's enjoy it. Let's get this Mills thing into some sort of shape. Then we can enjoy winning Iowa. It's important to *enjoy*.' He reached into the fridge door and pulled out a miniature vodka and handed it to her.

She refused it with her hand.

'I don't drink vodka any more,' she said.

'Oh, I'm sorry,' he said, a little too formally, and shook his head as if to say, so what are you drinking these days?

'I'll just take a One-Cal,' she said.

He handed her the can and a glass and slipped off his jacket and threw it over the back of one of the sofas. He nodded towards the other and she went over and sat down. He tried to smile at her again, she was looking real frosty tonight.

It was in a hotel room, just like this one, in Alabama, where their last great scene had taken place. The fight had begun just like this one.

Catherine looked around the room, shaking her head. The similarity of the setting was all too apparent to her as well.

Alabama had been humid for the entire duration of that campaign two years before, so hot that she felt she had fever. Part of that heat had been from working with Elliot. Not just the pace of the campaign but the sexual current running between them had been obvious from day one. Everyone had noticed it, so much so that most of the guys in the office were running a book on it. She knew it, he knew it.

They finally fitted 'sex together' into the schedule – by mutual consent – in a room not unlike this one the night they heard that their candidate had tipped all his negatives over, and they were peaking the polls.

A week of furtive happiness followed, which they imagined they'd concealed from the rest of the staff, until it all fell apart in a blazing row. Just as their working relationship, which they'd somehow managed to preserve until now, was about to do tonight. It was going to be one hell of a firework display, thought Catherine.

It was not a natural way for adult people to live; going from state to state; professional campaigners, great highs and appalling lows with nothing level in between. You either won or you lost, there were no honourable draws. They lived their lives one vote between glory or disaster. They had the metabolism of racehorses.

She thought of something that Anne Clearwater had confided to her in a rare moment of honesty. That she couldn't even yell at her husband any more for fear it might be heard through the wall. They'd learned to hiss through gritted teeth, their fixed campaign smiles still absurdly stuck to their faces, turning constantly towards the door in case anyone should walk in.

'You know, Elliot,' she said, calmly laying down her One-Cal, 'Mills said something very interesting before he went to South America. And I can see why he got out of here and went. He really is a very intelligent young man. A thinker.'

'And that was?' said Elliot trying to shield his unease.

'He was worried about the appearance on the scene of that sleaze-ball of yours, Dale Warnock.'

Elliot flinched. 'He just came up with that photo. I don't see what the big deal is. You should be really glad he intercepted it.'

'The big deal, Elliot, is that it seemed to cross the boy's mind when the Dionne Mary-Belle story broke, that maybe we had punks like Warnock employed by this campaign, stashed away in some office that the rest of us don't even know about. Turning up shit like the McKenzie girl and her abortion. Our campaign would really stink if people imagined we were doing such things.'

Hudson got up and went to the fridge. He stared at the labels on the small bottles of twelve-year-old bourbon. She was still talking. 'And that there's a whole tranche of the whiter than white Clearwater campaign that is, shall we say, below the water line. Around about sewer level. That we have rats sniffing in the shit. That maybe Dionne Mary-Belle McKenzie was dug up and brought back to life by us somehow. Tell me it's a crazy notion, Elliot, dreamed up by a kid who doesn't want to be part of it all.'

He was pulling ice out of the tray and clunking the cubes into his tumbler. He wasn't going to blow it with her this time. In Alabama it was different. Their candidate really had no hope of winning, and the other side started playing dirty first. When he hired Dale to dredge up every hooker in Montgomery it was because he genuinely believed there might be something legitimate there.

Catherine had been right to be angry, he knew. If they'd been caught, and thank God they weren't, it would have been the end of both their careers. Didn't matter how innocent Catherine was, she'd have gone down with it too. My God, what was it she said that night in the room like this one? That she'd sooner lose.

Sooner lose? This was crapola. He turned around with his drink. He was in two minds how to respond. One way might result in her walking off the campaign, the other might result in her helping to make those icy cold Iowa sheets warmer tonight. He doubted the latter, and dreaded the former. He had a lot of work to do.

How could he explain that it wasn't like that for him? He really wouldn't *sooner lose*. Didn't she realise that if they had lost the Senatorial in Alabama then neither of them, neither of them, would have found any work this year in the Republican Primary? You're only as good as your last win. No-one heads for the White House hiring losers, there's a whole new century out there.

He knew that he was going to have to lie to her about the existence of The Warren. Only Clearwater and himself knew of it, and the punks that worked there. He wanted her very much, it ached, and it ate away at him every day. It wasn't just the attraction, it was the fact that he had tasted her once, and now it seemed as if that short emotional delirium hadn't happened at all. She didn't even acknowledge it.

He walked back from the fridge, swigging his bourbon.

'Come on, Catherine,' he said. 'You think I'd let Dale Warnock anywhere near us here if we had some kind of a bunker operation going on with him? You think I'd risk that again after Alabama?'

She held him with her eyes for a moment and he slowly smiled, his head tilting to one side. He didn't even blink.

'It's a big day tomorrow, what do you say we both get some rest . . .' That was her cue, if she picked it up, she picked it up. '. . . Just see if you can come up with some way we can calm our Millsey boy down a little bit while he's on his big expedition.'

Catherine stood up.

'Sure,' she said. 'Good night, Elliot.'

As she got to the door she almost smiled at him. She almost smoothed her hand across his back. Instead she walked to her room. He watched her disappear down the corridor.

After she had gone Elliot went into his combination briefcase and pulled out some notes that Dale Warnock had passed him just an hour before. Warren stuff.

Dale had an interesting writing style. His sentences were concise and brittle, and because of that faintly ridiculous.

He read:

Pan-American movement. *Hernandistas*. Dr José Gregorio Hernández. Weird Voodoo. Mucho factions. Biggest popular movement in Venezuela, Colombia, Peru. Fanatics. Assassination of Archbishop Morales involved. V. Anti-American, esp. the Ford Motor Corporation . . .

Elliot Hudson could read no more. It was looking fairly clear that Mills was involved in some bad shit down there. His time in England had made a *lefty* of him. The situation couldn't continue as it was.

The next evening Kyle Clearwater won the Iowa Primary with a landslide. All their careers were on-track.

14

It was dark when they got back to Merida but the lights were still burning in Cordillera Tours. They went in to see Jenny. The fractiousness of the first part of the journey between Tomas and Mills was forgotten now as they began telling Jenny about their trip. The relief of being safely back had made them excitable and they were all talking at once.

'We must call Father Leonardo,' said Mills. They went silent. 'We must call him to see if he's all right.'

Jenny hesitated for a moment.

'It's okay,' said Mills. 'I know you called him. You've got his number. Looks like you've got mine too.' He laughed.

'You don't mind?'

'No, no. At least it got me to meet the priest. He's quite a guy.'

'I'll call then,' said Jenny slowly, picking up the receiver and dialling.

They all fell silent.

'The Father will be okay,' said Carlos. 'Even the soldiers wouldn't dare . . .'

Jenny looked up with a fixed expression on her face.

'José Gregorio will protect him,' continued Carlos.

'The line is dead,' said Jenny. 'It's been cut.'

Tomas was the first to speak. He looked up sadly. 'This is very bad news,' he said. There were tears in Carlos's eyes. Finally Mills looked at Jenny.

'You think it's my fault? I shouldn't have gone there?'

Jenny shook her head. 'I guess they're just trying to stop him talking to the press. A few words from him could be rather inflammatory right at the moment. He's been so careful not to get involved with this assassination business.'

Outside the streets were growing quiet as the hour of curfew drew nearer. The police had broken quite a few heads in the last twenty-four hours. Troops were positioned about the town, waiting in trucks. Even the cathedral was locked and silent; all public gatherings prohibited. In the candle-lit atmosphere of the tour office they felt like conspirators meeting in the dead of night. Jenny broke open the rum.

Mills searched through his mind, running through the events in Isnotu again. 'That guy at the town hall,' he said, 'who organised dinner for us, you think maybe he told the authorities there was an American in town come to see the priest? And that's what brought the military? He saw the nun come to see me, didn't he?'

'I think this is possible,' said Tomas.

Mills put his head in his hands. 'Oh God, I'm a liability,' he muttered. 'It doesn't matter where I am, I can't do any-thing right.'

Tomas put his hand lightly on his shoulder. Mills had finally explained who his father was in the car coming back. He was surprised to find that he felt easier for it. Neither Tomas nor Carlos had ever heard of his father and it had gone some way towards putting things into perspective. Tomas was feeling a great deal more sympathetic towards him now, but Mills had begun to wish that it was Jude here with him. Jude would cut through the shit and know what to do right now.

'Jenny,' said Tomas, calmly, 'do you think Mills is in trouble?'

'I don't know,' she said. 'I'm sorry about the press guy that came in here. He really made me think he was a friend of yours. He said he'd been with you up in Los Nevados, he said he'd been with you in the riot in Caracas. It wasn't until he'd gone, and I was praying to José Gregorio, that I thought I'd better call through. I feel such a fool not to realise.'

'It can't be helped,' said Mills. 'He was in Caracas with me?'

'Yes.'

'He must have followed me. I've got to stop using my credit card.'

Mills began flicking through the file of Remington-typed

notes on his lap. 'The priest gave me these,' he said, passing them over to Jenny. 'There's quite a bit in here about how José Gregorio opposed the dictator Gomez. There's a section too about the people who are opposed to José Gregorio's beatification. It names names, enemies of Archbishop Morales.'

'Mmm,' said Jenny, thoughtfully. 'Strange he should give you this.' She read silently for a few moments.

'These are all the kind of things,' she said, at last, 'that Father Leonardo wouldn't be able to say to the press in Venezuela himself.'

'So why would he give it to me?'

'Perhaps,' said Tomas, 'he would like it to come from a third party, someone independent of the shrine perhaps? You.'

Mills sighed deeply. 'When we were sitting in his garden he told me so much about himself, about how the shrine began. Now I think back on it, it is as if he wanted to be remembered.'

'You have to look after this,' said Jenny. 'It's probably the only copy. I also think you should leave Venezuela. You should leave tonight.'

'Yes, I think so too,' said Tomas. 'Maybe it was you who the military were after, not Father Leonardo.'

'I've got to give this bloody American journalist, or whatever he is, the slip too, haven't I? I can't stand the idea of some dork trooping around behind me like a shadow everywhere. These tabloid guys are unbelievable, they'll print anything.'

'I think so, he's a clever operator,' said Jenny. 'I'll help you. I'll help get you out of here tonight.'

'You think I should fly back to the States?' he said sadly.

'I don't think you'll be able to now,' said Jenny. 'There's no flights tonight, and anyway, I hear the soldiers are mob-handed at all the airports. I'm trying to think where you could go.'

Mills thought for a moment. 'I could go to Don Emi's house,' he said. 'He'd do anything for Father Leonardo.'

'Don Emi?' said Jenny.

'In Colombia.'

'Colombia?' she said, smiling. 'Out of the frying pan and into the fire, eh?'

'I don't think it is a bad idea,' said Tomas. 'Don Emi has

bodyguards I would think. He's not far over the border is he? It can't be far.'

Jenny thought a little longer. 'Right,' she said. 'Then we have to get you over the border tonight. There has to be a way. Let me think.' She walked over to the map on the wall. 'You'll have to take the northern road, along the coast. Where is Don Emi?'

'Envigado, near Medellin.'

Jenny raised her eyebrows at the mention of the infamous drug city of Medellin. 'You're sure?'

'Yes.'

Jenny returned to her desk and began thumbing through a notebook. 'There has to be a way,' she said. Her eyes stopped on a page.

'Unofficial buses go that way, but it's a rough old journey, maybe ten hours by road. It's over the mountains.'

'It doesn't matter. But what about the border? What if I'm stopped?'

'These buses,' said Jenny, conspiratorially, 'don't stop at the border. They kind of lose their way a bit and accidentally turn off the main highway. But I really wouldn't recommend this route to a normal tourist.'

'I think we've already got beyond that. Where do I catch one?'

'It's a pirate bus service. You pick it up a little way out of town.'

'Is this the route that all the guide books warn you against?' asked Tomas.

'Oh, you've heard of it?' said Jenny brightly.

'It sounds like my best bet,' Mills said decisively.

'Why is this road that Mills will have to go on so dangerous? Because of the smuggling?' asked Tomas.

'Yes. All the drugs come out of Colombia on that road, and because the purchase tax is so high over there all the Venezuelans smuggle whisky and hi-fis and stuff across. The smuggling goes in both directions at the same time; it's quite unique in that respect. It means you don't really get any other kind of traffic at all. Everyone on these buses is smuggling something. You'll really have to keep your wits about you, Mills. Don't speak to anybody, sit at the back and keep your head down. Don't get off at the sandwich stands, tourists on their own get abducted. Don't speak to anyone, they'll think you're a DEA agent.'

'What is DEA?' asked Tomas.

'Americans,' said Jenny. 'The government's got an agreement with America to let their Drug Enforcement Agency guys patrol undercover here. Everyone hates them. They shoot them dead.'

'Are you sure you really want to make this journey tonight?' asked Tomas.

'It's better to go than to stay. I'll be okay. It's the best way of giving this journalist the slip, isn't it?'

He said goodbye to Carlos and his brother and got into Jenny's jeep. Tomas was coming along for the ride. Jenny drove to a place just out of town. It was silent and still under the hanging Spanish Moss swaying in the moonlight.

'You're sure this is the place?' Mills asked Jenny.

Jenny looked down. 'Yeah. I used to know a guy who made a regular run of it. This is it.'

'I think I'll be okay,' whispered Mills, smiling. 'It'll be fine.' He took Tomas's hand and shook it. 'I'll be seeing you Tomas, sorry that things got a bit hairy on our trip. Nice to meet you.'

'I wish you luck,' Tomas said.

'And thanks Jenny, you've been great. You'd better get back into town before curfew.'

'Yeah, yeah, we better had. You got my number on my card, call me when you get to Envigado.'

'I will.'

'I'll pray to the Doctor extra special. You still got your pendant on?'

He smiled. 'Yes, I've still got my pendant.'

'So you'll be fine. Goodbye.'

They hugged.

He watched them climb into the jeep and turn back into town.

After the roar of the jeep had gone it was strangely peaceful on the road, no traffic was moving. The night air was warm and the cover of the Spanish Moss made him feel as if he was sheltered from all harm.

There was a rustle in the bushes and Mills turned around sharply to see what it was. He caught the glimmer of eyes and teeth in the darkness. It was a young girl, a blanket wrapped around her shoulders. She had a weird, other worldly smile, her teeth reflecting the moonlight in a soft golden glow. She was quite beautiful, with a soft, incandescent expression.

Well, if this girl can make the journey, I can, thought Mills. It was hard not to smile back but he was determined to stick to Jenny's advice and keep himself to himself for the next ten hours.

There was the sound of a vehicle, coming up the hill at speed, with blinding lights. It lurched into the side of the road and stopped. It was the jeep. The door opened and Tomas jumped out. He had his pack with him.

'I am coming with you,' he said. 'It's safer if there are two of us. Two sets of eyes are better than one.'

'You're absolutely sure?' he asked.

'Yes, we'll go over the border together. It is best. And I have brought rolls with me, and sausage, so we won't have to leave the bus.'

'Anything to drink?'

Jenny silently handed over the bottle of rum. Tomas looked nervous, and scared.

Jenny waved to them from the jeep. They could already hear the whistles of the police down in the town moving people out of the squares. She turned and disappeared back into the night.

They stood by the roadside for an hour until they heard the engine of a truck without lights coming up the hill.

'I think this is it,' said Tomas.

The truck stopped. It had four windows on either side, it was pretty filthy, with a battered fender, but the engine sounded powerful enough.

A grisly-looking man in a dirty white shirt and gum boots was squatting on the tailboard. He helped the young woman up and then he turned to look at them. He was about thirty years old and there was a clump of hair missing from the side of his head where he looked as if he'd been in a bar room brawl. His hands were dirty and stained. He wore a heavy silver belt and the hilt of a large bone-handled knife was sticking out from the top of his boot. He didn't seem particularly welcoming.

'Colombia?' asked Mills. 'Maicao?'

The man stared at them, expressionless. Even though there was no movement in his face or in his eyes the process of thought was as evident as a bulletin in lights in Times Square. He turned slowly to look at Tomas's dreadlocks and concluded that they were indeed just back-packers. He held out a hand and pulled them up. There was no mention of any fare.

The truck was already heading off before the back had been closed. The interior was dimly lit; there was a bench running the length of each side of the truck and the man in the dirty shirt sat opposite them, staring, his expression still the same.

The young woman had settled herself down at the front. They were the only passengers. The truck could take about twenty people sitting, more if there hadn't been sacks of rice covering the entire floor, stacked up three deep in places. Out of the corner of his eye Mills could see the young woman. He glanced over to escape the gaze of the guy with the missing clump of hair. She smiled at him again and now he saw why her smile was so ethereal. All of her teeth were gold, every one.

Mills shuddered as he realised that the young girl was not as placidly innocent as she appeared. When she got over the border they would pull all her teeth; and send her back for more.

She didn't seem to be able to stop smiling at him, almost as if the teeth were too big for her. If we are boarded by the police, thought Mills, I dare say she'll keep her mouth shut then.

After an hour, heading into the darkness of the mountains, Mills stretched his legs and dislodged a sack of rice. His shoe hit against a whisky bottle. The man in the dirty shirt looked up at him sharply and Mills yawned and pretended to be so tired that he hadn't noticed anything. Neither he nor Tomas had spoken since they'd boarded the truck. They were relieved when it pulled into the side of the road and two more passengers got on. It was a young couple who immediately hid their bags under the sacks. The young woman with the gold teeth began talking to them, but still the man in the white shirt remained sitting opposite Tomas and Mills, his eyes on them.

The two young women at the front of the truck began

whispering to each other and giggling. Tomas broke their silence.

'They are talking about you,' he whispered.

'What are they saying?

'I think the girl with the teeth just said "this could be my chance to have blue-eyed babies".'

Whether it was true or not it was a turning point in the journey. Both Mills and Tomas almost laughed, and the tension it released in the back of the truck was palpable for everyone. The young man lit up a cigarette and offered the pack to Mills and Tomas.

The back of the truck filled with smoke and everyone was smiling now except for the man opposite Mills. Mills leaned over and offered him one of his own Marlboros. The offer wasn't taken up, his expression remained just the same; it had become irritating to Mills now.

'My name is Alvaro,' said the young man at the front, reaching out his hand to Tomas. 'How do you do!'

'You speak English,' said Mills.

'Yes, yes, I speak it. It is okay?'

'Yes, it's very good. Excellent.'

'Excellent!' repeated the young man happily. 'My chick, she doesn't speak none of it. This one here with the smile doesn't speak too. But me, I speak okay, yeah?'

'Yeah,' said Mills.

'Good. You two Americans?'

'I'm German,' said Tomas, pulling up Jenny's bottle of rum and offering it to him.

'Yes, I know German too,' said Alvaro. 'Adolf Hitler! Kraft-werk! BMW.'

Tomas almost choked. 'Your English is better.'

Alvaro laughed. The bottle was passed back.

It seemed to be irritating the dirty-shirted goon opposite that his passengers had begun to talk, and to be speaking in a language he didn't understand. Alvaro was already pretty tanked up and threw a dismissive look at him. The two girls were giggling again.

'What are they talking about?' asked Mills.

'You must not ask it,' said Alvaro, and laughed loudly.

'They're talking about me?'

'Oh yes, yes, very much.'

Tomas pulled a mighty chorizo sausage out of his inside pocket where it had been curled like a sleeping snake. As it came out the young Venezuelan fell about laughing, and the girls giggled even more.

'German sausage!' yelled Alvaro. 'It is very funny.' He shook his head for a while and the girls continued to giggle.

Mills was hungry and he took a bite, which caused even more laughter and whispering among the girls.

'What are they saying?'

'They are saying,' said Alvaro, almost incapable with laughter, 'four boys, two girls in the back of a truck. A lot of sausage.'

'I see,' said Mills.

Alvaro wiped his mouth from where his laughter had made him dribble. 'Major big fuggin gang bang!'

'How many hours is it until we reach the border?' asked Tomas.

'A few more hours.'

'Why are you going to Colombia?' asked Mills.

Alvaro pulled himself back into semi-seriousness. 'Carlita and me go when we have something. We need money to become married.' He pushed his foot against one of the sacks of rice where he'd hidden his bag. He pulled open the top to reveal the dull, lifeless glint of a small portable TV.

'Sony,' he said. 'Good to sell. We make money in Colombia. Then we go back home, and we have enough money for the marriage. It's good.'

The rum bottle was passed around again. This time the hood in the dirty shirt accepted a swig, but his expression still didn't change. Next time, thought Mills, he can beg for a slug.

Alvaro tapped him on the back of his hand. 'This is all you are taking, half a bottle of rum?'

'It's all we've got,' said Tomas. 'We got robbed of everything.'

'Too bad,' said Alvaro. 'This is why you travel cheap.'

'Yes,' agreed Tomas.

The young woman with the gold teeth had seen the way Mills had taken the bottle back and flashed him an admiring smile, then she whispered and giggled again.

'What is she saying?' asked Mills.

Alvaro had to reach for the bottle of rum and take another slug before he could reply.

'She says,' he began, but broke off to laugh, 'that she could give you,' he took another slug of rum, 'the most expensive blow job in the world.'

Mills looked towards her as she flashed her golden teeth. She had stopped giggling now and her expression was fixed and serious.

The atmosphere was cut dead by the sudden stamp of a gum boot, and the dim light caught the flash of the bone-handled knife. The sexual innuendo, in the confined space, was proving too much for the conductor, as Mills had labelled him in his mind. There was a dangerous fury in his eyes.

'Let's just cool it,' said Mills. They had broken every rule that Jenny had insisted upon when this journey was first proposed, and added to this, they were pissing off their host. Suddenly there was an atmosphere of danger in the air again. It would mean nothing to these particular bus operators to slit their throats and dump them by the roadside.

Everyone sat in silence for the next hour.

Mills turned to Tomas. 'What are you going to do when we get to Colombia? Are you coming on to Envigado to Don Emi's?'

'No, I don't think so. I think I shall just go to the beach. There are beautiful beaches.'

Mills thought for a moment. 'Did your parents wire you that money?' he asked.

'No,' he said. 'No they didn't. I will have to sort it out in Colombia with my bank.'

'You're pretty stuffed then.'

Tomas suddenly looked perturbed. 'I didn't think of this,' he said. 'It has all been so, so, well dramatic. I didn't think what I will do for the next couple of days. I have a little money, but not much.'

'Let me give you some money,' said Mills.

'You have enough?'

'Sure. I'll sign some travellers' cheques. Best I don't do it in front of our friend over there, but as soon as we get to Maicao, don't let me forget.'

'I won't be able to cash your travellers' cheques.'

'In Colombia? If they're already signed? Buy a cheap meal with them and keep the change.'

Tomas laughed. 'I suppose you are right. If it's signed they'll cash it?'

'I imagine so.'

'Tell me one thing,' said Tomas, serious again. 'What do you think it would be like?'

'What?'

He sighed. 'Gold teeth . . .'

There was a screech of brakes and the smell of rubber as the tyres burned on the loose gravel road and the truck came to what was evidently an unscheduled stop.

'What the fuck?' said Mills, and then quietened himself like everyone else in the back of the truck. The light had gone out, but the moonlight picked out the dull metallic shine of a gun barrel, in Mills's peripheral vision, as the guy opposite him pulled it from his breast pocket, and in the same motion leapt to the small window beside Mills's head. The crescent of the moon was caught in both his eyes and his breathing immediately became erratic. The two girls were sinking slowly to the floor. Alvaro looked more terrified than anyone. Tomas gripped the rum tighter.

For two minutes they listened to each other's breathing. Then the engine started again, and the rubber of the wheels burned, the gun was pulled away from the window, and they were on their way again.

'What was that?' Mills whispered to Tomas.

'I don't know,' he said, and there was no explanation. Even three hours later, descending the *cordillera*, there was no explanation. What had happened had happened, no-one was the wiser except for the expressionless man with the lost tuft of hair. The night was becoming a long one and no-one could relax, or sleep after that. Both Tomas and Mills had become nervous and they avoided the faces around them, all of them sinister in their own desperate way.

Everyone began to sense the border at the same time. Maybe it was the body language of the conductor, just a nervous tap of his boot, or a sudden flicker across his expressionless face, that alerted them, but whatever it was they all felt the increased tension at around about the same time. They began to look at each other's faces again with equally furtive expressions. If only the night weren't so silent; if only there was the comfort of the sound of other traffic.

Alvaro offered his packet of cigarettes around again. 'You know what?' he said.

'What's that?'

'My chick and me, we've been saying, how much are you two guys worth?'

'Uh huh?'

'For kidnap? Like, if things get bad, we could always say to the bandidos we got two Americanos, how much, and they'll let us go, yes?'

'Sure,' said Mills. 'You tell them that.'

'I will,' said Alvaro, laughing. 'Maybe you'll come up on their list.'

'What list is that?'

'Oh, you don't know? In Colombia they're real organised, not like us dumb Venezuelans. They don't take every tourist, only the best. Every day they kidnap three people, every day! We say it is Colombia's biggest import!'

Tomas laughed uneasily.

'So what's this list?' asked Mills. Alvaro's sense of humour was beginning to grate.

'Computer print out. They got ten thousand names of all the rich and important families in the world and if your name is on the list you go up into the hills with them.'

'Well,' said Mills. 'It's reassuring that they're so organised.'

'It's big business,' said Alvaro.

They all immediately went silent again, the truck was on a rougher road now. The conductor had his knife on his lap, playing with it, catching the reflection of the blade in the moonlight and reflecting it across Tomas's throat.

The truck veered sharply to the left, the sacks swelled against their legs, the dim light fused, and they all fell about in the back at the sudden stop. The sound of the engine was gone and was replaced by the aromatic sense of gorse and heather, of fresh mulch, in a lower pasture of the Andean mountains on the Colombian side. The conductor had wrenched the back of the truck open and was signalling to all of them to throw the sacks of rice out onto the field. The driver sat looking back, urging them on, shouting at them to make it quick. It was the first time they had heard his voice. Down in the field the conductor was screaming at them, they banded together and threw out the sacks; they passed down the bottles of whisky, and plastic bags that cluttered like a collection of a child's building bricks.

'Computer chips,' said Tomas, 'worth more than gold in weight.'

'We must be in Colombia,' whispered Mills.

'I think so. At least we got over the border okay. They'll relax now, as soon as they've got rid of all the gear.'

They were conscious of other people; figures moving in the darkness. There were half a dozen motorbikes lying in the field and the men were dividing the contraband amongst them. The first of the bikes, with bulging pillion sacks, set off across the black scrubland, churning up the grass and heather. Then the driver of the truck lurched suddenly towards them and grabbed Mills by the arm, pulling him down from the tailboard. Tomas jumped down beside him. The driver was pointing to the sacks and indicating that they should help load them into the pillions. They moved as quickly as they could; there was an atmosphere of panic about the whole thing.

The cycles were about twenty feet away from the road and the terrain was scattered with sharp rocks and sudden dips amongst the spiteful gorse bushes. Tomas yelled out as he snagged himself in the thorns and dropped his sack. He struggled to free himself. Then a sudden bright light from a torch swept across the darkness and a gunshot rang out. There were more shots and the sound of people scattering. Tomas looked about him, he couldn't see Mills. He tore his leg away from the gorse bush, threw his sack to the ground and turned back for the truck. People were running in all directions and returning fire.

Tomas reached the tailboard of the truck and threw himself in. As he landed he smashed his mouth against the bare floor and the sweet taste of blood trickled down his throat. He was gasping so deeply he could barely breathe. He heard the driver returning to the cab. He searched around for Mills; Alvaro was still there, along with the two girls, huddled on the floor at the front.

Outside the shooting went on. The engine started up and the wheels spun on the loose gravel of the road. The doors of the truck were still open, looking out across the barren moonlit landscape. The truck jolted and began to move. Then with a crash Mills landed in the back of the truck and huddled there in a heap, gripping his head between his knees.

'Are you okay?' asked Tomas.

'What the fuck happened?' said Mills, raising his head and looking back out of the doors.

There was another burst of gunfire. Tomas grabbed Mills and pulled him across the truck, which jolted again and slammed them both against the small window. There, in the moonlight, they saw that the man who'd sat opposite them with the bone-handled knife, was staggering from side to side, trying to make it back to the truck. His white shirt was steeped in blood.

The truck was moving at speed. The driver didn't even look back to see the desperate straits he'd left his accomplice in.

The passengers sat in silence on the bench.

The town of Maicao was still twelve kilometres distant. Alvaro leaned over to them and spoke in a low panting voice.

'Be very careful,' he said. 'Now is when it begins to get dangerous.'

'You're kidding, right?' said Mills.

Alvaro's face remained fixed.

'Maicao is lawless. No police, nothing. You won't last five minutes in the street, you must move real fast,' said Alvaro. 'When the truck stops, you run like shit to the official bus station. I will show you where. The bus station has big steel doors, they will let you in.'

'Where do buses go from there?' asked Tomas.

'Everywhere. They go everywhere in Colombia. Good buses. Air con. You will be okay.' He leaned over to look out of the window. 'I will tell you when,' he said.

The unmade streets were filled with people; many of them still drunk from the night before. The shops and the roadside stalls were stacked high with electrical goods. There wasn't even a semblance of an attempt to hide the town's trade in contraband.

Every couple of buildings along the street places were burned out where rival gangs had fire-bombed each other. Suddenly Alvaro seemed to panic and slapped Tomas on his arm.

'Shit,' he said. 'We are going the wrong way. It is the wrong way. Get your things together.'

Mills and Tomas scrabbled for their bags.

'We have passed the bus station already, back there. You must go, you must go very quickly. Run like shit.'

Alvaro jumped up and kicked open the doors. 'Goodbye friends,' he said, and pushed them out of the back of the truck.

They both landed badly, sprawling in the dust and trash but were up and running before anyone in the street had fully comprehended the sight of two dazed gringos throwing themselves right into their arms. Many of them were carrying batons and guns.

They saw the metal doors of the bus terminal to their left and fell crashing against them. As the people in the street began to realise what they had in their midst, Mills and Tomas beat on the doors. Two guys had pulled out their guns and were heading towards them.

The doors opened and a uniformed man pulled them in. As the doors closed again they sank to their haunches, gasping for breath. Behind them they heard the sound of bare fists banging on the doors, and it served to get them back up onto their feet again.

The uniformed man led them down the ramp. At the bottom they came out onto a concourse. Smartly dressed people were sitting around on bucket seats; there was a small cafe serving coffee, and ahead of them was a row of airport-style check-in desks for the executive bus companies, with pretty young uniformed girls sitting before computer terminals. The floor shone and smelled of disinfectant; it was weirdly like a shopping mall in Beverly Hills.

'I got to use the bathroom,' muttered Tomas.

'Me too,' Mills gasped.

In the silence of the washroom they leaned against the wall.

'We are okay,' said Tomas. 'We are okay,' and he began to laugh a little.

'You know something,' said Mills. 'We never paid any fare.'

They both slid down the wall and laughed some more.

'Well,' said Tomas. 'I have done what I wanted to do. I have crossed the border. Thank you, I couldn't have done it on my own. Now I can go to the coast.'

Mills smiled. 'I don't think we had much choice. Let's get these travellers' cheques sorted.'

He signed and handed them over to Tomas.

'You are very kind to help me.'

'Don't worry about it, I've got it to spare.'

'I also have an idea,' said Tomas. 'You said in Merida that you shouldn't use your credit card. They can trace you, yes?'

'It's pretty easy I'd imagine.'

'Why don't we buy my ticket to the west coast with your card?'

They went up to the check-in desk to buy a ticket to Envigado and another to Cartagena. They used the credit card as Tomas had suggested for the trip to Cartagena.

An hour later Tomas prepared to board his bus west. 'Maybe I will see you on the coast. I am going to Zipatola, it's very nice, very peaceful.'

'Sure, maybe you will,' said Mills taking his hand. 'Thanks for helping me out.'

'It's no problem. With any luck your journalist man will get very lost now.'

'I think he will. He's probably lost already.'

'This is good, no?'

'Well,' said Mills, 'there's always another to take his place.'

They exchanged addresses.

'Say hello to Don Emi for me, I hope everything is all right with Father Leonardo, and, er, thanks for the adventure.'

'Don't thank me, I think it just comes included down here.'

'I am looking forward to not having any more.'

The bus driver was urging everyone on.

'Goodbye,' said Tomas.

An hour after that Mills was himself on his way to Envigado in an air-conditioned Mercedes bus with hostess service. As the sun took possession of the morning landscape the country gradually grew more civilised by the mile and his fellow passengers chatted amicably and read paperback books. From the idyllic view of the cattle in the fields and the villagers who paused to wave, no-one could have known that the problems of this country were ten times worse than the one Mills had just left.

15 ∫

Mills took a cab from the bus terminal in Envigado. The driver had been silently impressed when he'd showed him Don Emillio's business card, and nodded deferentially. It was mid evening when he arrieved at Don Emillio's gates; a humid evening, cicadas rasping everywhere in the exuberant foliage like drummer boys on the eve of battle.

It was a grand house with a central courtyard hung with large modern religious paintings. Servants in uniforms hovered around; they were simpering and effeminate in contrast to the six armed men who had guarded the main gate.

'We are so pleased, we are so very pleased,' boomed Don Emillio as he crossed the courtyard and threw his arms around him. 'Welcome to our *finca*.'

'It's a beautiful house, a very beautiful house.'

'It has been in our family for two hundred years. It was here when there was none of the town you see around you. Just a hill *finca* growing arabica beans.'

'Your family must have grown a lot of coffee.'

Don Emi laughed loudly. He led him with his arm around him past a fountain bubbling with illuminated water, to where lights were burning in a long gallery and his family were seated at table.

'Let me introduce you,' he said in English, 'to a remarkable young man I met in Isnotu. He has an interest in our beloved José Gregorio.'

Twelve people were sitting at the long dining table, and they looked up to smile broadly. At the head of the table Don Emillio's chair stood where he'd pushed it aside when he'd been told that there was an American at the door. Sitting next to the head of the table was a young man of Mills's age who looked up but didn't join in the general welcome. He looked sour, and not at all pleased by Mills's arrival. He had round steel-rimmed glasses, with incredibly thick lenses.

The table was heaving under the weight of food on porcelain platters. A servant set a place for Mills, and poured him a glass of wine.

'You look tired, young man,' said Don Emillio.

'I am tired,' said Mills. 'I've just come by bus from Venezuela. It's one hell of a road.'

'By bus?' said the young man at Don Emillio's elbow with the sour expression on his face.

'Uh huh.'

'You must be mad,' he said. 'No-one comes to Colombia by bus. Didn't anyone tell you that?'

A young woman, sitting next to him, with long flowing hair and breasts that were only just contained by the frilled edging of her top, laid her hand on his arm.

'The bus across the border?' she asked, astonished.

'That's right.' He had the whole table's attention now.

The young woman turned to the rest. 'He must be Christopher Columbus,' she said. Those who understood English laughed, then the others joined in afterwards. Don Emillio laughed louder than them all, he loved his daughter's sense of humour. His son, sitting beside him, scowled as if he was jealous of his sister, and disapproving of his father's indulgence of her.

Mills took a glance at him. He had a pleasant face, but the thick lenses made his eyes look strangely bulbous. In Isnotu, over lunch, when Don Emillio's miracle son had first been mentioned Mills had naturally presumed that he was going to be a kid of eight or nine. He was perturbed. The boy he'd been invited to meet, who'd actually seen José Gregorio Hernández, didn't look as if he could even see to the other end of the table. He wasn't expecting him to be in a Hugo Boss mohair jacket and silk tie either. What was obvious, however, was the fact that he didn't seem at all keen to talk to Mills. Perhaps he was sick of the José Gregorio business by now. Maybe he'd gone through it all a million times with the Vatican investigators. Maybe he'd made it all up as a boy and was now of an age to seriously regret the whole thing. He sure as hell didn't look like he wanted to talk to another guy of his age about it. Mills would just have to be gentle about it.

'But didn't they put you into a cage when you got to Maicao?' the young woman asked.

'Well, yes, they did,' said Mills smiling, and the whole table laughed.

'In a cage! They put him in a cage!' she shrieked with laughter.

'I've never met anyone who has done that journey by bus,' said the young man. 'Either you have inexpressible courage, or you've run out of money.'

'No,' replied Mills. 'Stupidity. An inexpressible amount of stupidity.'

The company of people laughed. None of them looked as if they'd ever been on a bus. They were the Colombian seriously rich, and he rather enjoyed the notion that they thought he was a poor Yanqui back-packer. Their wealth had made these young people so superior that they seemed to presume no-one else came from such grand, and rich, and complicated families, whereas Mills had been brought up to believe that everyone did.

He could understand why they were surprised by his bus journey, and delighted by his time in the 'cage' in Maicao.

'Don Emillio,' said Mills. 'Tell me, how is Father Leonardo? Have you heard anything from him?'

Don Emillio looked down at the table cloth silently.

'I called from Merida,' continued Mills, 'but the line was dead.'

'Yes, yes. I telephoned too, the line is dead. It is dead at the shrine also. I have sent one of my men over there. We hope everything is all right.'

'I hope so.'

'He is almost a saint himself. You have those notes that he gave you?'

'Yes, I have them,' replied Mills.

Don Emi merely smiled and looked thoughtful.

After dinner, Don Emi's daughter, Marta, asked Mills if he'd like to go with her to the opening of a new nightclub in town.

'Señor Mills is tired,' said her father. She looked coquettishly crestfallen.

'No, no. The meal's revived me,' he said.

Don Emi looked at his son, who scowled again and took off his glasses and cleaned them. Rafael nodded begrudgingly. If his sister was going out to a nightclub it would mean that he had to go too. No respectable girl from a family like this went out without her brother as a chaperon.

One of Don Emillio's security men drove them into town in Rafael's BMW. He was a big, silent man and not once did he presume to join in the conversation. He reminded Mills of one of his father's men.

'Envigado is a remarkable place, Rafael,' said Mills, looking out of the smoked glass window at the gleaming luxury apartment blocks. 'The streets are so perfect, no pot-holes. Everywhere is so clean, it's like California.'

'Oh yes, Mr America,' said Rafael cynically. 'It's just like California. All the streets are perfect and all the poor are fed.'

'There are no beggars on the streets,' Mills observed. 'No vagrants. You should see Britain, where I live. Every town is full of drunks and kids with dogs on bits of string begging outside the supermarkets. You don't have any of that in Envigado?'

'No,' said Marta, sitting next to him in the back seat. 'This is the cleanest town in the whole of Colombia. It's nice here, no?' She took the opportunity to take his arm, and gently squeezed it.

Rafael let out a low growl.

'Well, we do have beggars actually,' he said at last. 'You've got to understand, Señor Mills, that most of the money in this town is made from trafficking. The capos live here, they like it to be nice. They don't like their wives and daughters to see dirty poor people on the streets. They have something of a reputation for keeping the place clean . . .'

'Like Robin Hood,' said Marta, 'they pay for the street cleaners, and build the hospitals. They're good men, they help the poor.'

Rafael laughed. 'Oh sure, the capos built the hospital, they keep it pretty busy too. You live in a dream, Marta, you really do.'

'I do not,' she said petulantly. 'I am wide awake. At least I can *see*.'

He flinched. 'I'll tell you why there are no beggars on the streets of Envigado. It is the same reason why there are no beggars on the streets of Bogota. Two weeks ago the capos sent a truck round with their men in the back armed with machine-guns. They mowed down about seventy beggars where they sat with their bowls. It's a regular service they provide. That is why all the streets have shiny sidewalks, it's easier to hose down the blood.'

'Rafael, you exaggerate, you always exaggerate how it is,' said Marta.

'Yes, well maybe I do. Maybe they only gunned down fifty.'

'Yes,' agreed Marta. 'Can we have some music on the radio please?'

The driver switched the radio on to a salsa station that he knew she liked.

'It will get us in the mood to dance,' said Marta brightly. 'How do you dance, Mills?'

'Pretty badly,' he said.

'Oh no, I don't believe it. Here in Envigado, in the nightclubs, we all dance, sometimes all night.'

'What do you think?' asked Rafael as they looked around the nightclub awash with tinted mirrors and naked plaster statues. Six vast plate glass windows looked down into the street.

'It's quite something,' said Mills.

'It's shit,' said Rafael. 'It's as if the designers have set out to disgust us. I'm grateful that most of it is a blur to me.'

Mills smiled and nodded.

'Well I think it's very beautiful and very *exclusive*,' said Marta. 'Look there's Teresa and Isobel, let's go see them.' As she swept over to kiss the other two young women, Rafael tapped Mills on the arm, and held him back for a moment.

'Watch yourself with these two,' he said, 'they're real killers.' Rafael's attitude towards him had begun to thaw just a little.

'I can see that,' said Mills laughing. Teresa and Isobel were enormous girls, with round piggy faces and thighs like hams. They were squeezed into terrifyingly expensive clothes. Their dresses looked like those fancy lace things they put over loo rolls in seaside guest houses in England, but blown up to enormous proportions. They looked as if they'd dressed and then someone had put a foot-pump to them. To magnify the horrible effect even more, God had chosen to make them twins. They were eighteen years old, and had both recently had nose jobs that were still in the early stages of recovery. The thick make-up couldn't hide the bruising. Their eyes looked like a panda's.

'My sister wants to show you off,' said Rafael, as they drew near. His tone was a little easier with him now, perhaps because they had a common enemy. 'She wants to show them she's got a handsome young American with her. The twins eat pretty boys for breakfast.'

'They get boyfriends?'

'Sure,' said Rafael, 'they get the best looking boys in town fawning all over them. It's truly disgusting.'

'I wouldn't want to have to watch.'

Rafael laughed. 'You're not like most Americans.'

'No?'

'Shouldn't you be a little more arrogant?'

'I don't see why. Why do you Colombians hate Americans so much?'

'Huh!' Rafael laughed. 'You don't know?'

Their burgeoning conversation was suddenly cut short as the shadow of the twins fell across them. They both shook their hands, and then the twins demanded a kiss. It seemed unwise to refuse them. The two boys sat down at their table and the twins called for more champagne at two hundred dollars a bottle. Everyone who passed nodded to the twins as if they were paying court.

Mills followed Rafael to the restroom.

'I can't get the one next to me to stop sliding her hand down the back of my trousers,' said Mills. 'What the hell do I do?'

'I think we'd just better leave. Once they've got their claws in it's a nightmare. I'll have a word with Marta.'

'She won't go though, will she? She wants to stay.'

'I'm sure she'll go if you invite her for a moonlit walk by the river.'

'A moonlit walk round here sounds pretty dangerous to me.'

'I promise you,' said Rafael, laughing in his cynical, staccato way, 'it's much more dangerous in here with those two *harpies.*'

They drove a little distance in the BMW and pulled into the walkway by the river. The three of them got out into the moonlight and the bodyguard followed at a distance of ten yards.

'Anyway,' said Marta, 'I didn't like too much the music there. It was too fast.'

'We can go somewhere else before we go home,' said Rafael, 'if you really want to.' He didn't want to take her back to his father looking as if he'd been a spoilsport.

'Yes, I would like that,' she said, threading her arm into Mills's. 'Would you like that Millito?'

'It'd be great,' he said. Millito? *Little Mills.* Cheeky bitch.

'At least it was better than the last nightclub that opened there,' said Rafael, laughing.

'That was just unfortunate. It was a real shame for them that night,' said Marta, defensively because the last manifestation of that nightclub had been a surprise birthday present for the twins from their father.

'Unfortunate? It was hysterical!' said Rafael, laughing. He was on the other side of Mills and took his arm as well.

'You should have seen it, Mills. The whole thing had to be called off even before it opened. The place was entirely destroyed. Those great plate glass windows you saw were blown out all across the street.' He laughed again.

'There was a bomb?'

'No!'

'It was a terrible shame for them,' said Marta.

'But a great boost to the town,' continued Rafael. 'You know what happened? The twins had insisted on the biggest sound system ever to come into Envigado. As you noticed, everything has to be *big* with them. And during the sound-check in the afternoon they pushed the volume up so loud it blew the fucking windows out. Destroyed the place.'

Rafael laughed, and Mills joined him.

'So many people in this town have got more money than sense. They just don't know what to do with it. You know, at the height of Escobar's power, the whole town filled up with artists. You know Pablo Escobar, the drugs lord? This was his town. There were artists everywhere; terrible portrait painters, and those daubing merchants who knock out lurid seascapes and vermilion palate-knifed sunsets. They were selling them to the capos for fifty thousand dollars a shot. The capos thought if it had a signature, and the paint was thick, it was art.' He roared with laughter again.

'I think some of the painters here are very good. They have real talent. We have places here that are just as good as Montmartre in Paris, in France,' said Marta.

Rafael sniggered again.

'Anyway I am glad we went to the nightclub and I am glad to have introduced Mills to Teresa and Isobel. Did you see how jealous they were, Rafael? Did you see how they ate Millito up with their eyes?'

'I did,' muttered Rafael. 'That's why we had to get out.'

Marta stopped in her tracks.

'That is why?' she said, and looked at Mills. 'I thought Millito wanted to walk with me.'

'Oh come on, Marta. You know those girls are evil. I won't have you going around with them. And God knows what would have happened to Mills if they'd have decided to take him from you.'

'Hey, just a minute,' said Mills. 'I'm my own man here.'

'That remains to be seen,' said Rafael.

'But you do want to walk with me by the river?' she said turning to him. 'You are enjoying our walk?' she said, squeezing herself against him.

'Of course,' he said. 'It couldn't be more charming.'

'I don't know how you can like the twins,' continued Rafael. 'They were the most unpopular girls at school. Everybody hated them.'

'They were not unpopular. I liked them very much,' said Marta. 'You liked them too, really, didn't you Millito?'

'Well . . .'

'Of course he didn't. I'll tell you how popular they were at school, Marta. You seem to have forgotten their fifteenth birthday party.'

'It was lovely. I wore Chanel for the first time.' She turned to Mills. 'Not just the perfume, you understand, but the cocktail dress.'

'You looked like a French tart,' said Rafael.

She smiled. 'And you, my dear brother in your evening suit, if my recollection is correct, looked something like a short-sighted waiter.'

He winced. It still hurt every time he was attacked about his eyes.

'I'll tell you what their mother did,' he said looking at Mills. 'To make sure people came to their birthday party she promised a new Renault car to everyone who turned up.'

'But Daddy sent ours back,' said Marta, determined to cut his exaggerations dead.

'We have BMWs, he was insulted.'

'What does your father do?' asked Mills.

'He's a benefactor,' said Marta. 'He's a commodities broker. Do you understand *futures?*'

Mills looked at Rafael. Rafael said nothing.

'Marta, you remember those two cute brothers that the twins were dating six months back?'

'Which ones?'

'Those poor kids from the *barrio* that couldn't believe their luck.'

'They were really nice guys. The twins loved them. It's kind of romantic, twins going out with brothers. Don't you think so, Millito?'

'Romantic is what it was,' said Rafael. 'And you know why they loved the twins so much? Because they gave them an Alfa Romeo each. That's why.'

'Only so that they could drive them around.'

Rafael sniggered and turned to Mills. 'And you know how it all ended? One of them was seen out with another girl one night.

His real girlfriend from the *barrio*. Both of them were found the next day, down here by the river, their tongues had been torn out and they both had a bullet in the back of the head.'

'It's not true,' said Marta. 'You're exaggerating again. They didn't tear out their tongues.'

'It's a dangerous thing to accept gifts from the twins. Nobody knows how many dates they've had their father's henchmen shoot dead.'

'It's incredible,' said Mills, disturbed and looking around the path in case the bushes held any more of their recent conquests.

'You're very lucky that they only put their hands down your trousers, Mills.'

'When you said they were killers I didn't realise you meant it literally.'

'Oh I did. They're two fat eighteen-year-old serial killers.'

Mills fell silent for a moment. Thinking about the girls, whose champagne he'd been drinking, made him feel sick.

'Don't listen to him, Millito. Rafael imagines these things just to depress people, and ruin their nice walk,' said Marta, squeezing his arm tighter and looking up into his blue eyes.

Rafael said nothing.

'I just can't comprehend anyone being able to do such a thing,' said Mills.

'Oh come on,' said Rafael. 'If it was that easy, like it is here, wouldn't you have bumped off failed dates at eighteen? They can't think about anything else. And I don't know if you've noticed but daddies in Colombia do like to indulge their little girls . . .'

They walked past a wall with overhanging oleander blooms, and high standing nicotina, their nocturnal scent filling the air. It was like being in a private garden. It was all so perfectly kept that it seemed incredible to think of it as a dumping ground for tongue-less teenage corpses. Perhaps this was where the twins had walked, arm in arm like they were now, with their young men from the *barrio*. He could picture their faces; their perfect olive skin, their delight at being given cars. Look mama, look. Look what the rich girls gave us. We're gonna look after you, mama. You're going to be all right now. We won't go hungry any more. We got cars.

And mama will have thought of those words too, as she followed the double cortège, held up by her friends dressed in black on either side.

'Let's go to another club now,' said Marta. 'Let's go to the Flamingo.'

The Flamingo was much bigger than the first club. It was on several levels of terraces and held about two thousand people. They were asked to check in guns at the door. Their security man handed over a large silver automatic, but in deference to his employer it was discreetly handed back. They had a liberal door policy.

'Let's go to the upper bar and have cocktails,' said Marta. 'Let's have margaritas, a big jug of margaritas with ice and umbrellas.'

From the upper bar Mills stared down onto the main dancefloor. The people were dancing in long lines, all of them facing a vast mirror on the far wall. The dancing was incredibly formal. There were fountains and a cascade of water running from the top terrace to the bottom where it was pumped back up again, the cigarette butts craftily filtered out.

There were all ages in the club, and everyone was very smartly dressed. But on the topmost terrace the clubbers were mostly young.

A group of guys, seventeen- and eighteen-year-olds, were gathered at a table next to them. They were calling to the girls below in drunken voices, a couple of them had girls on their laps.

'Sicarios,' said Rafael.

'They're just low class kids,' said Marta. 'We don't have sicarios in Envigado any more. They only have sicarios in Cali. My brother imagines them everywhere, Millito,' and she turned her head away from them. She was eager to take Mills to the dancefloor.

'Sicarios?' he asked.

'Uh huh. You can tell them by the money they flash about and the Nike trainers. There are hundreds of them. The capos recruit them and take them out to training camps in the hills. There they teach them to ride motorbikes and shoot sub-machine guns from the hip. Another drink, Mills?'

'Nonsense,' said Marta, turning back to the conversation she had been trying to ignore. 'There are no camps.'

Mills held his glass out silently towards the jug as Rafael poured. Marta started singing along to the music, a passionate tango, the old style that she liked, a romantic break between the thudding tracks.

'They'll kill anyone you like for five hundred dollars. They shoot from their motorbikes and are gone.'

'But they're so young, they're not even our age. They look like they must still be in school.'

'Yes. Well, they don't live very long you see. Twenty-three is old for a sicario. They think of themselves as kind of post-modern matadors. Which means killer anyway. All of them get killed. Very often after they've done a job the same people who hired them kill them when they come for their payment. They had, after all, accepted the offer of very little money to kill an important person and shouldn't be surprised when their own life is worth less. Usually, though, they average about ten assassinations before they get it themselves. That's a pretty good average. That's what they expect. They don't mind dying. They think it's cool to get shot, they've all seen the elaborate funerals their friends get. It's a kind of sentimental thing with them. They know they're part of contemporary Colombian mythology.'

'What makes them do it?'

'They love their mothers.'

'So?'

'So their fathers are all drunks; they like the idea of being the head of the family. All they want is designer clothes, a hi-fi, a microwave for their mum. Just like any kid. Being a sicario is the best way to get those things quickly. They'd sooner live today and die than be poor for another thirty years like their folks before them.'

Marta stood up. She was cross. 'Are you still talking crap, Rafael?' she said. 'When are you going to dance with me, Mills? When is he going to ask me?' She appealed to her brother's sense of decorum. Girls in Envigado do not ask.

One of the sicarios looked across at her and wolf whistled. He was from out of town and didn't know better. The young guy in his Calvin Kleins came over and their bodyguard stood up.

Rafael and Mills felt duty bound to do the same, to defend her honour. But Mills was standing nearest to him.

The sicario laughed and raised his glass to them as if he was going to throw it into their faces. Then he looked at Mills and said, 'Americano? Bastardo?' He pulled on his shoulder, drawing him closer. Then he reached into Mills's shirt and pulled out the leather twine of the pendant around his neck, intent on winding it around his fingers until it cut into Mills's throat. He looked at the pendant and replaced it slowly.

The sicario laid down his drink and held out his hand to be shaken. Timidly, Mills took his hand. There was a long scar across the palm. Mills could feel the raised skin as he shook the man's hand. Then the killer apologised for disturbing them and went back to his table.

'What was that all about?' asked Mills.

'These boys are very religious,' said Rafael. 'They always get a blessing from the priest before a job. They ride along with their rosaries in their underpants in the hope it'll save them from getting their balls blown off. He's obviously got a job to do in the morning. That's why he's out to get laid. He saw your pendant of José Gregorio Hernández. It would have been severe bad luck for him to have picked a fight with you if you're under the Doctor's protection.'

'I'm beginning to think I am,' said Mills.

'If he'd fought you, he'd have had to kill you outside afterwards. It would have been a matter of honour in front of his friends. But at the same time, bad luck with that around your neck.'

'So okay,' said Marta, snapping her fingers. 'Now that's done can we have a dance please, Millito?'

At least the subject of José Gregorio has finally been acknowledged, he thought.

It was two o'clock in the morning, the music in the club was still blaring but the margaritas had loosened them all up considerably. The sicarios had even sent over another jug as an apology, and Mills was beginning to believe that Colombia was enjoyable.

'Tell me, Rafael,' said Mills, shouting over the music. 'What's it like being investigated by the Vatican?'

Rafael took a long draw on his drink and swilled an ice cube around in his cheek. He'd taken his glasses off, he didn't need them when he was in a place where you had to be very close up to someone anyway just to be heard above the music.

'It's a real pain in the arse,' he said, finally. 'They hauled me up before the bishop. Then they put me in a hotel for two weeks while the investigators talked to me every day. They brought in the doctors too. At the end I had to sign a statement, which the doctors witnessed. It was like being arrested. And still they come back for more. I've got to go through it all again in another couple of weeks. Or at least I think I am. With the assassination of Archbishop Morales everything's a bit confused right now.'

'When did it all start?'

'You mean when was the miracle?'

'Yeah, I guess I do.'

'Four years ago.'

'I take it you were really ill?'

Rafael laughed. 'No, no. I was quite happy as I was. That's the sad irony. I was very fit, sixteen years old. I didn't have any real problems with anything. But I was blind.'

Mills shuddered.

Rafael reached into his top pocket and pulled out his milk bottle glasses. 'When people who don't know me see these they think I must have diminishing eyesight. They couldn't be more wrong. My eyesight gets better all the time. In another year I'll see as well as you, they say.' He laughed. 'I'll be able to drive at over thirty miles an hour.'

Mills, emotional with the drink, grasped his arm and squeezed it. Marta was singing along to the salsa again.

'Had you always been blind?'

'No, I was born entirely sighted, but by the time I was five it had deteriorated so that there was just complete blackness. So cruel, when you think about it, because by five years old you have begun to take stock of the world, from judgements of your own. And you can remember things from when you were five. Until I was sixteen I remember them just as about half a dozen photographs.'

'So you knew what the world looked like?'

'Well, I thought I did. But I didn't at all of course. When you grow up with everything being entirely tactile, well, you dispense with colour for a start. You have to. You kind of reinvent the look of things I guess. When my sight returned that day four years ago, nothing was as I expected it to be.'

Marta sighed with boredom. 'Shall we be getting home now?' she said. The boys carried on talking.

'When the doctors told me my sight had returned I didn't believe them because I couldn't really see anything.'

'You couldn't?'

'No. It really annoyed them. Medically I should have been able to see, but I couldn't. I had lost the ability to focus you see, I couldn't judge distances. And you know that our retina actually sees things upside down and the brain learns to reverse it, well I suppose it was like that. I just didn't have the mental proficiency any more to process the visual information I was being given.'

Marta had the hiccoughs now and she was exaggerating them to illustrate her boredom.

'And it just happened, that's why it was a miracle?'

'Good God, no,' said Rafael. 'What do you take the Vatican for? They want a bit more meat than that.'

'What was the meat?'

'Well for a start, my condition was congenital. My mother was blind as well. Blind until the day she died. Blindness in fact, I suppose, killed her.'

'How did she die?'

'I was fifteen when she died,' his misty eyes glazed over slightly and he took another swig at his drink. 'She was such a warm person, so soft, and she always smelled of fresh flowers even though she couldn't remember what they looked like. She never could get her head around the concept of colour, however hard my father tried to explain it. She'd gone blind a little younger than me you see. At two years old.

'She was flying across Lake Maracaibo, you know, the vast lake on the northern coast that has perpetual lightning flashing across it?'

'Yes. I've read about it.'

'They had to pitch down in the water. The engines had blown. Everyone got out of the plane except my mother. No-one helped her to find the exits.'

The two boys looked down at the dancefloor for a moment. A slow, tragically dramatic tango was playing and it seemed to briefly snatch their mood.

'It broke my father apart. He booked me into the University hospital in Caracas and said it didn't matter what it cost, they had to try the new surgery on me. They had to try to restore my sight. I was against it.'

'Why?'

'I was sixteen, I had things to do. I didn't want to be stuck in a hospital for weeks on end.'

'Not even to have your sight restored?'

'Mills, there was no sight to restore. It was a degenerative disease. It took five years to blind me, and it's taking five years for my sight to return to that I was born with.'

'It is truly weird,' said Mills.

'Yes, that's what they say. They say it's unheard of.'

'Why did your father send you to Venezuela, to Caracas, because it was José Gregorio's own hospital?'

'Exactly. My father has prayed to him for many years. He said if it would take a miracle to restore my sight then it would have to be done in José Gregorio's own operating theatre.'

'And it did?'

Rafael had gone suddenly silent. 'I think we'd better be getting home,' he said.

'But how did it happen, the miracle, did José Gregorio appear to you? The priest said you actually saw him.'

'It's nearly three o'clock in the morning, we really ought to be getting back.'

'But, Rafael . . .'

'The sicarios will all be drunk, and there'll be hoods in the street high on basuko, they just start shooting at anything and besides, the Twins have just walked in.'

Mills stood. 'I guess you've got a point there,' he said. 'Let's go.'

16

At breakfast the next morning Don Emillio turned to Mills.

'And how do your parents feel about your coming to our country?'

'That's a good question. I suppose I should write home.'

'And have you?'

'How could he possibly?' said Rafael. 'There's a national stamp shortage.'

'There is?' said Don Emi, not really believing his son, and embarrassed for his country, in front of their guest, if it were true.

'Yes. At Easter everyone sends cards,' he turned to Mills. 'They've run out of stamps again. It's ridiculous. It happens every year. You'd think the government would at least know the date for Easter. They only have to print more stamps. But no extra stamps were printed again. It's pathetic.'

'Is this true?' asked Don Emi of his son.

'Of course it's true. It's ridiculous. Typical of our rotten country.'

Don Emi scowled, a similar expression to the one Rafael had shown on his face at dinner last night, before they had become friends. It hurt Don Emi to see his son show his lack of love for his country. In Don Emi's books a young man's love for his country equated to his love for his father. The same kind of filial feelings were at work. He turned straight away to Mills.

'Then you must telephone,' he said. 'You must telephone your parents from here and assure them you are safe. If my son were in New York I would imagine every kind of menace.'

'And you'd probably be right,' said Mills.

Mills did want to call home, but not to speak to his parents. He wanted to speak to Jude. To test the water at the mansion he first asked to speak to his grandmother. The woman on the switchboard put him straight through to Catherine Sirteema.

'Oh, it's so great to hear from you. Your father's holed up with Elliot Hudson at the moment,' she said, 'but I know he'd be thrilled to hear from you. He'll be available, I'm told, in just half an hour. Can you call then or shall we call you back? You want to give me your number?'

'No,' said Mills. 'I want to speak to Grandma and to Jude. Are they there?'

'Can you hold?' said Catherine. 'I'll see.'

She came back on the line. 'Can you give me your number and I'll locate them?'

'I'll call back,' he said.

'Give me ten minutes,' said Catherine.

'Sure.'

In the moments before his call was expected there was frantic activity in the mansion. Four of them gathered in the Bunker Room: Catherine Sirteema, Dale Warnock, Dan Resnick and Elliot Hudson.

The new Bunker Room just about epitomised the atmosphere amongst the campaign staff now. Every office was swept for bugs twice a day, but this room had been designed to be impenetrable. Only a select few had swipe cards for it. It was stuffed with technology and it resembled, if anything, the cramped interior of a space station. It was deep down in the bowels of the mansion. The mansion was a hot-house of intrigue now; of distrust and internal dealing; sensing victory everyone was jockeying for position; thinking of their glorious futures. No-one trusted anyone. Their ranks had been swelled by security men of every shade: people who were getting off on the smell of power, and being in the national limelight. The organisation was becoming increasingly riddled with mavericks. Everyone was dreaming of the White House. It was only these four people, down in the bunker, who could keep the great ship on an even keel. And they knew it, they were bound together whether they liked it or not. Not one of them liked the other.

'Oh, Mills,' said Catherine Sirteema when he called, 'I'm real sorry about this but your grandma's still not located. So how's it going? You having a great trip?'

'Well, yes, it's interesting. You know I think I'm going to have a real story to tell when I get back.'

'That's great, that's really good Mills. And how is the weather?'

'It's weather,' he said. 'So how's Dad doing? What are his points like, happy?'

'We couldn't be more pleased with the way things are going. We won Iowa hands down, and New Hampshire looks pretty much going our way. Should be a landslide.'

'Okay, you got it Dan?' said Elliot Hudson sitting with him in a corner of the bunker.

'Yeah, we got it,' said Dan Resnick. 'Give me a couple of minutes to run it all through . . .'

He didn't really like this sort of thing. They'd put him in a tight spot professionally, but then he could always justify it. A father worried about his son. The security of the family. It'd be okay using such resources. Sure it would. And who would tell in any case?

Within a few minutes, while Catherine kept him talking, Dan Resnick had done his work. He was scratching his head and his arse at the same time.

'Well?' said Elliot Hudson.

'Well, it ain't diddly squat,' said Resnick. He looked long-sufferingly grave. 'It sure ain't diddly squat. The number's apparently known to us. It's in Envigado, Colombia.'

'Colombia! Fucking Colombia!?' said Hudson exploding, but keeping his voice down at the same time lest Mills should hear him on the line. He turned to look at Sirteema. 'Shit,' he said and held on to the corner of a desk. 'Colombia. It's the worst Goddamn country on earth.' He shook his head again and muttered, '*Colombia.*'

'And it's Envigado too,' said Resnick, brushing a stray grey hair from his nice new suit. 'Just about one of the worst towns in Colombia.'

'Shit,' said Hudson. 'Fucking shit.'

'Old Pablo Escobar's personal playground. More bad guys per square inch than any other place in the world. *Official.*'

Catherine was still stringing Mills along on the telephone. She'd seen Jude that morning in the Team Room with Grandma, and as usual he'd looked up at her to see if there was any news. He didn't ask any more, there was no need, his expression said it all.

'I guess he must be downtown,' she said in explanation to Mills. 'Maybe he's gone up to Lake Travis. Yeah, now I think about it he was going up there for the day with one of the volunteers.'

Mills went silent on the phone. His friend seemed to have settled into the life of the Wasps' Nest pretty well, and the campaign too; better than he had ever done.

'You want me to give him a message?' asked Catherine.

'No, no. No message,' said Mills sadly. After the activity of the last few days he suddenly realised that he was feeling lonely. It was time to move on from Don Emillio's house. For a brief time being down here had given him a certain freedom to connect with other people; most probably because he knew he'd only be with them briefly and there was no commitment required; beyond looking out for each other.

'Well, it's been great talking to you, Catherine,' he said finally.

'You want me to give your dad your best?'

'Whatever . . .' he said, and his voice trailed off.

'Why?' said Hudson, looking directly at Catherine Sirteema. 'Why's he there? Why didn't you tell me he would be there?' He dashed his hand against a whole sheaf of papers and sent them to the floor.

'Let's not overreact right off,' said Catherine. 'We don't even know who this Emillio Guzman character is. They could just be some decent family, couldn't they?'

'Well no, I'm afraid not,' said Dale Warnock, pleased to be flicking through his Deep Research notes again, having picked up on the name. 'Don Emillio Guzman is one of the richest men in Colombia. Anything on him, Dan?'

'Queer, ain't it?' said Resnick. 'We got diddly squat. The cleaner they are down there, the deeper they must be in.'

'Well I got something,' said Dale Warnock. 'Thought I recognised the name. I have it on the best information that he's a major funder of the Hernández outfit. So whatcha got on that then, Danny boy?'

Resnick was momentarily offended by this amateur pressman's familiarity, but he let it pass. He let it pass because he did have something. These two were playing tennis too.

'When it comes to the drug cartels,' he said with authority, 'they like nothing better than to destabilise the government in Bogota. The weaker the government is the more they can get away with all their tricks. And sure as hell these Hernández riots have destabilised the Venezuelan government already. I guess there's folks, like our Mr Emillio Guzman, who'd kinda like to see it spread over there as well. And there ain't nothing moves faster than a grass fire when it's dry.'

'Shit,' said Hudson. 'Oh God, shi-it. We got to do something now. These motherfuckers are trying to break everything down between the Colombian administration and our own. I just can't countenance Mills even having a whiff of that about him. It could cost us very badly. All Dionne Frigging Mary-Belle McKenzie did was to get knocked up. Our fucking kid is trying to knock-up US Latin American Foreign policy, for fucksakes. What y'all got to say about that?'

'Let's just calm ourselves,' said Catherine. 'Let's take this piece by piece.' In this hot-bed of office paranoia, she was determined to remain level.

'I want that kid out of Colombia and back in the bosom of his family by the end of the week,' said Hudson. 'I want him in a white suit standing next to his dad waving to the crowd. It's your department, Sirteema.'

'Okay, okay,' said Catherine. 'But let's do it gentle. Let's get him out of his own accord, or at least get him away from these people – the chances are they know who he is and are just using him – let's get him visiting art galleries and having a regular vacation. Let's get him interested in pre-Columbian art, let's getting him trekking, white water rafting, for God sakes. Anything.'

When Mills returned to the table in the courtyard Don Emillio had gone into his office, but Rafael was still sitting there in the morning sunshine.

'Let's go and see something of the town,' he said. 'You want to go for a stroll, walk off our hangovers?'

'Sure,' said Mills.

Marta passed under the portico, her head held high. She'd been disappointed by her handsome American. She wanted more than anything, this morning, to talk to her father about the possibility of employing a hit man, like Rafael said the Twins did. Mills had hardly talked to her last night. He deserved to have his tongue torn out. She took the stairs to the upper gallery, the tinkling sound of her Walkman still audible as she dissolved into the shade.

'Let's go,' said Rafael.

They picked up a bodyguard from out front and went off for their walk around town in Rafael's BMW.

The town looked different this morning without the glare of neon and the thud of nightclubs trying to outdo each other. The designer shops were doing brisk business with the rich young kids of the town. People sat out at pavement cafes talking into mobile phones.

No-one was being gunned down by teenagers on motorbikes with sub-machine guns. It was a perfectly lovely day.

They drove a little way out of town, where the villas were set further apart and the homes had sweeping lawns with black vultures silently picking about on them, like garden ornaments; they gave the impression that they were hopeful of something dreadful about to happen, as vultures do. They looked like the bored secret-service men of the avain world.

There'd been a sudden downpour that morning and the grass, and everything, glistened perfectly.

They got out of the car.

'Let's take a walk in here,' said Rafael, leading him through an archway with a cross on top, and angels smeared with mildew on either side. It was one of the town's many cemeteries, and packed with elaborate tombs; there was barely the room to squeeze between them. Each one was like a little chapel or a house.

'Interesting place, isn't it?' said Rafael. 'It took me some time to ask what it was after I got my sight back. I thought maybe it was a little town the capos had built for midgets to live in. Look at the inscriptions.'

Mills tried to read the Spanish, but it defeated him. The dates he could understand, they were all recent and they were all of young men between the ages of sixteen and about twenty-three.

'These are the tombs of the sicarios that my sister says don't exist in Envigado any more. I guess there must be someone living here who exaggerates even more than I do and, at certain expense to himself, has had to construct all of these tombs to back up his lies.'

There was no love lost between brother and sister.

They passed a tomb that had been fitted with a sound-system, and a cable ran across the other tombs like a washing line to power it. Heavy metal music thumped and fizzed from the damp sodden speakers inside. The young man, Fernando Maria Ortiz, could not have been resting in peace. The soil around his grave vibrated as if his coffin was being inched back up to the surface by the heavy bass rhythms of Black Sabbath.

'What does the inscription say?' asked Mills.

'My mother gave me the gift of life, and I gave her all my eternal love and a refrigerator. Rock'n'Roll Forever.'

'Bizarre.'

'Yes.'

'So,' said Mills, 'I see why you wanted to bring me here.'

'You do?'

'Yes I do. You wanted to prove to me that what you said last night is true. That it wasn't just the drink talking.'

Rafael began to smile. And then he laughed to be caught out.

'Yes, exactly. I'm tired of talking about the *milagro*. But I guess you want to know? Yes?'

'Yes, I do.'

'Why? Why are you so interested?'

They passed a woman of about forty, dressed in black, tending the tomb of her young son. She had brought a small plastic washing-up bowl, and as she washed down the tiles with a soapy sponge she read the inscription again and again until she was on the edge of tears.

'Well?' said Rafael.

'Who knows?' said Mills, but he felt that the gravity of the place demanded more of an answer than that. 'I've never really been interested in anything in my life,' he said. 'I love books, I love reading, I like to get lost in their small interior worlds. But my parents kinda bashed any interest in real things out of me when I was a very young kid.'

They passed four grave-diggers taking a rest. It was getting too hot in the day now for physical work. A part of the walled cemetery had been taken down to extend it into the field beyond. A young bull, with a disconsolate face, had got in through the breach.

'You never really told me how you got your sight back?' said Mills.

'Well,' said Rafael, taking a breath. 'There are operations now that are restoring sight to some blind people,' he said. 'And the operation they performed on me was along those lines. So you make up your own mind about its miraculous side.'

'So why have they selected you, among all the hundreds that claim miracles, to be the one the Vatican investigates?'

'They are investigating two.'

'Yes, but from what I read in Father Leonardo's notes, the other was in 1964 and it was investigated at the time. The file's closed on that one, now they just need you,' he said. 'Two proven miracles and he's a saint is the way it was explained to me.'

But they both knew, without saying, why he'd been selected. It was because he was young and articulate, the son of a rich and important family. He wasn't some elderly lady whose testimony could become shaky with religious fervour. If anything, Rafael struck you as something of an agnostic. He was a credible witness. Mills felt some sympathy for him, and drew some parallels with himself.

'You've done your homework, I see,' said Rafael. You've visited the shrine, haven't you?'

'Yes.'

'I loved the stained glass. It was one of the first things they took me to see when my eyesight was restored. Imagine! Taking me to see modern stained glass! It's barely intelligible to the perfectly sighted.' Rafael laughed.

Mills didn't believe for a moment that Rafael was fabricating any of his story. He seemed a very direct man. Almost obsessively so. His sister was more blind than he, when it came to what was true and what was false. She couldn't see what was under her nose here in Envigado. Couldn't or wouldn't.

Rafael lit up a small cigarillo, it would have seemed disrespectful in any graveyard other than this with its heavy metal music. Mills lit up a Marlboro.

As Mills blew his smoke away, distracted by a large black bird in one of the trees, he looked up. It was mid-morning, the weather perfect, the sky as clear as a newly cleaned pool.

'I'll tell you what I did last night when I lay down to go to sleep,' said Mills.

'That was?' said Rafael.

'I took the crucifix down from the wall above my bed and held it and said: "José Gregorio, please let me see you tonight. Just let me dream about you. Come and tell me what to do if your hand is really at my back."'

'And you saw him?'

The bird flew out of the tree and took a swooping flight above them.

'No,' he said. 'I didn't see him. I woke up so disappointed. What does he look like?'

Rafael nodded his head, pulled out his glasses and polished them.

'I was under anaesthetic of course, when he appeared to me. Now you think that might not count. But there's the oddest thing about it.'

'I'm sure there is.'

He laughed. 'Not having seen anything since I was five, I couldn't possibly have known what he looked like from pictures of course.'

'No, I suppose not.'

'And when they took me into the operating theatre I was not

only blind but unconscious. After I came round there were bandages still on my eyes. The doctors thought I was asleep but I heard them telling my father that, as they had predicted, the operation had not been a success, that I would never see. At that point I reached out and found my father's hand which was resting on my arm, and I said, "But I can see". "What do you mean?" they said. I said that I had woken up in the middle of the operation. They said I hadn't. I said, "Yes I did, I saw the new surgeon come into the operating theatre and take the other surgeon's hand and say, no, not like this, and gently guide the laser." "What new surgeon?" they asked, "there were just two of us". "No, three," I said. "The third surgeon, the one with the moustache and the deep brown eyes. I saw him take the first surgeon's hand and move it, and I heard him say, 'Now he will see.'" There was dead silence. And then the first surgeon said, "What did he look like?" and I knew his voice to be that surgeon. I said, "You have freckles on your face, ginger freckles." I could hear them all breathing in deeply in the silence. How could a blind boy have known that from touch? Then I heard that surgeon sit down and exhale. "It's true," he said. "During the operation I felt someone take my hand and guide it. There was a moment of blankness in my mind," he admitted later, "all I could hear in my head were the words 'now he will see', with exactly the same intonation as you had repeated those words after the operation."'

Mills was absolutely silent.

'Then the second surgeon said to me, "So if you saw this so-called third surgeon, you must have seen the operating theatre too." I said I had. After the doctor with the moustache said I would see I looked all around me, and I saw the operating theatre. "So maybe you'd like to describe it to us while it's still fresh in your memory," the surgeon said to me. I didn't like the sound of his voice, he suddenly no longer sounded like a doctor, and I could hear what he was thinking. He was thinking that there was no way a boy who'd been blind since five could possibly describe something as alien and complex as an operating theatre. But I did. I described it down to the last detail, still with the bandages on my eyes. Every piece of equipment, even the students who were standing around. Two days later when my bandages were removed the surgeons came scuttling back. I had the beginnings of sight.'

Mills nodded. 'What was José Gregorio like?'

'He struck me as a rather impatient sort of chap. Wanted everyone to get on with everything.'

'Have you seen him again?'

'No, but then I've got so many other things to see now, haven't I?'

Mills drew a breath. 'And the two surgeons concerned have testified to all of this?'

'Oh yes. They were quite astonished. They had me back in the hospital of course, because the surgeon with the freckles was convinced he'd made a slip up during the op. It turned out, of course, that José Gregorio had been absolutely right about that small detail. It made all the difference they say. His command of the new technology was exemplary. I don't understand the details myself. Eyes are pretty delicate things. But it makes all the difference, apparently. They reckon it'll soon become standard procedure. Something of an innovation.'

'But how does it make you feel about life? Doesn't an experience like that make you think on an entirely different plane to the rest of us? I know it would me.'

'No, I don't think it would. You can have no idea what it takes to change a person's mind about things. With miracles, which I guess are God's operations after all, I think He kind of gives you a bit of an anaesthetic as well, but afterwards. He doesn't want those he blesses to have to suffer the brunt of the mystery of grace, does he?'

'Doesn't he?'

'No, I don't think so. If anything, now I can see the place I live in; in this shocking disgusting town, I would rather not have certain facets to experience that ordinary vision gives.'

'After all of this you call the gift of sight *ordinary vision*?'

'Yes, that's exactly what I call it.'

There was a commotion behind them, and a woman began screaming. The black bird flew away. It was the bereaved mother who was cleaning her son's tomb. The young bull that had got in through the breach in the wall was lurching and dipping its horns towards her as she screamed hysterically.

They watched, frozen for a moment, as did the young grave-diggers. The woman threw herself against the iron grille of the door that opened onto the sanctuary within her son's tiled tomb.

The bull hoofed at the rubbly ground as she pulled at the iron grille and broke it open. She squatted in there, cowering under the low ceiling and shrieking as the bull prepared to thrust his horns through the metal bars and into her. The bull was young and angry, confused not to be in the simplicity of his field. He was furious about being involuntarily caught in this small, cluttered town of tombs; of undersized houses; he felt as if he must be a giant; so mighty.

Then a clod of earth, catapulted from the spade of one of the young grave-diggers, hit him on the side of the head.

He turned his nostrils up to the air, snorted and turned; beginning to break into a canter, which in bulls looks like an almost equestrian effeminacy. His muscle-bound body went careering into the monuments, dislodging their saints and angels, and sound systems, as he looked, disorientated, for the breach in the wall.

They drove back to Don Emillio's house in silence.

'May I make another call?' Mills asked when he got there.

He called the mansion again and got through, this time, to his grandmother.

'Well, you son of a bitch,' she said. 'So where have you run off to this time?'

'What's the mood of my folks?' he asked.

'It ain't good,' she said. 'We're planning a lynching.'

'I guessed you would be. Where's Jude?'

'Not with you?'

'With me?'

'He's gone haring off, but don't tell anyone.'

Mills laughed, his grandmother was drunk, as she liked to be before lunch.

'Where? Where has he gone, Grandma?'

'Don't ask me,' she said. 'I just give him the money out of my handbag.'

'So he's gone back to Oxford?'

'I got a bit of paper,' she said, her voice coming and going on the line as she flailed about with the telephone receiver. 'A funny place,' she said. 'Looking for you.'

'And whose idea was that, Mom and Dad's?'

'Don't think so. We've been sitting out on the porch together, he's a good kid, so I helped him out with a bit of cash.'

Mills steeled himself. 'Grandma, please, try to find the piece of paper.'

'He's gone to the Amazon, he said.'

Mills was silenced for a moment. 'He has?'

'Hang on, hang on, I think I got it.' He could hear lot of fumbling through handbag noises coming down the phone.

'Nope,' she said, 'thought I did but now I haven't.' Grandma's handbag was always bulging with dollar bills, she hated going to the bank. He could hear her turning everything out onto a glass-topped table.

'Come on Grandma, where did he go?'

'Left this lunchtime,' she said. 'You only just missed him.'

'But where?'

'He took a flight to Bogota.'

'Bogota? Then where?'

There was silence on the line for a while and then he heard the sound of chuckling, and a hoarse old smoker's cough.

'I got it,' she said at last. 'I got the piece of paper. You want me to read it?'

'Yeah, I want you to read it.'

'He said for me to read it if you called. Says this,' she said, and there was another gap on the line as she tried to interpret the scribble.

'Says: "Tell Mills I'm at the end of his journey". That's all it says.'

'That's what it says?'

'That's what it says. You know where that is?'

'Shit,' said Mills. 'I know where it is.'

He had a vision of his friend wandering around the Amazonian town mentioning his name to everyone he met.

Before Mills left Envigado he asked to see Don Emillio and met with him in the long gallery around the table they had eaten at the previous night.

'Something has come up,' said Mills. 'And I wonder if I could ask you a very large favour.'

'Of course,' said Don Emillio, 'it will be my absolute pleasure.'

Mills explained to him about the worries he had about the notes that Father Leonardo had given him, and told him the real reason for his coming to his house; it hadn't been to meet his son at all. Now that he'd met him, of course, things were different, and he promised to do all that he could.

'But,' he said, 'I think I have misjudged a friend. My friend Jude is on his way to Leticia, and I have to find him there.'

'Leticia?' said Don Emilio, shaking his head. 'How can I help you?'

'I'll pay you back,' said Mills, 'but can I borrow some money? Cash. So that I don't have to use my cards or travellers' cheques; cash is the only way I can preserve my anonymity.'

'It is,' said Don Emi, laughing and smiling broadly. 'This is no problem. You want to leave now? We will organise the flight. We will make sure you are safe.'

17 ∫

It was mid-afternoon when a taxi pulled into the main square of a small dusty town six miles from the Colombian western Pacific coast. The square had a neat white church, its bell ringing mournfully to celebrate some local atrocity. The taxi driver was having an altercation with his passenger. The driver was insisting that his passenger get out.

The passenger glared at him. What did he mean get out? The guy had agreed to take him all the way to the coast.

But this is now the way it is, the driver told him. That was then and this is now. It was way back at the airport I agreed to take you all the way to the coast, he said. Taxi drivers agree to anything at airports, didn't he know that? Was he born yesterday?

I'm this close, the passenger said to himself, I'm this close to snapping the bastard's fat neck. Did *he* know *that?*

The taxi driver explained that he was only protected this far, beyond here they'd be pulled off the road at gunpoint by the local collective. They were the only ones who could run a taxi service to the coast. Who did he think he was, Pancho Villa?

Leave them to me, the passenger wanted to say, leave this collective to me. But for the sake of the overall good of his task here he had to accept it. He was dressed as a kind of ageing drop-out as well, what he called California clothes. They were too loose and casual, there was no constriction to them, nothing to bite into the flesh a little. He'd sooner be in his own jeep too, but it was better to travel anonymously, even if it meant being constantly ripped off by this sub-human species of cheap racketeers.

The new taxi was nothing but an open backed Dodge truck,

onto which the enterprising locals had lashed a garden shed with ropes. It had been waiting for him across the square. The shed was windowless and had been fitted out with benches like the pews of a church. He was the only passenger except for the pig upfront with the driver. He hung on to the underside of the bench in the windowless shed as the truck took the bends of the coastal road. As the road got rougher he found himself being thrown about and his box of tricks skidded across the floor of the shed. He banged on the wall behind the driver's head and shouted: *why don't you let the fucking pig drive?*

When they arrived he staggered out into the light, staring back at the shed as it performed a reckless 'U' turn and shot off back to the town, leaving him with just the laconic silence of the place and the smell of tyre-rubber as it burned on the dirt-track road.

He pulled his hat down over his face, put on his Polaroid sunglasses, and rubbed his hand over his upper lip.

He looked about him. There wasn't much to the place, just the one stretch of squalid huts running along the beach front. An awful stench was blowing up, and it seemed as if an unseen power was lifting the dust from the road in fistfuls, and throwing it into his face. He spat on the ground, it was so hot he expected it to sizzle on the dirt track.

The place was called Zipatola, an Indian name which meant 'killer beach'. The surf could get up to thirty five feet high. Anyone attempting to swim out more than twenty yards had the choice of being crushed to death by a wave as it pounded them into the shingle, or, if they got beyond it, being swept out by the evil current to a point of no return; getting themselves washed up dead and bloated on the Playa del Amour a mile down the coast. Ruining everyone's beach party.

Then there were the rip tides; formed where the returning surf crashed from right and left into deep gulleys in the sand, doubling its strength. Even people walking idly in the surf could be suddenly dragged into the damning sea as the sand and shingle were torn relentlessly from beneath them. There one moment, enjoying the sunset, gone the next.

The stray dogs that haunted the bars in packs went nowhere near the water's edge and they wore a look of resignation on their faces for those that did. They'd seen too many of their compatriots dragged howling away.

He set himself down behind a dune that was scattered with old oil drums, took out a small pair of field glasses and surveyed the beach front.

Zipatola had been the haunt of New Age travellers for the last ten years. They tipped up there, dirty and unshaven with disintegrating back-packs to rent hammocks on the beach. They lived by bumming cigarettes and boiling black beans on just a few pesos a day. It was the very end of the line for many of them who had been wasting away on the great South American trek. They had begun with the excitements of Canaima and the Angel Falls, with the Llanos and the vast wastes of pampas grass blowing in the wind; the coypus splashing about in the swamps; the sloths, the anteaters, the splendours of Macchu Picchu, and the vistas of the magical, breathless, High Andes. Finally many of them crashed-out here in a Colombian wasteland amid the misfits of the world in a drug-induced stupor. For money they made attempts at selling jewellery to each other that they'd fashioned out of shells and sea-rolled brown beer bottle glass. They sat on the beach all day, stoned, twirling lengths of wire, swapping bits of 'amber', and gazing blankly at the waves.

A small town had grown up around them; just a couple of beach bars; a thatch-covered disco that had lost half its dancefloor to the spring tides, and on the rock above the beach there was a quasi-Buddhist commune that dominated the skyline with panoplies of palm, and ringing wind chimes. On the surface it looked idyllic, a hidden haven where for hundreds of years buccaneers had beached for fresh water and better times.

It was a place beyond the law; and that had its attractions for the travellers. The greatest of which was that they could go naked here, and that was almost a point of honour among them. The locals capitalised on this and in the nearby town of Puerto Antonio they advertised daily trips to *See the nudi people!* It was as if the travellers had now become an exotic tribe themselves, to be viewed on excursions by the locals. Some of them even bought their beer bottle craft works. But the offer to see the nudi people was mostly taken up by the local business men who paraded along the beach every afternoon wearing reflective sunglasses.

He quickly checked the clients of one of the beach bars, and ordered a *refresco*. He wiped the sweat from his forehead with his sleeve.

The surf was in a mighty fury. He looked at the local accommodation: rows of hammocks slung from poles that had been driven into the sand.

The sun was just beginning to get lower in the sky, a swipe of brilliant orange already lay behind the Buddhist temple on the rock above, setting the thatch of its domes and parapets in dramatic relief.

He began a recce along the beach. The hippies looked so sorrowfully lethargic it gave the impression that a bloodless slaughter had taken place. Those who moved were like the walking wounded.

He stopped by a group of three people who were staring out to sea.

'Hi there you guys,' he said.

'Look at those poor suckers,' said one of them, with glazed eyes, wearing nothing but flip-flops.

He turned towards the sea and could just make out a couple of heads bobbing away, a quarter of a mile out, beyond the big waves, slowly moving out of view.

'What gives?' he asked.

'Like, they're drowning, man. They gone beyond the big crashers and they just ain't getting back. They'll, like, never get back now.'

He stared at the two figures in the sea as they struggled helplessly and waved for help.

The girl offered him a toke on her joint. He took it and handed it back. 'Anybody doing anything about it?' he asked.

'There's a lifeboat, I guess,' said the guy.

He looked again as the figures waved wearily to the beach. They didn't look like people, their heads were going under, there were just their arms plunging in and out of the water. They looked like sea birds swooping for fish.

'So, we just stand and watch?' he said.

They looked at him blankly. 'Well, like, what do you suggest? They should know not to go beyond the crashers. It's death for certain beyond there.'

'Is that so. Is that so really?'

'They should know better.'

He looked along the beach. People were sitting up on their haunches, watching and smoking as if it were afternoon TV. Just by them there was a boat with peeling police livery painted on the side. Two Colombian officers were sitting by it, their heads hunched over a backgammon board. They were the official presence of the lack of law, a Colombian notion often difficult for the visitor to quite understand.

'There's a couple of cops over there, why don't they take the boat out?' One of the policemen smacked a backgammon piece around the board and the other sighed with irritation.

'Guess they don't want to get it wet,' said the guy.

'The police don't do much round here I guess.'

'No. We just got the two, they're okay. They don't do nothing, it's cool.' Things couldn't be better, almost paradise.

'Well I guess we could get some kind of a team together ourselves and go out and save those guys.'

'Yeah, that'd be really something.'

They watched as a towering seventh wave crashed its mighty fist down and spat pebbles and rocks out of the white water.

'Man, did you see that one? That one was a real *mother.*'

'Sure was something.'

'I reckon,' said the guy, 'if we all went in together and like, kinda held hands, we'd get to them.'

'Yeah,' the other two agreed. 'But maybe we'd all be washed away, huh?'

'We could, like, rope ourselves to people on the beach. Like attach ourselves maybe to one of the beach bars?'

'Neat.'

'Or we could lash some planks together, make a sort of shield against the surf, or a raft . . .'

'That's an awesome idea.'

'Yeah,' said the girl. 'Like if it was chimpanzees out there, or maybe elephants . . . I mean, a troop of apes would do something, or a herd of elephants. They help their own, don't they?'

'Yeah.'

The next group of people along had lost interest now and

were building a sand castle, aimlessly pushing a mound of sand together with their feet.

The swimmers were now just naked dots.

He walked on. None of these people deserved to live out the rest of the afternoon.

It was a beautiful late afternoon, almost viciously so, with an indigo and vermilion sky, a clear already risen moon, and the sun still hanging in the casuarina trees above the rock. He looked out to sea again. The water was pink and milky.

The dots had gone.

He walked on his way to check-out the rock above on which stood the town's only hotel. There was a kid on the desk.

'I want to see your register,' he said.

'I'm sorry sir?'

'Give me the register.'

'I can't do that.'

'I think you'll find you can.'

'Why?'

'I'm looking for an international political activist who is a threat to the security of the state.'

At first the boy smiled, and then he became uneasy.

'In what name?' he asked.

'Mills Clearwater.'

'Oh,' he said. 'Yes. We know.'

'What do you know?'

'The German boy with the dreadlocks. He tried to cash a travellers' cheque but he didn't have identification. So he paid cash.'

'You didn't do anything about it?'

'No. It's common here. Stolen cheques are common.'

'Where is this boy?'

'On the beach I guess.'

He went back down to the beach. People were beginning to gather up their things and were heading for their hammocks or the bars, or the disco with the walls lurching towards the sea.

He got himself a beer and stared at the sea as the white foam was illuminated by the burning torches of the bars, and the fires the hippies were lighting.

The he saw two figures, two naked figures, pulling themselves exhausted out of the surf. One of them was a young guy with dreadlocks. His beer bottle stopped at his lips, his muscles suddenly tense and keen.

It had taken an hour or more, while the sun went down, but somehow those naked dots from earlier had fought their way back, through the big crashers to the shore. He watched as the one with the dreadlocks laid his hand on the other guy's shoulder. They turned to each other and laughed helplessly for a moment. Then they shook hands, rather formally for two men who'd been drowning together, kicking their heels in the surf, as if they were daring the rip tides to take them back in again. He watched as the kid walked up the beach, picking up his clothes, towards the bar where he was sitting.

He smiled quietly to himself.

The boy took a beer from the bar and steadily drank it down, he looked pretty pleased with himself. When he'd drunk it he got up and began walking along the beach, towards the rocks, where it was dark and quiet.

He followed and watched as the boy climbed up onto a set of rocks that stuck out into the surf and pulled a ready-rolled joint from his pocket. He followed him up onto the rock.

'Hi there,' he said casually. 'You picked yourself a neat spot.'

Tomas looked at him and mumbled a 'sure'. He assumed that the guy was looking for some dope.

'Been here long?'

'Three days.'

'So where's the action?'

'Draw, you mean?'

'Whatever.'

'It looks like it's pretty casual all over.' He didn't really want to but he passed the man the joint he was smoking. He couldn't not.

'So you been travelling a while?'

'Couple of weeks.'

'Travelling on your own?'

'Yes.'

'Pretty tough on your own I bet.' He took a toke and handed it back.

'Yeah, it can get tough.'

'You'd think it'd be easy to hook up with other travellers.'

'Well, I did for a bit.'

'Oh yeah?'

'Yeah. We had a truly terrible time crossing the border. I've never been so scared, thought I was going to die.'

'He didn't come down here with you?'

'No.'

'That's too bad. So where'd he go on to?'

'I think he must have gone down south, he said he might. But it's rough country down there. I wanted to come here, I reckon it's one of the only safe places in Colombia. Beautiful too.'

'Yeah, probably is.' He looked out to sea. 'Where'd he go exactly?'

'Why d'you want to know? It matters?'

'Uh huh, it matters a great deal to me. Where'd he go?'

'I told you, probably a town down south.'

'You didn't say which town though. You want me to write it on a piece of paper for you?' He laid his index finger on Tomas's chest and slowly pushed him back onto the rock. His finger began scribbling out words as he spoke. *'Which town did Mills go to, my German friend?'*

'You know his name . . .' said Tomas in a low, frightened voice.

'It ain't such a hard name to recall. So are you going to tell me and we'll be friends, or do you want us to fall out over this already?'

'I just . . . I just don't see why you want to know . . .' Tomas's mind was racing. He'd felt so relaxed here on the beach, now he was in a panic again. Mills had managed to disappear at last, with his connivance. This was probably the journalist that he'd been trying to give the slip, or was it someone working for the Venezuelan government? It had all back-fired on him. This had to have something to do with the trip to Isnotu. Please God the guy didn't know he was there as well.

He was close to him now, leaning over him as he knelt on the rock. He heard a click and felt the sensation of something cold and pointed at his side, just at the base of his rib-cage.

'Okay, okay,' said Tomas. 'I'll tell you, just don't knife me, please don't hurt me.'

'That's better, so where?'

'He went to Envigado . . .'

'Oh, come on, my man, some precision please,' he pierced the boy's skin with just the tip of his knife. 'You underestimate my seriousness about this matter.'

'I don't, I don't, please . . .'

The knife was twisted a little, just to irritate. As the boy screamed with pain the man held a hand over his mouth, and at the same time smashed his head against the rock. Blood was flowing now down Tomas's side, and down the back of his head. His eyes were wide with fear.

He felt the pressure of the boy's screaming subside beneath his hand. He sighed with relief. This was exactly as it should be; first they scream after they register the pain, and then the real fear sets in and grips them tight like young petals around a bud, then they're silent. Silent as a forming bud.

'Where's he going?'

Tomas had barely any voice. 'He talked about the Amazon, I don't know where.'

'Well that's a pretty big river.'

'I don't know.'

The boy was trying to sob now. His fear was so complete that it was clear that if he had known he would be telling him. He forgave him for that, he patently didn't know. He absolved him of this sin.

He pulled the knife away.

'Well, thanks for doing business with me,' he said.

'Thank you . . .' Tomas muttered.

Then he slid the knife slowly under the boy's rib-cage, placing his hand over his mouth again, until he went silent, and the pressure of his breath grew soft against his palm.

He relaxed and stubbed out the boy's joint. He sat for a moment with the moonlight on his face, then he rolled the boy over so that he tumbled off the rock and into the sea where the waves crashed white and perfect with their foam smashing against the rock.

Down to the Colombian Amazon, he thought.

PART 3

The Amazon In Flood

18

Leticia was a river trading town down in the furthest flung part of Colombia in a corridor of empty rain forest jungle that had been captured from Peru, with great loss of life, in the nineteen thirties. It was Colombia's only port on the Amazon, the place where all the base-cocaine grown along the river in Peru enters the country for processing in the 'laboratories' hidden in the surrounding jungle. No-one really has any business being there other than a specialist chemist.

Just a fortnight before, a journalist who had been asking questions around town had been shot dead in the street by sicarios riding Suzukis. All Americans were regarded as probable DEA agents, and all Brits as members of the SAS or MI6 training and advising the Colombian Security Service: the DAS. All this added to the particular atmosphere of the town.

Jude arrived by Fokker from Bogota at eleven in the morning. He'd had a two-day wait for the flight in Bogota, sitting impatiently in a cheap hotel and going for strolls around the beautiful city, blissfully impervious to the danger on the streets. In fact Bogota had been rather quiet due to the presence of the Farc guerillas out in the suburbs who'd thrown a cordon around the city, effectively laying seige. The president, fearful for his life, hadn't emerged from his underground bunker in over a month.

Jude hadn't bargained on the fact that there would be only two departures a week for Leticia. He'd expected to have arrived there a great deal sooner and wondered now if Mills was even there, and hadn't already returned home, crossing him in the air.

When Jude arrived the Amazon was in flood and had risen fifteen metres, flooding the bankside villages. The ramshackle restaurants were submerged up to their tin roofs, the enamelled Pepsi-Cola signs glowering under the moody swirling waters, many of them a few hundred yards out in the river away from the sand-bagged bankside. Some people said it was the melting of the polar ice-caps that caused the tremendous rise in the Amazon these days, others that it was the deforestation. The water just came rushing down from high up in the Andes with no trees to draw up the volume of the torrent. Thousands of square miles of the forest were flooded.

It made a moody river doubly severe, and impossibly vast. Even there, one and a half thousand miles from its mouth, it was three miles wide. It was an incredible sight.

In the summer the river was a characteristic orange colour, but now, the water was black.

Jude stared down at the river from the vantage of the mud and duckboard street where the taxi from the airstrip had dropped him. The Fokker from Bogota had stopped at isolated jungle strips before landing.

He walked along the main street where the hotels stood. They were rather faded looking places, stuffed with plants and with mildew on the walls. He breathed in the equatorial atmosphere, dank and musty, but was pleased, very pleased to be there. From the plane as they flew in it had been nothing but an endless spread of green, with the great black river winding through it like an exhausted worm dying on Astro-turf. You could get no sense of the scale of the Amazon from up there, and you got even less on the ground. This was the place where all of Mills's pencil journeys in his atlases led him to. He'd showed the town to him several times before on maps back in The Stables. It had possessed his imagination; the place on the edge of nowhere, where the dark Amazonian back-waters began, and river tributaries were still to be named. The maps were blank for hundreds and hundreds of miles. The nether reaches of the Amazon. A place of 'real anonymity'. A place where even his father's publicity-obsessed minders couldn't track him.

Two teenage boys came running up to him, clutching a photograph. One of them grabbed him by the arm.

'Señor!' he shouted. 'You want to buy my picture. Picture of a big anaconda. Very big snake.'

It was an odd thing to want to sell. He looked at the picture. The anaconda was about thirty foot long and pictured, black and shiny, where it had just been pulled from the river. A group of people were standing proudly around brandishing poles with hooks at the end.

'It's a big snake,' he agreed. 'But I don't want to buy it.'

'But look, look, señor! Look at the big lump.'

A third of the way down the snake's length there was a bulge.

'So?'

'Person inside!' said the teenager excitedly. 'He swallowed a nine-year-old boy.'

Jude shook his head and walked on. They followed for a short while and then tired of him.

The sun was falling through the breaks in the slowly moving cloud and he watched the people making their way up from the river on duckboards, straining with the weight of heavy loads of catfish or alligator skins slung over their shoulders. He watched the nuns in their tropical white habits walking purposefully across the square to the bleached concrete church streaked with green-growing damp, its steeple cheerily decked out with coloured fairy lights. He couldn't wait to find Mills. Mills would be so astonished to see him. It was going to be a great moment.

He walked into the first hotel, the Paradiso. It was a fine looking place with individual thatched-roofed rooms set around a pool. It had been built for the rich Colombians from Bogota who wanted to come down here to make trips to see the Indians. Everything was perfect, the pool, the palapas and the lounge chairs. The noise of the street was muffled by the palm fronds. But the place seemed deserted. As he looked closer at the tables around the bar he saw the moss that was growing on them, and the bar itself wasn't stocked and a large spider had woven its web from the shelf that once had held the optics. The only guests now were bats and tarantulas.

Jude heard a voice and a security guard came striding over, his hand on his revolver.

'Oh hello,' Jude said. 'I'm looking for a friend, I wondered if he was staying here,' trying to shield his unease about the gun.

'No, señor. Your friend is not staying here.'

'Well, he could be, um . . .'

'I have told you, señor, your friend is not staying here. You must go.' The guard glared at him and moved his hand slowly up to the hilt of his revolver. It was an act he was so unused to that he found himself staring.

Jude pulled himself together and walked steadily out of the place without looking back. He went a little way down the street. Soldiers in full combat gear were leaning on the corners chewing gum and spitting into the mud. The whole town was a jungle fortress; more troops than inhabitants. Boat loads of Brazilian tarts came up river in the evenings. On the outskirts there were armed men in watch towers, he'd seen them on the way in from the airstrip. Automatic weapons poked out from sand-bagged emplacements at the side of the road. Spent ordnance lay in the gutter.

All the food was hauled in by cargo boat, tired and tasteless. Anyone half respectable went to bed by nine. The people dealt in fish, in cement, in money exchange. There was often the sound of gunshots. It was a place known as the home of drug traffickers and had a reputation for being riddled with informants, DEA agents, and opportunists. At lunchtime soldiers slept beneath the trees after a night patrol on the river, and black vultures sat in the branches above them shitting on their helmets.

Jude looked into the darkness of a shack he was passing. Several men were drunk inside and throwing darts at a live mouse on the floor. They'd disabled its back legs with an elastic band. This was not what he'd imagined from Mills's maps. There were no other tourists in the street at all. He'd been the only one on the Fokker, and now he was feeling uneasy, and anxious to see Mills as quickly as possible.

But he'd seen this sort of cruelty, he reminded himself, and now he'd need all those survival skills that he'd learned on the Kidbrook Estate as a teenager. There were drug dealers there too, and walking the deck-developments after dark was to run a gamut of evil characters willing to do you harm just for looking at them. Just for being there sometimes. He tried to smile at the sad irony that substances which began their life here ended up back home in his own mother's veins.

Jude was, by necessity, a great deal tougher than his bookish and solitary manner suggested. The darkness of dangerous streets frightened him, but he had a sense at least of how to navigate them. He wondered how his friend Mills could be faring in this atmosphere which no doubt would be decidedly alien to him.

He was hungry, and was beginning to shake with the lack of food.

He turned into a restaurant. Again, the place was absolutely deserted. It also had rooms for tourists, but there was no sign of any guests there either.

He sat there for ten minutes before another guard, this time with a kind of sawn-off shotgun, came and stood in front of him.

'I guess you're closed too,' he said, trying not to look too nervous.

'Yes, sir,' said the guard. 'We are closed. Very closed indeed. You are American?'

'English.'

'I am learning English,' he said, and broke into a smile. 'It's a good thing to know. Pick up properly expressions from the visitors and then all is hunky-dory and ding-dong.'

Jude smiled back. The man might have had an unnerving looking gun but he seemed quite pleasant with it. Just a tool of the trade, like a swagger stick.

'You are visiting to us here on our river?'

'Yes, I'm visiting.'

'This is an excellent thing.'

'It would be if I could find somewhere to stay.'

The guard began laughing, rocking his head back. 'Have you considered Peru? Or maybe Brazil,' he said.

'Why is everywhere closed? The other hotel I went into was closed.'

'The Paradiso?'

'Yes, I think that was it.'

'Ah, yes. It's closed.' He lit a cigarette and offered Jude the pack. He took one.

'It was a great hotel,' he continued. 'Owned by a young

American entrepreneur. Visitors used to come to stay at his hotel all the time. But then, *phew.* He's gone. Gone to a jail in Miami. All banged-up for certainly. Throw away the bloody key.'

'What for?'

The guard registered surprise and blew out his smoke awkwardly, as if he hadn't been smoking for very long but the boredom of this job had led him to take it up.

'The young entrepreneur was a trafficker, señor. What else?'

'And this place? Why's this place shut up? Gone bust?'

'Ah, this place. Everybody used to drink in here. Everybody. Regular water-hole. Now only me left to guard it until it is sold, or whatever happens to it *with the best of British luck.*'

'Who owns it?'

'Oh,' he said casually, 'a young American entrepreneur. He too in Miami also. Throw away the bloody key.'

Jude reached into the top pocket of his shirt where he had a photo of Mills.

'I'm meeting up with a friend,' he said. 'Do you happen to have seen him around?' He handed him the photograph. The guard handed it straight back.

'I don't know. I never seen him. I don't know. So, please, you must go away now. We are closed. We are all shut down. We are gone bust.'

His face had changed entirely. It was as if the sight of the face in the photograph had just broken his dream; a dream that he had every night in which every day a person came into the bar at this time with the same photograph. Finally, at the end of the dream the boy in the photograph himself walks in and shoots him dead. Well, that, anyway, was something like the oddness of the expression on the man's face, thought Jude. He knew that look of sudden nervousness and fear in people's faces. He'd see that walking in the stairwells in Kidbrook too, when the lifts were disabled by urine, and someone took him to be a mugger or a junkie. It was an odd reaction though. It was almost as if someone else had been around before, asking the same question.

As he walked out and back into the street the guy didn't even say goodbye. For a moment there'd been some contact in this foreboding town. Now he felt suddenly cold.

There was just one hotel that was open, and a scattering of cheap flop-houses. Jude toured them all with his photograph. It was already beginning to disintegrate in the leaden, thick damp of the equatorial atmosphere. Rain clouds vaster than he'd ever seen were gathering. The skies looked inconsolable.

There was a floating bar just beyond the riverbank that looked like the sort of place any back-packers who were around would drift to. He walked out, across the single plank that was supported by sandbags. In the bar he pushed his pack under the table and ordered a beer.

It began to rain; a deluge from a cloudburst that turned the surface of the river white. It came down in an instant, as if a water tank at the top of the house had burst. He watched as a man waded through the water towards the bank, almost up to his neck. He was pulling on a rope, and behind him was his two-storey house floating on a pontoon. Two young children leaned out of the porch as their father dragged their home nearer to the bank. Perhaps they'd been washed down river in the night. It was a Herculean effort on the part of the man to get his home and his family back to the shore.

Half a mile out into the river was the island of Santa Rosa, still Peruvian territory, and moored up against it was a rusting hulk of a cargo boat. Jude could just make out its gaunt silhouette against the rain.

He stared out into the middle distance of the darkening waters. The heavy cloud had taken away the light, it was almost dusk now anyway. Beside the bar was a pool hall, set up on stilts with the Amazon flood water lapping around, mangoes and broken breadfruit knocking against the wood. Two members of the Amazon Police leaned against the rail, their bush-hats beaten by the stripes of rain. From time to time they glanced over at Jude. He seemed to be an irritation to them.

He watched as a floodlight, hung from a telegraph pole to illuminate the board walk, fused and caught fire. The sparks and flames licked along the flex and blue smoke drifted towards him as the lights in the bar and the pool hall failed. The pool players continued their games in half darkness, the clack of the balls appeared to grow louder in the gloom. A blue smoky smell of rubber from the flex drifted across, attacking his nostrils with its astringency.

A brace of abandoned catfish were gasping on the board walk, the rain prolonging their agony, blood spurting from their gills. Jude sat in the bar for an hour and the fish were still alive. The stevedores stomped about heavily in gum-boots, searching for tarts, wearing black rubber ponchos, looking like cormorants who'd given up hope of ever drying their wings.

Out of the squall on the swirling river a dug-out was approaching the landing stage beside the pool hall. An old man was hunched over his paddle at the stern. In the fore was a tall figure in a black rubber poncho standing up, as the dug-out rocked, to grab the landing stage.

Jude leaned out over the rail of the bar and watched. The rubber hood was covering the man's face, but through the gloom Jude could see the whiteness of the young man's hands as he pulled on the slippery wood of the jetty. Then he leapt up out of the boat and turned to give his hand to the old boatman. '*Muchas gracias, señor,*' he was saying.

Jude jumped onto the plank that led ashore. He put his hands up to his mouth to shout 'Dr Livingstone, I presume.' But instead he just kind of hollered Mills's name in a ridiculous quasi-American accent, such was his excitement, overtaken by the moment.

Mills looked up, but didn't see Jude through the rain. He began walking along the landing stage. Through the sound of rain on corrugated roofs, and the *clack clack clack* of the filthy pool hall, he heard his name being called. He hurried on. Damn, he said to himself. Damn.

Jude pursued him across the duckboards that went in all directions between the waterfront shacks. He turned down a dark narrow passage. It came to a sudden end, a drop down to the floodwater below. Jude watched as Mills leapt into the air and disappeared down. In his black rubber poncho he looked like some almighty bat.

Jude got to the end of the plank and looked down. Beneath him Mills was lying in the bottom of a dug-out holding his foot. He looked up.

'I thought you'd be a bit more pleased to see me than that,' said Jude.

'My God,' said Mills. 'You're really here?'

The rain had let up now in Leticia. Mills took Jude to the Hotel Doral where he was staying; a place with two iron barred doors covered in padlocks that first had to be opened with a whole bunch of keys, and then secured again afterwards. All the way there Mills had muttered, 'It's incredible. I can't believe it. You're insane.'

But Jude was shocked by the Hotel Doral, it was an appalling place.

'You're really staying here?'

'I've been here two days. It's fine, I like it. It's a dollar a night.'

'You're being done,' said Jude as he looked around. The dark dingy rooms were set around a squalid little courtyard with a few palms growing in plastic tubs and the glass of broken beer bottles unswept on the oily boards. His shoes were sticking to the floor.

The rain had stopped as suddenly as it had begun, and the air was hot and humid and it seemed to be sweating. It felt so thick and heavy on the lungs that the bestial jungle calls melted into it as if it had a voice.

Mills pulled a couple of beers from a rusting fridge that hummed in an irritated way beside an old radiogram that served as a front desk. They sat on stools around an upturned oil drum Mills had appropriated as a drinks table. He had a flower pot as an ash tray.

'For God's sake why are you staying in such an almighty dump? It's really not you at all,' said Jude.

Mills laughed. 'Exactly,' he said. 'I had a pressman after me. I thought I'd be a little less public here.' He began to recount his adventures; talking in an over-excited, almost febrile, way about the mysterious figure of José Gregorio Hernández, whose hand, he said, was *at his back*. Jude really couldn't keep up with him at all, dizzied by Mills's launching into the story of the assassination of the archbishop, and how it affected the Papal succession; and how that in turn would be reflected in a destabilisation of South

America; how the administrations of these countries kow-towed to American policy in return for aid and holding off on an all-out drugs war, which would bring down most of the politicians that the US currently recognised . . .

Jude really couldn't keep up with it as it tumbled out of Mills's mouth.

Then Mills suddenly stopped dead, in the middle of telling him about the sicarios in Envigado, and how his pendant of José Gregorio had saved him yet again.

'Did my parents send you?' he asked. 'To see what I was doing? Talk me into going back to Oxford like a good boy?'

Jude looked down at his beer.

'No-one sent me,' said Jude, suddenly looking sad. Mills must have been more deeply disturbed in Austin than he'd realised if he preferred to run away to this. He had to help. Mills's hair looked filthy, there were mosquito bites on his face. He'd lost weight.

'It's true,' said Jude, 'that I took money from your grandmother to come here. She's worried about you,' he said. 'But your parents didn't ask me to come. They weren't even at the mansion when I left. I had to come and see you.'

Mills smiled, and then he leaned towards Jude and put his arms around his neck. But there was a strange expression on his face.

'What's the matter Mills, what has happened?'

Mills took a deep breath and began to tell him about the business with Father Leonardo and why he'd had to leave Venezuela so quickly with the notes that the priest had given him. He told him a little of what was contained in the notes. Among the catalogue of miracles, and anecdotal stories from José Gregorio's life, there was also a section on the assassination of the archbishop. There were people in government and in the security services, just as in all other walks of Venezuelan life, who were passionately loyal to the cause of José Gregorio, and to Father Leonardo who was himself a national figure. They had, naturally, opposed those who wanted to rid themselves of the radical archbishop. Two days before the assassination, Father Leonardo had received a visit from a senior member of the security service. He had urged him to intercede with the archbishop; to ask him to preserve a period of silence on José Gregorio; and to receive the Papal envoy at his residence, not at the airport. The archbishop, of course, had refused. It had been a warning that the state had set itself against the church; they were colluding with the US in wanting an elderly conservative Italian to succeed John Paul, so the status quo would be preserved. Latin America would remain under the US thumb, there would be no awkward outbursts of hot-headed nationalism that had already, at the end of this century, made a mess of vast tracts of eastern Europe.

Jude listened attentively, and at the end he said: 'So what do you do now? What are you going to do about it?'

Mills shook his head.

'I've got absolutely no idea.'

'You must have some idea.'

'Well, I suppose I could quite easily get a story published in the US. It wouldn't be difficult; but what would it achieve? Maybe more riots in the streets, maybe the Venezuelan government would fall, it's on its last legs in any case. But does that do anyone any good?'

'But what about the truth? If it's true that people right at the top of their government ordered the archbishop's assassination, it's got to be told . . .'

Mills looked down. As he'd mulled all this over in his mind over the last few days, he found himself coming to a political conclusion: if he went to the US press with it it would only serve to bring more attention on himself; it would compromise his father; it was a price to pay.

He took Jude's hand again and laughed. 'It's pretty big of you, you know, Jude, to come and find me down here. I was just so wired the night I rowed with Dad.'

'I know, it's okay. I understand. It was a fairly wild night all round. I don't know what was more ferocious – you or Hurricane Wendy.'

'Oh God, I'd forgotten about Dad's hurricane. He'll kill me. Did he go down and get his picture taken with the wreckage?'

'In Galveston, yes.'

'And you just worked out that I'd be heading here?'

'I just put two and two together. I really wanted to come and see you. I couldn't let it go the way it was if you thought I was hatching some kind of terrible plot with your mom.'

'Funny thing is, though, and I don't suppose you'll believe this . . .' Mills gripped both of his forearms, 'you didn't come here to find me.'

'Huh?'

'I came here to find you. After I spoke to Grandma.'

He began to laugh very loudly.

19

Mills rather startled Jude by announcing that he had been invited to dinner at the home of the owner of the photographic print-shop in Leticia that evening.

'How come?' asked Jude. 'You've only been here two days. You've got friends in this town already?' Considering that this was Mills, it was completely absurd.

'I got talking to the guy next to me on the plane down from Envigado. He's been sent down here to teach the owner of the print-shop how to use the processing machine that he's bought. Bit of a boring assignment for him I guess. I mean, there's absolutely nothing to do here in the evenings. The whole town just shuts down.'

'It does? I thought you said it was the centre of the Colombian cocaine trade. What do the locals do? They must do something.'

'Last night I was walking along at about nine o'clock and I saw a couple of people in their house playing Scrabble. If you want any action you have to go over the border to Brazil.'

'How did you get invited to dinner?'

I saw the guy from the plane in the street this morning and he's bored out of his brains in his hotel.'

'And he just invited you to another person's house?'

'Yeah. Antonio, I think it is, the print-shop man. Jaime is setting the shop up for him.'

'Isn't that just a bit odd?'

Mills considered for a moment. 'No, I don't think so. Jaime is okay, he's a great guy. He's very keen on José Gregorio Hernández. We talked about him all the way on the flight. I promised I'd go to this guy's house for dinner with him tonight. You'll come along?'

Jude looked around the courtyard of the decrepit hotel. 'Well I'm not staying here with the cockroaches playing Patience.'

'Great!'

Jude was surprised. For all Mills's tension over the notes that the priest had given him, and his inability to decide what to do about them, there was also a side to Mills down here that was considerably more relaxed – especially in the way he'd begun making friendships. Jude was a little jealous of course that Jaime was such a great guy, but it was still good to see his friend beginning to flex his wings. It could only make him a happier person.

They met Jaime Souza in the square at seven-thirty and polite handshakes were exchanged all round.

As they walked to Antonio Silva's house, in the humid early evening along streets lined with jacaranda trees, Jaime and Mills chatted about José Gregorio Hernández. Jaime was a devout believer in the Doctor and was impressed by Mills's knowledge and his enthusiasm to find out more.

Jude watched as Jaime Souza occasionally took Mills's arm, to make a point, or to agree. He'd obviously developed a genuine affection for him and he had an eager way of picking over and savouring every part of their conversation, as if he were a man starved of any stimulation or discussion down here in his enforced exile on the river. He gave the impression that something had recently brought him to a crossroads in his life and had forced him to view his existence more metaphysically; overseeing print shops was dampening his spirit. But despite his inner thoughtfulness his physical demeanour was that of a do-er and a fixer, a man of action. He was a strikingly handsome forty year old with a great flop of jet-black hair and the pale, perfect complexion of the hills. He still moved with the exaggerated grace he had learned when he was a young matador in Bogota.

They talked about the Venezuelan dictator, Gomez, who had kept an iron fist on the country for twenty-seven years until his bizarre death in 1935. Although entirely senile he'd continued to rule the country from a ranch in Maracay. When it was finally discovered that he was dead, and had been for some time, the people of Caracas rioted and hanged his chiefs of staff from the telegraph poles.

Father Leo's Remington notes had told a story about Gomez's hatred of José Gregorio. He was jealous of him in his lifetime and when his brother fell seriously ill Gomez sent for all the most eminent doctors in the country; all but José Gregorio. For six weeks his brother deteriorated under their care. Gomez had no choice but to send one of his ministers to ask José Gregorio to attend his brother. The Doctor complied and effected a full recovery. Gomez despatched his minister of finance to ask how much his bill was. Hernández replied 'nothing'. The minister was sent again and came back with the same reply. It was a matter of honour to Gomez not to be beholden to a man he despised. 'Okay,' said José Gregorio, 'two Bolivars.'

The money was duly sent, a sum less than a street trader would expect to pay for cough medicine.

'Why do you think Gomez was so offended?' asked Jaime Souza.

'I suppose because he was saying that his brother's life wasn't worth anything.'

'And by implication his own was worth nothing!' said Souza, thoroughly enjoying the process of the debate.

Jude smiled as they walked through the evening scents of mud and blooms, listening to them talk about the mythical doctor, chewing over the incidents of the fateful lunch at the restaurant when Hernández had been called away to treat the man's dying mother. It was a fabulous sort of story and Jude gave up any attempt at trying to understand it, or why it was suddenly so important to Mills. If this 'great guy' Jaime was anything to go by, it seemed to be true that the whole of South America could talk about this doctor for every hour of the day. He was a very important figure to them and appealed to their Gothic imaginations; a universal doctor to cure all ills, physical, spiritual and political. Was there anything left that he couldn't fix?

Jude checked himself and pulled back on his natural cynicism. Mills was pretty volatile right now and if this outlandish tale had served to fix his mind onto a spot, then good for it.

Back from the grime and the dark labyrinths of the water front the residential district of Leticia was really rather middle class. Jude could well believe Mills that here, at the cocaine trade's heart, they spent their evenings quietly playing Scrabble. Neat detached bungalows stood on three or four streets that stretched out of the town for half a mile before they were suddenly halted by the jungle. The roads didn't taper out, where the concrete abruptly ended so the dense trees began. The big toads, that Mills called 'the jungle night shift' were out and croaking; fruit bats were dropping like dead weights from the eaves, launching themselves into the night, swooping around their heads in squeaking pre-historic flight.

People were swinging on their porches on hanging seats and their gardens were filled with growing fruits; guavas and tamarillos and great spiky jackfruits. Every now and then they passed quite magnificent houses with high beamed ceilings and satellite dishes: the homes of those who made their fortunes in the chemicals of the river. Those who lived comfortably down here lived very comfortably indeed; on their porches armed guards were enjoying the clement night and the clean sweet smell of recent rain.

Antonio Silva's house was more modest but kept spotlessly clean by Carlotta his wife; no small achievement in the equatorial humidity. They were a young couple with a small boy and all three were as timid as each other; slight of frame; a family scraping to make ends meet. Carlotta served small slivers of Welsh rarebit as the three of them sat down in the easy chairs. At the window was an elaborate wrought iron grille open onto the night. On the coffee table stood an onyx cigarette lighter and a vase of artificial flowers. There were several vases of silk roses all around the room as well, which seemed rather unnecessary in the midst of such natural abundance. Perhaps the Silvas had pretensions to the affluence of the city.

Antonio put on a CD of Mantovani music.

Jaime Souza smiled politely.

Antonio's brother-in-law, Paco, arrived puffing from his pop-pop bike. He was a large man with a big belly that swirled around as he walked into the room as if it was still full of beer, though he was perfectly sober. He wore a baseball shirt which showed off his mighty arms and enormous hands and broke around his thick collarbone in a V. He had an enfolding grip when he shook their hands, his hand like the mouth of a conger eel devouring a mackerel whole. The first thing he said to Mills was: 'I once lived in Queens, New York, USA', and his smile was about nine inches wide.

Paco was the real reason for the evening's dinner party, Jaime had told them on their walk to the house.

During their long hours together tweaking the machines in the print room Jaime had disclosed his Gift to Antonio. And this had led Antonio to think Jaime's Gift might be the solution to his brother-in-law's problems. Jaime, in turn, had shared this information with Mills.

Paco was a big bear of a man, but with it came a strength he couldn't always control. Deep down, there was a disturbance which led him into sudden mindless rages. Even Paco himself didn't know when this awful black mood, which he called his *gloom*, would descend on him and he would become uncontrollably violent. He got into bar-fights, if he was in a bar when the *gloom* took him. Two weeks ago it had taken him in the plaza and he'd tried to kick a dog to death. He was riding around now, looking ridiculous on the pop-pop bike because he'd crushed his own car with a slab of concrete he'd torn from the sidewalk when it had stalled on him. He was frightened that he would beat his wife, or his children; he was beside himself with worry about his *gloom*.

Jaime's Gift was the talent of being able to hypnotise people and regress them to their former lives. He'd joined a spiritualist church in Bogota and they had discovered his Gift. He believed that regression unearthed their personal demons and therefore exorcised them. It was planned that after dinner Souza would regress Paco. It was quite a prospect and Jude was looking perplexed.

'Welcome to South America!' said Mills by way of explanation.

Paco was very nervous about the ordeal and over the meal of corncakes and catfish he could talk about nothing else. What would it be like? Would he be in a sleep? Would he be able to remember it? Would it be like being in a dentist's chair?

Each time Paco worried about it Souza soothed him with his

calming voice; so much so that everyone thought he might be reduced to a trance then and there, and his great buffalo's head would come crashing down into his plate on the table.

'I'd feel better about it,' said Paco, at last, 'if I wasn't the only one.'

Souza looked around the table. Mills was intrigued by the whole business.

'I'll join you if you like,' he said.

'You will?' queried Paco, smiling.

'Sure,' he said. 'Do you think you can regress me too, Jaime?'

'I think you'll make an excellent subject. The more labyrinthine the mind, the more deep tunnels of the past we may shine our torchlight into.'

Jaime was already getting himself into the mood to exercise his Gift and his language had become filled with suggestive images.

'Can you regress a person to a particular time exactly?'

'Oh yes, yes. It is best to fix on something particular, an incident in your childhood, or a time in the distant past that you feel some inexplicable affinity with. They are the markers, fixed like the buoys above a wreck in shallow water. You have a specific time in mind, Mills?'

'Oh, yes.'

Jude rubbed his hand across his chin. Mills seemed somewhat under the man's spell, as well as the big man with the *gloom*. Throughout the meal Jaime had continually glanced over at Mills, judging his reactions to turns in the conversation. It seemed glaringly obvious to Jude that this 'great guy' was inordinately interested in Mills. He couldn't help but wonder if Jaime was all that he seemed, and if their meeting had been the coincidence that Mills had described. He was concerned about what his friend might reveal under hypnosis. Jude felt uneasy about the whole thing.

After dinner they took their coffees out onto the porch, to calm themselves in the evening breeze before the hypnotism began.

Antonio Silva was re-arranging the furniture inside and Carlotta his wife was lighting candles to create an atmosphere.

'How much do you have to pay for a photo processing machine?' Jude asked Jaime.

Mills looked perplexed, it was an odd question to ask.

'You'd need about sixty thousand dollars for the whole operation,' replied Souza.

'How does a person like Antonio afford that?'

Souza laughed, and flashed a look inside the modest house to see if he were in earshot.

'You may have noticed while you've been in our country, Jude, that there are print-shops and photocopy parlours in every street; those and pharmacies. All these places are owned by the cartels; all the equipment has to be imported, it is a perfect way of laundering drug money. We have more print-shops and photocopiers per capita than any other nation on earth.'

'Yes?'

'Yes. When Antonio married Carlotta she made him promise he'd give up working for the cartels. So now he has an independent shop, a rare thing.'

Souza had reduced Jude to silence with his answer, but as they walked back into the house Jude realised that he hadn't actually answered his original question, about where the money had come from, and what his part in it was.

The hypnotisms began.

The big man, Paco, was to go first and Jaime sat him in an easy chair, the most comfortable in the room, and began to work on him. His voice was low and methodically soothing, but although he was speaking in Spanish it was obvious that the script was much like that of any stage hypnotist. After he had relaxed him by smoothing his forehead and arms, and got him to clench his hands together so tightly that he couldn't pull them apart – having induced a mild cramp – he began inviting him to imagine he was walking towards a distant light. He picked up a candle from the table and passed it slowly before Paco's eyelids.

He asked him if he could see a distant light and Paco slowly nodded his head.

Now, he said, you are coming into a beautiful garden. Can you see the flowers?

Paco didn't seem so certain that he could. Can't you smell

them? Jaime asked, and he signalled to Carlotta to hand him a rose from a vase. He passed the flower under his nose.

'Smell,' he said, 'smell the flowers.'

Jude wanted to snigger, the man was entirely fraudulent, and, added to this, he hadn't realised that the flower was made of silk and had no smell except for the dust caught in its fading fabric petals.

Paco sneezed. Then he opened his eyes. Jaime thrust the rose behind his back to hide his cheap trick from Paco's decidedly un-hypnotised gaze.

'It's not working,' he said, and slapped his hand down on the arm of the chair, gloom descending on him, and an uncontrollable anger beginning to well up.

'Relax,' said Jaime, 'we'll try again later. Mills, do you want to sit in the chair?' Perhaps if he went under it would encourage Paco. Jaime obviously had great confidence that the lively and labyrinthine nature of Mills's mind would make him an ideal subject.

Mills went to sit in the chair. This time Jaime's script was in English.

Jude looked on incredulously.

As he began relaxing him Mills spoke.

'You know where I want to go back to, Jaime,' he said.

'I think so,' said Souza. 'The 19th of June 1919.'

'Yes, and make it lunchtime. In Caracas.'

Jaime led him successfully towards the distant light and into the garden to smell the flowers, this time without any props. Everyone in the room was now absolutely silent and concentrating on Mills's face, which was beginning to take on a kind of ethereal distance as his chin slowly lowered onto his chest. The street outside was now silent as the lights in the houses went out and the people went to their beds. Just occasionally a fruit bat would flutter by, but there was a supremely somnambulant feeling now. The whole room, except for Jude, was willing the hypnotism to take place, so much that they were almost in a trance with him.

'You have come upon an avenue of marble monuments,' said Souza softly, 'column after column, stretching through a dusty street in ancient times . . .'

'Yes,' said Mills, quietly. 'It is Petra, ancient Petra.'

He was under.

'Before you there are steps, stone steps, leading up to a great steel door; go up the steps; push open the door. Inside there is a great library, there are many books, too many books to count, as many books as there are people in the world. By the window there is an old woman, you cannot see her face; she has a veil; but her head is turning towards you; she is the librarian. Ask her for a book, ask her for the book of your former lives, where everything is recorded; all the incidents of your other lives are kept in the pages, because while you live now you cannot know them. That is why they are kept for safe keeping in your book. You can only know them if you can get to this ancient library, where the books were written before the first of your lives began. Ask her to take you to your book. She is leading you through avenues of many books, can you see the book that is yours?'

'Yes.'

'Take it down and lay it on the table beside you, and open the book. Turn the pages towards the twentieth century, have you found it?'

'It's in the middle.'

'Open it at the first chapter and turn the pages to 1919. Have you found it?'

'Yes.'

'Turn to the 19th of June.'

'Yes.'

'Now lay your hand on the page and turn to look towards the window, what do you see out of the window?'

'A street, there is a tram-car across the street, there is a restaurant.'

'Are you there? Can you see yourself?'

They watched as Mills pursed his lips together, as if he was refusing to answer. Everyone leaned closer in to watch him. Even though Antonio and Carlotta spoke little English, they were mesmerised by Mills.

'Tell me what is happening in the street.'

'There is a man leaning against the doorway of the patisserie, the tram-car has stopped. The man is looking over at the restaurant where people are having lunch.'

'Why don't you go over to the restaurant and see who is having lunch?'

'Yes.'

'Who is there?'

'José Gregorio, he is sitting by himself, he has a dish of *pabellon criollo*, he is reading the newspaper.'

'Do you want to speak to him?'

'No.'

'No?'

'I have to go now. I have to go.'

'Where to?'

'To the corner.'

'What corner?'

Mills was beginning to respond to Jaime now as if he thought he was stupid, as if he presumed he should know what was going on in the street in Caracas in 1919, and why he couldn't stay here, at this moment in the restaurant.

'The corner at the end of the street,' he said tersely.

'What is there?'

'The Ford.'

'The Ford? It is coming round the corner?'

'No. It is parked, of course, waiting.'

Paco and Jaime were following every part of the story now, but were exchanging rather surprised looks. Jude was feeling decidedly uneasy.

'Pablo is coming now.'

'Who is Pablo?'

'He will go in to tell José Gregorio that his mother is dying. That he has to come and help her.'

'Who is in the Ford?'

Mills was silent again.

'An American,' he said at last.

'What is he like?'

'He is sweating. He is very hot.'

'What is happening in the restaurant?'

'Pablo is speaking to the Doctor. José Gregorio is getting up, he is going to the door. Pablo has stopped. He is letting the Doctor go first. Now the man across the street in the patisserie doorway is waving his newspaper to the corner. The Ford has started coming down the street. No wait, wait . . . something's wrong.'

'What is wrong?'

'José Gregorio has left his hat in the restaurant. He is going back for it,' he said, a nervous edge to his voice. 'The man waves the paper again. The Ford has stopped.'

'What is happening now?'

'José Gregorio has his hat, he is running out of the shop. It is all wrong. The man is waving his paper again. The Ford is moving again. José Gregorio is out of sight behind the tram-car. Pablo is waiting on the steps of the restaurant. It is too hot, too hot.'

'Okay, okay, just be calm, try to be calm.'

'I can't be calm.'

'There is lots of time, everything is in slow-motion, you have time, tell me what is happening.'

'There is a thud. There is a scream. The fender is crumpling. The Ford has hit José Gregorio. His hat is falling into the road. I can see it in the air.'

Mills expelled a great sigh. 'I want to come back now, I want to come back. I shouldn't be here.'

'Okay,' said Jaime. 'Return to the library and replace the book. Walk down the steps and back up the avenue of ancient columns. Go through the garden, find the tunnel. This time the light is at the other end. Walk towards the light, when you get to it you will be back here, fully awake. Can you see the light?'

'Yes.'

'Hold out your hand and touch the light and you will be back.'

Jaime clicked his fingers and Mills opened his eyes.

'Shit,' he muttered.

They were all silent for a few moments. Paco was shocked and he turned to Jaime.

'It was a plot,' he said. 'They had him killed? They killed José Gregorio?'

'Yes,' said Jaime. 'Gomez, Gomez the dictator had him killed.'

'My God,' said Paco. 'It was murder. We should tell the police.' He'd been entirely caught up with it and wasn't thinking straight, there was a fury in his eyes.

Mills shook his head from side to side.

'The American in the car was an assassin?' asked Jaime. 'Hired by Gomez?'

'Yes, and I know who he was,' said Mills. He expelled another sigh. 'It was me. I drove the Ford. That's why I couldn't always answer you when I was under, I couldn't believe it was me.'

Jaime and Paco gasped.

'God save us,' said Jaime reaching for his whisky. 'This is why you are so interested in José Gregorio. This explains why you are, in this life, so drawn to him. And why he is calling you. Why his hand is at your back.'

Paco shook his head from side to side. 'I would never have believed it if I hadn't heard it with my own ears,' he said, and stared at Mills again, shaking his head a little more furiously.

'It explains everything,' said Jaime.

Antonio and Carlotta were sitting attentively with their necks straining, perched on the very edge of their sofa, they were looking between Jaime and Paco, with their mouths open too.

'What has happened?' they asked. They hadn't understood a word of it but they could sense the drama in the air.

Both Paco and Jaime began to explain to them in Spanish at the same time that Mills had murdered José Gregorio and their mouths fell open even wider as they darted glances at Mills, now sitting there with his head hung low, occasionally wiping his brow and shaking his head too, with remorse. Carlotta's eyes fell upon the toasted crumbs of the Welsh Rarebit that remained on the empty plate in front of the American that she had welcomed into her house and happily served with food only a couple of hours before.

Jude surveyed the scene and reached for his glass of whisky. He had experienced his first taste of the weird surrealism that was inevitably induced in people who ventured even just a little way into the mood of this continent, and was enjoyed on a daily basis by the people who lived there. The dark side of the imagination was accepted here more as fact than the grind of the daily round. But is it wise, he wondered, to go to a dinner party and tell your hosts that you were the murderer of their national hero in a former life? He couldn't help but smile at Mills and slowly shake his head.

20 ∫

After a downpour in the morning they went to sit in the bar on the waterfront beside the pool hall. Mills was thoughtful today and was gazing out across the water towards the island.

'I wonder,' he said, 'where that cargo ship is going. It's been moored up there ever since I got here. I wonder if it's going further up river, it'd be great if it was.'

'Why?'

'We could join the crew.'

'Of a Colombian cargo boat? You must be mad.'

'It's Peruvian actually, that island is on the Peruvian side of the river. We should go over there tonight, the Peruvian beer's better and the bars stay open until the last man drops.'

Mills's 'performance' of the night before hadn't really been mentioned today. Jude was still mildly amused by it but was so confused about the whole business of this doctor with the incredibly long name, which he couldn't remember with a hangover today, that he thought it was a subject best left alone.

Mills looked longingly towards the cargo boat again. It was a great brown rusting hulk of a thing but there was something about its blunt shape as it sat in the water against the backdrop of the Amazonian trees that made him ache to be on it. As a boy he'd often spent hours in the Jardin Anglais staring at the paddle steamers on Lake Geneva, planning to stow away one day, escape the American School, and sail off across the sea. He'd been very disappointed when he'd discovered that they only went to the other end of Lake Geneva, turned around and came back again. After that he had no regard for them. They may have been big and lavishly arranged with decks and saloons, and had fine names, and flags flying from the mast, and deafening whistles blasting from the stack: but they went nowhere. They were a sham, trapped in a lake in a country without a sea, like a lion in a cage in a miserable city zoo. But this Peruvian cargo boat, she *did* look right; she was in her element and he'd like nothing more than to be sitting in her wheelhouse as she ploughed ever deeper into the steam and the mist of this most exotic of rivers.

Dusk was coming on and the prospect of a dull evening in a half closed town was making Mills agitated. They had spent the afternoon talking to the tourist guides in the Hotel Anaconda trying to organise a trip into the rain forest. No-one was interested in taking them. They couldn't make a trip with just two people, they said, come back tomorrow, maybe there will be more tourists arriving on the flight from Bogota. Mills had thought that since they appeared to be the only tourists in town the guides would jump down their throats to take their money, but it wasn't the case. They'd even tried to get a table in a restaurant and had been refused. No-one seemed to want to do any kind of business with them at all.

'It's odd, isn't it?' observed Mills.

'It is. It's almost as if someone's been going around town ahead of us and telling everyone not to have anything to do with us. It's like we're under a kind of house arrest.'

'Except in a whole town.'

'Yes. It's weird.'

'You think maybe they think we're Drug Enforcement agents?'

'We're a bit young.'

'I bet they use back-packer types as informants. It's very strange that none of the young guys on the board-walk have offered us any drugs. They just get out of the way. It's strange.'

'It's very odd here all round, Mills.'

They took a dug-out over the water to the island of Santa Rosa where the cargo boat was moored. Its name, the *MV Ulysses*, was painted on the side in a rather sloppy way. Mills sighed.

'She's quite a ship,' he said.

'But she doesn't look like she ever goes anywhere. Looks like they've left her there to rust away.

On Santa Rosa there were just two bars, a house, and a hut where you got your entry and exit stamps in your passport. But there was no need for that if you'd only gone to Peru to drink. If you insisted on a stamp for your passport then the guy who did it was in the bar anyway, but it wasn't always appreciated if you woke him up.

They had a couple of bottles of the Peruvian beer in the bar and as it grew dark Mills saw that there was a light burning in the stern of the *Ulysses*. There was a plank leading up to the bow.

'Let's go and visit the boat,' said Mills.

They climbed up the plank. It was a vessel of a hundred and fifty feet with two decks and could have been constructed any time from the nineteen hundreds. She was an old lady, that was certain. The *Ulysses* was painted brown to cover the rust.

Then they heard the sound of the crew playing backgammon in the stern and jagged Peruvian music coming from a small transistor radio. Steam was drifting about the lower deck where an old guy was boiling rice in the galley. The hulk smelled of metal and grease, and an acrid stench which turned out to be chicken shit.

As they walked towards the stern, where the bare bulb was illuminating the backgammon board, a voice called out to them in English.

'Good evening, young sirs!'

It was almost as if they were expected.

'I am the captain,' said a man stepping into the light, smiling at them broadly. He was a thirty-five-year-old dressed in a crisp white shirt and cream slacks. It seemed impossible that he should have been able to keep them free of grease and rust stains for more than ten minutes on this boat, but he had. He was wearing an expensive gold watch. His features were smooth and refined, but he was carrying quite a bit of weight.

'How can I help you?' the captain asked.

'Just wondering where you were headed,' said Mills.

'Iquitos,' he replied. 'Up river.'

'How far is that?'

'Ten days. Four hundred and fifty kilometres.'

'When do you sail?'

'Tomorrow at five in the afternoon.'

'Do you need any extra hands?' asked Mills, attempting to sound vaguely nautical.

The captain smiled broadly again. Jude coughed. In Mills's mind he might be seeing them as Huck Finn and Tom Sawyer heading up the Mississippi, but Jude didn't entirely share that idyllic vision. Neither did he believe that either of them would make useful 'hands'.

On the table there were bowls of horrid looking soup going cold.

'It's a galley-mate we need,' said the captain. 'Have you sailed before?'

'Sure,' said Mills, recalling the time his father had forced him out onto Lake Geneva in a dingy and had spent the entire afternoon shouting at him in an unknown language until finally he'd yelled 'going about' and Mills had been knocked senseless by the boom.

'Can you cook?' asked the captain.

'Certainly,' said Mills. 'I'm a great cook.'

While Mills had conducted several culinary experiments at the Stables, this was rather stretching the point.

'Good,' said the captain. 'You come along then. What about your friend here, what can he do?'

'Welding,' Jude replied. 'I was a welder's mate in a paper mill,' hoping that this would sound entirely inappropriate for life on a ship.

'Heavy work,' said the captain.

'Very heavy,' said Jude.

'So you'll make a good deck-hand then.'

'Great!' said Mills, and shook the captain's hand, sealing the bargain. 'We'll see you at five tomorrow.'

As they went back later that evening Jude stared out at the black water. The light from the ship's one bulb was stretching behind them, wiggling across the current. He turned and looked into the moonpath from the further bank. Every now and then a log or a tree trunk floated by; sometimes a piece of someone's house that had succumbed to the flood waters.

'Thank you, Mills,' he said. 'You really know how to give a friend a help up in life. Imagine, little old me, rising to the position of deck-hand on a Peruvian cargo boat. You're not really serious about this are you?'

'It'll be an adventure,' said Mills, undaunted.

'I don't doubt it.'

The next morning Jude expressed his doubts about the captain of the *Ulysses*.

'He looked like a bit of a fast one to me. Did you see his expensive watch? He's probably running drugs. I just have this vision of us being blown out of the water by a Colombian gunship.'

'Or maybe they'll just rob us, slit our throats, and throw us overboard,' said Mills.

They reported for duty at five o'clock.

The sun was bearing down moodily on the river from behind a tower of billowing cloud and the first boat load of good-time girls from Brazil were on their way up river. It was difficult to judge which was putting on the more garish display.

Jaime Souza had stood on the dock-side waving them goodbye and shaking his head as he gazed towards the prospect of the rusting hulk that they were giving themselves up to.

Although the *MV Ulysses* was sailing shortly the casual attitude remained on deck. The captain was sitting in the bar next door, that stood over the water on wooden stilts. He was eating an enormous plate of food.

'Don't think he trusts your cooking,' said Jude. They pulled up their packs from the dug-out, and with them a sack of beer Mills had bought in one of the chandlers on the waterfront along with hammocks, and another black rubber poncho to match his that they'd be needing on deck during storms and downpours. It was the stuff of a *Boy's Own* adventure to Mills. This was to be their river. They were going to breathe it, and live it, and become part of the water-life; members of the teeming details that made up Amazonia. His mind had already encapsulated this voyage as both a symbol of escape and the thing itself at the same time. He loved gestures, he'd inherited that from his father who'd built a career on them, and this was his. Nothing would deter him from joining the crew of this ship.

There were just five other regular crew members. There was Pablo, a man in his sixties, primarily the engineer whose task it was to tickle the vessel into moving at all. He looked as if he'd spent his life on the oceans. He was just as an old sailor should look. His face was lined beyond his years from the sun and the salt; his hands were calloused from the pulling on ropes, and he was already flat-out and drunk at the back. He was singing to himself and between his thumb and forefinger he was holding a bright green frog that had climbed the side of the ship mistaking it for the bank. What he proposed to do with the frog was at this point unclear.

There were two muscly lads, Juan and Gonzalo, swinging in their hammocks resting from having loaded six sacks of rice. Ernesto, a serious looking man in his mid-twenties, was sitting in his wheelhouse in the prow trying to re-connect some electrical wiring without much success. The last of the ship's complement, Jiminez, was late. He was still in town having his hair done.

Six o'clock came and went and nobody seemed too bothered about it. The captain was still in the bar next door. Jiminez hadn't arrived, and Pablo drunk at the back had long released the tree frog which was now flipping about the deck. It appeared to be going to Iquitos too, a rather ambitious excursion for a frog. The ship's complement consisted of a dozen chickens, which lived in a cage on the lower deck, and two parrots. At the moment they were sitting on a beer crate by the galley, the smaller parrot cowering under the bigger one's wing. They were both a yellowy green, the colour of sea-sickness, and rather shabby and dissolute. They didn't scream *anchor's away*, or sing snatches of sea shanties like ship's parrots are supposed to do. They just sat there like an elderly couple waiting for a bus in the rain. When anyone passed by they shuffled as if they'd been splashed from a puddle. They really didn't look as if they could face another voyage. Perhaps in the whole of the rain forest they hadn't yet found the right tree to settle down in. It certainly wasn't for the love of human company they were here.

Ernesto came out of the wheelhouse and pointed out to Mills

and Jude, who were still standing aimlessly, where to hang their hammocks on the upper deck.

'We should have brought mosquito nets if we're going to be sleeping in the open like this,' said Jude.

'Is okay,' said Ernesto, surprising them. He'd given no indication until now that he could speak a word of English. 'No mosquitos.' There was a sly smirk on his face as he dealt with their inexperience.

'There have to be mosquitos, it's the rainy season,' said Mills.

'At night we don't stop no place,' said Ernesto, helping them roll out their hammocks. 'So we sail in the middle of the river. There's no mosquitos in the middle of a river.'

'Well I never knew that,' said Jude.

'There's nothing to bite,' said Ernesto as if it should have been obvious.

When their hammocks were slung they broke into a couple of beers and lay back.

'I must say it's not quite how I'd imagine joining the Royal Navy. What's the time?'

'Who cares?' said Mills.

There was a sudden small slap and Jude fell out of his hammock. It tipped him out most expertly onto the greasy deck as if this inanimate thing were an experienced vaudevillian, which over the next ten days that hammock was certain to become. There was a laugh from Ernesto, and the two lads swaying at the other end of the deck.

'What the fuck was that?' said Jude, standing up awkwardly.

'Think it was another flying frog,' said Mills, 'or maybe even the same one,' still swaying and staring out across the water towards the twinkling lights of the town that they were glad to be leaving.

It was interesting that Ernesto had told them to hang their hammocks here, while theirs were at the far end. We're not members of the crew of a Peruvian cargo ship yet, thought Mills, but wait till I get cooking.

'This is going to be,' Mills said slowly turning to Jude, 'a kind of perfect evening.'

'You think so?'

'It's a *thing to do*,' said Mills, expressing his excitement.

'What's "MV" stand for?'

'MV?'

'As in *MV Ulysses*,'

'Merchant Vessel,' said Mills authoritatively.

'It's the same in Spanish?'

'It's the international language of the sea,' he said, seriously, gently swaying himself with his foot.

'So this really is the Peruvian Merchant Navy?'

'I don't imagine it's all of it.'

At that moment a dug-out with an outboard came clattering alongside and a young man with a high pitched voice was yelling and screaming, *'Disculpa, disculpa!'*: I'm sorry. The two strapping muscle-bound lads, Juan and Gonzalo laughed. It was the fifth member of the crew, Jiminez, back from the hairdresser's in Leticia, struggling to get on board in his tight jeans, high Cuban heels, and a woman's blouse. He came trotting up the iron steps to the upper deck and threw his arms wide, smiling at Juan and Gomez. Then he ran his hands through his long perfectly coiffed hair, and flashed his eyes. He was wearing just a hint of lipstick.

'Well I guess we are in the Peruvian Merchant Navy,' said Jude.

Jiminez turned to look at them in their hammocks. He looked startled, and suddenly self-conscious. He walked briskly to the stern and sat down with the others to get a more detailed opinion of his bouffant. Both the lads felt his hair between their fingers and commented on the quality of the conditioner that had been used.

There were sounds from the steps again and a woman appeared in a bright floral frock, struggling with bags, and carrying a baby in a papoose. A little boy of two and a girl of four, also beautifully dressed for the voyage, followed her up, helped by Ernesto. She hung a family sized hammock beside Jude's and dropped her children into it. They looked tired. None of them made a noise.

They were the passengers that Mills had been hired to cook for, he presumed. The children were heartbreakingly pretty, and perfectly silent. They stared, unabashed, at the two gringos as if they had never seen such things. But then, they'd probably never tasted TexMex either.

Another dug-out arrived and a young *mestizo* – half Spanish, half Indian – boarded with a suitcase, another passenger bound for Iquitos. He had a handsome face, and was dressed smartly, but he had a distant, troubled look on his face. He didn't look much like a talker. He was breathing heavily, indicating that he'd had to make a dash down to the waterfront to catch the boat. He flashed a look at Mills and then turned his head swiftly away.

Another boat load of tarts from Brazil were in mid-stream. Juan and Gonzalo leaned over the rail calling and waving to them as they approached. All the men in Leticia were obsessed with Brazilian girls, fascinated by them; they found them exotic and different; the lure of creatures from another land. The fact that they looked identical to the Letician women, and only came from two miles down the river, spoiled the fantasy not a bit for them.

The captain got up from his seat in his favourite bar on the Amazon and walked up the gang plank – which in this instance was just a plank – and hauled himself up to the wheelhouse.

'Let's go up front,' said Mills. 'I reckon we're going to sail.'

'Sail' seemed an incredibly romantic and optimistic term for what this heap of rusting steel, that was now making the most appalling grinding sounds, might do when it was finally released from its tethers, but Jude followed him up front nevertheless.

They took their beers and leaned over the rail by the wheelhouse as Ernesto steered the ship with a groan of its engines and a throwing up of muddy water away from the disintegrating bank. They'd taken a considerable chunk of their mooring with them. The waitress from the bar was waving to her captain. The other drinkers were waving too, not much else would happen here for a while now that the *Ulysses* was sailing.

Mills was beaming wildly. 'I've been looking forward to this so much. I can't tell you how much. The fact that you're here makes it just kind of perfect.'

'Well, thank you sir. I guess I call you sir as I'm only a deck-hand?'

'No, be serious. Be serious now,' said Mills. There were tears at his eyes.

'It means something to me. It's a kind of perfect freedom isn't it? Look at this! Just look at where we are, that amazing sky, and this black water, right here on this river. Look at those lights going out over there. Doesn't it mean something to you?'

Jude didn't know what to say. Even less emotion had been expressed in his home than perhaps Mills had experienced in his.

'It's one of those great places on earth, I suppose,' said Jude finally. 'It's a little too much to take in really. It's much easier, right now for me, just to contemplate the difficulties of being a decent deck-hand, considering what I have to work with.'

'Stop talking,' said Mills, quietly. 'It's just beautiful, look, the electrics are going to start in a moment, the sky's going to go wild and crazy.' He clunked his beer bottle against Jude's. They were already into the descending darkness of the river, just the mighty swirls visible by the few bare bulbs, and the searchlight that was scanning the bankside for drift-logs. Suddenly the ship was operational, a real ship in its dark element of swirling water. Moving into the water brought a sudden silence; the engines and nothing more. The music of the bar was gone now, the river-fowl had retired. There was a sudden nothing, just the water and the engine.

'I've done it,' said Mills, quietly. 'Got away from them all, even their photographers. Try and let them check up on us now, Jude. We've slipped away quietly, very quietly indeed. We're away from the bank.'

Mills was in a rather dramatic mood, but they both smiled with pleasure. This was to be it: hammocks slung on the Ulysses, with just two paying passengers, three kids, a dozen chickens, two parrots, and seven crew with themselves, including one transvestite and a frog, for the next four hundred and fifty kilometres of the Amazon.

'It's kinda like heaven,' said Mills. He stared back as the lights of Leticia faded and disappeared.

They were in absolute blackness now. Then suddenly Jude looked up into the sky.

'What the hell is that?' he said startled. 'What is it? I've never seen anything like that before.'

They stared over the rail at the sky, open-mouthed.

It wasn't lightning, it was something more. It was silent, there was no rain, nor thunder. The entire sky was lighting up in great blocks of colour: silvers, vermilions, lilacs and pinks. A dozen of these giant spectacular bursts going off at a time in adjoining parts of the sky. Their lights lingered too, and played across the black water. While the energy was concentrated in specific areas there were so many of them that they *melded* together and formed a whole that drew the eye this way and that, until you began to relax with it and watch it like some great celestial light show. From the middle of the wide river there was a great deal of sky to see, and all of it was lighting up.

'It's some kind of phenomena. A build up of electricity I guess. I've got my own theories about it, but no-one I've spoken to believes me,' said Mills. 'I think perhaps José Gregorio has laid it on especially.'

It was the first time he'd mentioned him that day.

'It's like a sort of aurora borealis caught in the clouds,' said Jude.

'Ah, you see,' said Mills. 'You see why I wanted to come here and just be? Like this old river hulk we don't have to hurry.'

'What does it?' said Jude still staring out. 'What makes this happen?'

'I reckon it's the day expending itself. All the heat and moisture, all the rising currents of air that have built up so much electricity, the moment the lights are turned out it just has to come.'

Jude put his arm around Mills. 'I'm so glad you're alive and didn't expire on that mountain, or get shot on the border.' It was a rare gesture, helped by the beer and the intensity of the moment.

'You're beginning to *see*,' said Mills softly. 'We're free, Jude, we're really away from it this time.'

21

'Elliot?' said his secretary, 'I got Morris Vangressen on the line. Says it's urgent. Says you'll want to know this one.'

'Can't take it right now,' he said. He was on another line trying to reason with Catherine. She was hitting him from every which way today. She was asking him about the depth of Warnock's involvement with the campaign again.

'He really says you'll want to know,' repeated Elliot's secretary.

'I don't want to know,' snapped Hudson.

'They're giving us a front page negative. Blow the whole thing apart, he says.'

'What?' said Hudson. 'I'll be right back,' he said to Catherine, and switched to the call.

'Well, hello, there Mr Vangressen, how's it hanging with you guys?'

Vangressen was the senior political pundit at the Washington Post. Their relationship had always been excellent, greased by a great many good dinners and the lion's share of their exclusives.

Elliot wiped his brow with his cuff.

'So what's this front page negative you got?' he asked him.

Vangressen gave out a short laugh. 'I thought that'd get your attention,' he said. 'I needed to speak to you.'

But Elliot's heart was still pumping, he found it hard to slow it down these days, even when a crisis had passed.

'We've got a story over here that I thought you'd like to hear something about. Before you start chewing into the phone on me, just let me say no decision has been made yet about running with it, so don't go crazy.'

'It's that bad?' said Elliot trying to employ his customary good humour with the press. But it was a struggle now. Since the despatch of Dirk Fontenay, one of Dale Warnock's men, to Colombia, the full reasons for which were a great deal more serious than he'd told Catherine, he was a nervous man. He was only just holding it all together.

The whole fucking thing's going to come tumbling down on us, he thought.

'We've had this picture of Clearwater's son, down in Venezuela,' said Vangressen.

'Uh huh. He's down there right now on a trip.'

'Picture of him punching the air.'

Shit, thought Hudson, that bastard of a stringer. They'd paid that guy quite enough to suppress it, and he'd sent it to the Washington Post anyway, it's fucking unethical.

'I see, yeah, I seen that picture too,' said Elliot, building up to his spin.

'Well, we decided against taking it. It's pretty poor when the kids get roped into this terrible business all round, don't you think?'

That was a bit barbed, thought Elliot, he'd obviously guessed that they'd given them the Dionne Mary-Belle McKenzie story.

'It certainly is,' he replied cheerily.

'And anyways, it wasn't much of a picture. I mean, he could be in the crowd at a football game for all that picture says.'

Elliot felt cold. He was right. God, they'd over-reacted to that snap, they certainly had. It was just a kid, after all, with a whole bunch of smiling people, punching the air.

'Anyways . . .' Morris Vangressen continued. 'Thing is this. We've had to send one of our guys down there.'

'For what?' asked Hudson, he was feeling stronger now.

'Well it seems that the guy who took the picture, his agency kept him on the story, and he turned up some pretty interesting stuff. I mean, nothing that we'd be majorly interested in; associations with some kind of weird political religious movement down there. Not really my kind of thing, kids are kids.'

'Thing is this,' said Vangressen, dropping his voice a tone. 'The photographer, a Mark Graham. He's been killed. Knifed in Colombia. Town called Leticia, down on the Amazon.'

Elliot shuddered. He remembered his words to Fontenay, *dissuade and discourage*. He sat down into his chair.

'They got a lot of street crime over there, and if he had a whole load of expensive camera equipment with him . . .'

'Oh no, Elliot, this was a very professional job. His hotel room had been cleaned out too. Not a roll of film left in it. Weird for a press-man huh? No exposed film?'

'Who knows?'

'It was his wife who contacted us. He'd been phoning home, telling her everything he was up to. She's absolutely certain he was killed by someone trying to protect your boy Mills, from whatever it is he needs protecting from. Pretty weird all round don't you think?'

'Well that sure is a wild assumption.'

'Assumption yes. But you have to face it that Mills Clearwater is somehow connected to the murder of an American press photographer. You got any comments on that, Elliot?'

Elliot stammered for an answer, he could see the headline: Candidate's son linked to pressman's murder. He couldn't help but wonder how the photographer had managed to track Mills down. Fontenay, he knew, had had the devil's own job after he'd left Envigado. Elliot's only conclusion was that the Democrats were up to a similar game as themselves and using their resources to keep a pressman on his tail in case anything should turn up.

Elliot felt debilitated by the realisation that the theatre of operations, in which this part of the campaign was possibly now being played out, was a slither of land away down in Amazonia.

'You're running this in tomorrow's edition?' he asked finally.

'It won't be tomorrow, no. We'll need some time to do background, and to be honest, our guys are not even down there on-site yet, but for old time's sake I thought I'd give you fair warning.'

Here is a journalist, thought Hudson, who doesn't want to queer his pitch with a future Chief of White House staff. So he still had some movability.

'You want some time to get back to me?'

'Sure,' said Elliot. 'I'll get back to you, that's a promise. We'll have some black and white.'

He leaned back in his chair and he felt a numbness beginning to inch into his fingers as he reached up to touch away the clammy sweat forming on his forehead.

He called Dan Resnick.

'Dirk Fontenay,' he said. 'Can you run a screening on him for me, Dan?'

'He's not screened already?'

'Well, yes, of course, but we don't have the resources you do. Can you go a little deeper?'

Resnick sighed, he was getting a bad feeling; their campaign was beginning to sound as if it had a rottenness about it at the core. Everyone was going to have to hang on tight if they were all going to make it to Pennsylvania Avenue.

Elliot Hudson laid the phone down and sank back further into his chair.

There had been no contact from Dirk for days; there was an ominous silence out there that even the technical capabilities of the Bunker couldn't seem to reach.

Dirk called through to Dale Warnock.

'Oh hi there, good to hear your voice at last. You can give me an update?'

'Sure. The situation is now stable,' said Dirk rather dramatically.

'That's good,' said Dale Warnock, sitting at his desk in the Warren. 'I'm glad you've touched base. Hudson is giving me grief. Thinks we've got something going on without his knowledge.'

Dirk Fontenay laughed, it was a dry cracked laugh. He had no regard for Hudson any more, he was losing it and he looked to Dale Warnock now for his future.

'Through the vine,' said Warnock, 'I hear that the Washington Post are going to move on Mills. He is a priority for us. Nothing must get out of Colombia.'

Fontenay laughed again.

'Rest assured, Dale,' he said. 'He is safe for the next ten days.'

'That is so?'

'We have him on a very slow voyage to Iquitos.'

'That sounds excellent. You have tabs?'

'I have tabs.'

'You're a good man, Dirk.'

After they had spoken Warnock called through to Clearwater's private number and told him about the voyage of the Ulysses.

22

Mills was in the galley assisting with the evening meal for the passengers and crew. There was quite an expectation about it on deck where everyone was assembled around a table. It was a bizarrely arranged dinner party: a place had been set for Ernesto, although he couldn't possibly leave the wheelhouse and take it up; a hammock had been hung beside for Pablo who preferred after his exertions (mainly at the neck of the rum bottle) to dine recumbent in the Roman fashion; and placed beside Jude was the woman with her baby and two small children all piled up on one chair with a kitten surmounting them. There was no conversation, as such, but an oddly restrained behaviour that stood for formal manners. Jiminez had found himself a small striped apron and was standing by ready to perform his duty as a waiter. A duty he prized above all others. His place was set at the head of the table, the most sensible place for any waiter to sit, where he could oversee the progress of the courses.

'Galley' was, perhaps, a rather grand term for the conditions in which Mills was working. There was just a butane gas stove, a filthy corroded sink, a block of fearsome looking knives, and the whole thing was partitioned off in a kind of wooden cage at the stern. It was identical in design and construction, in fact, to the hen coop in the prow, complete with chicken mesh.

Things were not going well. Pablo, the drunken old engineer who also doubled up as chief cook was immovable over the menu for all three courses that he'd planned. He was also rather dangerous in a confined space. He was crashing drunkenly about with a fish paring knife.

Mills lifted the lid of the big pot to look at the soup course.

It was indistinguishable from the river water all around except that it had a handful of pulses thrown in (unwashed and still with grit) and one diced onion. Mills was so exasperated that he reached into his back pocket again for the Spanish phrase book he'd picked up before they left.

'*Donde estan las hierbas*? – where are the herbs?' Mills began muttering vainly, but Pablo just scowled until finally in exasperation he took a large swig of rum from his bottle, swilled it around in his mouth, took the lid off the pot and spat the rum in it.

'*Las hierbas*!' he barked, and slammed the lid back down. Mills was rigid for a moment.

'*Sopa de escupicadura*,' he mumbled – spittle soup. He returned the phrase book to his back pocket. Nothing could save this meal.

Mills had once learned a little Spanish and had incurred his father's wrath for it when he'd discovered he was taking the language as an option at the military academy. There was Latin, Greek, German, Russian. He forbade him to learn a language like Spanish. It only encouraged the Hispanic immigrants, he said. Mills was struggling now to recall any snippets from his one term's worth of classes, but in a kitchen such as this no language on earth could ever be expressive enough.

Pablo sent Mills to get the fish, which was also going into the soup, from the keep net hanging from a rope off the back of the boat. Mills hauled it up. The fish had drowned in the wake. He tipped them out on the chopping board and stared at them for quite a few minutes. They weren't fish at all, but some kind of crustacea, the ugliest sort of river offering; rather like large woodlice about five inches long. They were black and armoured in sections, they had spindly brittle legs and large hard flat heads. Mills asked Pablo for the paring knife to gut them, dreading what he might find inside.

'*Non, muchacho* . . .' said Pablo and grabbed the chopping board and swept them all whole into the pot.

He tried to ask Pablo, with the aid of mime, if he really expected the passengers to eat such horrible things.

'No,' said Pablo in Spanish. 'They are just for *decoracion*. All the more for us later.' Those that weren't eaten were to be returned to the net and hauled up again every time they made soup.

Mills had let the rice for the main course boil over and Pablo whacked him on the back of his legs with the flat of his cleaver. He watched through the mesh of his cage as Jiminez minced along the deck with the first bowls of soup and laid them with a flourish on a table that had been set up, around which everyone still expectantly, but silently, sat. Jiminez had learned the proper way of serving in the restaurants of Iquitos and tonight he was determined to perform his task with similar style and precision. He made sure to serve from the left and occasionally he wiped the edge of a soup bowl, where Pablo had slopped it, with a cloth he had neatly folded over his arm. Sometimes mealtime was chaos, especially just after the flood waters had risen and their decks had been filled with families moving down river for aid. But tonight was different, with the handsome young American on board, working in their galley. It gave him, he felt, an affinity with elegance, like those handsome young men in their bell-hop uniforms in the Hotel Presidente in Iquitos. He'd watched them through the smoked glass, gliding about the foyer, from the street outside, longing to join their ranks.

When they were all served Mills and Pablo joined them at the table. Jude was prodding the black creature tentatively with his spoon.

'What is it?' he whispered to Mills.

'It's rum and spit and monster soup,' said Mills, attempting a smile.

'Looks like it!' said Jude laughing. He began to eat. Mills stared for a while. The woman with her children looked up at him and nodded, she seemed to approve. The guy who'd boarded with the suitcase had already polished his off and seemed to be looking about to see if there was any more.

This surprised him more than anything he'd witnessed in the galley. Mills tasted it. The monstrous creatures had given the soup a real flavour, rather like a sweet lobster bisque. The rum seemed to work as well, and the little pulses popped on the tongue. It wasn't half bad, in fact, it was really rather good and he finished off his bowl too with an astonished look on his face.

During the main course, which was a splodge of over-boiled rice, a small piece of scrawny fried chicken, and tough fried plantain *tajada*, a thousand small flies encrusted themselves on the bare bulb above and generously fried themselves up as a garnish. Dessert was a banana each, delicately placed onto the table by Jiminez, making sure that they all pointed the same way.

Towards the end of the meal the young man who'd boarded late and panting introduced himself. His name was Ramon, a 'tour consultant' from Leticia, whatever that was.

'Where are you going?' he asked in English.

'To Iquitos.'

He looked rather serious for a moment and his dark eyes flashed around the deck in a manner that summarised their situation. 'You think you'll last the journey?' he asked.

'We're tougher than we look,' replied Jude.

At midnight Jude was called up front to perform his first duty as a deck-hand, with him were Juan and Gonzalo. Ernesto was Director of Operations, from his place of vantage in the wheelhouse.

The river was considerably narrower now, only about a hundred yards from bank to bank. He registered some surprise and turned to Gonzalo and indicated that the river was very small.

'Los Islas,' he said. They had entered the narrow channel between two islands; Isla Corea and the Isla de Los Micos.

Jiminez was perched up on the roof of the wheelhouse with a flashlight that sent out quite a beam. He swept it across the water from bank to bank so that Ernesto shouldn't run them aground. He had a look in his eyes which suggested that at any moment he expected Diana Ross and the Supremes to suddenly appear in sequins on the bank. The islands were thick with trees and dense undergrowth with no sign of habitation at all, but then as they turned towards the bank there was a small clearing. Although it was midnight the bankside was packed with people, the flash-light catching their dark eyes. Ernesto switched on a forward floodlight and lit up whole families, with small children on the bankside all waiting for the ship. Gonzalo signalled to Jude to pick up the end of the plank that was lying on the foredeck.

Gonzalo took the other end and began extending it out towards the bank. It was bloody heavy. Jude was conscious that all eyes were on him, they were mightily amused to see a pale-faced ghost like him struggling with a plank. At this time of night you couldn't wish for a better distraction, just when the hammock strings had begun to bite into your aching shoulders, and it made him very nervous indeed. Jude guessed that his end of the plank would have to rest on the deck but as he made to lower it his foot got snagged in some untidied rope and he slipped. He fell forward and sent the plank shooting off the front of the boat. There was a great splash as his end hit the water. Everyone on the bankside laughed and cheered. Juan and Gonzalo heaved a sigh of irritation. Ernesto came out of the wheelhouse to direct things. Juan leapt to the bank, and with some of them helping him managed to get the plank back out of the water and lever it up towards Jude and Gonzalo. They grabbed it and pulled it back to rest on the boat. Despite Jude's abject misery, everyone seemed quite cheerful about the disaster.

The people on the bankside all had branches of green bananas with them, most them about four foot long, they looked pretty heavy to Jude. He watched Gonzalo run down the plank. He and Juan both had a branch of bananas heaved onto their backs by the villagers. Then they each ran with them, at some speed, nimbly up the steep gradient of the plank and dropped them into the boat. The only way to get up a steep plank with such a heavy load, Jude concluded, was to do it at speed. Gonzalo nodded to Jude and he realised he was expected to do the same. The plank, of course, was wet and slippery now, where he'd dropped it in the mud and water. He looked back at Mills, heaved a sigh and set off for the bank. The idyll of the Amazon further disintegrated in front of his eyes.

Early the next morning the *Ulysses* pulled into the town of Puerto Narino where the bananas they'd taken on the day before were taken off again, and in their place the whole crew struggled to bring a crated generator on board, which then sat on the foredeck like a coffin in a state funeral.

Puerto Narino was a filthy place with rusted corrugated roofs and houses on stilts. Even the palms looked ragged, but for all that, in the morning mist that hung on the river there was a strange and awesome beauty to the dawn.

Mills took himself on to deck, clutching a coffee mug in the damp morning chill. He turned around to see Jude walking stiffly towards him.

'Just look at this morning,' he said.

Across the water was another cargo boat that had rusted itself into the water, died here, and gone no further. Its deck was still loaded with old disintegrating beams and it looked like another famous ship that had sunk here under the weight of trying to deliver the interior of an Italian opera house to the rubber barons many years before.

'You look cold,' said Mills, passing his coffee cup to Jude.

'Thanks. Yes, I'm cold. I ache too. Never slept in a hammock before.'

'We'll get used to it, I expect.'

'I hope so,' said Jude, trying to brighten up and passing back the coffee.

'Finish it,' said Mills. 'I sneaked some of Pablo's rum into it.'

'Rum, at six o'clock in the morning,' Jude reflected.

'It's a naval tradition,' said Mills.

Jude was still in the rubber poncho he'd spent the night in and he began flapping it around him and sniffing the air as if something unsavoury had crept under it in the night.

'You remember that kitten at dinner last night that the little girl next to me had on her lap?'

'I let it have some of my rice, I couldn't let the poor little bugger risk anything else. It loved it.'

'Well,' said Jude, miserably. 'I don't love it. I think it must have got under my poncho in the night and peed on me.'

Mills began to laugh. He stared out across the morning mist again. A crowd of fifty people had gathered to greet the ship and a few more passengers came on board and slung their hammocks. Some of them had roosters with them in palm frond cages.

Waving in the dockside crowd was another young man in make-up and inexpressibly tight jeans. He shrieked as Jiminez tripped down the plank, to everyone's delight. Jiminez seemed to be a very popular figure in the riverside towns, and he got a small cheer as he jumped ashore. Jiminez, it seemed, had a hairdresser in every port.

Jude laughed, at last. 'He's quite a character,' he said.

'It's fascinating, watching this river,' said Mills, dreamily. Nothing could break him of his adventure.

'That guy Ramon, at dinner last night, looked doubtful that we'd last the trip to Iquitos. Do you think we will?'

'Certainly we will,' said Mills. 'We have to.'

'Why?'

Mills thought for a moment. 'Because it's where the ship is going.'

As the sun dispersed the mist, Ernesto told them that they were to have no more stops that day, and hence no running up and down the plank for Jude. He began to relax.

By lunchtime Pablo had relaxed so much that he'd rendered himself unconscious and Mills realised that he'd be able to make a better stab at lunch. They'd even taken on a great bunch of coriander in Puerto Narino, and that encouraged him greatly, so he pinched some. He appropriated some of the chicken's new laid eggs too and used them to make a batter for some of their less fortunate friends.

In the afternoon, after a considerably more successful lunch – though it has to be admitted less tasty without Pablo's monsters – Mills and Jude lay in the sun on the foredeck, sipping Peruvian beer. There was very little other traffic on the river. Every now and then dug-outs would pass piled high with maize and with entire families sitting on top of the bundles, shielding themselves from the sun with brightly coloured umbrellas.

'Tell me,' said Mills, 'that this isn't the life?'

Ramon came and sat down beside them and Mills offered him a beer. Ramon pulled out a double pack of cards.

'You play?' he said.

Mills blinked in the sun, 'I've never played cards in my life.'

'I'll teach you canasta,' said Ramon, 'a South American game.'

Mills was enthusiastic.

Jude squinted at Ramon. The pack of cards in his hand made him look even more shifty than he did already. His hands moved so swiftly as he dealt them he gave the undeniable impression that he may well have spent his childhood hanging about on the waterfront in Leticia picking the pockets of the tourists.

The rules of canasta were a mightily complicated affair; filled with *melds* and *naturals* and *concealed hands*. It quickly exasperated Jude and he returned to sipping beer and watching the bank go by. Mills however, was doing rather well with it, and perhaps because Ramon was trying to encourage him, he was winning. When his conquest of Ramon was completed he was so pleased that he leapt up and gave himself a round of applause. It was all very unlike the Dark Satanic Mills of The Stables, he was like a kid on a pirate ship in a Walt Disney.

After the game Mills gazed out at the bankside again, at the white egrets, and the turtles sunning on the logs; he sighed with pleasure as the Ulysses steamed on in its stately progress.

23 ∫

In the early hours of the morning, on the third night of the voyage, with the river still pitch black and thick as oil, the *Ulysses* discreetly neared the bank and cut its engines.

The sudden loss of noise woke Jude. He was too tall for his hammock and was sleeping uneasily in his black rubber poncho which also served as a protection against the insects that did make it out to the middle of the river. They were mainly the big buzzing armoured variety that could manage long-haul flights but invariably crash landed, in a dazed and angry state, when they arrived: all legs and pincers and brightly coloured wings that didn't fold back properly into their shiny beetle jackets. Nevertheless, it was a shock when they hit you in the face.

Jude's back was aching and he swung his legs over his hammock to take a walk around the deck. As he got up he saw the eyes of the woman lying beside him, swaying with her babies in her vast hammock. She looked directly at him, and shook her head, she seemed to be warning him about getting up. But his back was aching so badly he had to stretch for a bit.

He picked his way across the oily metal deck and pulled a cigarette up to his mouth and lit it. He could hear muffled voices, and some rustling in the bankside undergrowth. He could make out the dark figures of Juan and Gonzalo leaning over the prow of the ship, the plank was out. Deck-hands were working and he wasn't a part of them. Then he saw the glint of half a dozen eyes on the bank, and a flashlight that created diffused spots of orange light on the ground. He saw the small cloth sacks at the men's feet. They were silently handing them to Juan and Gonzalo who were bringing them aboard. He heard the slide of metal as they removed a panel from the floor of the foredeck and gently laid the sacks in. Jude extinguished his cigarette with his fingers, it burned like hell, but it was better than being seen. This was not something he should witness. He crept back to his hammock. The woman was still staring at him.

He lay back in his hammock, his heart pounding.

In the morning he'd have to tell Mills about this. They'd had the adventure of running away to sea, now they were going to have to enjoy the thrill of jumping ship. They really were drug-running. He slept very uneasily.

When they were ashore during their fist stop of the day Jude told Mills about the cargo that he'd seen loaded the night before.

'Ridiculous,' said Mills. 'It was probably just rice.'

'Then why have to hide it behind steel?'

'So the mice don't get at it,' he said. He wouldn't have a bad word said about the Ulysses. Despite its essentially disgusting nature he insisted that this was living.

'Can't you see this boat is farcical?' said Jude. 'We take bananas on, we take bananas off. It's like some mammoth game of pass the parcel. You're at the back hauling up the same horrible river-monsters for every meal, and I'm at the front bringing on and off the same green bananas. And where does that captain make enough money in that to dress like he does?'

Mills slowly nodded his head. Finally he looked up to Jude as if he was going to admit that it was probably true. 'Oh God!' he said, his eyes twinkling, 'a-crewing on a drug-running boat!' He whooped with joy.

'This isn't a fantasy, Mills. This is real.'

'The sort of thing my folks sent you here to stop me getting up to,' he said.

'That was uncalled for.'

They were both tired now, the motion of the ship and the back-aching hammocks were beginning to take their toll.

'We'll look for an opportunity to see what's in those sacks under the deck,' said Mills at last.

Jude said nothing. That probably wasn't a very good idea either. He was almost beginning to sympathise with Mills's mother and father. Mills could be truly reckless, a danger to himself. He lived within the *idea* of a thing, not the reality. It was as if he wanted something to go wrong down here, something finite and cataclysmic that would get him out of having to face the future. A last burst of freedom before his father took office and he too would be assigned secret service men to protect him from kidnap and any wayward fundamentalist group that wanted to take an easy shot at America. As Jude thought about that he tempered his annoyance. It wasn't much of a prospect for Mills, and perhaps he deserved a last great burst of reckless freedom before his family entirely took him over. If only his parents had allowed him to get up to a lot more mischief as a kid, then it wouldn't have all got bottled up like this until now. They should have put him in some free and easy West Coast hippy school, and by now he'd have been rebelling so much he'd have joined the Marines, with the best shined shoes in the platoon.

That afternoon they pulled into a small village. The children splashed towards them in the water when they saw the white faces on deck. More bananas were loaded but, more strangely, also the steeple of a church. It was quite an endeavour, involving ropes and winches, and all the men of the village as well as the entire crew. The only place for the steeple was on the roof of the upper deck. It was fifty foot long and clad with copper. It took an hour and a half to secure it and slowly haul it up. It creaked and groaned, and lost its shape considerably. It was like a great trumpet as it lay on the roof and they lashed it down. The grass where it had lain waiting on the riverbank for days was yellow and wriggling with bugs that were being collected up by the villagers – presumably they fried up into a nutritious snack.

'Please God,' muttered Jude, exhausted, 'we're not taking the whole bloody church.'

Mills asked Ernesto why on earth they'd taken a steeple on board. Ernesto shook his head, he wasn't impressed with the cargo either, it made the *Ulysses* lilt to one side and would make it more difficult to steer.

'They're building a new church here,' he said. 'The priest is a bit too enthusiastic. There's been a miracle in the village and so he thinks they need a bigger church.'

'José Gregorio?' asked Mills.

'Yes, I think so. So the priest is donating the old steeple to a village up-river that lost their church in the floodwaters.'

The captain had disappeared the moment they'd arrived and taken himself off to what was his second favourite bar on the Amazon. Sensing that he was going to be there for some time the rest of the crew joined him. The villagers, grateful for the help they'd been given with their gift of a steeple, invited the passengers down for a *baile*, a dance with a barbeque of grilled fish. Already tired of Pablo's unchanging menu, even when Mills managed to vary it, they eagerly went.

'It's just us on the ship,' said Mills.

'Uh huh.'

'Let's get that bit of deck of yours opened and see what's in the sacks.'

Jude looked both ways. These villagers looked friendly and generous too. If need be they could jump ship here, hide in the forest for a bit until the Ulysses had gone, and throw themselves on the good nature of the people.

They sat themselves down on the foredeck as if they were taking the sun while Jude gently prized the portion of deck up. Mills took out his penknife and slipped his hand in until he found one of the sacks. He slit a small hole and dipped his finger in. He pulled his hand out and Jude slowly lowered the steel panel.

They both stared at his finger. It was covered in a light greyish powder.

'Basuko,' said Jude. 'It's cocaine paste. A guy I spoke to in Oxford warned me about this, it's the base they make the stuff from; it's like heroin.'

Mills put his finger in his mouth and tasted it. His face slowly crumpled in disgust.

'It's cement,' he said. 'They're bags of fucking cement.'

Jude didn't believe him and opened up the plate again for Mills to dip his finger in the sack a second time.

Mills pulled his hand out and held his finger up. Jude licked it. Then he coughed and spat on the deck.

'Fucking cement,' he said. 'We're on a cement smuggling boat,' he began to laugh. 'Steeples, bananas, cement; a life on the ocean waves.'

'Is cray-zee country no, señor?' said Mills, delighted. 'So you reckoned we were smuggling cocaine?' Mills laughed. 'Did you never stop to think how dumb that sounded?'

'Mills, we're exactly where it all is.'

'Oh yeah, sure, a very smart captain indeed who's running cocaine *out* of Colombia and *into* Peru, where they grow the bloody leaves. It goes the other way, you schmuck. We'll pick the cocaine up on the way back.'

By evening they were deep into Peru, almost up to San Mateo, and on either bank was one of the blankest parts of the still unwritten map of the world. Tonight Jiminez was in the wheelhouse and swooping his flashlight beam across the river, and there'd been a sudden downpour of lashing rain that had sent everyone running to take down their hammocks so that they wouldn't get sodden as the water came across the bow. After dinner Mills and Jude sat up front beside the wheelhouse in their ponchos, rain dripping from their faces, cowering their cigarettes under their rubbers. The downpour had served to bring everyone together a little. The woman's children, who swung next to Jude at night, had come out to stare at them, like little frogs after rain. One of them, the little boy, had now been bold enough to crawl under Mills's poncho and settle in his lap, delighting in the warmth of the rubber, and punching out at it with his little fist, much to the astonishment of anyone else walking past. It was chilly after rain. Jude was passing cigarettes to Ernesto as he held the wheel, and downstairs Juan and Gonzalo were slapping backgammon pieces. Pablo, more drunk than usual, was setting about the task of wringing the neck of one of the chickens for tomorrow's lunch, but it was evading him and fluttering about on the lower deck. Everyone laughed as they heard the sudden frantic cluckings shortly followed by the sound of Pablo slipping on the oil and falling headlong with a thump and a groan.

Ramon came up to join them.

'You're getting better on the plank,' he said to Jude. 'You're almost running now with those bananas. Did you swallow much river water the first time?'

'Quite a bit,' said Jude. The experience was still painful.

'You drank alcohol afterwards?'

'Shot of gin,' replied Jude.

'Good, only way to stop you getting river water sickness. Strong alcohol cures everything.'

'Yeah, Ernesto told us.'

Mills pulled his hip-flask of gin out from under his poncho. 'Take a shot?' he said.

'Sure.' Ramon admired the flask, twisted the top and took a short taste.

'So is it any fun being a tour guide in Leticia?' asked Mills.

'Not really,' he said. 'Most people are just permanently lost down here. I don't know if they really see anything of the Amazon either, they've always got a camera in front of their face.'

'Tell me,' said Mills, offering Ramon a cigarette, 'why's cement such a big thing down here?'

Ramon smiled, and then he dipped his voice a little as he spoke. 'It's illegal,' he said. 'So are some types of glue and kerosene.'

Mills and Jude looked bemused.

'You have to have a special import licence for those things round here, have to account for its use. It was *your* country, the US that insisted on it. Colombia imports more acetate and cement than any other country in the world.'

'They're trying to limit the expansion in the rain forest, slow down all the roads and deforestation?' said Jude.

'Get real,' said Ramon. 'Let me tell you something about the Peruvian national cash crop.'

'Uh huh?'

'Do you Yanquis actually know how cocaine is made? Have you ever stopped to think about what it is you're actually taking up your noses?'

Mills and Jude were thinking. They wanted to protest that not all westerners snort cocaine, but of course, that had never been the impression given to Colombia, or Peru, it was an argument they couldn't possibly win.

'My father was a cocaine smallholder, down here in Peru, before he died,' said Ramon and paused with satisfaction as he garnered in their total attention. 'Me, I have nothing to do with it. That's why I went to Leticia to improve myself and ended up a tour consultant. I spent all my childhood making cocaine. Every six weeks, when the boat came to pick it up, we'd stamp out another kilo or two. About four hundred dollars' worth, street price in America, God knows, fifty thousand?'

'So how d'you make cocaine?' asked Mills, interested.

'Got a piece of paper and a pencil? I'll give you the recipe.'

'I got a good memory, fire away,' said Mills.

Ramon explained that it was a fast growing plant that took less space and less husbandry, and paid more, than anything else the peasants could grow. It was as easy to grow as a busy lizzy on a windowsill. They didn't make the demand, they just met the supply.

Ramon described the process:

'After you have picked the leaves,' he said, 'the whole family gathers around and tears the leaves up into little bits, and scatters them into a circle on the ground. Then all the kids, grandma and grandpa, kids like me when I was a boy, stamp around on the leaves for a bit and mulch it all up. The leaves exude the coca acid. Then all you need is something alkaline to sprinkle over it to soak all the acid up out of the leaves. And the perfect thing is cement.'

Mills and Jude looked at each other.

'Then, when it's soaked it all up,' said Ramon, 'you gather all the cement and put it in a big barrel and pour in half water and half kerosene. The kerosene forces the acid out of the alkaline and back into the water. Syphon off the kerosene – usually by mouth with a pipe – and throw away the leaves. Boil up the water and leave to simmer on Gas Mark 4 for the rest of the day. What you end up with is a grey mush, like clay. Wrap in banana leaves and serve to the midnight crew of a passing coca-paste boat. The glue comes in later when it's taken to the "factories" hidden in the jungle and the big boys take over with their acetate to turn the whole mess into a chemical sulphate. The rest, as they say, is nothing more than a drugs war.'

At the end of Ramon's recipe, Mills and Jude were quite mesmerised by him. He was obviously a talented tour guide, but Jude still couldn't really feel easy about him. He was a smart guy, good looking, and wearing designer jeans. Why was he travelling so cheaply, and wasting all this time, on his way to Iquitos?

It was a very pleasant evening now and the boat sounded moodily atmospheric as the copper-plated steeple groaned and whined above. The chicken had got back into its cage, because drunken Pablo hadn't fastened the door, and escaped with her life; the backgammon was continuing amicably, the cement had been safely stowed away, and all was at peace on the Ulysses.

'Why are you going to Iquitos, Ramon?' asked Mills.

Ramon thought deeply for a moment and a conspiratorial air came over his face, as if what he was about to say would have to be dragged out of him with ropes.

'Well . . .' he said, at last, and sighed. 'All a bit of a mystery really.'

Their attention was captured again. The little boy who had been curled on Mills's lap came back and leapt up onto Ramon like a monkey. Ramon held him in his arms and stroked his hair.

'One of our guides came in with some craft-works that he'd picked up in Iquitos and none of us could work out which bunch of Indians it had come from. Wasn't like anything we're used to. A lot of Amazonian tribes, the real difficult ones to contact, are nomadic. That's why it's difficult, obviously. So we reckon there's a tribe out there that's wandered down and set up home for a bit, a tribe that's uncontacted.'

'What do you mean by uncontacted?' asked Jude.

'Means that we don't know who they are, the government doesn't know who they are, the anthropologists have got nothing on them. It'll be their first contact with the outside world if we go and meet up with them.'

'Well, sounds like someone's already met up with them if you've got their craft-works,' said Jude, cynically.

'No, we don't think so. They traded them with another lot of Indians that we do know. It's not unusual for one tribe to give gifts to another, especially if they're new to the area and want temporary land rights, a bit of territory without being molested.'

'So where are these nomads exactly?' asked Jude.

'If you don't mind me saying,' said Ramon, 'that's a pretty dumb question to ask about nomads.'

'So why are you going?' asked Mills.

'To see if it's possible to make contact; see if they'd be receptive to visitors.'

'Tourists, you mean,' said Jude.

'Well yes. It's an attractive package for the higher end of the market.'

Jude sniggered.

'So that's what a tour consultant does,' said Mills.

'Yes,' said Ramon, 'That's what we do.'

'I suppose this kind of thing is very good for business,' said Jude, dourly. 'It drums up interest, people want to come down and see something new. National Geographic and the like splashing money about. A good earner for your company, eh?'

'Oh yes,' said Ramon. 'Charge top-rate for this one. Why'd you think I was going to Iquitos?'

Jude liked him a little better for that reply; at least he was honest about it.

'Well,' said Ramon. 'This little boy has given me cramp now, so I guess it's time to return him to his mother. Thank you for the shot of gin.'

Ramon ambled confidently away and dropped the boy into his mother's hammock, like an actor discarding a prop as he walked into the wings.

'*Hey Jude! . . .*' said Mills.

The night before they were due to arrive in Iquitos, Ramon was re-packing his suitcase of craft-works and asked if Mills would like to have a look over them.

He brought out strings of beads made from forest seeds threaded between jaguar and piranha teeth. Some of them had half coconut shells hanging from them. Then Mills gasped slightly and reached his hand into Ramon's suitcase and pulled out a small carved figure.

'What is this?' he asked.

'That is the biggest mystery of them all,' said Ramon. 'We really can't work it out at all. We can only presume that at some time in the tribe's distant past they must have had some contact with the early explorers of these parts. It's clearly the figure of a westerner. Very unusual among Amazonia craft-works.'

'No it isn't,' said Mills, plaintively. 'It's not a westerner or an explorer at all.'

'Oh he is,' said Ramon, 'look at the black hat he's wearing, and the moustache. Indians can't grow moustaches.'

Mills handed it to Jude. Jude nodded slowly. 'It is, isn't it?' said Mills.

'It certainly looks like,' Jude replied quietly.

'What?' said Ramon. 'What are you saying?'

'Maybe they've had contact with someone who's given them a picture of him?' offered Jude. 'A missionary perhaps?'

'Who knows?' said Mills. His mind was working, he was thinking again of the Doctor.

'What is it?' asked Ramon. They could see the lights of the outlying settlements of Iquitos now, in the early morning they would be there.

'This is a figure of José Gregorio Hernández,' said Mills. 'You've heard of him?'

'Well, yes of course, but I'm not religious,' replied Ramon. He picked up the figure and turned it around in his hands.

'I think you're absolutely right, it is José Gregorio,' said Ramon. 'We're so used to seeing those plaster and plastic figures it didn't occur to us that this wooden thing might be him; and coming from such an unlikely place.'

'It is possible that there wasn't a meeting with an explorer or a missionary. It's possible that they saw this man much more recently than that.'

He turned to Jude. 'Why shouldn't he appear to people like that? Uncontacted nomads? I'd call that pretty conclusive evidence, wouldn't you? It's practically another miracle!'

Mills's eyes looked like fire, sparkling wide. This time Jude had no reasonable answer. None at all.

After dinner Mills and Jude stood on the prow watching the lights coming slowly closer.

'It's strange, meeting Ramon. You have to admit it's strange? Wouldn't it be great if we could go along with him?' said Mills.

'Into the forest?'

'Yes. Don't you want to see the forest now?'

'Well, of course, but . . .'

'But what?'

'He's hardly likely to want to take us with him. And if he does he'll charge a fortune.'

'It would be a thing to do though, wouldn't it?'

Jude smiled, he had to admit that it would. In the afternoons as he'd gazed out from the ship his imagination had led him into the cavernous by-ways of the forest.

'I feel as if I've been given a sharp reminder,' said Mills.

'By José Gregorio?'

'Yes. His hand is still at my back.'

24 ∫

The town of Iquitos made the boast that it was the furthest jungle town from any other habitation in the world. But everything down here was the biggest or the furthest – and this piece of tourist-guide detritus floated with the rest as the Ulysses was being roped up at two o'clock in the morning.

At the end of the gang-plank the captain stood, waiting to shake their hands, and they felt as if they'd made landfall more as the passengers of a cruise liner than of the vessel that had conveyed them. Already the experience of being part of that most bizarre crew was beginning to leave them. They were only ever honorary members of it; however many bananas and steeples, and contraband sacks of cement Jude pulled up the plank; and however much rice Mills battled to prepare; they had the over-whelming feeling of having been merely visitors on the Ulysses, tolerated like house-guests on a cultural exchange. Jiminez watched them leave the wheelhouse, an envious look on his face, knowing that they would be going to stay at one of the big hotels into which he could only stare from the street. They were on the last stage, and as they stood on the wooden boards of the dockside pontoon they felt like puppets being dangled from very long strings by distant puppet masters. In many ways they were.

Iquitos rose above the water on stilts, awash with river debris. The boom time of the Amazonian port had been in the nineteen hundreds, when the demand for rubber for the newly invented pneumatic tyre had transformed the place. Until then the small port had been ignored. The rubber barons prospered and built Portuguese-style villas all along the river front, that had now fallen into decay.

It was just before midday, on the following morning, when Mills and Jude walked across the main square to meet Ramon at a restaurant on the corner. The Hotel Presidente, while it had no water in the taps, or for the shower, did have a pool where they'd swum after breakfast. It had served to relax their muscles from the exertions of the boat and they were both enjoying the sensation of smelling faintly of chlorine, and feeling clean.

They stopped where a crowd had gathered round an orator in the square. He was holding forth to a packed circle of men intent on his every word. They were staring down at the paving stones – at first they thought they were hanging their heads in shame at the orator's words. Then as they eased themselves in the circle they saw what the speaker had taped to the pavings: dozens of enthusiastically explicit pornographic photos. Photographs of men and women wildly copulating in all manner of positions; and stranger still the men were examining pictures of other men, standing proudly and pointing to their elephant-like members.

There was a little laughter, but on the whole the oration was taken very seriously, as if it was the first time they had ever heard of such things.

At the end of his speech, which concluded with violent thrusts of the speaker's pelvis, he produced a small vial of brown liquid: the fabled aphrodisiac.

There was a shout from the cafe on the corner. 'Hey!' called Ramon.

Ramon was in a state of excitement and high anxiety and was already making his report before they'd sat down at the table. They'd need a boat and a boatman; they'd need gasoline, they'd need water and rice, tinned meat, cooking equipment, and sun hats. Especially *sun hats* for when they were in the open on the Rio Mammon. Also, he said, they'd need Jorge, his brother who lived here in Iquitos, and was a guide too. He knew the rivers round here better than him. And Jorge would need Carlita, his wife. She could do the cooking, the washing, and keep Jorge happy at night. And they'd need a lot of regalos, presents for the Indians.

Ramon had spent the morning, he said, visiting the various tour-guide offices that lined the streets up to the Plaza de

Armas. He now had a very definite idea where they would find the Indians who had made the images of José Gregorio. The local tribes had christened them the *Mano-Tinkas*, which, roughly translated, said Ramon, means 'the people who've got absolutely no idea where they are'.

Mills looked across at Jude.

'So it's back onto the river, then?' he said.

That afternoon Ramon introduced them to his brother Jorge.

'Big fukken trip!' said Jorge. Jorge's English wasn't as good as his brother's but was a great deal more picturesque. He looked about sixteen but was older than that, and where Ramon was as tall as they were and had a city manner about him, Jorge was much more the descendant of his forefathers. He had the vaguely Polynesian eyes of the true Indian and an open placid face. He was short and smiling, cheerful in his disposition, and had none of the hardness and opportunism of Ramon. Carlita, his wife, stood silently behind him, wearing her best dress to meet the *Yanquis*, and she looked as if she were about to perform a dance. She was fifteen or sixteen years old and they made a curious couple, more like a child's dolls of a bride and groom than the actual thing.

Mills enjoyed the afternoon touring the chandlers along the waterfront, Ramon reeling off all the things they would need for the excursion and Jorge bartering for them with the locals.

Ramon's list seemed to be endless. Just when Mills thought it must be enough, Ramon would suddenly stop in the street and gasp 'Cigarette lighters!' or something equally inexplicable.

They duly bought a dozen plastic disposable lighters, which, said Ramon, would make excellent presents for the *Mano-Tinkas*. They would be amazed by such things, he said.

Jorge seemed to be mildly amused by the whole enterprise and he insisted on portering the greater bulk of their provisions; the sacks of rice; the gasoline; the tinned food and the whisky. Then Carlita spoke for the first time, tugging at Ramon's arm.

'*Proctor y Gambol*,' she said urgently.

'Soap-flakes!' gasped Ramon, stopping in his tracks again, and turning them all around to walk back along the way they had come to buy soap-powder.

'Soap-powder's essential?' asked Jude.

'You want to have clean clothes, don't you?'

'Well, yes . . .'

'Everybody falls out of a dug-out some time. If Carlita wants soap-flakes, we get soap-flakes. They are making this trip at a very special rate for you, being my family.'

'Of course,' said Mills. 'We can stretch to soap-flakes.' But he'd long suspected that this entire 'provisioning' expedition was part of some arrangement between the tour-guides and the shop-keepers. The afternoon ended with Mills handing over two hundred dollars in cash to Ramon so that he could make a deposit on a boat and a boatman down on the waterfront.

'We'll come with you,' said Mills.

'No,' said Ramon. 'I will go alone. If they see rich *Yanquis* like you, they will charge double for the boat.'

So Ramon walked off across the Plaza de Armas, dissolving into the early evening crowd.

'And that,' said Jude, 'is the last we'll ever see of Ramon.'

After a dinner together, just the two of them, they returned to the hotel and sat and talked in Mills's room. There was a knock at the door. It was one of the hotel staff from the front desk.

'Señor?' he said, and then his eyes gently swayed across the scene in front of him: the sacks of rice, the gasoline, several loaves of bread; lengths of rope for pulling fallen logs out of the way, and an enormous box of soap-powder. He pulled himself back to the task in hand.

'You have a visitor, sir, while you were out.'

'A visitor?'

'Yes.'

'Was it Ramon? Our guide?'

'No, sir. A big man. Forty, maybe fifty. He wants to know if you are here.'

'He gave a name?'

'No, señor. He gave no name.'

'He'll come back?'

The desk-clerk shrugged his shoulders. He'd delivered his message, and that was all he had to do. He stood now with his right hand wavering around his waist, waiting for a tip.

When he'd gone Mills turned back into the room and shrugged his shoulders too.

'Whoever it is,' said Mills. 'He's clever to find me up here. Maybe it is time to go.'

The next morning at first light, there was a banging at Mills's door. It was Ramon, with Jorge and Carlita.

'Hey! hey!' he said. 'It's time. Let's get everything up to the port. We have to go early!'

'Too fukken early,' mumbled Jorge behind him. He looked as if he'd had a night on the town on the proceeds of whatever was left over from the cash that Ramon and he had relieved Mills of the afternoon before.

'We're going?' said Mills, pleasantly surprised.

'Of course we're going!'

He supposed that things had turned out pretty well for Ramon; he was a clever operator, he'd come to find these *Mano-Tinkas*, and had managed to get Mills to pay for the whole thing.

Half an hour later, Bernado the boatman, was steering them out of the filthy port floating with almost everything that can float: breadfruits, dead dogs, and pieces of the dockside bars and slices of people that had broken off in the knife fights of the evening before.

As soon as they were out on the water Jorge treated them to a burst of his tour-guide spiel, but due to the mighty hang-over, he found it hard to enthuse.

'Amazon, big *fukken* lot of water,' he said. 'Look out for fish.'

'We will,' said Jude. 'Piranha?'

'Yes, piranha. Cayman, manatees, fukken dolphins.'

'Dolphins?' queried Jude. 'In a river?'

'Yes. I see two already this morning. *Pink* dolphins.'

'I bet you did,' said Jude.

Mills laughed.

They took the river to where the Amazon finally splits in two: the Maranon and the Ucayali, and by evening they reached the narrow Tigre river. The dug-out, with its outboard, had been lithe and fast in the water.

'We are,' said Jorge, 'miles and miles and many miles more from any-fukken-place. Is most very fantastic?' He was feeling better now after having requisitioned a substantial part of the whisky ration for medicinal purposes.

They were a good hundred miles out of Iquitos in a world of nothing but black water. It was sometimes dappled with light as it came in shafts through the over-hanging trees. The bankside of the Maranon had been punctuated by the occasional tall teak tree, and towering palms hundreds of years old. But here the trees leaned over them and the surface of the water was still and stagnant-like with a scummy layer of palm oil drifting across. Mills had been at the tiller for the last hour but now Jorge said he'd better take it. 'Sometimes we just shut up and paddle. Don't want no *fukken* arrows coming *thwack*.'

Ramon had been silent for most of the journey, he seemed a little tense. He was a town boy, perhaps he was uncertain of himself in this place so far from the shops. He asked Mills for a shot from his hip-flask. Even though it had been filled with the same whisky as Jorge was brazenly sneaking out of one of the sacks, it seemed to be a matter of honour for Ramon, who was senior to Jorge on the expedition, to drink from the hip-flask. In a very short while he was a little drunk too, and clutching the flask on his lap as if it was going to be taken away from him.

'We here now,' said Jorge. 'Hip-hooray!'

'At the *Mano-Tinkas*?'

'No, at the big hotel. We stay in hotel, yes?'

'A hotel!' yelled Mills. 'Here?'

'Oh yes, Millito, very big expensive hotel, right here. It's a miracle no, I bring you to such a top-notch place.'

Mills looked dazed, as if he'd been hit on the head again by one of the over-hanging branches. Jude was sniggering. Bernado took the tiller and brought them up to a short wooden jetty. He hadn't imagined, after all their provisioning, that they'd be staying at a hotel. He wasn't happy, either, that Jorge was already calling him *Millito*.

'We make our base here,' said Jorge. 'It very nice. Beds, sheets, a bar. Pin-ball machine. Tomorrow we go into the forest for a walk. Maybe we find the *Mano-Tinkas*, we will telephone them from here,' he said.

'Sure is the best way to get in touch with an uncontacted tribe,' said Jude.

Mills was looking perplexed. 'I think Jorge has seriously lost the plot,' he said.

At the end of the landing stage a sign in English and Spanish read: 'Very much welcome to the Hotel Tigre Lara'. Above them on a small hillock that had escaped the rising floodwaters was a set of grand *palapas* and behind them there were individual huts arranged in a square. There wasn't anything else but the forest.

They walked up the steps to the dining-room.

'Now,' said Jorge, 'we have good long drink at the bar, then we have dinner. Then we talk about poisonous snakes that are here.'

Ramon nodded in agreement. 'This is a very good plan,' he said approvingly, as if he were a captain praising one of his subalterns. 'Jorge has the right idea. We should eat well, to keep our strength up for the forest, and then Jorge can talk to us about the dangers.'

Mills and Jude realised that Ramon was himself a little nervous of the forest, and, without his brother's knowledge, would be entirely lost here himself.

They stared around the dining-room of the hotel. Some of the tables had collapsed where their legs had been eaten through with rot. There was the smell of decay in the air.

Jorge took the box of beer and the whisky that he'd brought up from the dug-out and set it down behind the bar. He pulled a handful of bottles up onto the counter.

'You want a beer, Millito?' he asked, smiling. 'I am barman, now.'

'Where is everyone?' asked Mills.

Ramon laughed. 'Who's everyone?'

'The staff, the other guests?'

'We are,' said Jorge. 'No-one been in this hotel for two years. No staff, no guests. Carlita, she will find a broom, sweep up a bit. Carlita will get the fire going in the kitchen, cook the dinner. Good we bring her, no?'

Bernado, the boatman, was over by the pin-ball machine, which was actually an old wooden *bagatelle*, but the spring had rusted.

'So just tell me,' said Jude, 'the place was owned by an American and he's now in jail in Miami?'

'You knew him?' said Jorge. He laughed. 'So we have our own hotel!' he said triumphantly, throwing his arms open wide.

'In that case,' said Mills, 'as I'm paying for all of this, and all the provisions, I reckon I'm the boss. So I insist that I am head barman. Let's get these glasses washed.'

Jude looked around him. It was true, this hotel was indeed deserted and left to decay in a distant part of the jungle. No-one had stayed here for a long time and it was theirs. It probably wouldn't be that comfortable, but it was, as Mills would say, a thing to do.

Mills settled himself behind the bar to serve the next round of beers. 'What a great place, what a great place,' he kept muttering. 'Got my own hotel.'

The light was fading and as they filled the lamps with the kerosene from the boat there was a sudden thumping on the door to the dining-room.

'Martan!' shrieked Jorge, with joy. 'Martan is here, maybe Alfredo is still here too? Long time since I been here. Maybe they here too!'

Mills looked towards the door. The knocking had become more urgent but in the darkness, through the mosquito net, all he could make out was a short guy shuffling about impatiently.

'*Entra!*' called Jorge. He looked to Mills. 'Martan will be wanting beer. You will have to give him one of your beers, Millito.'

Mills got up and went to the bar.

Then the door crashed open and in came Martan, shouting and swaying about. He ran straight over to the bar, leapt up onto the bar stool and grabbed the bottle from Mills's hand.

Martan was a five-year-old woolly monkey. He climbed up on the bar and tipped the bottle into his mouth with both hands. He had deep chocolate-coloured fur and a long thick tail that he used to anchor himself down to the bar.

'Very good handy thing to have,' observed Jorge.

Martan had perfect little hands, and a pleasant constantly questioning face.

'He is so pleased to see us,' said Jorge.

Martan could certainly guzzle beer, and the whole time he drank he didn't look up. Then there was another knocking at the door.

'Alfredo,' said Jorge, 'Alfredo has come too.' He got up and went to the door, Alfredo was having difficulty with it.

'I suppose he wants a beer as well,' said Mills.

'No,' said Jorge, 'Alfredo doesn't drink. Never touch the stuff.'

'Glad to hear it.'

Martan had guzzled the beer so quickly that he'd given himself the hiccoughs now and was unashamedly farting on the bar-top in a kind of heartfelt syncopation.

Alfredo came into the room, much less hectically than Martan had done. He looked around rather dismissively at everyone, but proceeded, nevertheless, to the bar. He was a four foot long shimmering blue macaw. He walked with his head held high, seemingly looking down over his beak rather as if he imagined himself to be the General Manager of the place. Martan turned to him and shrieked, this was *his* party and he seemed to regard Alfredo as a gate-crasher. There was an evident hatred between the animals.

'They live here?' asked Jude.

'It's their hotel now. They used to be part of the staff here. Entertain the guests.'

'They were the cabaret?'

'Yes, the entertainment. When the hotel was abandoned, all the staff left very quick, escape drug agents. They leave Martan and Alfredo behind.'

'Well,' said Mills. 'Tell 'em they've let the place run to rack and ruin.'

'What do they live on? How do they survive?' asked Jude.

Ramon laughed, and looked at Jude as if he was the most stupid tourist he'd ever met. The drink made Ramon belligerent. 'This is the forest,' he said. 'It's where they come from. They live off the forest. Not bars and tourists. These are *real* animals.'

'They don't look it,' mumbled Jude. They looked very glad to have their old jobs back again as the cabaret act at the hotel Tigre Lara. They hadn't seen lights in the dining-room for a very long time.

After breakfast the next day Jorge said that they should 'take a walk' into the forest. 'So I show you how to walk,' he explained. 'Walking carefully because of snakes.'

It was necessary he said, before they went deeper in to find the *Mano-Tinkas*. No-one must be bitten, or 'big *fukken* trouble for everyone all-round'.

They walked out across the grass and Jorge led Mills and Jude over to a large hollowed out log that had slits cut in the side. Jorge called it a *cilindro*. 'It is the telephone,' he said. 'We can tell them we are coming on the *cilindro*.' He picked up an old club-like stick and beat on the log, it gave out a deafening sound that vibrated throughout the trees.

'Can be heard for miles and miles and many miles,' he said smiling. Ramon took the club from him and began beating out a frantic rhythm.

'Who are you calling?' asked Mills.

'He just tells everyone,' said Jorge, 'that we are here.'

'Don't do that,' replied Mills. 'They'll *all* come over and drink the beer.'

Jorge and Ramon began cutting staffs from a tree. 'For when you fall in the water we can pull you out. And we can stab the path. No snakes.'

'That makes them run away does it?' said Jude.

'Yes. Snakes, they don't want trouble either. They know you're there and they get out the *fukken* way. Except for ones who don't get out the *fukken* way, then you do.'

In the distance they heard the sound of another *cilindro* being beaten. An erratic rhythm like the one Ramon had thumped out.

'I think that's probably for you, Ramon,' said Mills. 'Or do you want me to get it?'

Jorge was laughing, he understood enough of Mills now to know that he was taking a shot at Ramon's ridiculous pride. 'You know what they're saying?' he laughed again. 'They're saying *yes, we are here too.*'

'The *Mano-Tinkas*?'

'No, not them. There are Indians back down the river, that is from them. Used to turistos a bit. They like to be funny with us.'

Ramon was looking anxious again.

Jorge returned to his favourite subject: snakes. 'Even in camp,' he said, 'you all be careful, be very smart.' He turned to Carlita, who was nervous of the forest too, and said the same in Spanish. Then he turned back to them. 'Sometimes we get bushmasters.'

'They sound fearsome.'

'Oh yes. Very much. Bushmaster snakes grow big, twelve feet. And they don't *fukken* run away. They like to kill, they enjoy it, and they hunt you. You are out here, walking to your hut at night, and you don't know. Following you is a bushmaster. And then he jumps, he jumps, oh, how far? He can jump nine ten metres like a whip. And when he hits you, the bushmaster tears a whole piece, like this,' he held up his hand making a fist. 'This much flesh from your back, or your leg, and his poison is inside you. Then you fall to the ground. And the bushmaster he sits beside you, watching you. He waits until you die and then he goes back into the forest. Like he is invisible. He's a definite mutherfukker is Mr Bushmaster.'

Jude and Mills were absolutely silent, but Ramon looked truly terrified.

'So, shall we go for our walk?' said Jorge.

Martan and Alfredo joined them for dinner again that evening. Mills and Carlita had joined forces in the kitchen to produce quite a spread, and when Martan leapt onto the table in excitement he spread it all a bit further. They sat now in their post-prandial state as the oil lamps flickered; Alfredo still mooching about cleaning the dinner plates and Martan on Mills's lap enjoying a cigarette. He was very sly when it came to easing Mills's pack out of his top pocket and pulling out a cigarette. If Mills tried to stop him he simply went off with the whole pack up into the rafters. It was better just to let him have one when he wanted it. They weren't lighted, of course, he just liked to strip the paper off and chew the tobacco. But charming and highly intelligent as Martan was, too much beer made him a bit of a bore. He'd begin to get aggressive with Alfredo and they'd shriek at each other and then both of them would start throwing glasses about. It was amusing at first, but when Martan grabbed the oil lamp by its handle, they feared for the consequences. A four foot macaw doused in flaming kerosene flying around in a confined space with a thatched roof would have caused something of an emergency.

Ramon was sitting moodily on the step, taking slugs from Mills's hip-flask. Jude was lying in a hammock holding his stomach. He'd taken another spill into the water on their walk in the forest and had swallowed mouthfuls of it in his panic to get back to the bank. There were caymans and piranha around, and even though Jorge said that they rarely ate any-one 'these days' he really didn't feel too comfortable about trusting to Jorge's appraisal of the recent culinary fads of South American alligators. Instead he had thrashed about in a panic grazing his arms on the bankside thorns and screaming for help.

Mills was still sitting at the devastated dining table with Martan, chatting to Jorge about the *Mano-Tinkas*.

'You really think we'll find them tomorrow?' asked Mills.

'Don't know,' he said. 'I don't think we will find them, no. It is too difficult. You cannot see far in this forest. You can't see as far as that wall.'

'You mean you think we won't find them at all?'

'No, I don't think so. I think it is not possible.'

Jorge was drunk now and had dropped his tourist-guide bit and was probably speaking the truth.

'But Ramon had no doubts after he spoke to those people today?'

During their 'walk' they had come across a small settlement, just four huts with a few pigs smooching about and dark eyes staring out from the thatch. Ramon had gone to talk with them and had come back saying that they had heard of the *Mano-Tinkas*, that they'd been up there and traded with them. That they had given him precise instructions to where they were, and that they should set off tomorrow, they were only a couple of hours off.

Jorge had, frankly, not believed him and a small altercation had ensued at the end of dinner: hence Ramon had taken himself off to sulk on the step.

'But Ramon is so certain,' said Mills.

'What does my cousin know? He don't know *fukken* shit.'

'Your *brother*,' said Mills, correcting him.

Jorge laughed. 'I don't have a brother. Ramon is my cousin, I think.'

'You think? You don't know if he's your cousin or not?'

'He says he is.'

'What? But how long have you known him? You must know if he's your cousin.'

'I just met him in Iquitos,' he said. 'He asked me to make this trip for him to the place up-river from here where he says your Indians are. I haven't heard anything about no new Indians.'

Mills looked over to Ramon where he was still moodily smoking and drinking on the step, letting in all the *fukken* mosquitos.

'Why did he say you were his brother?'

'I don't know. It is something tour-guides say. We say this to the tourists. It makes them happy, makes them trust you. They say, oh well, *Jorge* he is okay. He is a nice boy his brother he must be nice too. And then two of us have jobs not just one, and charge you double.'

'So I didn't even need Ramon along on this trip?'

'What does he do?' said Jorge, bitterly. 'He just drinks your beer. He don't know fukken shit about the forest. He's never been in jungle, I know. Look, he don't even get in a boat very good.'

'He says he's got to be back in Iquitos in two days anyway. If we don't find the *Mano-Tinkas* tomorrow, we can keep looking, yes?'

'Yes, sure. For certain. Thirty dollars a day. If they exist or if they don't.'

'You're a tough old breed, you tour-guides.'

As they went silent the whole room felt as if it was enveloped in the forest sounds, the cries and the skirmishes, and the heavy flop of the giant toads making their way under the dining room.

'You're okay, Jorge.'

'Sure I'm okay,' said Jorge.

25

Ramon was banging away at the *cilindro* before breakfast.

Mills walked up to him. 'You're telling them we're coming?' he asked.

'Yes, then they will expect us.'

'Well, tell them to put the kettle on.'

'For what, what do you mean? I don't understand?'

'It's just a saying, something they say in England,' said Mills. His attempt at humour had fallen flat. Like everyone else he was exasperated by the man. Ramon seemed twitchy again this morning, his eyes were dark with a hangover. As the two of them stared at each other for a moment, Mills realised that there was no way he could possibly be related to Jorge. Ramon was tall, the same height as himself, and his face was angular and chiselled where Jorge's was soft and boyish. He had the devious eyes of someone who'd had their hand in the till. It was going to be a long day.

'You really think we'll find these guys? Are you sure we're going in the right direction?'

'Don't worry,' said Ramon, with his supercilious smile. 'Relax.'

Ramon, himself, was anything but relaxed. 'After breakfast we get in the boat. We go just two hours up river, you will see the Indians, and we will be back here for dinner tonight. We will have a big celebration. Drink a lot of beer!'

'Well, we'll see,' said Mills.

He walked with him up to the dining-room for breakfast. Jorge and Carlita were already at the table with Martan, who was having his corn flakes, or at least he had his head in the box.

'Where is Jude?' asked Jorge.

'I don't know, I guess he's still in the hut. Lazy bastard. I'm keen to get going.' He drank some coffee and ate a bread roll. He understood now why Ramon had insisted on bringing so many provisions with them, even though he still believed he must be on some kind of a kick-back with the store-keepers. After they'd been up the river today both Mills and Jude had decided that they'd like to stay on in the place for as long as their provisions lasted. He'd thought that the corn flakes were a particularly ridiculous touch when they'd bought them, and now that he saw the box, torn to shreds, and corn flakes in Martan's hair and everywhere else, he realised that it was. But it made a fine photograph. Ramon annoyed him again when he wouldn't pose with the others. Ramon had been incredibly camera shy throughout the trip. He'd even ducked out of shot when Mills had taken photographs on the Ulysses. He had another coffee and went down to rouse Jude.

There was just a groan from inside the hut.

'My God,' said Mills. 'What's the matter with you? You look green.'

'I've got the runs,' he said. 'I don't think there can be anything left inside me. I've been turned inside out.'

'It's a hangover from hell, yeah?'

'Yeah. I've been like this all night, I feel awful.'

'You sound it. Do you think it's the river water you swallowed?'

'I reckon it must be. I'll be okay.'

'You want to try some breakfast?'

'No, no, I don't want anything.' He hadn't even moved out from under his mosquito net which was lying flat on top of him like a shroud, covering his face. He'd felt too rotten the night before even to hook it up.

'You think you can make the trip up the river in the boat?'

'Yeah, sure, sure.'

Mills pulled back the mosquito net.

'Look, don't worry. We'll postpone it. We'll go tomorrow.'

'You can't do that. They're nomads, what if your *Mano-Tinkas* wander off again?'

'Jorge says he doesn't think we'll find them today anyway. He thinks it'll take a couple of days searching all the little tributaries.

Even if they are there. He's agreed to stay. At least we'll be shot of miserable old Ramon.'

'Then you go,' said Jude. 'I'll just rest today. How long do you think you'll go for?'

'Well, it's dark by six, so we'll have to be back here before then. Jorge says it's two hours up river. We'll be back by tea-time.'

'I'll be okay. Leave me some water, maybe a couple of bread rolls'll stabilise my guts a bit.'

Mills went up to the kitchen where Jorge and Carlita were canoodling over the washing up. He felt uneasy about leaving Jude behind for the day.

'Jude is bad,' he said. 'Bad stomach,' he said, rubbing his belly.

'Ah!' said Carlita smiling, it was the first time she'd even attempted to speak to him. She left the kitchen and came back with a handful of long grass. She boiled it up in water.

'Forest medicine,' said Jorge smiling. 'Everyone gets it we bring up here.'

'Yeah?'

'Oh, yes. Don't last, soon better. This stuff cures it.' The grass smelled a little of camomile and a little of lemons as it boiled. She made a big jug of the tea and Mills took it down to Jude's hut.

'This'll probably kill you,' he said, pouring some into a cup. 'Apparently you've got to keep sipping it.'

'It looks like boiled grass . . .' Jude muttered.

'Are you sure you'll be all right here on your own?'

'Sure, I'm okay really, just got a bit of the squits.'

'I presumed Carlita would be staying behind, but apparently she's coming. She's an Indian herself and speaks dialect, that's why Jorge brought her along, so he says.'

'Yeah, right, yeah,' he said weakly. 'You go, I'll be fine. I'm feeling better already.'

'You do?'

'Yes. I'll see you at tea-time. I'll be fine by then, but I don't fancy rocking in a boat right now. This boiled grass is quite nice,' he said.

'If you get really bad, like, if you feel you need medical help or anything, telephone me.'

'Telephone you?'

'Yeah, just bash that drum thing a few times. Dot dot dot dash dash dash dot dot dot. It's *SOS*. We'll hear you, won't we?'

'You see,' said Jude, smiling, 'it was worth going to military academy after all.'

Ramon was cross. 'But he has to come,' he said. 'We need him to balance the boat.'

'Well he's not coming and that's that,' snapped Mills. 'Come on, let's go and find these *fukken* Indians.'

Jude had made it down to the landing stage and waved slowly as they pushed out into the lagoon.

The mist was almost cleared from the surface of the Rio Tigre now and egrets and turtles sat on the floating logs. Every now and then they heard the splash of a rotten bough plummeting down into the water. The floodwaters had taken away all definition to this part of the river.

'And there's yet another tributary?' Mills asked Ramon. Ramon pulled out his map.

'Yes,' he said. 'It is here,' pointing to an area of green with no marks on it at all. 'There's no river on the map, because it's not on the map yet,' he said.

'The Indians you spoke to were certain this is where they exchanged gifts with them?'

Ramon heaved a bored sigh. 'We have been through this a dozen times,' he said. Mills wished that he'd been able to speak to them, or the guys in Iquitos, himself. When he'd asked to meet them the afternoon they were provisioning he'd been told that they'd already left on a trip. He began to believe that Ramon had made this whole route up himself.

The sun was now burning strong through the window of the hut and Jude was feeling worse. He'd begun to feel slightly delirious, he was quivering, and the bed sheet was soaked with his sweat. There was a terrible smell and he realised that he'd been sick again, but he felt too weak to even move himself away from the mess he'd made on the bed. He kept imagining he could hear voices. He thought he could hear people chatting by the hotel pool, and the clink of glasses on the waiter's tray. But there wasn't a pool. Then he began to realise what it was. It was coming from the dining-room. Martan was in there with Alfredo rehearsing their cabaret for tonight. There was a great crash and the sound of breaking bottles. Martan had pulled the crate of beer down from the top in the bar. There was a chorus of shrieks, and then silence.

Jude dozed for another hour and woke to hear his door creaking open. It was Martan coming quietly and slowly towards him, clutching a bread roll in his hand. He seemed to be holding it out to him.

Oh, bless you, Martan, he thought, you've come to see how I am. He'd felt too weak even to reach for the roll that was on the table by his bed. He could hear Martan making his funny little clicking sound with his throat that he did when he was worried.

'Come up here, little man,' he said, softly. 'You come to cheer me up?'

Then the bread roll hit him hard on the side of the head as Martan shied it at him. He heard a sullen thump and looked down to the floor. Martan was lying flat on his back with his arms outstretched. The room was reeking with beer fumes.

'Martan, you're drunk, you useless little bastard.'

There was a wavering little groan from the floor, and then another thud. Martan had pulled himself up onto all fours and was pulling at the bed sheet on the other single bed. After a bit of heaving and sighing he pulled himself up onto the bed, belched, and fell back with his head on the pillow, his arms outstretched, staring at the ceiling.

'What time's nurse coming round?' muttered Jude. Alfredo – who didn't touch drink of course – was already at the door, banging his beak.

'You're a mess, you know that, Martan?' Martan grunted in reply. He didn't want to talk. 'You're like all those old colonials who go to seed and turn to drink in the jungle. Except you were bloody born here . . .' Martan sighed. 'I know I'm sorry, I'm rambling, I'm feeling delirious.'

Thank God Alfredo couldn't open doors. He wondered if Martan often spent his afternoons like this, having a kip in one of the rooms to get away from Alfredo's moralising. He certainly looked at home in the bed.

An hour later he heard voices in the dining-room again. He looked towards the bed. Martan was still asleep. He guessed it must be Mills back and dragged himself out of the bed and opened the door. Slowly he began walking towards the dining-room, all the time looking around him for a bushmaster. When he got to the dining-room it was deserted, just as it had been left from breakfast, except he fancied he could still hear voices, a distant echo of voices. Then he heard an outboard start up. He looked out of the window and down to the landing stage on the lagoon. Two men were leaving in a boat. One of the men looked back, and the sun caught the angry scowl across his face, and the glint of what could only have been a gun in his hand. The face suddenly came into sharp focus; the hypnotist from Leticia: Jaime Souza.

'We are there,' said Ramon, and turned to Bernado the boatman directing him to a landing gap on the bank. Bernado cut the engine and the dug-out glided in the black water until they hit the bank.

'There's no-one here,' said Mills. 'Wouldn't they have heard the noise of the outboard?'

'Yes,' said Ramon. 'We have to walk now, a little way through the forest. Just ten minutes and we will be there.'

'But I thought they were by the river?'

'Yes. But not this river. The tributaries do not connect. It is quicker to walk than take the boat.'

Mills turned to look at Jorge. Jorge shrugged his shoulders. It was an odd way to go about the forest when it was in flood.

'Bring the machetes,' said Ramon. 'We may have to cut through.'

The machetes were evil looking things. Ramon took one and gave the other to Bernado.

Bernado wanted to stay with his boat. He didn't like the look of it.

'No,' said Ramon. 'You come too Bernado.'

'Bernado doesn't come, he stay with boat for safety,' said Jorge. Bernado always did this. There was a definite air of tension.

'Well Jorge is in charge of the boat,' said Mills. 'Whatever he thinks best.'

'No,' said Ramon. 'I am in charge now. You must trust me, I have the map. Relax. Bernado must come and help machete.'

Jorge signalled to Bernado to get out of the boat. Bernado shrugged and complied. Ramon seemed more unsure of the *Mano-Tinkas* than he'd previously led them to believe.

Mills turned to Jorge and whispered: 'Do you know where we are, Jorge?'

'No,' he replied quietly. 'I think at first I did. I know this river a little. People live here, another tribe, the *Boros*. But now I look and see, I don't know.' He sounded a little nervous. Carlita was smiling as usual, she always smiled as if she didn't know the expressions for worry or sadness, she was wearing her best dress again today. Ramon was thwacking the foliage with his machete, though it really wasn't necessary. He was just swaggering and being wilful.

It was hot, steamy, and dark as if the whole of this part of the Amazon basin had been put in a pan to be simmered. The air was filled with the searing sound of insects.

'You have got your *regalos* with you?' said Jorge.

'Sure,' said Mills. He hadn't forgotten his presents for the Indians. The Bic lighters were a piece of low-tech magic. Mills's pockets were stuffed with them, all in different garish shades of translucent plastic.

No-one was speaking now and sweat was dripping from their foreheads, they no longer had the breeze of the fast moving boat to cool them. Mills's shirt was sodden with sweat and every breath tasted of the decaying foliage. He could hear Jorge tutting and complaining to Carlita behind him. Where was Ramon leading them? As far as he knew he'd never been in the Peruvian jungle before, surely he couldn't be so sure of this track just from an x mark on his *fukken* map?

There was a bird-call, loud and repetitive and Ramon stopped for a moment. Mills turned to Jorge. 'What's that?'

'It's not a bird,' said Jorge. 'I know that call. That's Indians.'

'Well, I guess we'd better get ourselves ready.' Mills pulled a cigarette out of his pack and offered one to Jorge.

'Anyone got a light?' he said. Jorge slapped his pockets and looked at him seriously for a moment. Then he laughed. Mills lit their cigarettes and they marched on behind Ramon, his machete under his arm now like a baton.

They came to a stretch of water, no more than thirty feet across. This is my unnamed river? thought Mills. The *Rio Millito*, it certainly lives up to the name I wanted to give it. A couple of thin tree trunks had been laid across it, but they sank somewhat in the middle.

Then they all stopped suddenly, as they looked through the over-hanging gloom. There were a dozen Indian faces, some of them gesturing with spears and baring their teeth. Naked children were knee-deep in the water, they could make out the shapes of a couple of women. The men with spears were growling. They were wearing nothing but a wrapping of beaten parchment around their waists, their faces were painted with the whiskers of a jaguar.

Ramon looked more shocked than any of them to see the Indians, it was as if it was the last thing he expected to encounter. He quickly pulled himself together.

'We must walk forward,' said Ramon, briefly turning. 'We must smile and walk to the bank.'

'Smile?' said Mills, incredulously. Jorge shrugged his shoulders. Carlita was smiling, albeit nervously.

As they crossed the makeshift tree-trunk bridge the warriors shook their spears at them and growled louder. Ramon turned around and looked at Mills.

'It's their greeting,' he said. 'To threaten and not attack in these cultures is commonly the same as a welcome.' He raised his hand imperiously to them. Mills turned and looked at Jorge. Jorge raised his eyebrows as if to say, that's a new one on me.

But when they got up onto the bank there was a small clearing with a puddle of light where the sun came through the rare gap in the trees. There were about forty of them, all smiling and excited, but looking a little nervous too. Every time Mills looked at one of them in particular they filled with embarrassment, took their hands away from their naked private parts and covered their faces.

Everyone who was dressed was dressed much the same.

'The skirts that the men wear, what are they made from?' Mills asked Jorge.

'Tree bark,' he replied. 'They peel it and beat it and beat it many more times. Like paper, no?' He smiled, feeling confident in his tourist guide stuff. The bark was white and had been decorated with loosely geometric brown painted patterns. Everyone looked the same, as if there was just one fashion for make-up and couture here this season. He was gradually seized by a growing excitement. He was genuinely off the map.

They moved slowly through the clearing while the children pulled and tugged at them, and the women giggled, and the men repeated a bit of cursory spear shaking. They got to where it grew darker again. They only seemed to have cleared about a dozen trees, not much of a break in the rain forest canopy, just a single beam of light in the darkness.

Mills felt he was twelve feet tall. Ramon and he towered above these people and they seemed pretty impressed by how big they were too. A woman, with pointed breasts, came up to him and reached her hand up to touch his blond hair while all the other women giggled, hiding the sound of it behind their hands.

Then they were left for a moment with the women and the children while the men seemed to go into a bit of a conference. The children began to crowd around, looking up at him and muttering what sounded like *'daddy, daddy, daddy.'*

'What are they saying, Jorge?'

Jorge shrugged his shoulders.

Everything went silent, and they all turned to look as the men parted and stood in a line. In the middle of them was an old man, of about four foot two, made marginally higher by the fact that he was wearing as a hat the head of a jaguar. He looked very solemn.

'Head man,' whispered Jorge. 'The chief.'

Then nothing happened at all for a few moments.

This is the time when I have to do something, thought Mills. They've put on quite a display. Now I have to go and do something.

He pulled a turquoise Bic lighter from his back pocket and

walked over to shake hands with the chief. But these *Mano-Tinkas* didn't shake hands so he improvised by slapping his chest twice and presented the chief with the lighter.

'*Daddy*!' said the chief, smiling and nodding his head. There was a general murmur of approval from the crowd, it seemed to satisfy, and Mills breathed a sigh of relief. The chief breathed a sigh back, and everyone smiled. He had been as nervous as Mills was. Mills was moved. He could understand why José Gregorio Hernández had chosen this tribe to appear to; they were simple and pacific and had a quiet dignity.

Then the chief led him to a small, shaded, palm construction, which had a single thin pole suspended twelve inches above the ground like a limbo dancer's bar.

'I think you gotta sit down now,' whispered Jorge. Ramon had hung back, he just seemed to be flashing glances all around like one of Mills's father's bodyguards.

Mills sat on the pole. He felt like Elizabeth II on one of her post-Imperial tours to the Sandwich Islands.

Now that he was sitting down the entire tribe just stared at him, smiling happily. There seemed to be a general sigh of relief that the first part of the visit had gone to plan. After five minutes of this hovering about, Mills's 'crew' having retreated to the shadows, the old chief called his men together in a football huddle. They didn't seem to know what to do next. The younger men were disagreeing with their Head Man. Then he seemed to insist, that was it, he appeared to say: We have to do a dance. That's what we do.

Mills watched and smiled. The pole hurt like hell. He looked over to Jorge again, who helpfully repeated his favourite gesture of shrugging his shoulders.

Mills signalled to him. Jorge came over.

'I think they're going to do a ceremonial dance, is it okay if I take pictures, or will they be offended? A lot of tribes think you're stealing their soul, don't they?' It would be important to have pictures of them, as evidence.

Jorge replied in a low reverential voice. 'I don't know if photographs are possible. I think no. First you must win their trust. They know nothing of the outside world. They will not know why suddenly you cover your face, and then flashes of light come out. It could frighten them. There may be panic. Already I have seen the chief trying to get the top off the lighter you gave him to drink the gasoline.'

'Take my camera,' whispered Mills. 'If you get a chance take photos. This tribe has never been recorded on film before?'

'No, Millito.'

'It'd be quite a thing.'

'Yes, Millito.'

Mills watched as the men began their dance. At first they seemed to be forming a snake as they wove in a wayward, slithering line. Instead of music all they had was their own breathing, and sudden grunts, and their stamping of a complicated rhythm on the forest floor.

After their dance the men went for a good sit down while the children invaded the dancefloor, as they would do at any cheap wedding in a function hall. They jiggled about and bit each other. They were rather taken by the stamping on the ground that they'd seen their elders do.

Mills was beaming. Well, he thought, if they're not standing on ceremony, I'm not. He went over to the chief and embraced him, laughing.

Ramon was looking cross. He turned to Jorge and Bernado.

'We have to go now. These Indians could turn on us and kill us.'

'Don't talk rot,' said Jorge, in Spanish. 'Everybody's having fun. Mills is no fool.'

Ramon looked at the ground. He watched as Mills gave out the other Bic lighters and for his pains was mobbed by the enthusiastic Indians. He now had the chief's hand in his and much to the man's bemusement he was shaking it up and down.

The chief had taken a shine to Mills's white straw sun hat. He was offering the head of the jaguar that he had in exchange. It's only polite, thought Mills, to accept. He gave him his hat.

The chief broke his hand away from Mills's and sat down on a log. He began chattering away. Mills nodded and smiled, he couldn't understand a word of what the man was saying, but the chief didn't really seem to realise that. It was pleasant just to talk.

Nothing here was as he'd imagined it would be.

'We must go now,' said Ramon, taking his arm with that nervous look on his face again.

'We only just got here,' said Mills. 'These people are extraordinary.'

Ramon expelled some air and walked off.

'Carlita,' called Mills. He turned to Jorge. 'Tell her I want to speak to the chief about José Gregorio.'

Jorge explained this to his wife and she began speaking to the chief. The chief pulled Mills down on to the log beside him.

He stared up into the gap in the trees, almost blinding himself with the sunlight.

'Tell him,' said Mills, translating through Jorge, and Jorge through Carlita to the chief, 'that I have seen the figures his people have made of José Gregorio.'

Jorge spent a great deal of time nodding his head and then finally he translated. 'Carlita says that their dialect is very strange. Hard to understand, but she thinks he says, what figures? We don't make figures, we're not very good at carving wood.'

'Say to him, the figures of the white man with the hat and the hair above his lip. The man they have seen in their dreams?'

There was a pause.

'The chief he says he don't know what you talk about,' said Jorge.

'Ask him about a great doctor who has come to heal his people.'

Jorge listened and shook his head again.

'He doesn't know anything about doctors. Since they settled here they don't get sick any more. They've got all the medicine they need from other tribes.'

'But they're nomads, they've just arrived?'

Jorge and Carlita spoke again. The clouds were building up in the sky for a torrent and it made the clearing they were in turn suddenly and irrevocably dark.

'He says no,' said Jorge. 'They are not nomads. They've lived around here since his grandfather brought them down.'

Mills looked around at the simple temporary dwellings. Some of the structures were made of green wood, fresh. He didn't believe it. He knew enough to know that this was a new habitation.

'Tell him I can see that they are nomads by their habitation here.'

Mills sat and waited for the translation and the reply, toying with a small carved wooden snake that one of the little boys had pressed into his hands.

'The chief says he'd thought you come here to help, not to ask big question.'

Mills took Jorge's hand. He felt very close to Jorge today, and his sweet young wife, who was still sitting there smiling, waiting for her next phrase of translation for the chief.

Mills spoke in very slow English so that he was sure Jorge understood him.

'Ramon has lied to us. We are in big trouble,' he said. 'These are not the *Mano-Tinkas*, this is something, I think, that Ramon hadn't planned for.'

'I know this is all wrong,' said Jorge. 'Where is Ramon?'

'I don't know. He's wandered off.'

'Wandered?' said Jorge.

'Gone. Vamoose,' explained Mills.

'Yes,' said Jorge. 'But Bernado the boatman is still here. He's not gone far. He can't get away from us without a boat. You think he has gone with your money?'

Mills shook his head.

'Maybe he has another boat somewhere,' said Mills. Jorge didn't understand. 'Ask the chief the same question again. I think we've left him worrying long enough. Ask him why their village is so small if they've been here so long.'

Jorge turned to Carlita, who was looking worried herself now, she could hear the quavering timbre of her young husband's voice.

Jorge turned back, his face entirely blank.

'He says this isn't their village. They have very good village but not here, over there a mile, they built this place because they heard that the hotel is open again and they will be able to sell their beads again like they used to.'

'Who told them that?'

Mills waited for the translation.

'The men that came from the city,' said Jorge.

'I'm worried now. Ask him who came to speak to them.'

They spoke. Jorge turned back to Mills.

'He said it was seven days ago. He came in a fast boat with guns.'

'Then it couldn't have been Ramon. We were still on the *Ulysses* then, so who was it?'

Jorge tried to translate all of this to Carlita, and her smile slightly diminished with the complexity of it all. She translated it again to the chief. His reply was brief.

'Who was it?' asked Mills.

'"You", he says.'

Mills thought for a moment, and held his head in his hands. 'I came here?' He looked up. 'He means an *American*, or someone from the city. I think we've got to get ourselves out of here or we're going to be killed.'

Jorge looked shocked. 'By these Indians?'

'No, Jorge. He means someone came here and set up this trip. Doesn't he?' Mills looked down at the ground.

'But why?'

'The Venezuelans,' said Mills. 'Or the Colombians, or God knows who. It's a long story, I met this priest in Venezuela, and the military . . .' His voice trailed off. 'The whole thing's been pretty elaborate all round,' he said. 'They don't want me to publish Father Leonardo's notes, and they knew a story like this would lure me up here into the middle of nowhere. Then they can kill me.' It all seemed so blindingly obvious now. The Venezuelan secret service, or the Colombians, wouldn't dare kill the son of a presidential candidate where it might be discovered, but here it would be perfect, his body would never be found. They had pulled him up this river like a fish on a hook. He felt sick in his heart.

'Millito, it's okay, no?'

'No, Jorge, it's not okay. I don't know why this is, or what, but there's just too much of it. I can't think straight. We're in a trap, and we have to be pretty smart now to get out of it. These poor Indians have been duped and so have we.'

Jorge didn't understand a word. The chief just sat there silently, still hoping that his civic reception had been okay. They're a funny kind of people, the chief seemed to be thinking, but they were troubled men, they'd brought a little bit of magic, and a lot of worry with them. About time they went.

They re-crossed the bridge made of the thin forest saplings. There was still no sign of Ramon. None of them spoke, neither Mills nor Jorge nor Bernado. Carlita wouldn't have spoken anyway. No-one asked what had happened to Ramon.

Mills was disappointed. No great miracle of José Gregorio's had been forthcoming. It had really seemed to him that here, in the back waters of the Amazon, with this simple tribe, such a miracle had a rightness about it. It should have been. Instead they had used the Doctor against him; to trap him.

He thought of Jaime Souza and his enthusiasm for the doctor, and what a coincidence it had been meeting him on the plane down like that. He shook his head. Perhaps he had overtaken them in one of the speed boats while they were on the *Ulysses*.

The fake carving of José Gregorio was a clever touch but, he supposed, simply done. And Ramon had, as a result, made a great deal of money out of him during the low tourist season. It was probable that Ramon wasn't even from Leticia at all. But would Ramon now go as far as killing him, even here in the forest where it was so easy to do?

'What is that?' said Jorge, suddenly, as they walked back through the darkening forest towards the dug-out.

'What?' said Mills.

'There are people here,' he whispered, 'other people.'

Mills listened but could hear nothing, just the dense rasping of the forest. But Jorge, whose ears could separate these sounds, was sure. They were suddenly feeling very vulnerable, there was just Bernado the boatman to look after them, but when he had reached for his machete to depart, it had gone. He was looking white and nervous now, unhappy without his boat.

Suddenly they found that they were trapped in a fork of the trodden trails that the Indians had made from one riverbank to another. It didn't seem to be the way they had come. Bernado was leading, feeling certain he could find his way back to his boat, and keen to get to it.

There was a movement in the forest around them again. It

wasn't an animal, it wasn't silent enough. It wanted its presence to be heard. They stopped and froze.

A voice spoke through the sultry gloom. 'Well, good afternoon, Mills.'

They froze and Carlita whimpered and clutched her young husband's hand.

'Who's that?' said Mills, though he recognised the voice.

There was a short laugh.

'It's the Bushmaster,' said the voice.

There was the sound of a swish of feathers; the flight of an arrow.

Bernado fell to the ground, but even before his heavy, silent body hit the leaf floor another three arrows had pummelled in to him. They came with force out of the trees.

Then the other arrows came out of the darkness. Even as Carlita died she said nothing, just folded into Jorge's arms, and they died together.

26

Night had come on and with it the cacophony of the forest around him. Jude felt lost and alone, and confused.

Martan wasn't there any more, just the rucking of the sheets where he'd fought with them.

Where was Mills? thought Jude. Perhaps they won't be back tonight, perhaps the Indians have invited him to their bosom and he's enjoying the notion of being some great explorer in the chief's hut tonight?

In the afternoon Jude's fever got worse and he began to wonder whether it was malaria.

Night came again and broke him out of his delirium. He got out of bed and made his way across the grass, loaded with fat toads like land mines, towards the dining hut. There were no lights burning.

Martan and Alfredo enthusiastically joined him, expecting dinner. But there was no dinner. He collapsed feverishly into the hammock, the short walk had nearly finished him. He was weak from dehydration and the lack of food.

He stared out into the pitch black night. He was worried now. Why hadn't they returned? Mills wouldn't leave him like this. Mills, he knew, was in trouble, and in his weakness he began to weep. That night he slept in the dining-room.

The next morning he realised two things, one: that the fever came in waves and there were always a few hours in the day when he was able to function, and two: that Mills was not returning and that he was stranded here with no boat.

In his periods of strength he got out of the hammock and got himself to the kitchen. He needed to eat, he kept passing out with hunger. He saw the boxes where the bread was and the rest of the cereals.

The entire supply had been eaten by termites. There were just two plastic bottles of water, one of them had been left without a top on and was now a cloudy green. The other had been chewed through by Martan, and was lying dry on the floor.

He pulled himself slowly towards the lavatory, to drink the water, he was desperate for water, but that too was green.

He collapsed into the hammock and another night passed.

He woke early the next morning, his throat painful with dryness. *There has to be a way out of here*, he said to himself. But he couldn't see how. There was no view of the river here, they were at the end of a small water gulley that formed a lagoon, he couldn't even wave to a passing boat, no boats passed. He didn't have the energy or the courage to swim in the black water the quarter mile to the Rio Tigre. The hotel was closed, no-one would be coming. He had no strength to weep any more.

Late in the afternoon when the wildlife was preparing to change shifts for the night, and the mosquitos were irritating the ears, Martan came in with a large dark fruit in his hand. He had bitten through the hard peel, and inside was a luscious dripping pulp the colour of watermelon.

Jude held out his hand towards it. Martan snatched it away. Jude tried to speak to him, but all he could produce from his dried out throat was the kind of guttural clicking that Martan himself uttered when he was worried.

Martan moved nearer to him and pressed the fruit slowly to Jude's mouth.

Jude nodded and ate it. Martan went to the door and disappeared. Then he came back with another.

Yes, thought Jude, as long as I can keep this feeling like some sort of game, he'll bring me these fruits.

Martan had no consistency. He'd do a thing three or four times in succession, but then, experience had taught him that humans get bored with it. So you stop and try something else.

Hang from the rafters maybe, or steal their cigarettes. Piss on the table.

But Martan brought him another fruit, he seemed to understand the man was ailing, and didn't do much without fruit. Maybe he even understood that Jude, like them, had been abandoned in the hotel and would have to live again from the forest.

There was still another hour of light left. Strengthened by the sweet pulp of Martan's tree he began to think more coherently. *Dot dot dot dash dash dash dot dot dot*, he thought, remembering Mills's last words to him. The *cilindro*. He hadn't thought of it. He didn't have to reach the river at all, there was the *cilindro*.

He pulled himself over to where the log drum was. The club was still lying there where Ramon had left it.

Unable to stand, he knelt down by the *cilindro* and raised the club high above his head. He brought it down onto the resounding drum.

Jaime Souza had been on the river for six days now. He was bitten and he was tired. The two accomplices he had with him were becoming exasperated. Their heart wasn't in this.

'Cut the engine,' he said suddenly. They did as they were told, but they'd have to be turning back now anyway, they'd need their floodlights soon to get them back to Iquitos.

'Listen,' he said. They listened.

'A *cilindro*,' he said. 'I thought I heard a *cilindro* thumping.' They shook their heads. The forest had so many sounds in it.

It was dark now and the jungle noise was flooding the hut. Jude lay on his bed, giving up hope. He pressed his face into the mattress. Tomorrow he would have to drink the river water, and that would make him more sick. There was nothing that he could do. Martan had stopped bringing him fruits and he'd seen him from the mesh of his window walking slowly back into the forest, without looking back.

He didn't see the torch flashes as they swooped around the dining-room.

'Someone *is* here,' said Jaime Souza, 'look, someone has pushed

all the breakfast things from the table. It can only be the boy
Jude. He must have hidden from us. We have to find him.'

'The animals,' said one of the agents. 'No-one has been in this
lodge for years.'

'We search the place,' he said.

'We cannot, there are snakes.'

'We search the place.'

Jude thought it was Martan returned and called out to him. Then
he saw Souza's face bearing over him. He felt sure that he was
delirious again and closed his eyes. But then as he heard him
speak he realised that his fear was real.

'Get him into the boat, we take him to Iquitos,' said Souza.
'He's sick. He doesn't know where he is.'

They gave him water on the boat.

'Where's Mills?' was the first thing Jude said as the lights of
the port began to startle him awake.

'Drink some more of the water,' said Souza, looking down into
his deathly grey face as the reflections of the black water from
the boat's floodlight played across him.

Jude's head flopped to one side.

As they got into the waterfront of Iquitos in the dead of night,
Jaime Souza took charge of the bag of things he'd collected from
Mills's room in the lodge. Inside were the notes that Father
Leonardo had given him.

'Okay,' said Souza, 'let's get him in a car and go.'

They took him to an apartment in one of the decaying
Portuguese palaces that lined the stinking waterfront.

'We'll take turns to watch him through the night,' said Souza.
'Go and find a doctor. Tell him to bring a re-hydration drip and
antibiotics.'

Souza laid Jude on a bed in the corner and settled down on a
chair in the darkened room, his pistol on his lap. He was tired
after days on the river, his eyes were sunken and his flesh pallid;
he shook his head slowly from side to side like a lamp swaying
on the deck of a ship.

It was an hour before they found a doctor. He was a short man
and nervous to enter the room. He stood for a few moments in

the doorway, his beady eyes darting about the room. This sort of thing was not unusual in this port, but nevertheless he was surprised to find his task was re-hydration and not a gunshot wound. It suggested that the people who wanted the boy treated were not, in this instance, his friends.

'Do the best you can,' said Souza. 'He'll live?'

'He's very sick,' said the doctor. 'His throat has closed. We'll see.'

In the morning Souza pulled the curtains back and looked out into the street. A tribe of Indians were being driven by in military trucks.

It was the second day of the investigation at the Portuguese hotel and the heavily armed soldiers kept their guns trained on the Moro Indians as they brought them again from the barracks. As they drove them across the plaza a man had thrown a rock and caught one of the Indian children on the side of the head. Blood streamed down his face, but he just stood there, as if nothing more could possibly increase his misery; his eyes were fixed and frightened. The mood of the crowd in the square had been ugly this morning. The Indians stood in the trucks, holding on to one another.

The chief was still wearing his jaguar's head-dress, but it looked a battered and sad thing now. Four soldiers in full battle-gear stood around him propping him up with their rifles.

When the military had brought the Indians in on the gunship they had gone entirely silent at the sight of the vast town that seemed to them to be rising unnaturally out of the floodwater. None of them had ever ventured out of the forest. They had heard of The World, and they had met some members of it, but they had never hoped to see it themselves. It was more terrifying than they had imagined. It looked a brutal hard place without flowers or birdsong. In the gloom of the forest they lived by their ears, but here there was nothing but a deafening roar of sound where the calls were indistinguishable one from the other.

The rubber barons who'd built Iquitos at the turn of the century had brought Indians down the river too, much like this in belching old gunships, for slave labour, and most of them had died. These same palaces that their forebears had stared up at from the waterfront, quivering while being sold off as slaves, were now decaying themselves in the obdurate heat. Since that time the tribes that had roamed the back-waters had feared Iquitos. It lived in their legends as a Hades, a place far worse than their own conceptions of hell.

The Indians were unloaded from the truck and they stood there still blinking in the sunlight, used only to a life spent under the dark canopy of trees. How could these people live here without cover? Where is their food? What can they hunt here? But in their hearts they knew that these people of The World did not need to hunt, because they didn't need to eat; they didn't need cover of trees in hell; because all these people were already dead. The dead had come to their village and captured them alive; now they stood them in the courtroom, to barter over their meat; and now they would be dead too, and their spirits would never get back to the forest. They were lost.

People in the crowd screamed '*Asesinos!*' at them, and they were holding copies of newspapers with Mills's photo. The crowd cursed them for destroying their tourist trade.

There were just forty of them, the entire tribe, and the men and women were topless and the children naked. The sky was beginning to collect bulbous clouds and they could smell the forthcoming rain. They stared blankly at The World.

The crowd screamed at them as they were led towards the court house created by the military out of the old tiled ballroom of the Portuguese hotel.

They led them in at rifle point.

Jaime Souza watched from the balcony.

These wild Indians looked pathetic as they passed under the darkness of the portico in their skirts and their now faded whiskers. He shook his head sadly and walked back to stand under the cooling draught of the overhead fan. It was a terrible business and it gave him a sick feeling in his gut.

He'd heard that when they had brought the diminutive chief up on to the stand he had barely been able to see over the rail. The hundred or so people packed into the former hotel ballroom were sweating in the heat and fanning themselves with whatever came to hand. The Indians just quivered and blinked. The prosecutor had held up Mills's charred hip-flask and made a great thing of LBJ's initials. But the liberal press around the world were coming out heavily against the trial and nothing the Peruvians did was working in their favour. There was real anger in America at Mills's murder. The atmosphere in the courtroom was very tense. The whole affair was a mess. So far the only thing the Moro chief had done was to mutter the word *Daddy* at the prosecutor. With the scrutiny of the world's press it would be a difficult task to get the survivor of the incident out of the town undetected. Souza angrily stamped his foot.

Kyle and Anne Clearwater were standing on the lawn in Austin, dressed in black mourning, facing the press. For days the news media had been waiting for Clearwater's formal announcement that he was pulling out from the presidential race after the death of his son. Finally they had emerged, walking with their heads down, holding hands. For the first time in their lives looking like defeated people.

Clearwater came up to the microphones and began to speak in a cracked voice. He began by listing the reasons why he had entered the race: the *preservation of the family* and now he added to this the pressing responsibilities for America in the twenty-first century, whoever it was that would be at its helm. He wished whoever that was Godspeed. Chief amongst these responsibilities he added the rather ambitious notion that the whole world should become a place where everyone could live without the fear of violence; whether that be the sidewalks of New York; the settlements of the West Bank, or, indeed the jungles of Peru. His voice gradually regained its former strength of purpose, but slowly.

'I have come to say to you today that I can no longer continue this, with so much cost to the family I love . . .' his voice broke again, momentarily. 'The tragedy that we feel, in the young life of our son being snuffed out is, I know, a tragedy that America shares. Wherever he went on the campaign trail there were groups of young people waiting outside the hotels. It wasn't me they'd come to see. They'd turned out for him. Just this morning I got a letter from a young woman who'd been in the crowd the night we were down in San Antonio. I'd like to read that letter to you as a tribute to my son's memory.'

Anne Clearwater squeezed him around the waist and they looked into each other's eyes for a brief, pain-filled, moment, as the camera lenses zoomed in and held them in a misty shot. Then he fumbled with the pink scented paper in his hands and began to read the young girl's letter: 'I have cried myself to sleep every night since I heard the news on CNN. Mills Clearwater was my hero and I have his picture from a magazine cover above my bed. I thought I couldn't go on without him. I only met him once but he had such a big smile and was so full of life. But I can go on because Mills has died a hero, and he will always be a hero, he has become part of a special band of people who will never let us down.'

Clearwater, the defeated man, slowly folded the letter and handed it to Anne, who held it to her breast for a moment.

The press corps were silent.

'He died a hero,' repeated Clearwater. 'No father could ever have admired, respected, and loved a son so much as I . . .'

He broke down and couldn't go on. The press began to clap quietly.

He exhaled a great sigh, and then, pulling Anne closer towards him, they both slowly closed their eyes and began to walk away from the microphones sadly back into the house. Briefly Clearwater turned and gave the press a single wave.

Jude was still delirious, and his throat was so damaged he was unable to speak, but the news of Mills's death seemed to have penetrated his consciousness as they had talked about it in the room on the waterfront. He wept silently. He muttered, sometimes he appeared to click his throat like a jungle monkey. Then he opened his eyes fully wide and looked into Souza's face.

'Why?' he mouthed.

Souza shook his head.

Mills's body was to be flown back to the States in a couple of hours, where the Clearwaters were due to meet it on the tarmac in Austin, draped in the Union flag. The whole thing had been timed so that the arrival could be covered live on the main evening News.

'No-one knows you're here,' said Souza. 'We have to get you out of here.' He looked across at the doctor, who shook his head. 'He's too sick to travel.'

'He has to travel, we leave in two hours. Get him as good as you can. We got medics on board Don Emillio's plane.'

The doctor nodded.

'And do yourself a favour and forget you ever came here or you'll be dead too,' said Souza, in as kindly as way as he could to the doctor.

On the plane, a private jet, the Colombian medics were preparing to administer an anaesthetic. Jude's breathing was worse now, the moment was critical, the infection that had taken hold of his throat was threatening his windpipe. They were preparing to perform an emergency tracheotomy. Jude could hear the roar of the jet's engines as they headed towards Colombia. Once again he turned to Souza and mouthed the word 'Why?'

Souza took his hand, Jude didn't have the strength to pull it away.

'I think you can understand me,' said Souza. He spoke in a low hypnotic voice, just as he had that night after dinner in Leticia, but there was a quiver of emotion to it.

'I wasn't entirely straight with your friend Mills, was I?'

Jude's eyes glared at him.

Jaime shook his head. 'I followed him to Leticia because Don Emillio asked me to. I work for Don Emillio. He was worried he would come to harm . . .'

Jude felt the needle of the anaesthetic at his neck, and saw the flash of steel as the surgeon moved in.

Jaime looked away, he couldn't bear to see the boy suffer any more. How could he explain to him the guilt they felt? That they had used his friend to advance their cause and now he was dead, and they didn't even know who had killed him.

Jude looked up. One of the doctors was speaking to him. He didn't seem to be taking part in the operation, but was leaning over him insistently.

'Look,' he said, and he pointed towards the ceiling. 'Look up, don't look at the scalpel.' Jude looked up, and there on the whiteness of the ceiling he felt he could see a ripple of water, the current of the river, and then the trees. He could still faintly hear the low soft timbre of Jaime Souza's voice.

He saw a small group of people in the darkness of the under-growth, and then he heard the swish of arrows. He saw the dash of confusion in the darkness. Then he saw Ramon, walking white and dripping with sweat towards the water's edge. He watched Ramon get into Bernado's boat. Two bowmen, two young sicarios from Envigado, were standing on the bank.

'I didn't know you meant this, not this,' said Ramon, he was quivering and his eyes were white with fear.

A man on the bank laughed. Ramon looked just like Tomas had done on Zipatola beach, just as he'd begun to slip his knife under his rib-cage.

'You could do with a bit more charm, Ramon,' said an American voice, and Jude recognised him as a guy called Dirk Fontenay that he'd seen with Dale Warnock at the mansion in Austin.

'I was nervous,' said Ramon, in his defence.

'Well you don't have to be nervous any more,' said Fontenay.

'No?'

'No,' said Dirk. 'You won't have to be. Thank you for your assistance in creating a little American hero. It was good doing business with you.' He waved his arm to his bowmen and they let their bowstrings go. Both arrows hit Ramon in the chest, one passing through him to pin him to the wood of the dug-out. They doused him with petrol and set him on fire. Fontenay kicked the dug-out into the river with his foot.

Jude was showing visible signs of distress. Jaime Souza began to pray. He looked at one of the medics, he looked worried too, they had an airway now through his throat, but it didn't seem to be doing any good. Jaime pressed his pendant of José Gregorio into Jude's hand.

Jude was still watching. He was watching the burning dug-out, with Ramon's body in it, from the riverbank. He felt the warmth of someone taking his hand and turned slowly to look at him.

There on the riverbank with him was a man in a dark suit, a trilby hat and a moustache, looking deeply mournful over the events. Then the sicarios pulled revolvers from their Calvin

Klein jeans. There was a suddenly startled expression on the American's face. Then they shot him and kicked him into the burning boat as well. They hadn't trusted their pay-master.

'Look deeper into the flames, my friend,' said José Gregorio. 'Can you see?'

As the flames crept up Ramon's jeans Mills's hip-flask fell out, charred.

José Gregorio pulled him away from the river, and there in a distant clearing, where the light was falling through the forest, he saw a group of Indians. Mills was at their feet, an arrow in his leg, as they dragged him away.

As he woke, safe in Envigado at Don Emillio's house, he found he was gripping a small picture on a pendant of José Gregorio Hernández.

27

It was spring in Oxford again, and a rare bright morning. A small flock of barb-tailed godwit had arrived on the lawns of Cudlow Hall, and there were bittern sitting in the reeds.

Jude was in college and taking his seat in the third row from the front before the podium. The first rows were filled with dignitaries: the local Member of Parliament, the mayor, the British Foreign Secretary.

It was nine o'clock in the morning and the members of his college watched as he settled down into his chair; many of them were staring at him. He was never seen at lectures and the door to The Stables was closed to visitors. As yet he'd not confided in anyone about what had happened in South America and it gave him a kudos, and a mystery, among his peers which some of them foolishly envied. But for Jude it was a simple fact that he had no other place to be than Oxford. He had nowhere else to go; the reading of books, and the solitary hours as the spring moved greenly across the landscape, were a consolation of sorts.

The ceremony began. The block of masonry was hovering over its place suspended by chains. Words were spoken by the Master of the college about the importance of the laying of the foundations for an Institute of International Understanding, a place for scholars from all countries, but Jude found it hard to listen or concentrate. The dons on the podium, puffed up in their gowns, reminded Jude of the vultures on the lawns of Leticia. They all seemed mightily pleased by the financial legacy being inaugurated in stone, the money donated in Clearwater's name by a Texan billionaire with an interest in steam trains.

Then the Master welcomed Clearwater, who let go of his wife's hand and stood gravely from his chair, taking the sterling silver trowel from the Master, with which he was to tap the block of masonry, and he gave his blessing to the *Millburn Clearwater Institute*.

Jude stared for a moment as the trowel glinted in his hands.

Instead of the usual marquee for such a thing they were gathered in a bullet-proof galvanized steel construction like an aircraft hangar. Jude was due to take part in the ceremony, following the college string quartet, with a short reading that he'd been forced to submit for approval to Clearwater's staff.

As Kyle Clearwater spoke Jude looked at the faces ranged around. There was Elliot Hudson, whom he remembered from the Team Room, sitting in the row in front; now chief of White House staff. And Dale Warnock, he was recognisable enough these days, as the President's press spokesman. He took the press conferences with an impressive flair.

Of Catherine Sirteema, on the other hand, there was no sign. Jude had never heard of her again. He'd read a brief piece about her resignation before the election, but it gave no indication of what she was going to do. He imagined her living out in Cape Cod or somewhere, running her old dad's General Store, in a run-down weather boarded place.

Just before Christmas a senior member of the Venezuelan President's cabinet had drowned in a sailing accident, another had resigned, reported to have left the country and settled in Dublin: both were named in Father Leonardo's notes as being associated with the shooting of the archbishop.

Anne Clearwater, who was sitting on the chair where the President had left her as he'd gone to the podium, was looking younger, fresher, a hungry court champion again. Despite their grief they had managed, somehow, to return Washington to the Nancy Years, with balls, and glamour, and proper table manners again. Now, three months into their administration, they were on a grand tour of the capitals of Europe. They had been elected on a huge wave of public sympathy; none of the newspapers dared to attack the grieving candidate; no-one had dared to delve into the true cause of Mills's death. The notion that a brave young American should be murdered in a savage foreign place was too potent a symbol for their national introspection.

Jude settled back into the discomfort of his chair and listened as the new President wittered on, speaking again of Mills's least favourite theme: *family values*. As Clearwater's voice droned around the tin marquee Jude began to frame a few phrases in his mind that he might add to his own brief moment at the podium. The feelings that he really had about why Mills was sacrificed in the back-waters of the Amazon and who was truly responsible for his death. Just a few damning sentences in front of the world's media would suffice.

Outside the sky had darkened now and the rain began to fall on the roof.

Jude saw himself back on the *Ulysses* and a rush of adrenalin skimmed through his body as he recalled the comforting feeling of the rains on deck; the altered surface of the water and the stately demeanour of the great trees; as they huddled beneath a sheet of tarpaulin.

He thought of the beam from Jiminez's lamp in the early hours as it swung across the bow; the steam from Mills's cauldron of rice; the children in the afternoons paddling alongside in their dug-outs.

He thought of Jaime Souza, Emillio Guzman's man who'd been sent to ensure Mills's safety, and of Ramon, the clever young sicario.

He thought of the vision he'd seen of José Gregorio when he was being flown to the safety of Guzman's house. He tried once again to see that single image of Mills being pulled away from it all by the Indians.

When he had recalled his vision for Don Emillio and Jaime they had leapt to believe it, perhaps to assuage their own guilt and leave the dream of their saint untarnished.

The investigation of the Indians had been allowed to collapse quietly, and they'd been permitted to go back into the forest when the bullet-ridden body of Dirk Fontenay had been dis-covered, and the young sicarios who'd killed him were captured as they tried to escape on the river.

Although Jude very much wanted to, he couldn't believe now in his own vision of José Gregorio. He tried to fancy that Mills was back on the *Ulysses,* having escaped from it all, boiling his rice with Pablo; but that vision faded too, as much as the rice-steam drifted across the wide river.

He looked up, instead, to the real vision that was in front of him: a politician, and a father, who would countenance any amount of brutal mischief for his dream of power.

Clearwater was still speaking and using the name 'Millburn', and it suddenly stuck in Jude's craw and his body filled up with anger. In life Mills had hated the name. It was an offence to Jude's ears to hear his father using it so frequently now. None of the fine words seemed to accurately match his friend: a young man who had been completely mixed up by his parents; and because of them had got himself mixed up in dangerous things without intending it at all. He would rather wail and scream and accuse than make this valediction.

President Clearwater was still a little way off the end of his oration, and his audience and the TV cameras were following every word, but Jude found himself shaking his head disconsolately. Then he stood up, and removed himself from his aisle seat, looking first at the podium and then away.

He began walking slowly up the aisle towards the door.

Behind him he heard the President's voice falter, and a hush fell as he walked.

The congregation stared at him as he went, and his tutor's hand came out, to deter him on his way; but he walked on and left the place. A solitary figure in his dark suit, one left by Mills in the closets of The Stables.

He stepped outside, and pushed his way through the security men until he was alone in the quad.

At least they had let him live. He looked up into the darkening sky.

The Hall of the college stood before him. He crossed its threshold. It was still only a quarter past nine in the morning but nobody was left at breakfast; they were all listening to the President at the ceremony, or following it on TV.

He sat down at one of the long benches in the deserted, dimly-lit Hall; the portraits of the masters bearing down.

The silver toasters were still on the tables.

The rain was torrential now.

From the skylights above sparrows were swooping in and flying the length of the Hall.

Author's Note ∫

On my first day researching this novel I was caught in a riot in Caracas and sheltered from the gas in the church of the Candelaria. It was there that I first came across the figure of Dr José Gregorio Hernández and became interested in his story. On the whole, I have largely stuck to the facts of his life. I only depart from the truth when the story moves to the shrine at Isnotu. While the shrine as I describe it is much as it is, the plots surrounding Father Leonardo are an invention. There is, however, a priest there who has indeed built the shrine and the school, and who came there from Spain in the nineteen sixties after four Venezuelan priests had resigned in one year. I am very thankful for the time he spent with me and ask his forgiveness for building the character of Father Leonardo around him. The character of Don Emillio Guzman is an entire fiction, as are the episodes in the seminary in Barcelona.

I would also like to express my thanks to my friend Alec Howe, who may recognise The Stables that we shared together, but not, of course, his own noble parents in the shape of the Clearwaters. I should also like to thank Christian Blackman who came with me to Isnotu and whose adventures on the Colombian border I have shamelessly lifted. And to my Colombian friends in Bogota, Jaime Rojas and Matthew and Rachel Leighton, who wrested me from the embrace of the security services, thank you.

The cult of José Gregorio Hernández continues to spread across South America. The Vatican is investigating . . .